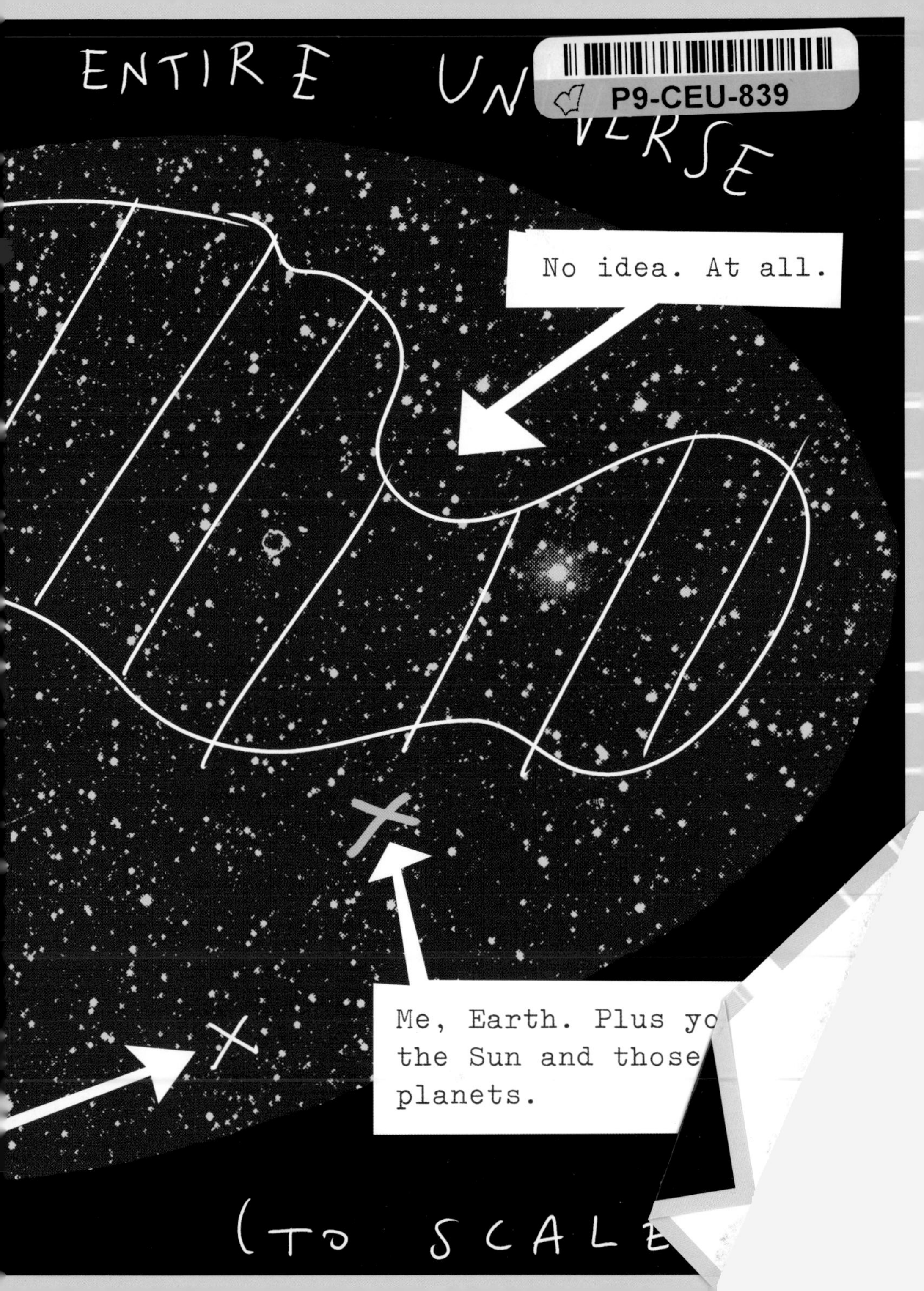
ENTIRE UN
VERSE
No idea. At all.
Me, Earth. Plus yo
the Sun and those
planets.
(TO SCALE

ASTRO-NUTS

Mission One: The Plant Planet

By Jon Scieszka

Illustrated by Steven Weinberg

chronicle books · san francisco

NNASA!

Many thanks to the Rijksmuseum for their use of the
engravings featured throughout the book. Command
Escape, Earth, and Mount Rushmore are all collaged
from images in the public domain under the Creative
Commons General Use License. More information on all
this is available at www.AstroNuts.space

For Amina —J.S. and S.W.

Text copyright © 2019 by Jon Scieszka.
Illustrations copyright © 2019 by Steven Weinberg.

Library of Congress Cataloging-in-Publication Data available.

ISBN 978-1-4521-7119-7

Manufactured in China.

MIX
Paper from
responsible sources
FSC™ C008047
FSC
www.fsc.org

Design by Ryan Hayes and Jay Marvel.
Typeset in Freight Micro, Typewriter, and Noyh.

10 9 8 7 6 5 4 3 2

Chronicle Books LLC
680 Second Street
San Francisco, California 94107

Chronicle Books—we see things differently.
Become part of our community at www.chroniclekids.com.

NASA!

5

AstroNuts ACTIVATE!

Emergency launch/launch/
launch has been triggered.

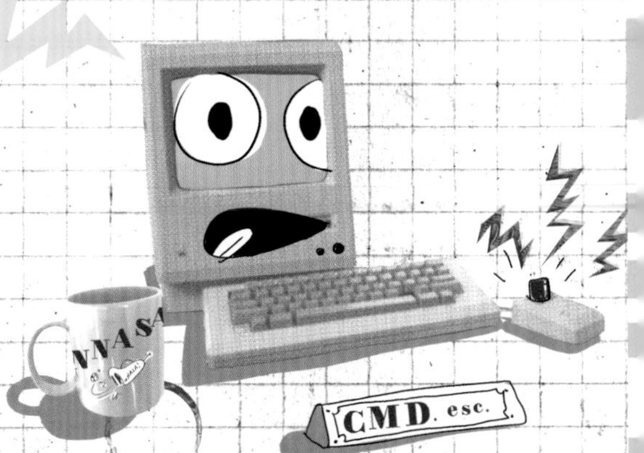
CMD. esc.

4

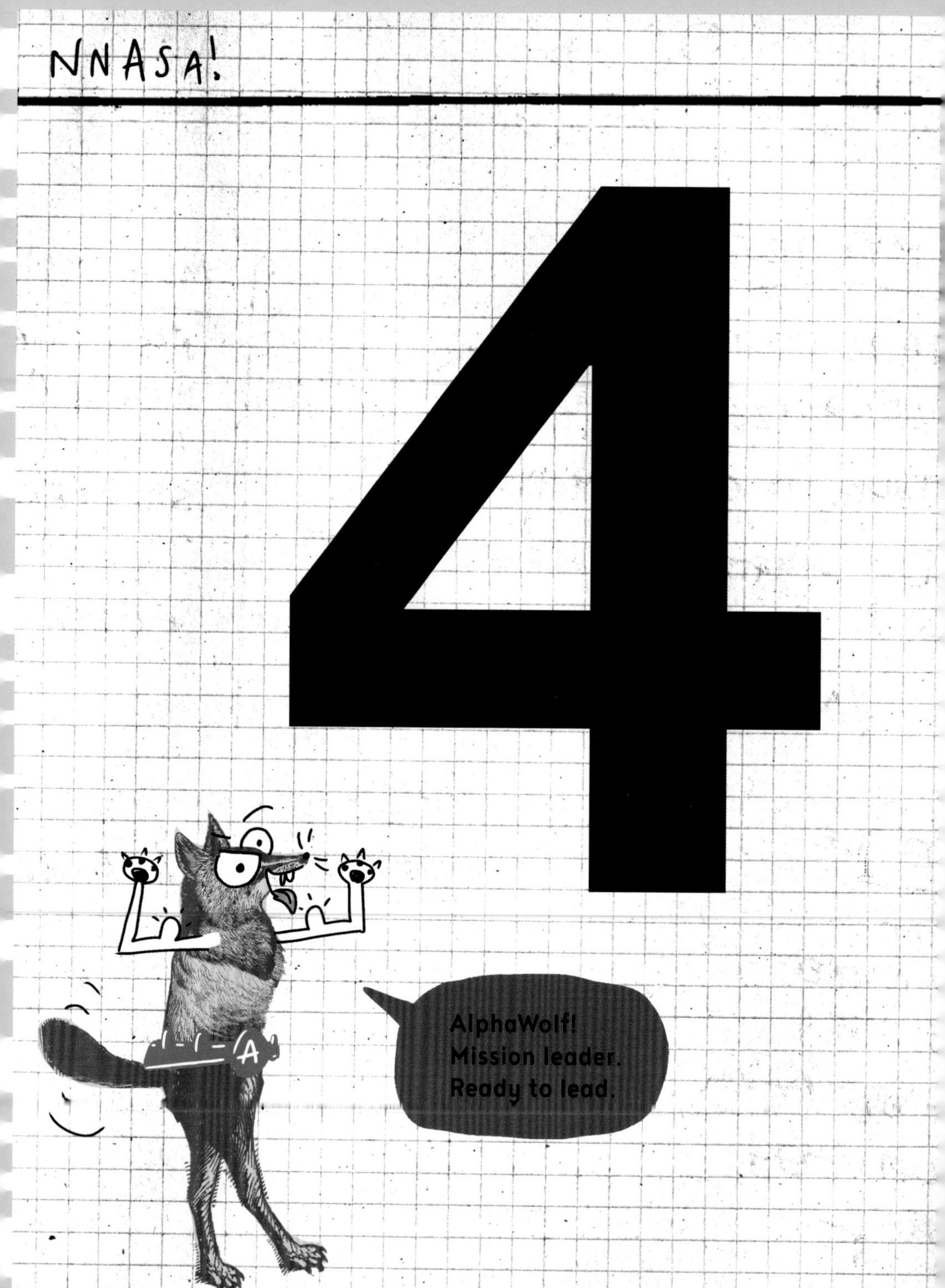
AlphaWolf!
Mission leader.
Ready to lead.

VNASA!

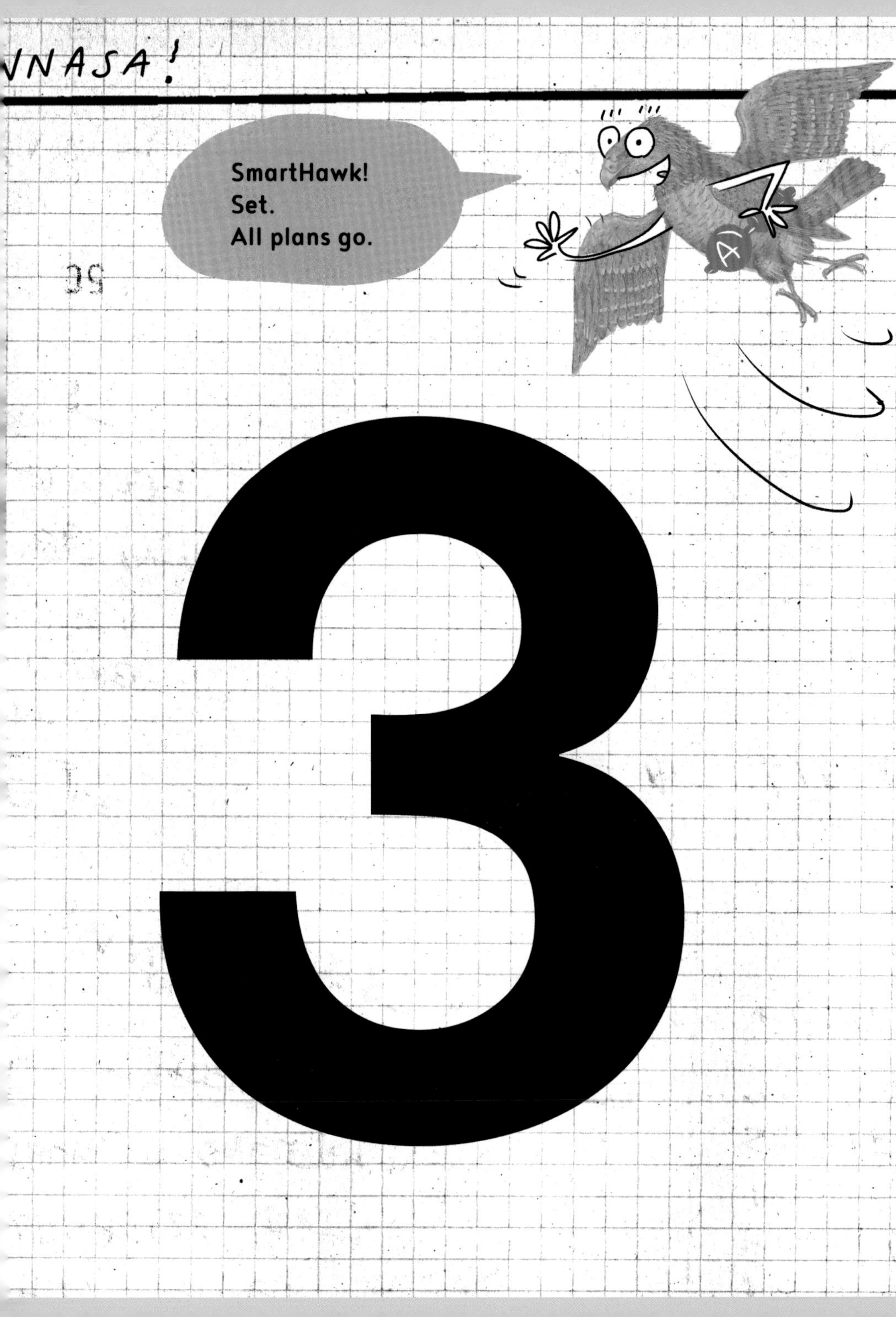
SmartHawk!
Set.
All plans go.

3

NNASA!

2

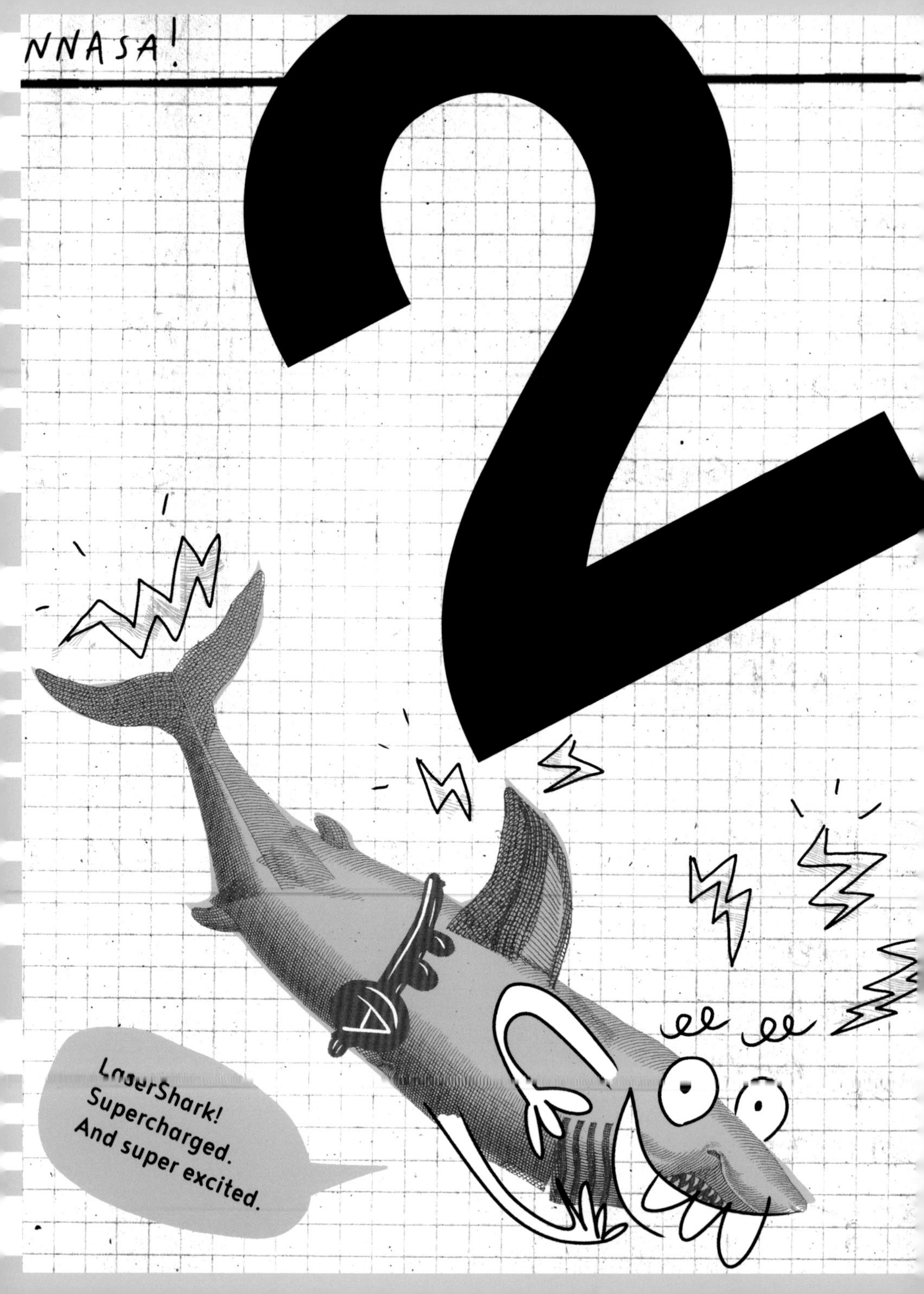
LaserShark! Supercharged. And super excited.

NNASA!

1

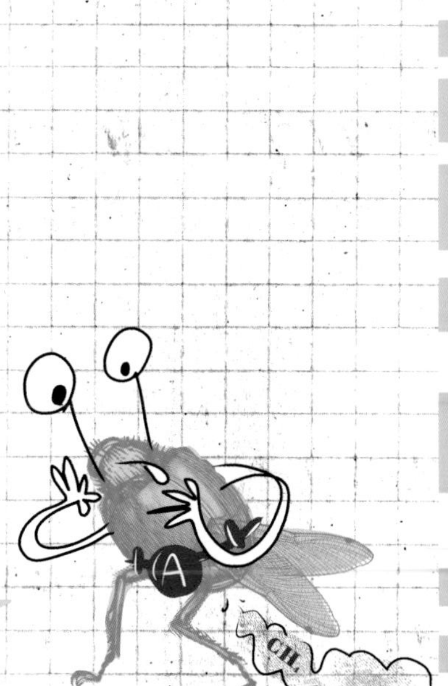
Oh, no. I knew this would happen.
Checking controls.
Oh — and I am StinkBug.
C.H.
C.H.

BLAST OFF!!

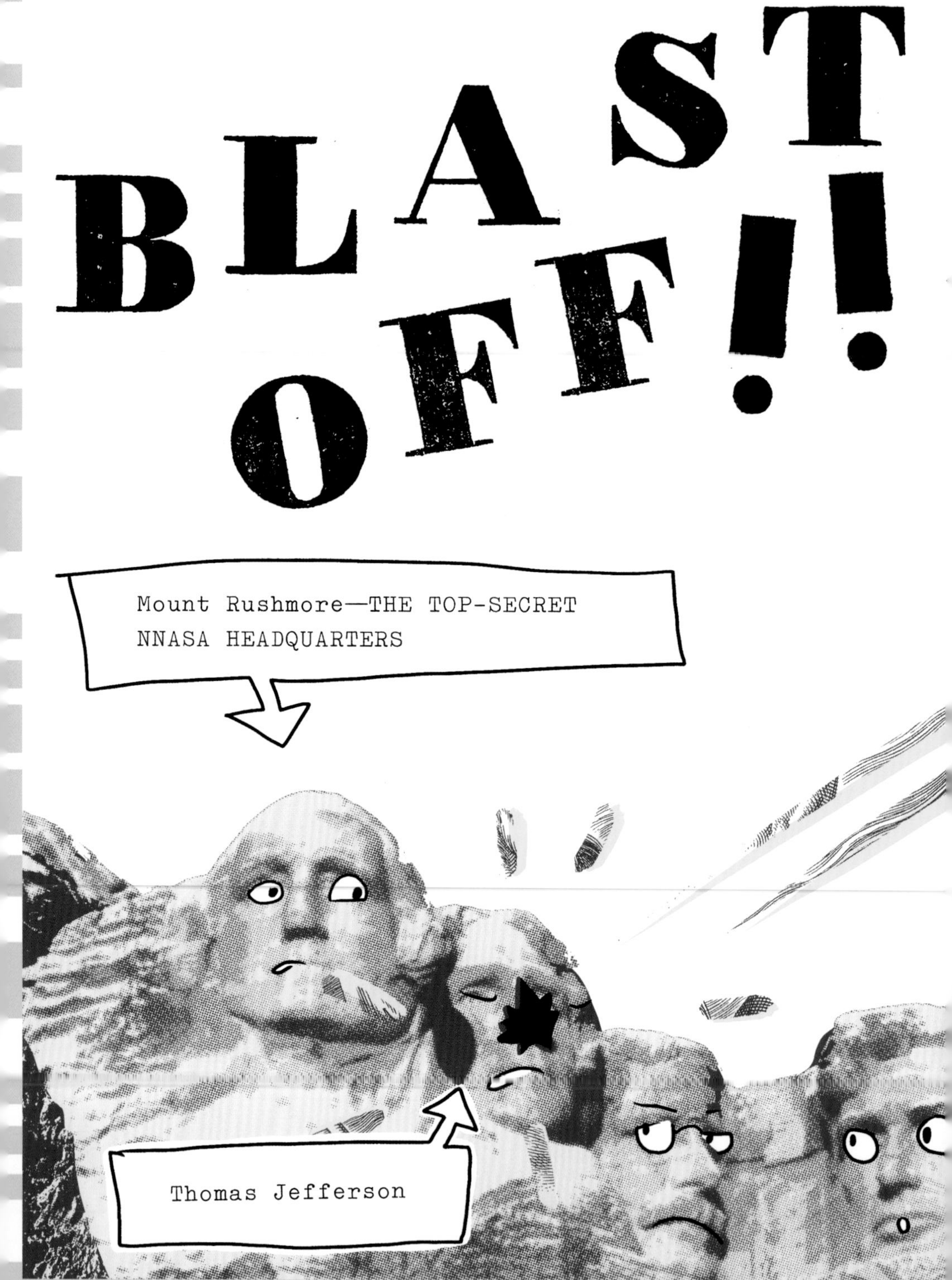

Mount Rushmore—THE TOP-SECRET NNASA HEADQUARTERS
Thomas Jefferson

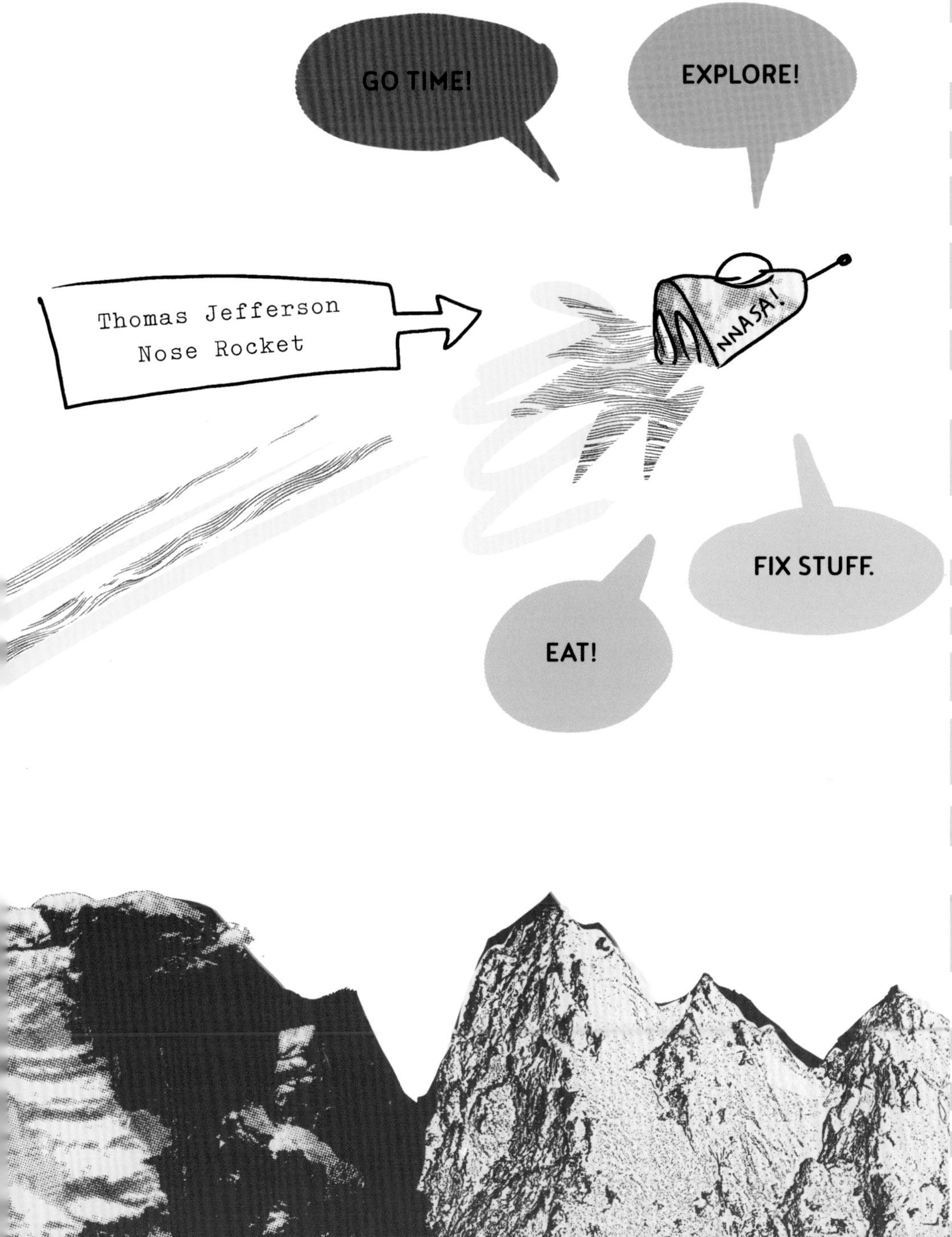
GO TIME!
EXPLORE!
Thomas Jefferson Nose Rocket
NNASA!
FIX STUFF.
EAT!

Yes, blastoff. How exciting.
Usually. But not this time.

This time, blastoff was scary and awful. Because this blastoff was a deadly emergency.

And it was all caused by you humans. You humans who finally crossed the BIG RED LINE by putting more than 400 PPM (parts per million) of CO_2 (carbon dioxide) into my beautiful atmosphere. Overheating my oceans, melting my ice caps, killing my plants and animals and even yourselves, and . . . well, more about that later.

Oh, hello. I'm Earth. Your planet. And boy, do I have a story to tell you.

Lucky for you humans, way back in 1988, a couple of your smart scientists working for NNASA (Not the National Aeronautics and Space Administration) in a secret lab inside Mount Rushmore built four superpowered animal astronauts. Because what a perfect place to hide what could be the most important program ever—right in plain sight, clear as the nose on Thomas Jefferson's face. These animals were designed in case of emergency—in case humans ever went over the BIG RED LINE—to automatically activate, launch into space, and investigate a new Goldilocks Planet. A place not too hot, not too cold, just right for humans to live on. Like I used to be. Before you got here.

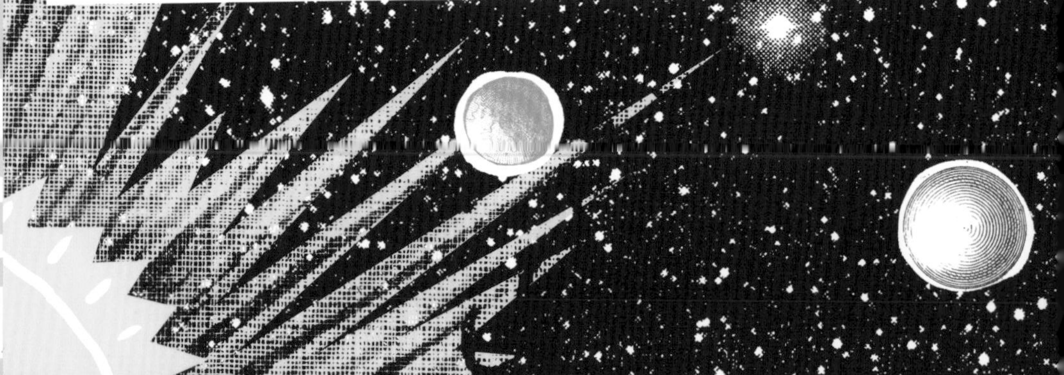

Well, that emergency finally happened.

Humans pushed the level of CO_2 in my atmosphere over 400 PPM, over the BIG RED LINE. In fact, you put more CO_2 in my atmosphere than there has ever been in the last two million years. So, blastoff.

That's right. Your best hope for a new planet was in the paws and claws of four experimental, untested animal astronauts.

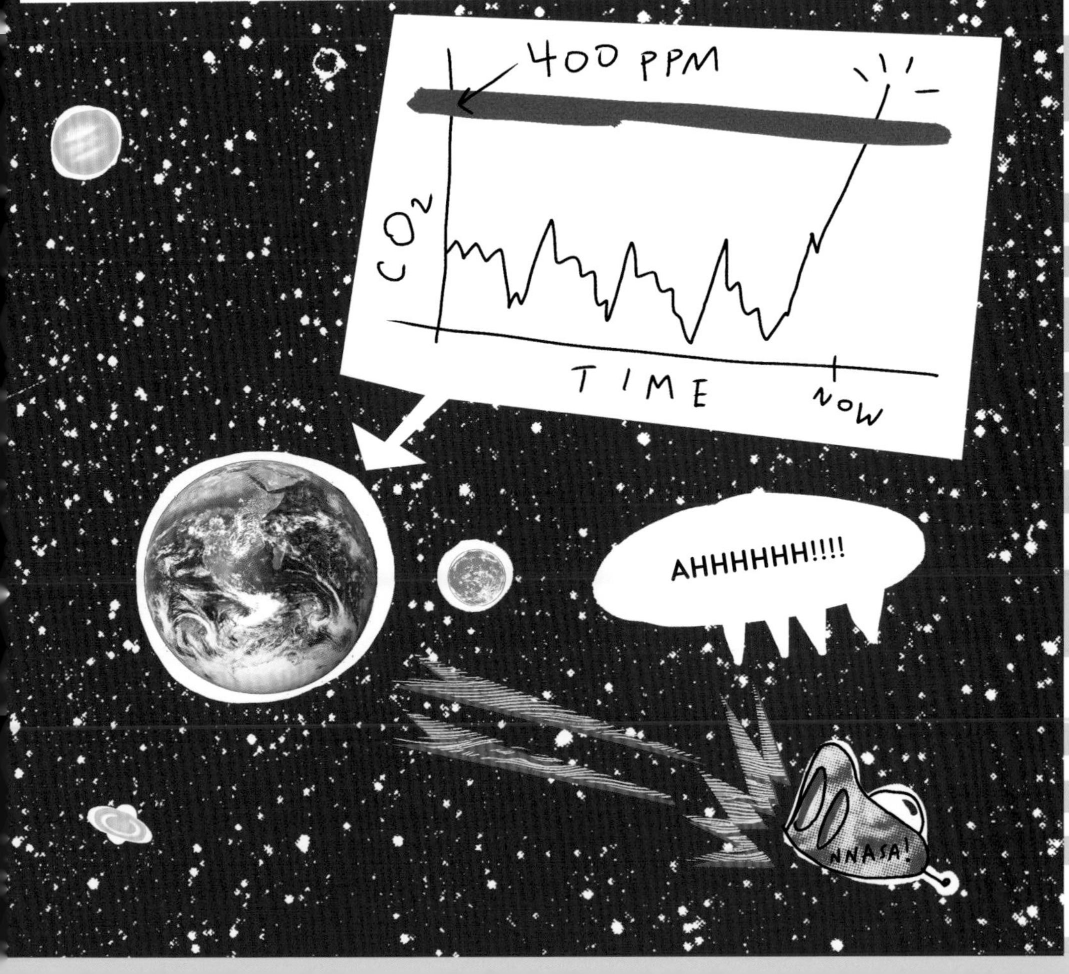
400 PPM
CO2
TIME
NOW
AHHHHHH!!!!
NNASA!

Chapter 1:
Ahhhhhhhhh!!!

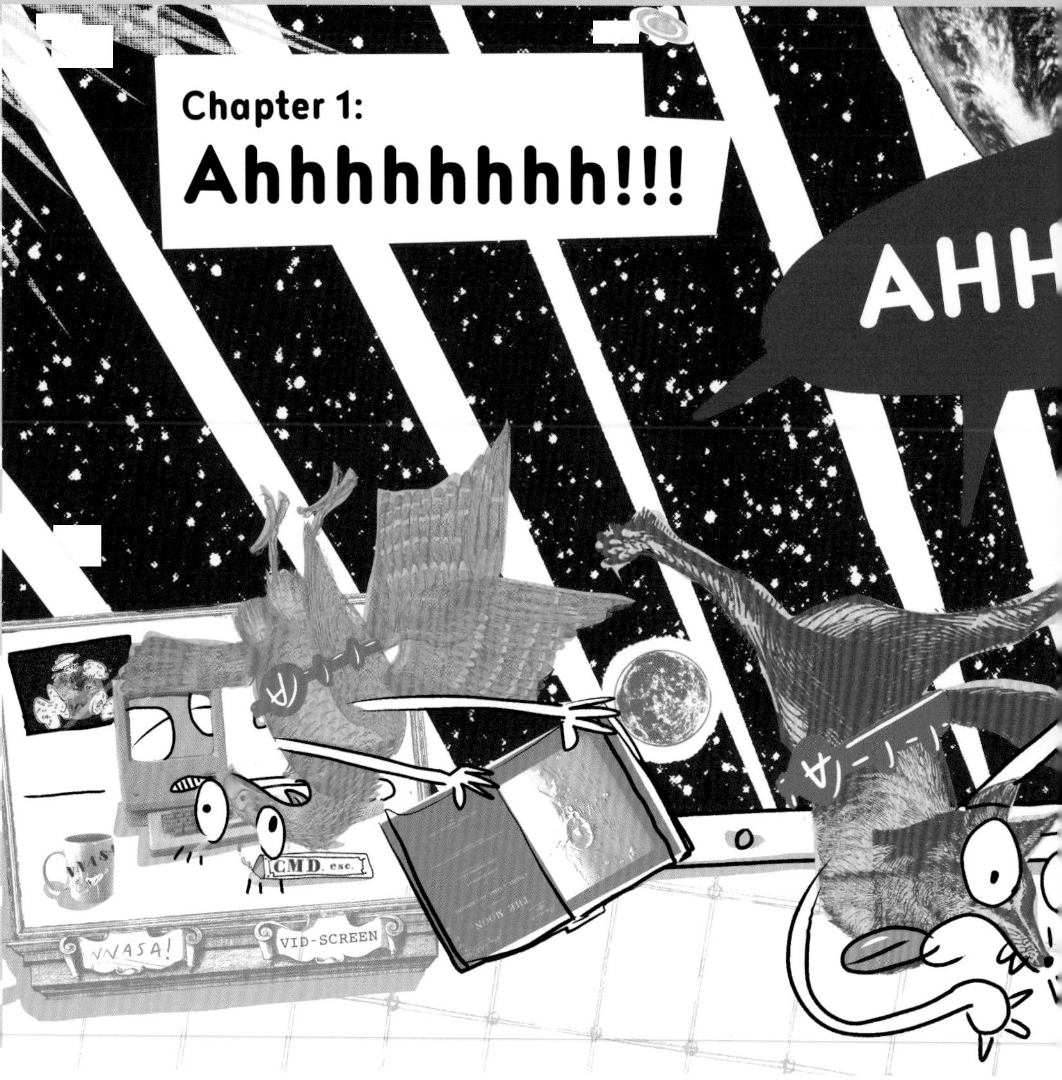
AHH
CMD. esc.
NNASA!
VID-SCREEN

Inside the Thomas Jefferson Nose Rocket, things got off to a rough start.

Maybe because the super animals had been in storage for more than 25 years. But maybe also because they had been made of oddball bits and parts.

They were superpowered, sure. But they'd never been tested.

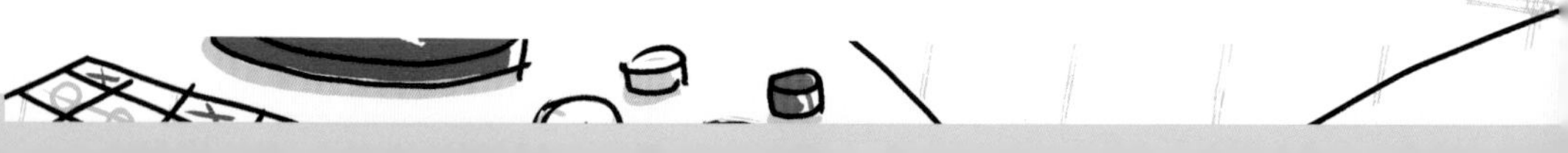

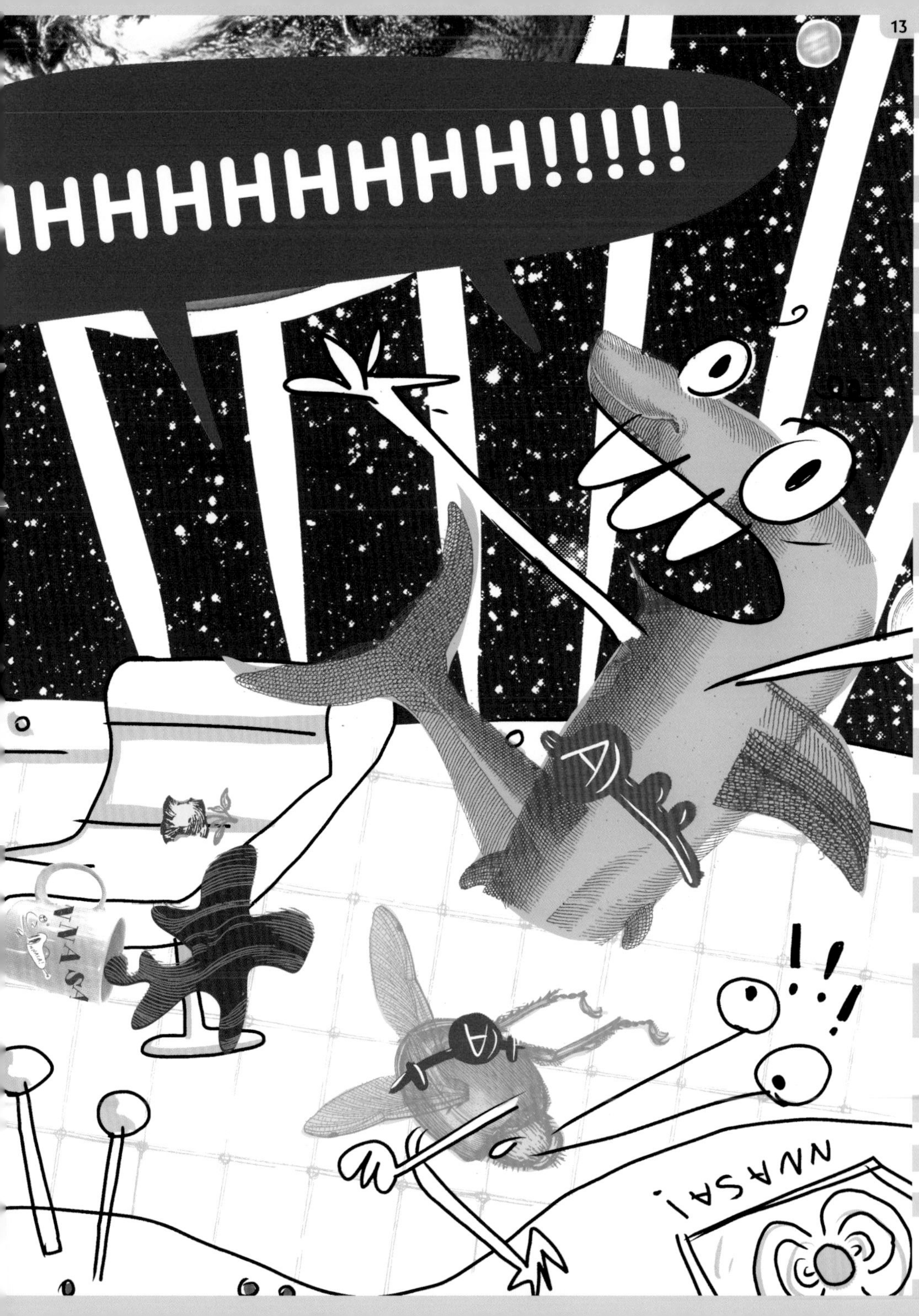
HHHHHHHH!!!!!
!!

Command Escape, the slightly rusty, very glitchy 1988 computer brains of the Goldilocks Mission, popped onto the Nose Rocket vid-screen.

Astronauts, welcome out of hibernation. You have been activated to explore/to explore the Plant Planet. It appears to be a very good Goldilocks Planet.

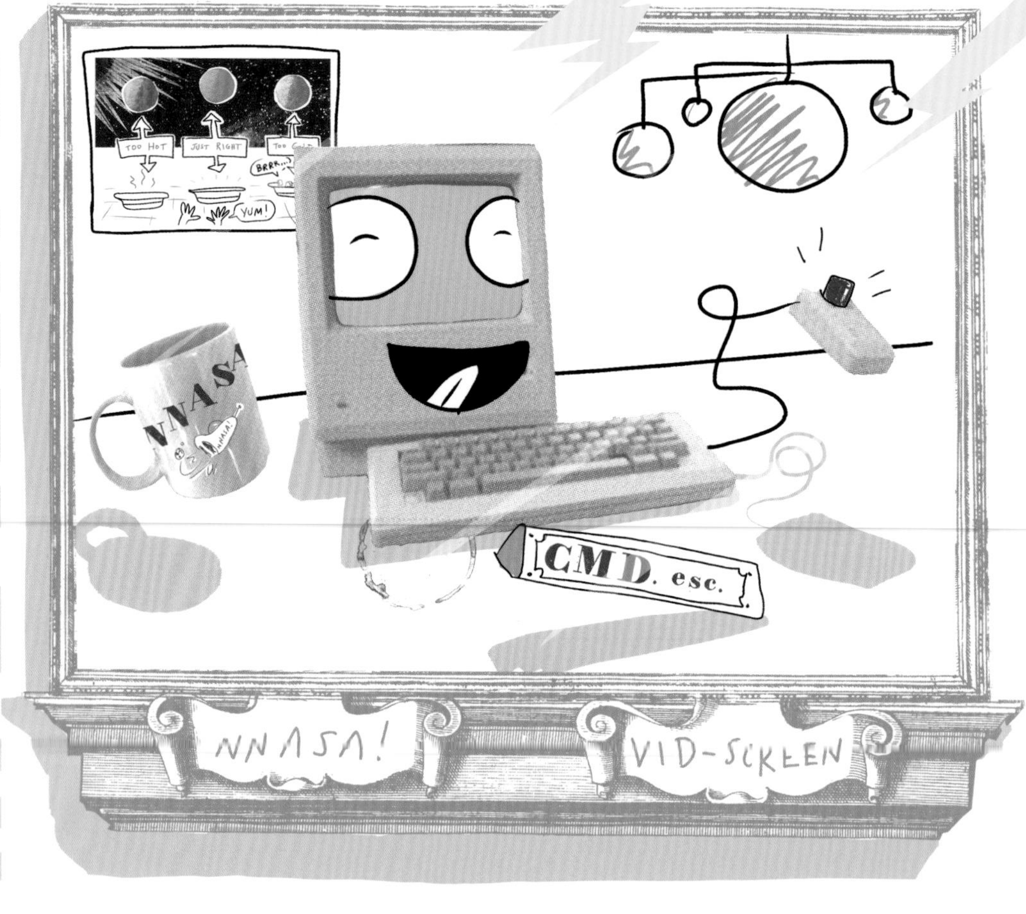
TOO HOT
JUST RIGHT
BRRR...
YUM!
NNASA
CMD. esc.
NNASA!
VID-SCREEN

It is not too hot.
It is not too cold.

You must use all of your superpowers/all of your superpowers/all of your superpowers and scientific training to see if humans can live there.

Without wrecking any existing life.

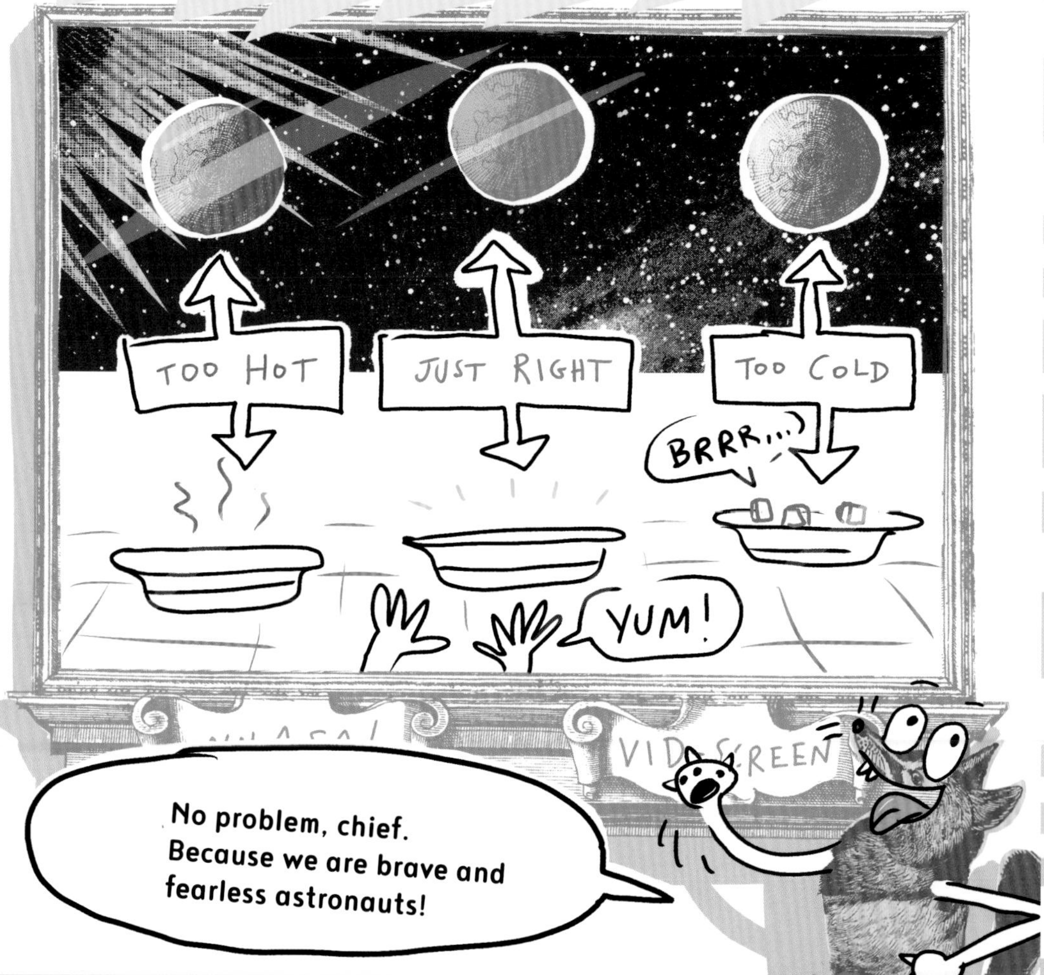
TOO HOT
JUST RIGHT
TOO COLD
BRRR...
YUM!
No problem, chief. Because we are brave and fearless astronauts!

////// Official NNASA transcript //////
//// of ASTRONUT MISSION 1 ////

Command Escape: Yes. About that/about that/about that. There has been one small change in your program.

LaserShark: Every day we get more fabulous superpowers?

Command Escape: Not exactly/not exactly.

SmartHawk: With each mission, we get smarter and smarter?

Command Escape: Hmmmmm . . . no.

AlphaWolf: We get gold medals right now?

Command Escape: No. Your NNASA PD-934 Program Description was misspelled.

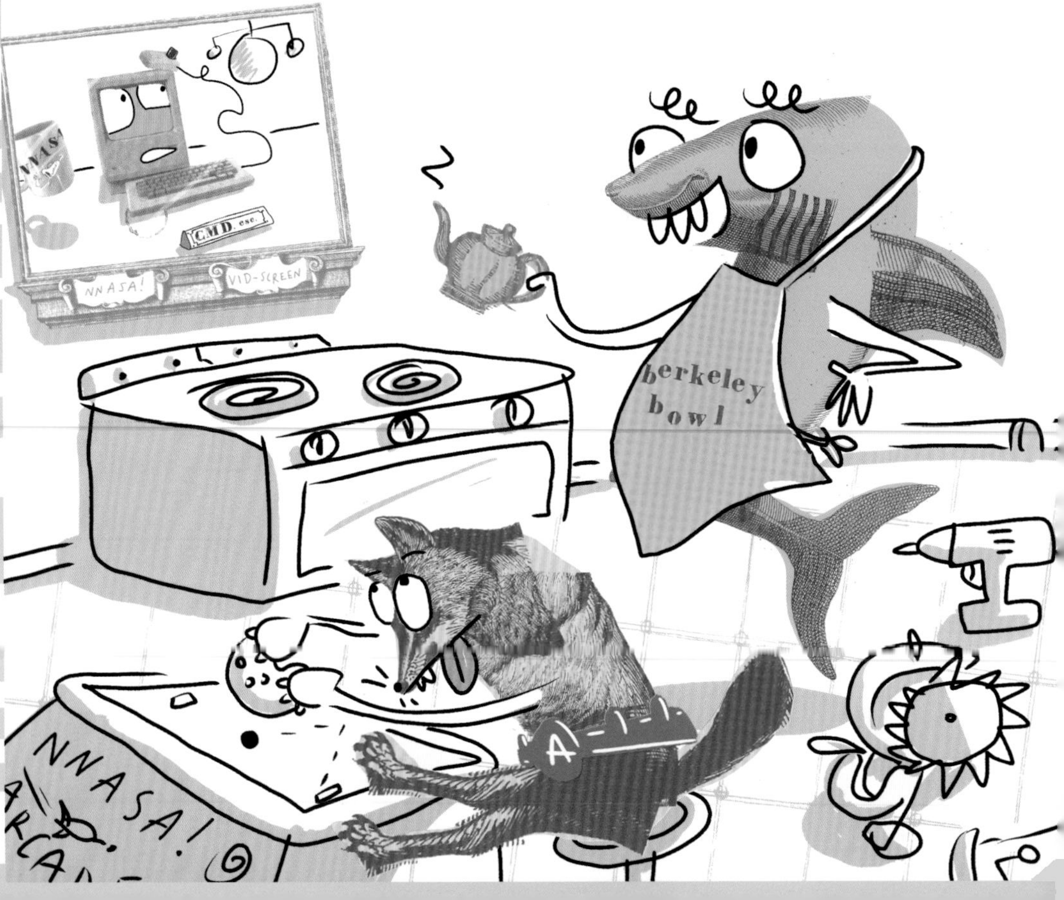

NNASA
CMD. esc.
NNASA!
VID-SCREEN
berkeley bowl
A
NNASA!

AlphaWolf: So we get our medals later?

Command Escape: So you are not/not/not astronauts.

AlphaWolf: What?!

Command Escape: You are AstroNuts.

StinkBug: Oh. That is not right.

Command Escape: I will file paperwork to correct the error. Do not worry about that. It is much more important for you to remember that, because of interstellar traffic, your exploration of the Plant Planet is limited to exactly two weeks/exactly two weeks/exactly two weeks/exactly two weeks/exactly two weeks/exactly two weeks/exactly two weeks/exactly two weeks/exactly two weeks/exactly two weeks/

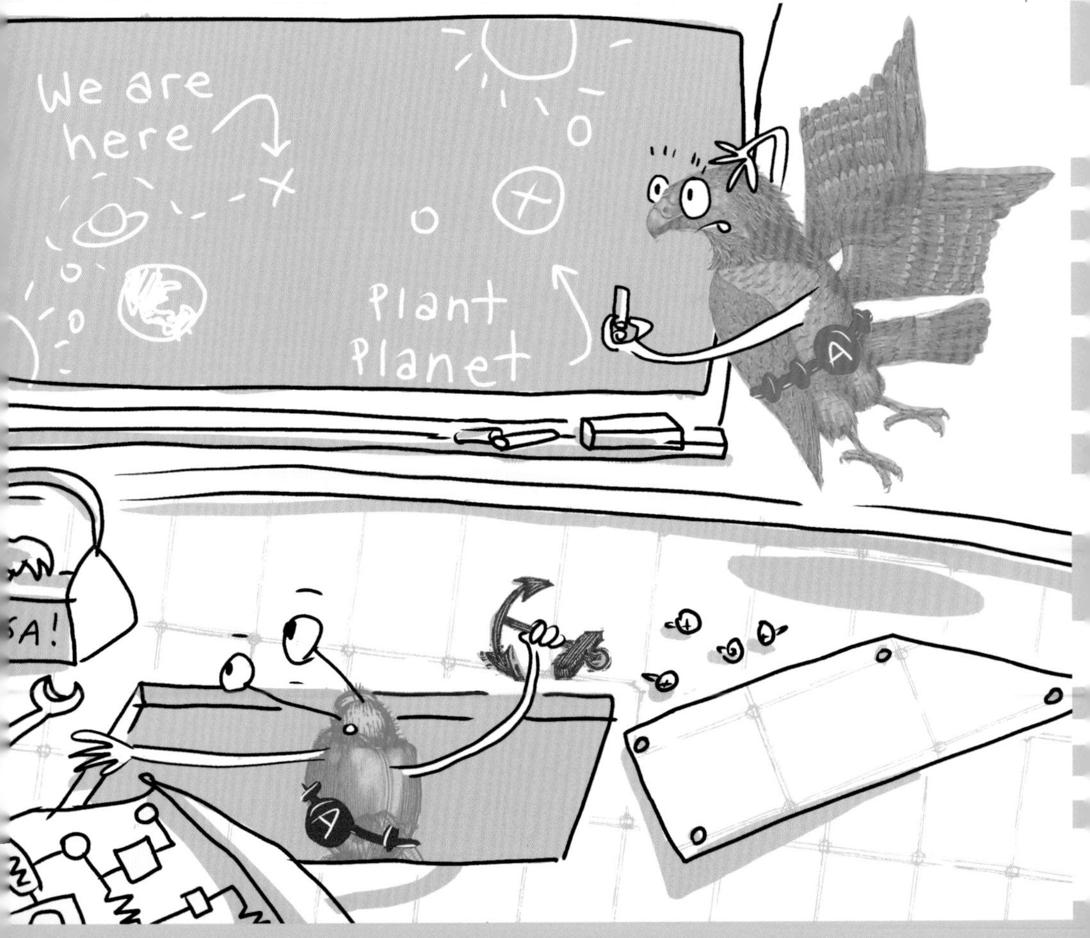
We are here
Plant Planet

exactly two weeks/exactly two weeks/exactly two weeks/
exactly two weeks/exactly two weeks/exactlytwo weeks/
exactly two weeks/exactly two weeks/exactly two weeks/
exactly two weeks/exactly two weeks/exactly two weeks/
exactly two weeks/exactly two weeks/exactly two weeks/
exactly two weeks/exactly two weeks/exactly two weeks/
exactly two weeks/exactly two weeks/exactly two weeks/
exactly two weeks/exactly two weeks/exactly two weeks/
exactly two weeks/exactly two weeks/exactly two weeks/
exactly two weeks/exactly two weeks/ exactly two weeks/

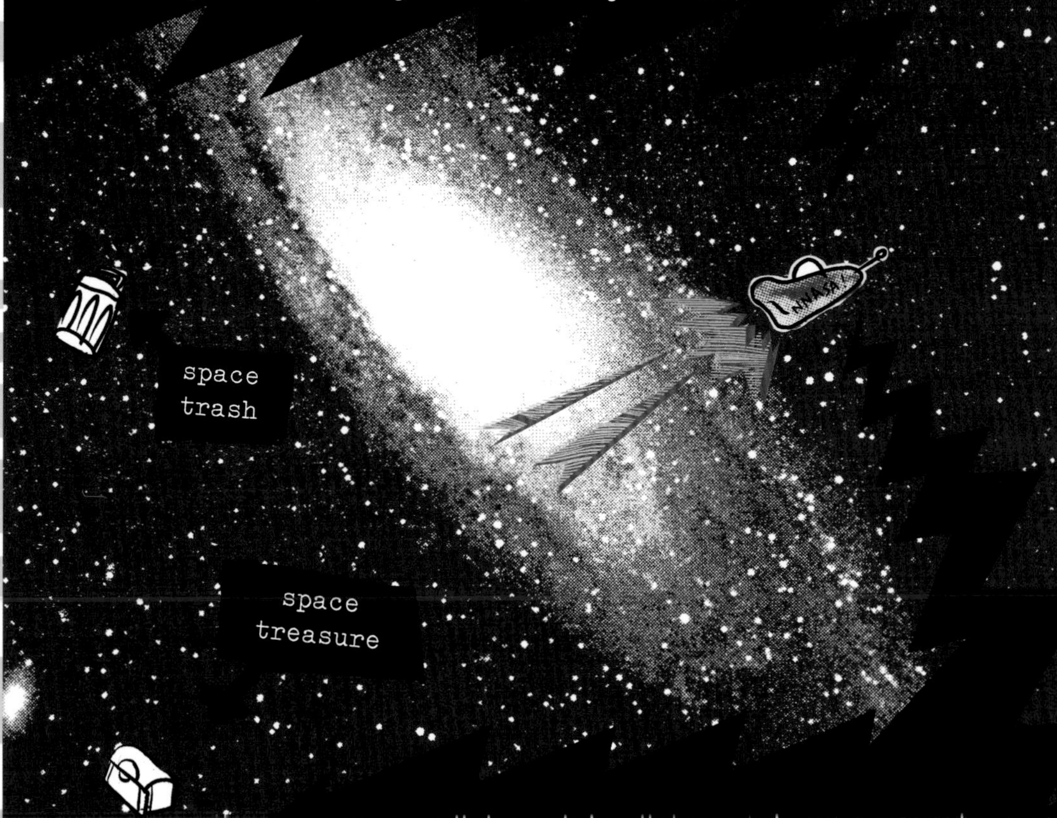
space trash
space treasure

exactly two weeks/exactly two weeks/exactly two weeks/
exactly two weeks/ exactly two weeks/exactly two weeks/
exactly two weeks/exactly two weeks/exactly two weeks/
exactly two weeks/exactly two weeks/exactly two weeks/
exactly two weeks/exactly two weeks/ exactly two weeks/
exactly two weeks/exactly two weeks/exactly two weeks/
exactly two weeks— ”

This was one of Command Escape's longest glitch sequences ever.

"Right," said AlphaWolf. "Got it. EXACTLY TWO WEEKS. JEEZ."

"—exactly two weeks/exactly—"

AlphaWolf accidentally-on-purpose leaned on the Command Escape OFF Button.

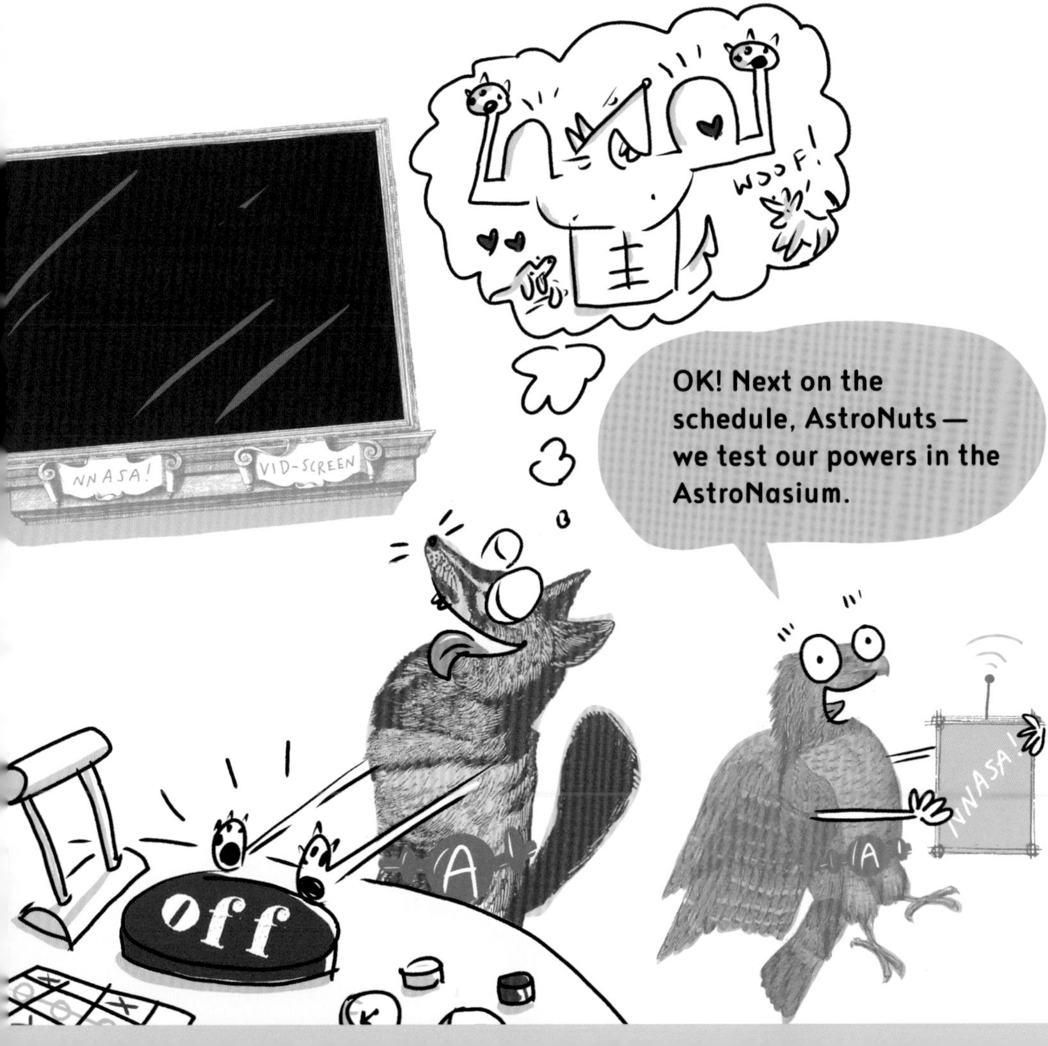
WOOF!
NNASA!
VID-SCREEN
OK! Next on the schedule, AstroNuts— we test our powers in the AstroNasium.
NNASA!
off

The AstroNuts headed to the AstroNasium. Now a curious person like yourself might wonder exactly where an AstroNasium might be in a Thomas Jefferson Nose Rocket—and exactly what else might be inside a Thomas Jefferson Nose Rocket.

Of course, the Nose equipment is Top-Secret and should never be shown.

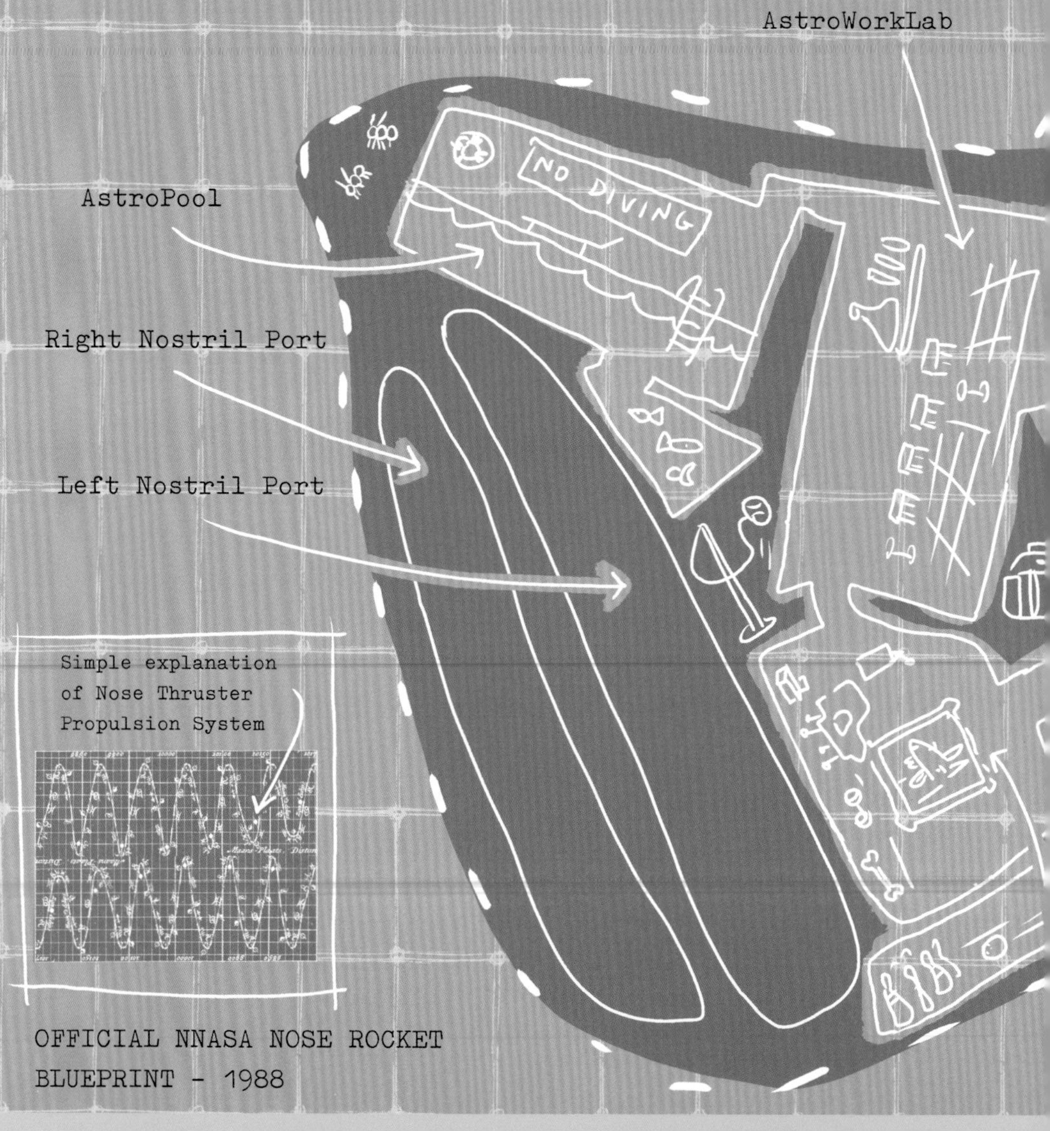
AstroWorkLab
AstroPool
NO DIVING
Right Nostril Port
Left Nostril Port
Simple explanation
of Nose Thruster
Propulsion System

OFFICIAL NNASA NOSE ROCKET
BLUEPRINT - 1988

But an honest individual like yourself could probably look at a classified Nose blueprint and not blab about it to everybody. Right? Now forget everything you saw here. Let's check out the AstroNuts' amazing AstroPowers.

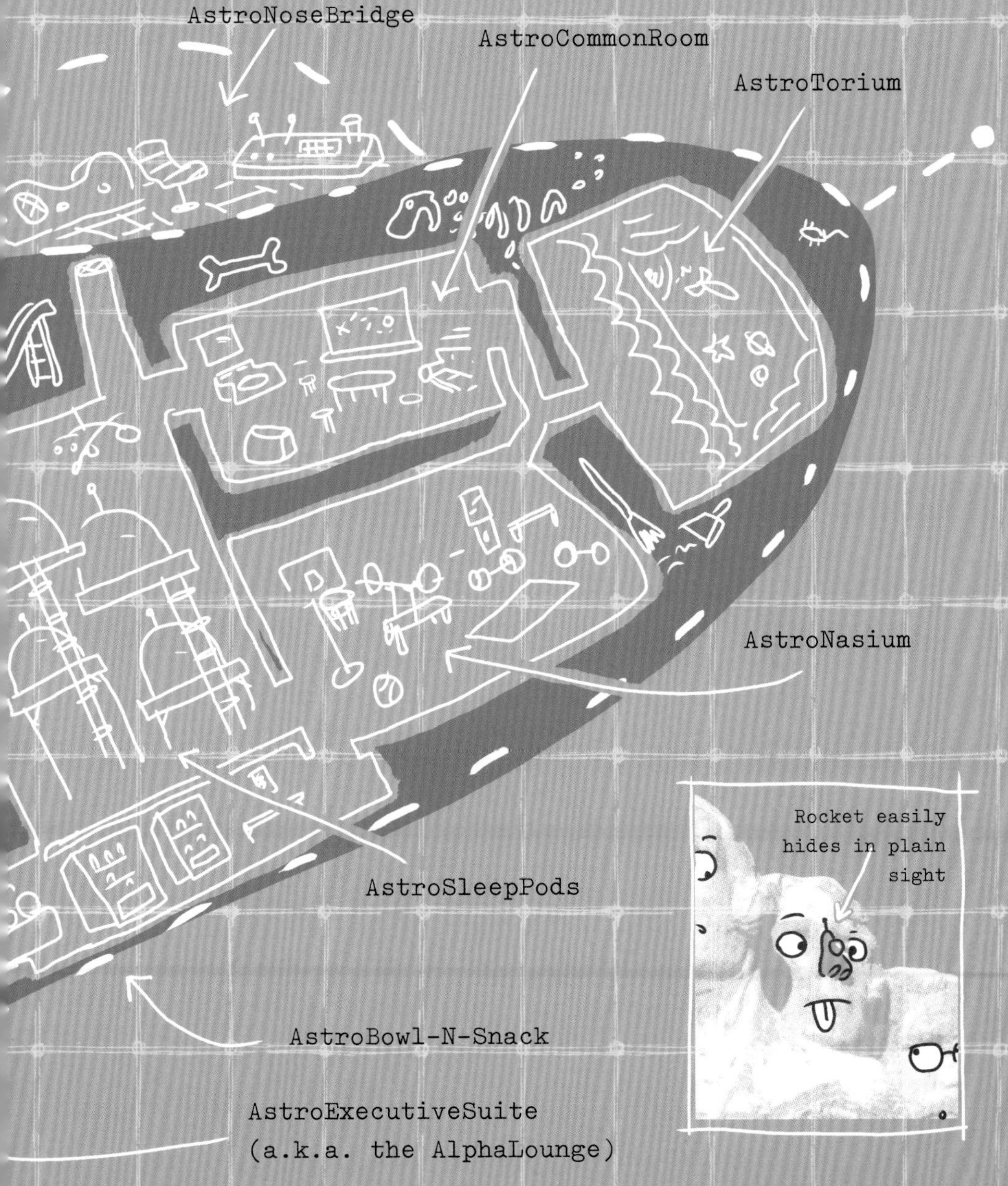
AstroNoseBridge
AstroCommonRoom
AstroTorium
AstroNasium
AstroSleepPods
Rocket easily hides in plain sight
AstroBowl-N-Snack
AstroExecutiveSuite
(a.k.a. the AlphaLounge)

Chapter 2:

AlphaWolf

I am AlphaWolf!
The greatest boss of everyone!
I tell everyone what to do.

ASTROSTATS

MISSION LEADER

Objective: Search target planet for INTELLIGENT LIFE.

Height: 6′1″
Weight: 175 pounds
Hobbies: Trophy polishing, bossing

Timber wolf habitat:

Most Greatest
REAL-STRONG-IUM
claws

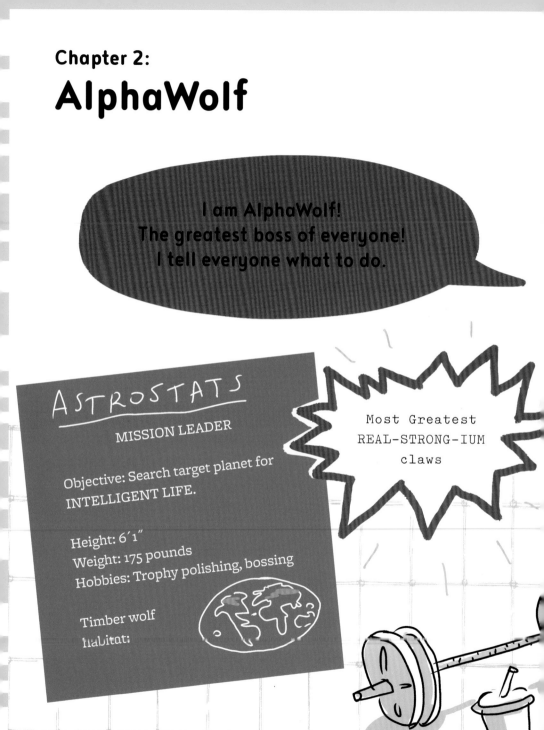

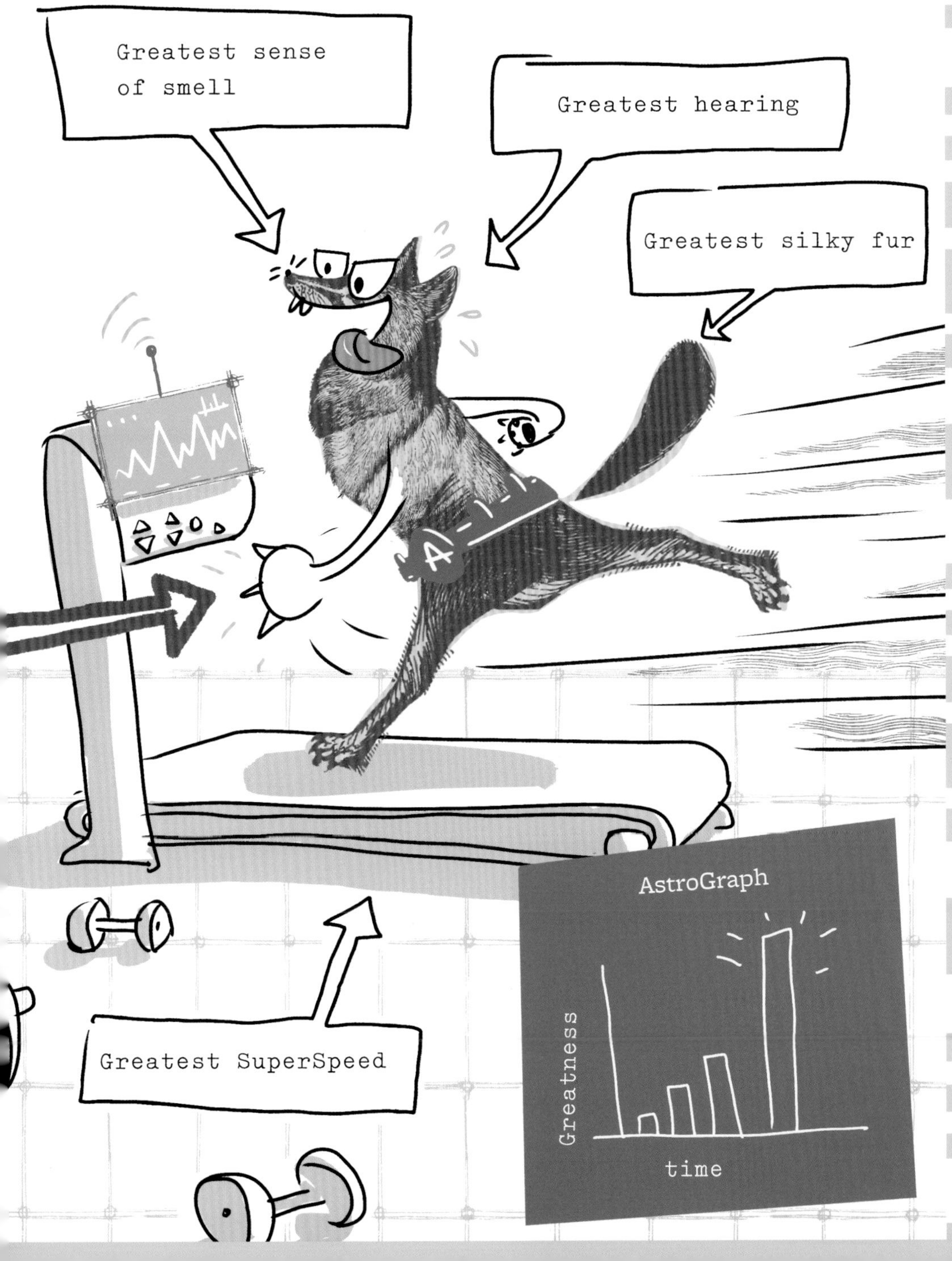
Greatest sense of smell
Greatest hearing
Greatest silky fur
Greatest SuperSpeed
AstroGraph
Greatness
time

Chapter 3:
SmartHawk

I am SmartHawk!
I am the perfect AP (AstroPlan) planner.
I keep everyone on schedule.

Perfect diamond-
edged razor beak

Perfect 120%
planning

ASTROSTATS

MISSION PLANNING
AND RULES OFFICER

Objective: Inspect and test
ECOSYSTEM and CLIMATE.

Height: 5'3"
Weight: 115 pounds
Hobbies: Spell-checking, planning

Broad-winged
hawk habitat:

NNASA!

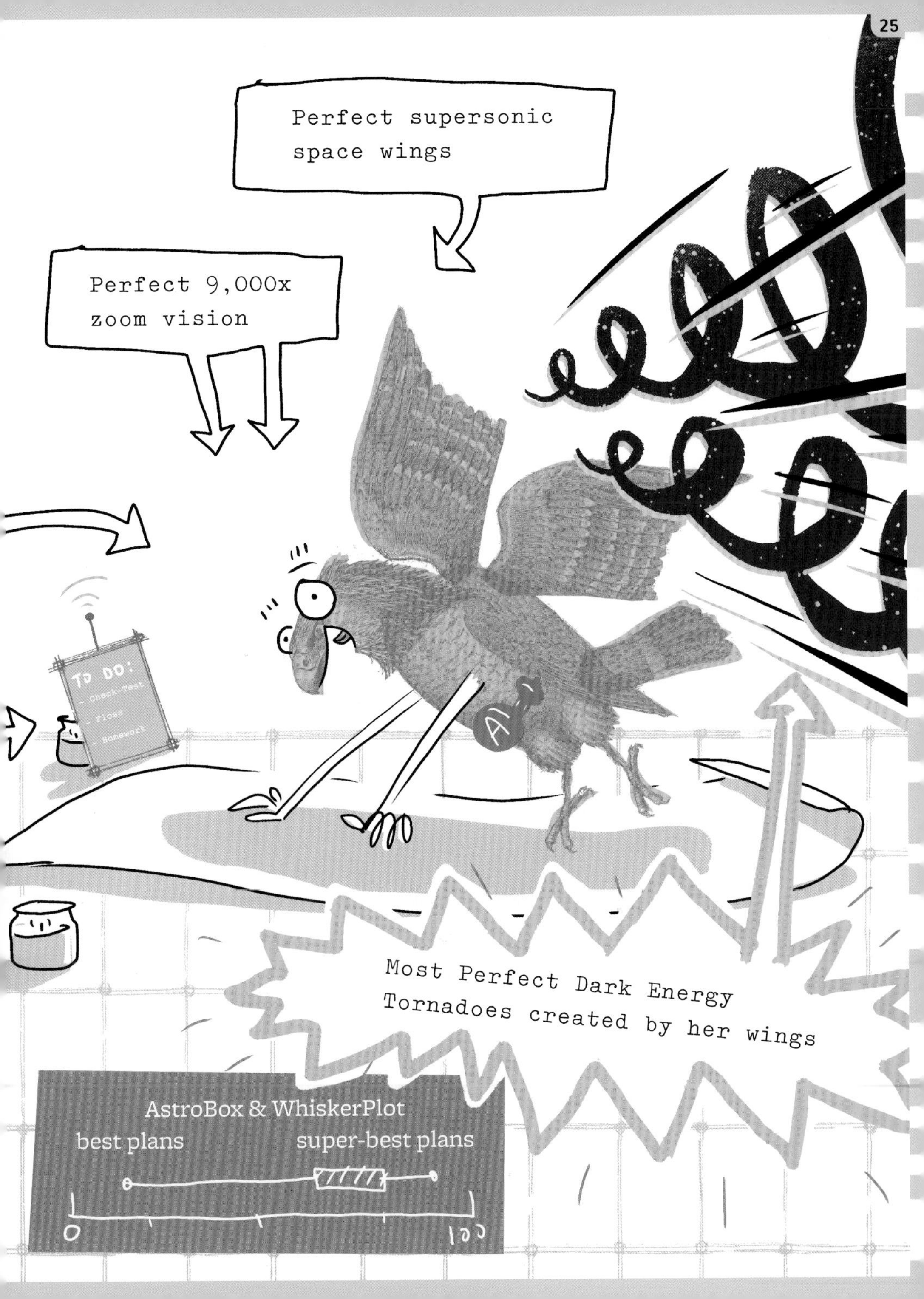
Perfect supersonic space wings
Perfect 9,000x zoom vision
TO DO:
- Check-Test
- Floss
- Homework
Most Perfect Dark Energy Tornadoes created by her wings
AstroBox & WhiskerPlot
best plans
super-best plans
0
100

CHAPTER 4:
LaserShark

I am LaserShark!
I am super!
I protect and feed everyone.

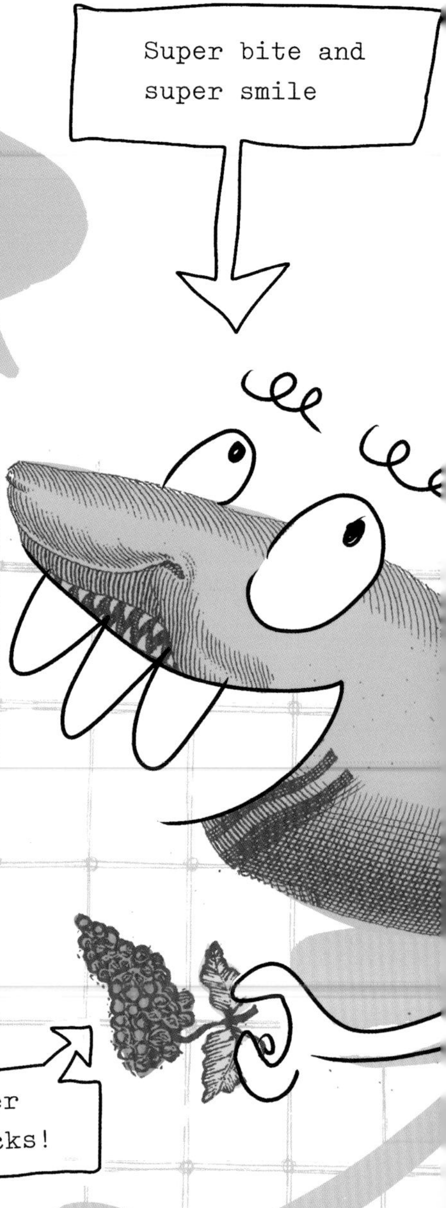

Super bite and super smile
Super snacks!

ASTROSTATS

MISSION NURSE, COOK, AND SECURITY

Objective: Search target planet for FOOD

Length: 14′2″
Weight: 2.3 tons
Hobbies: Making new friends

Great white shark habitat:

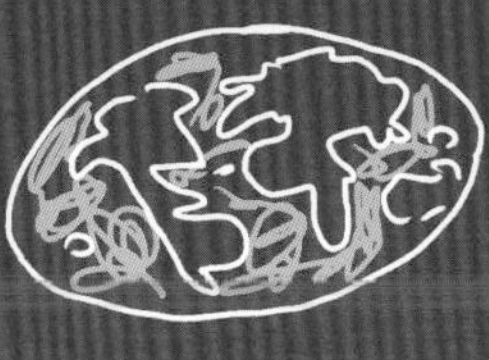

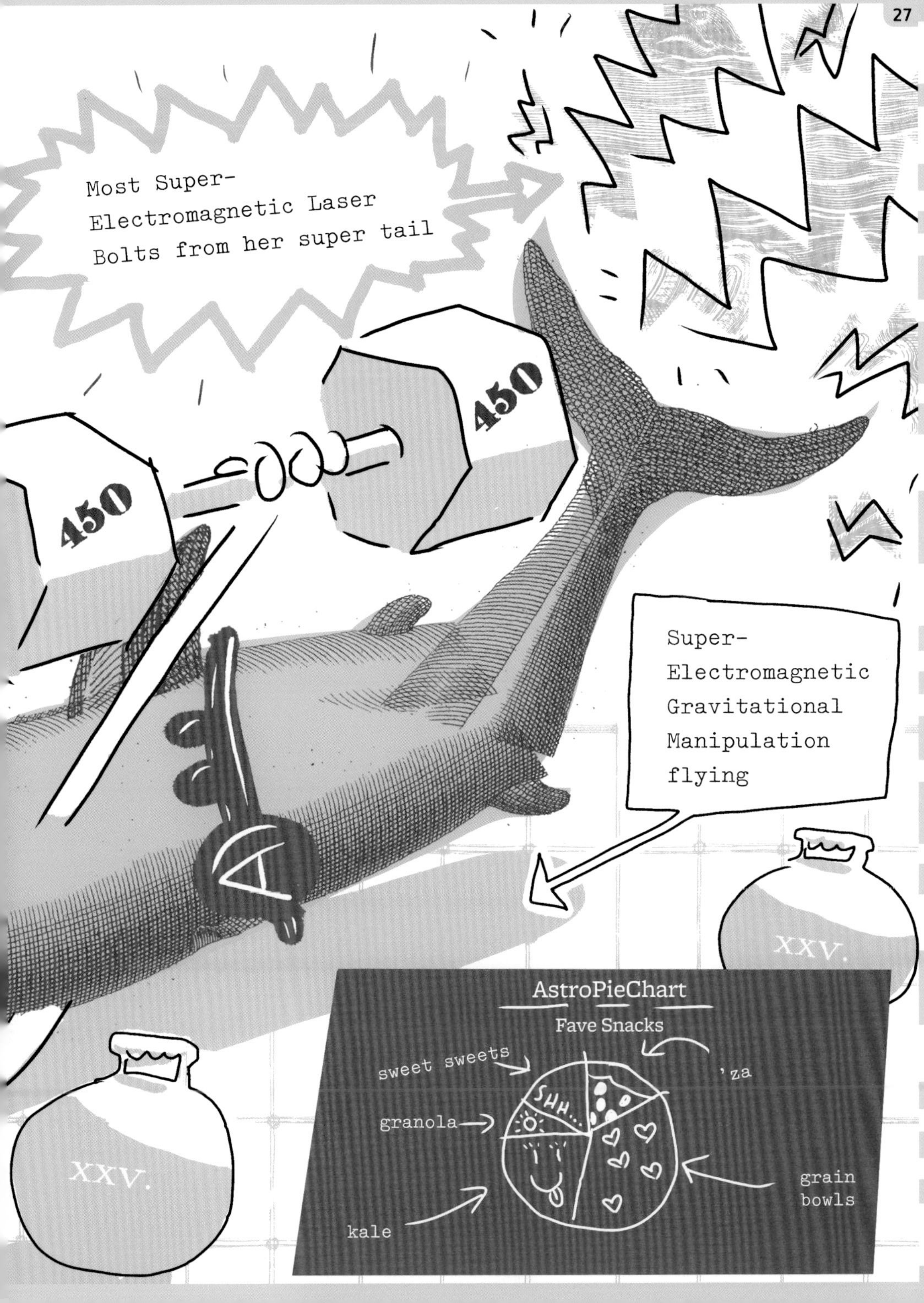
Most Super-
Electromagnetic Laser
Bolts from her super tail
450
450
Super-
Electromagnetic
Gravitational
Manipulation
flying
XXV.
XXV.
AstroPieChart
Fave Snacks
sweet sweets
'za
SHH...
granola
grain
bowls
kale

CHAPTER 5:

StinkBug

I am me.
Oh, I mean. I am StinkBug.
And StinkBug is me.
Aren't we supposed to watch our Video Briefing in the AstroTorium now?

Serious high-altitude jumping

ASTROSTATS

MISSION PILOT AND TECH OFFICER

Objective: Search target planet for SHELTER

Length: 3'0"
Weight: 14 ounces
Hobbies: Master LEGO builder, flower arranging

Dung beetle habitat:

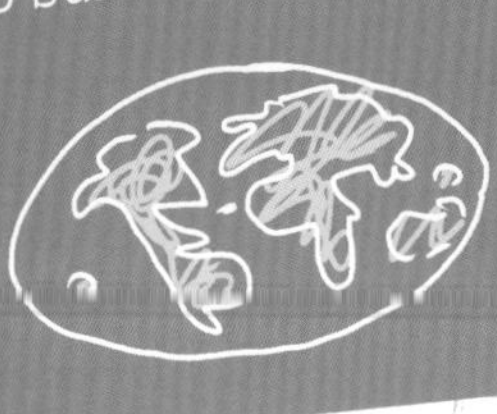

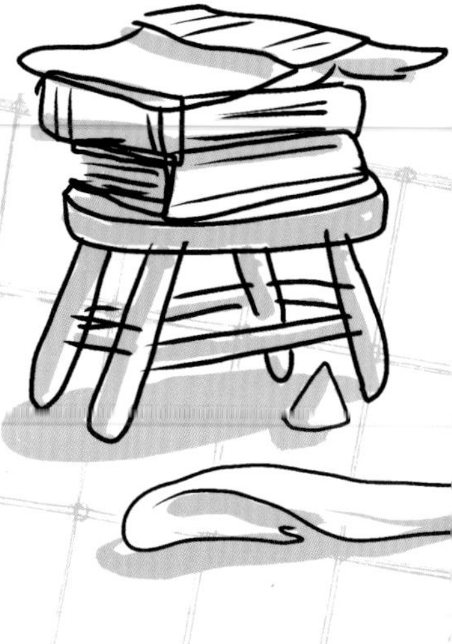

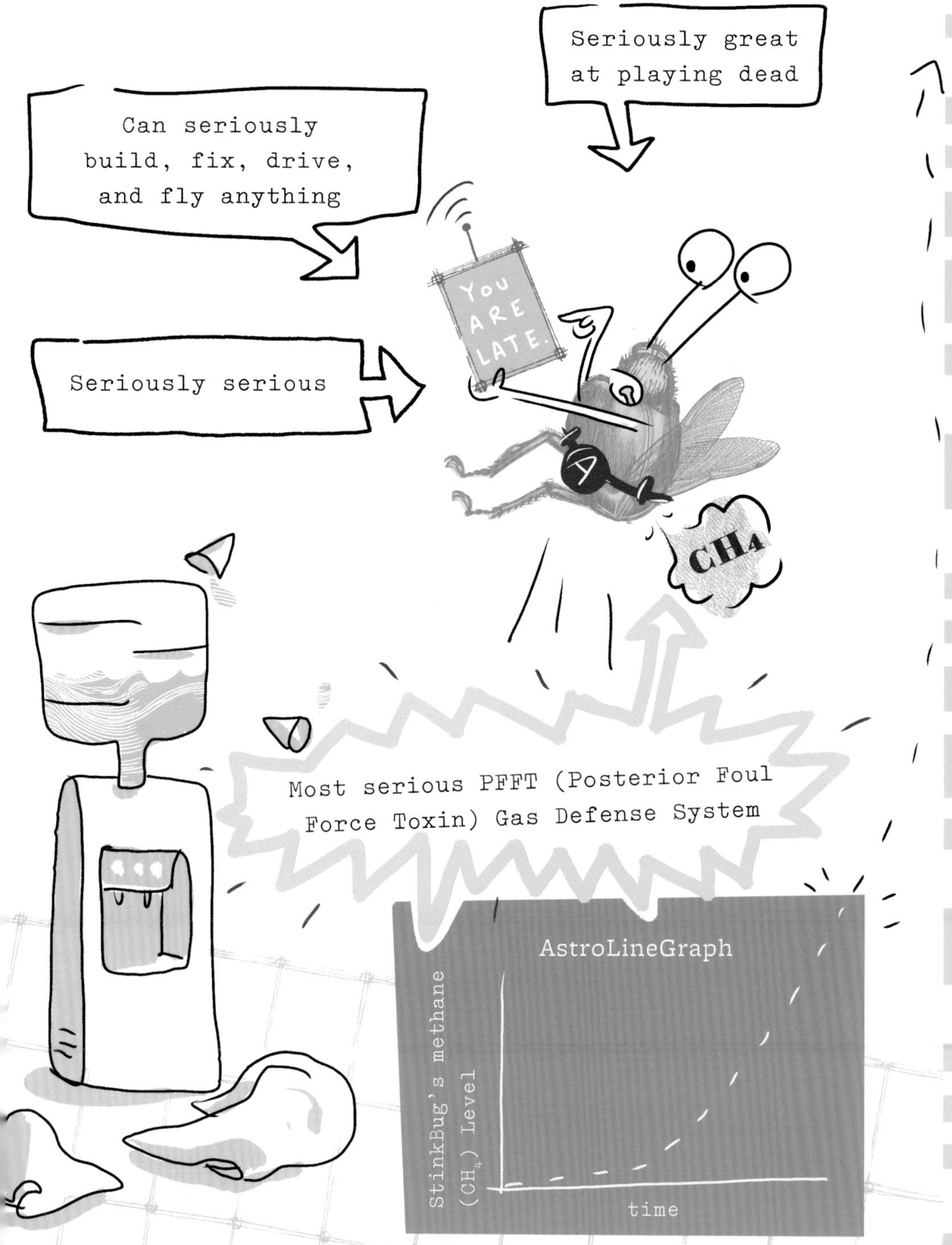
Seriously great at playing dead
Can seriously build, fix, drive, and fly anything
YOU ARE LATE.
Seriously serious
CH4
Most serious PFFT (Posterior Foul Force Toxin) Gas Defense System
AstroLineGraph
StinkBug's methane (CH_4) Level
time

CHAPTER 6:
Homework

Feeling pretty super about showing off their superpowers, the AstroNuts marched from the AstroNasium into the AstroTorium. They were superpowered, all right. But exploring a Goldilocks Planet takes more than superpowers. It also takes superhuman ability to watch videos, answer questions, and fill out forms.

If you saw *Why the Plant Planet?*, I think you would agree it is a fairly interesting film.

Did I miss the previews??

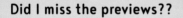

WHY THE

Temperature is just right.

80°

O_2 CO_2

N_2

Atmosphere is just the right mix of oxygen, nitrogen, and carbon dioxide.

Lots of beautiful shots of plant life. A very soothing voice talking about why the Plant Planet just might have everything a planet would need to support human life. Very solid science.

But can we talk about that weak ending?

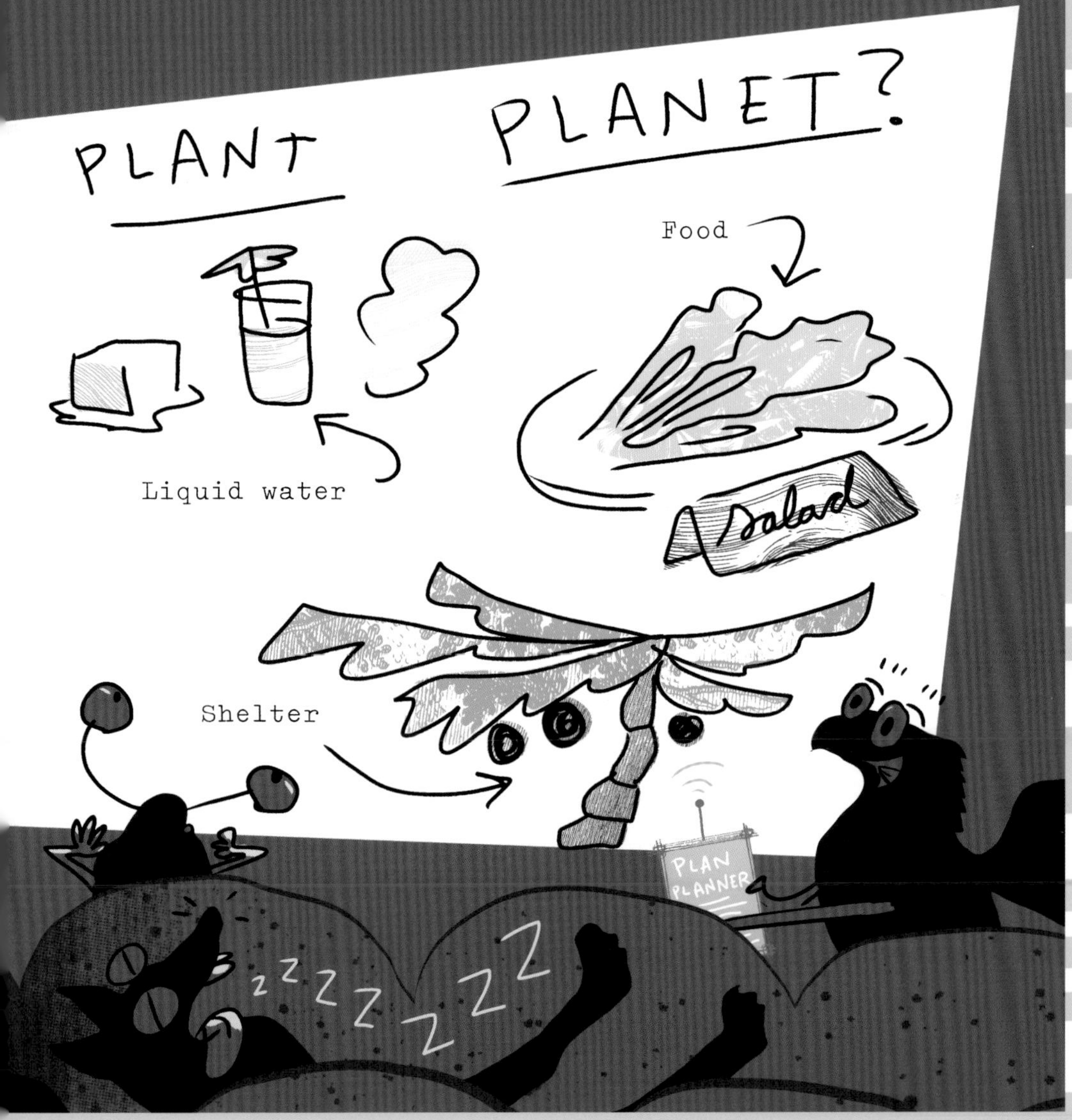
PLANT PLANET?
Food
Salad
Liquid water
Shelter
PLAN PLANNER
zzzzzzzz

The whole video ends with a blank Form 35-FGPR Final Goldilocks Planet Report.

Not the most exciting ending ever.

FORM 35-FGPR

FINAL GOLDILOCKS

Name of planet: ____________________

Temperature range: ____________________

Atmosphere: ____________________

Describe inhabitants: ____________________

____

____

____

____

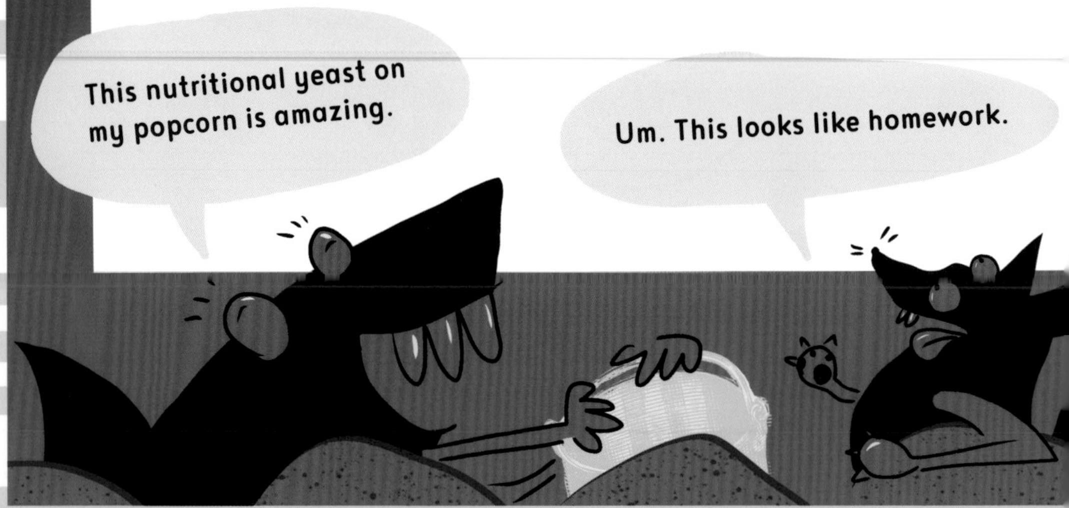
This nutritional yeast on my popcorn is amazing.
Um. This looks like homework.

The only good news about Form 35-FGPR was: The AstroNuts didn't have to fill it out until the end of their mission.

PLANET REPORT

Planet has liquid water:	TRUE / FALSE
Humans could find food and shelter here:	TRUE / FALSE
Planet ecosystem well-balanced:	TRUE / FALSE
No intelligent life harmed:	TRUE / FALSE

OVERALL RATING:

a) Great
b) OK
c) Not good
d) Terrible
e) Your head explodes

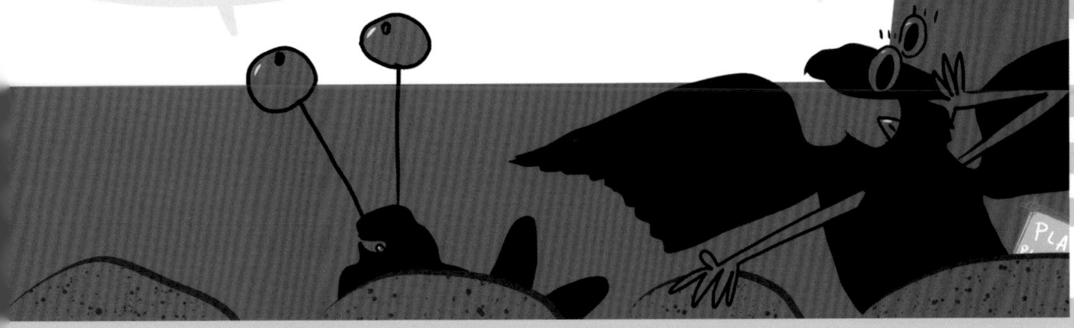
Oh, what a beautiful form! Short answers! True/false! Multiple choice!
Elementary.

The AstroNuts were ready. They filed out of the AstroTorium. They took their positions on the AstroNoseBridge, hurtling toward the Plant Planet at an intergalactic speed too fast to even be explained.

Just like that, they had traveled 39 light-years.

In 3 hours and 26 minutes.

Seriously breaking the Speed Limit of the Universe.

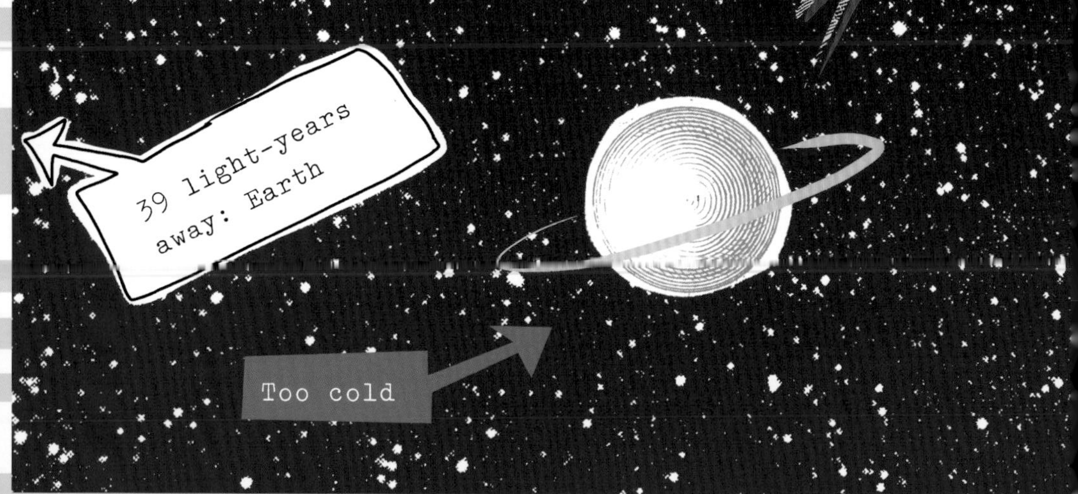
39 light-years away: Earth
Too cold

The AstroNuts were jazzed.

They were ready to explore everything!

They were also, except for StinkBug, completely clueless that they were very, very, very, very close to the Plant Planet.

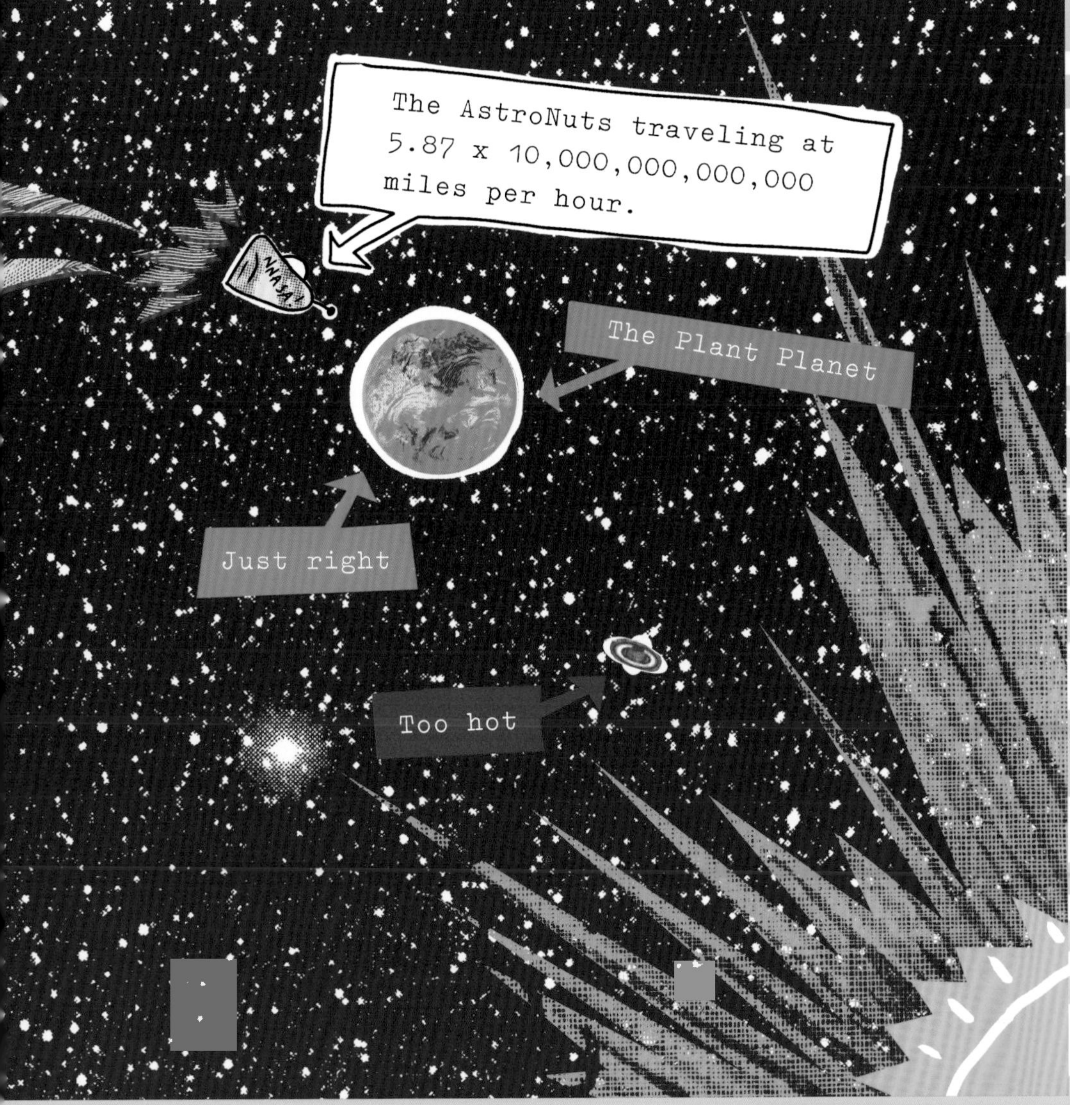
The AstroNuts traveling at 5.87 x 10,000,000,000,000 miles per hour.
NASA
The Plant Planet
Just right
Too hot

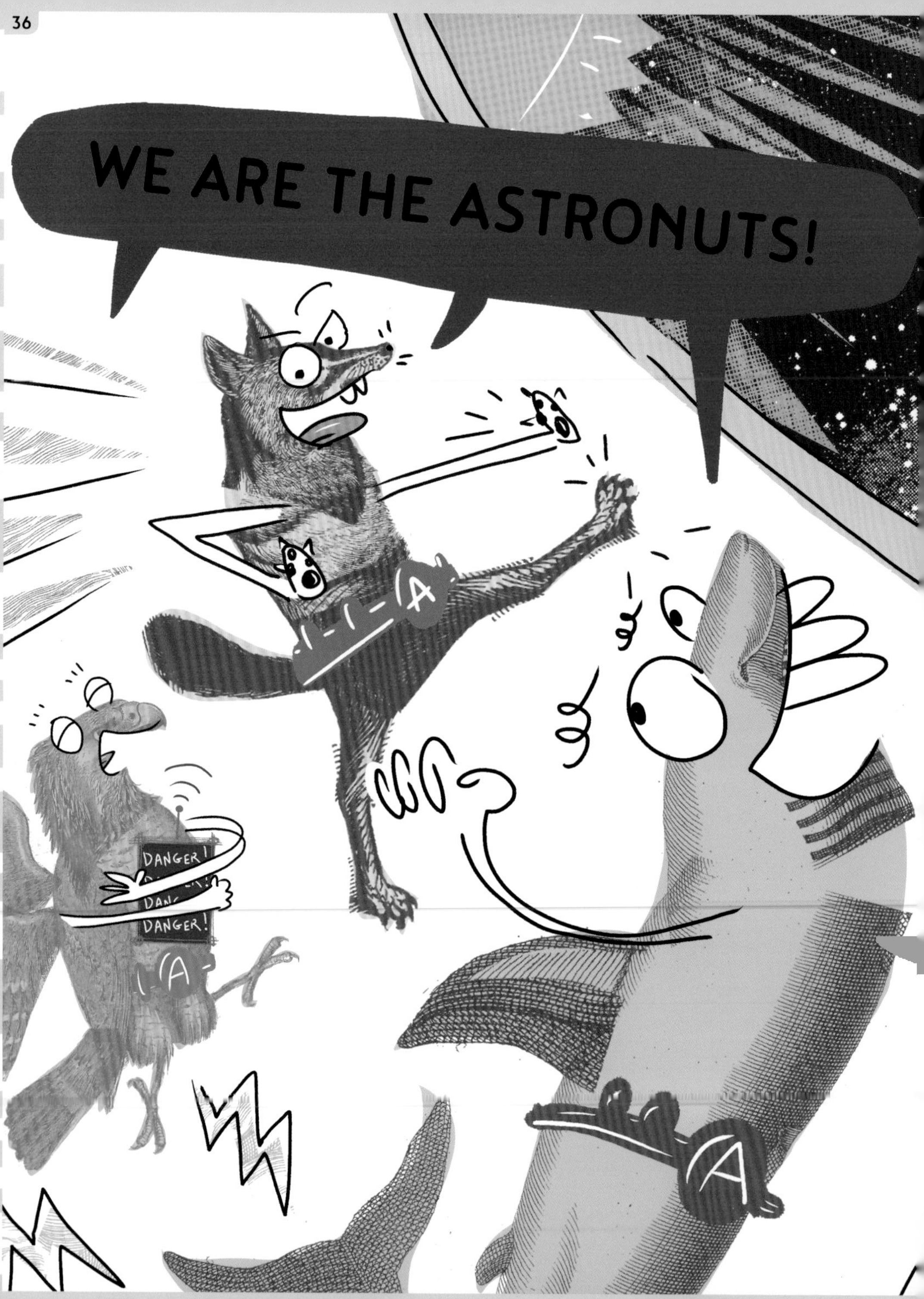
WE ARE THE ASTRONUTS!
DANGER!
DANGER!
DANGER!
A
A
A
A

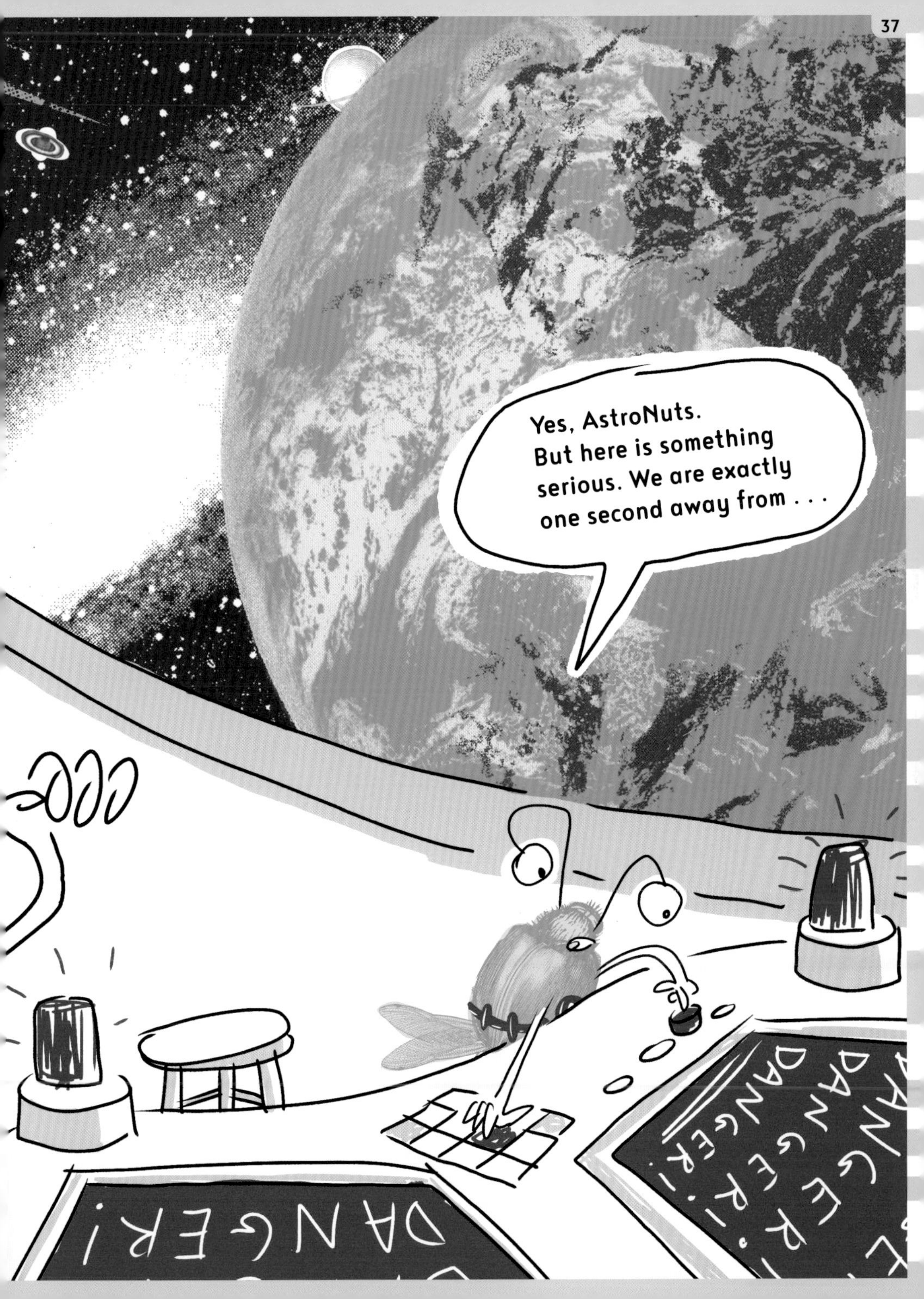
Yes, AstroNuts.
But here is something serious. We are exactly one second away from . . .
DANGER!
DANGER!
DANGER!

CHAPTER 7:
CRASH!!!!

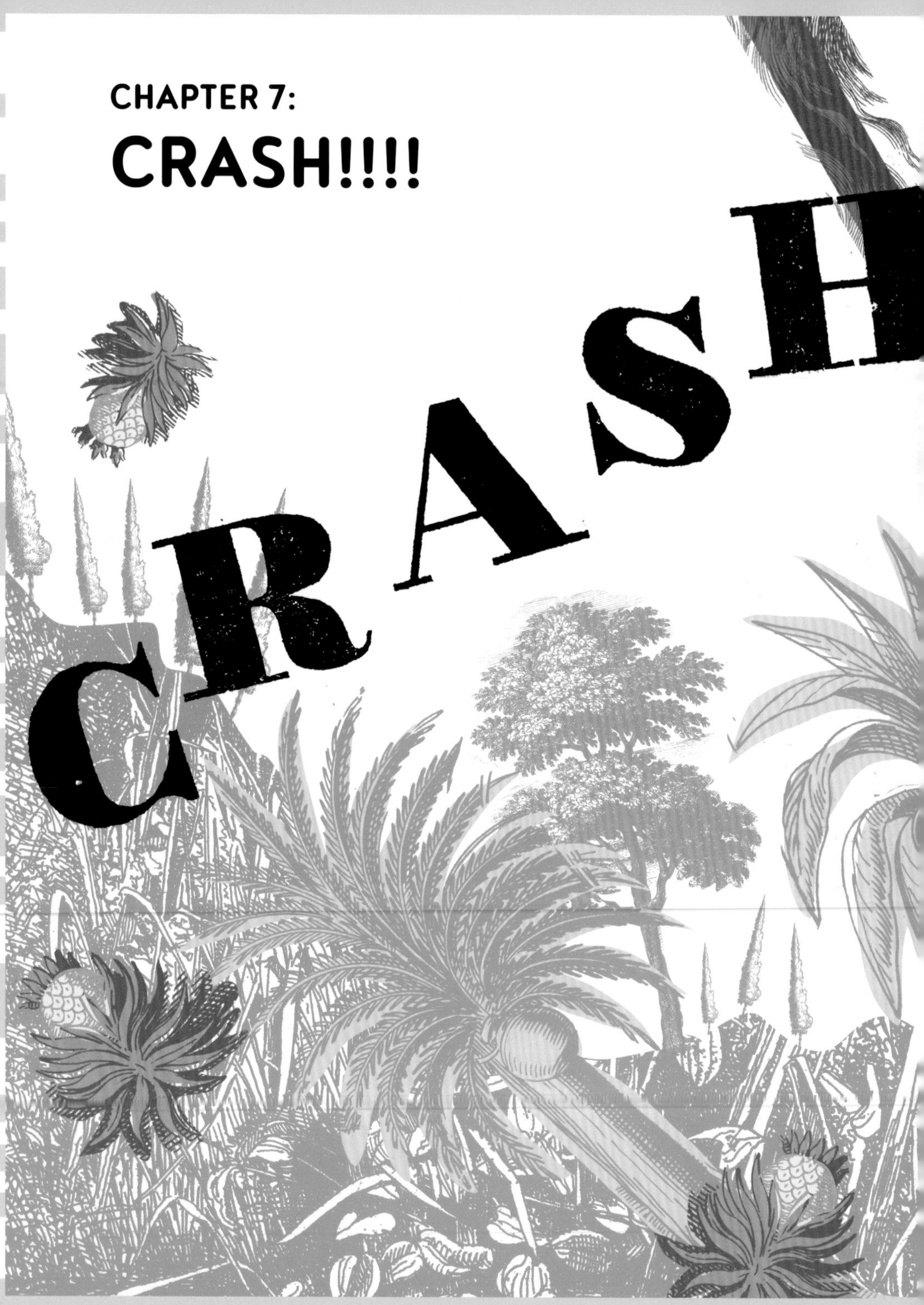
CRASH

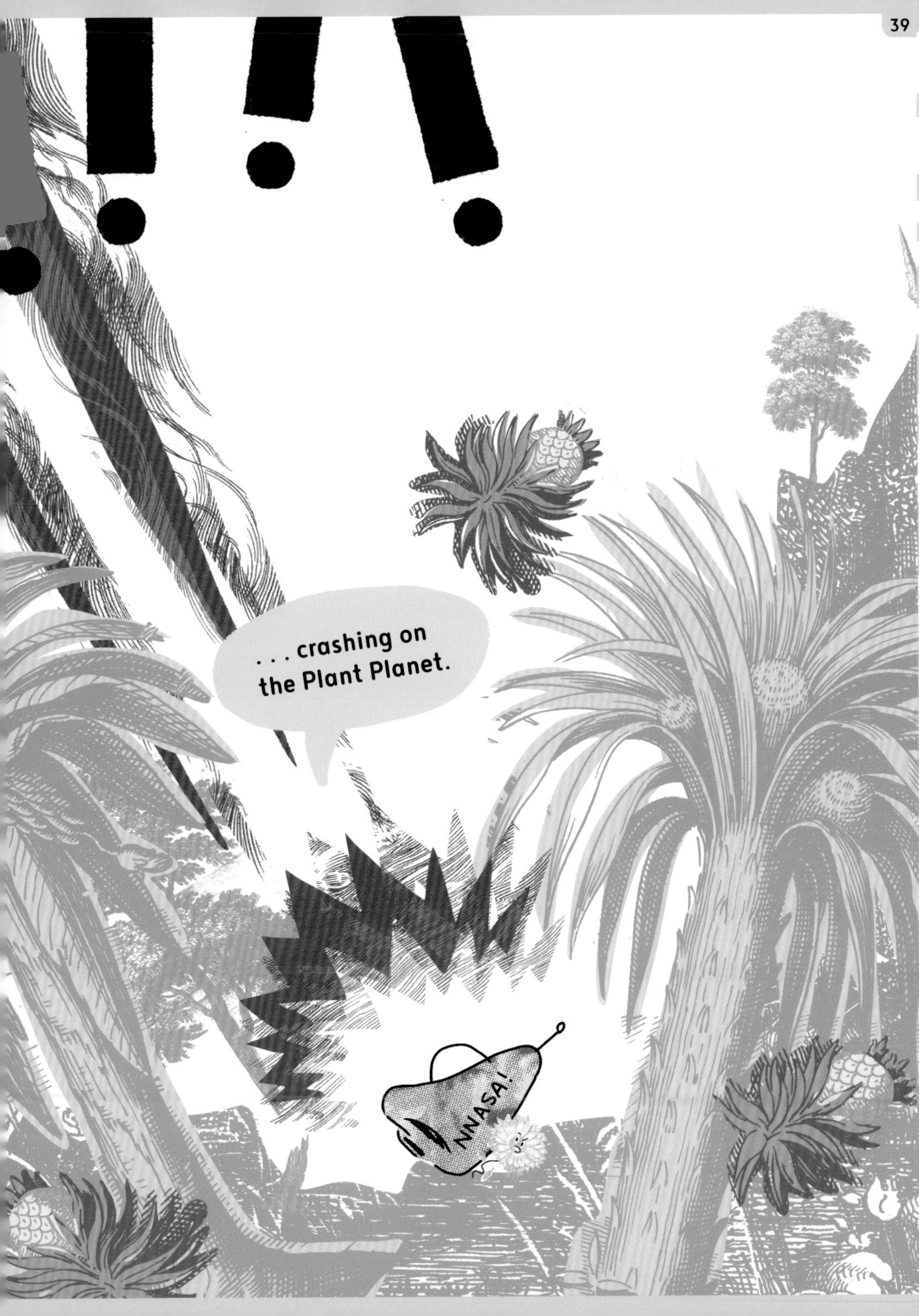
!!!
. . . crashing on
the Plant Planet.
NNASA!

CHAPTER 8:
Oh, No

Now, this is the part of space exploration—a first look at a new planet—that you would think would be the most exciting. The most dramatic. The most amazing.

But because these were the AstroNuts, it was not any of these things.

Because these were the AstroNuts, the nose of their Nose Rocket was stuck in 1.7 metric tons of Plant Planet plants.

And they were in complete darkness.

////// Official NNASA transcript //////
//// of AstroNut MISSION 1 ////

StinkBug: Great. Our crash-landing broke our exterior Nose instruments.
AlphaWolf: What are we going to do?!
SmartHawk: Well, we could use AstroPlan AP-123G (Gesundheit).
AlphaWolf: Oh, right. I was going to suggest that. One quick question: What is AstroPlan AP-123G (Gesundheit)?
StinkBug: Actually, I thought this could happen. So I redesigned the Nose Thruster to double as an Emergency Exit.
AlphaWolf: Is this going to mess up my silky fur?
LaserShark: It sounds like a thrilling ride.
SmartHawk: Genius. Now, before we blow out onto the Plant Planet, let's confirm our AstroAssignments.
AlphaWolf: Or we COULD . . . just head back to Earth. That would be safest. For everyone, of course.

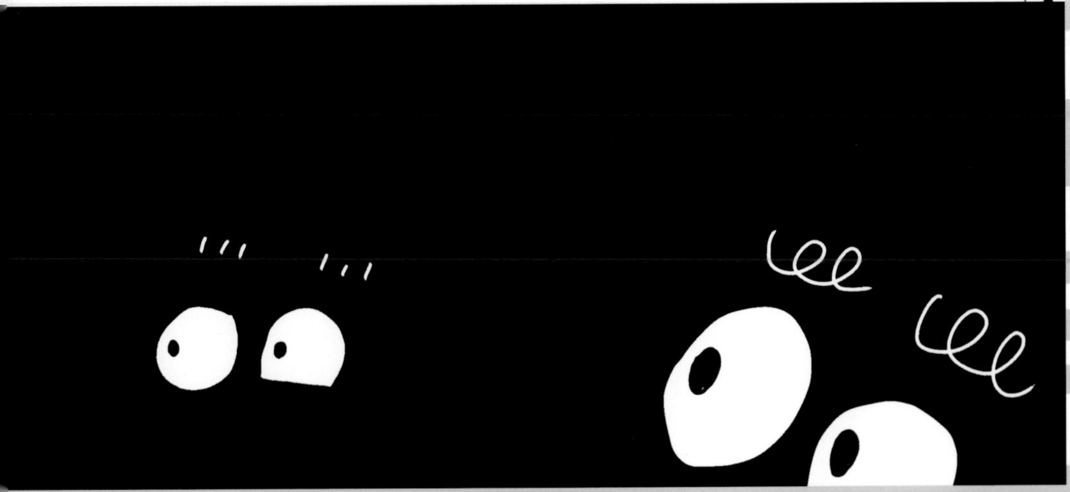

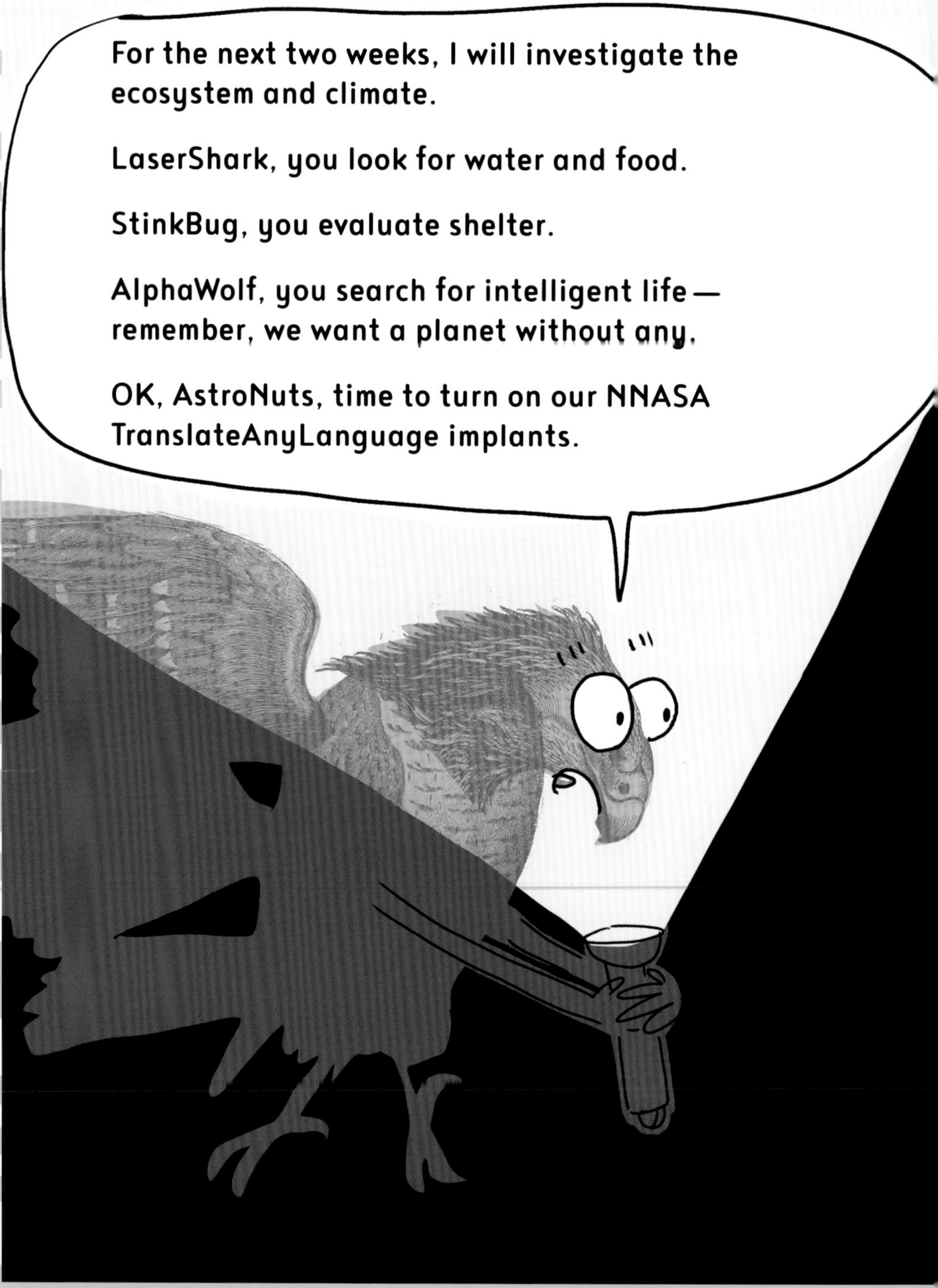
For the next two weeks, I will investigate the ecosystem and climate.
LaserShark, you look for water and food.
StinkBug, you evaluate shelter.
AlphaWolf, you search for intelligent life— remember, we want a planet without any.
OK, AstroNuts, time to turn on our NNASA TranslateAnyLanguage implants.

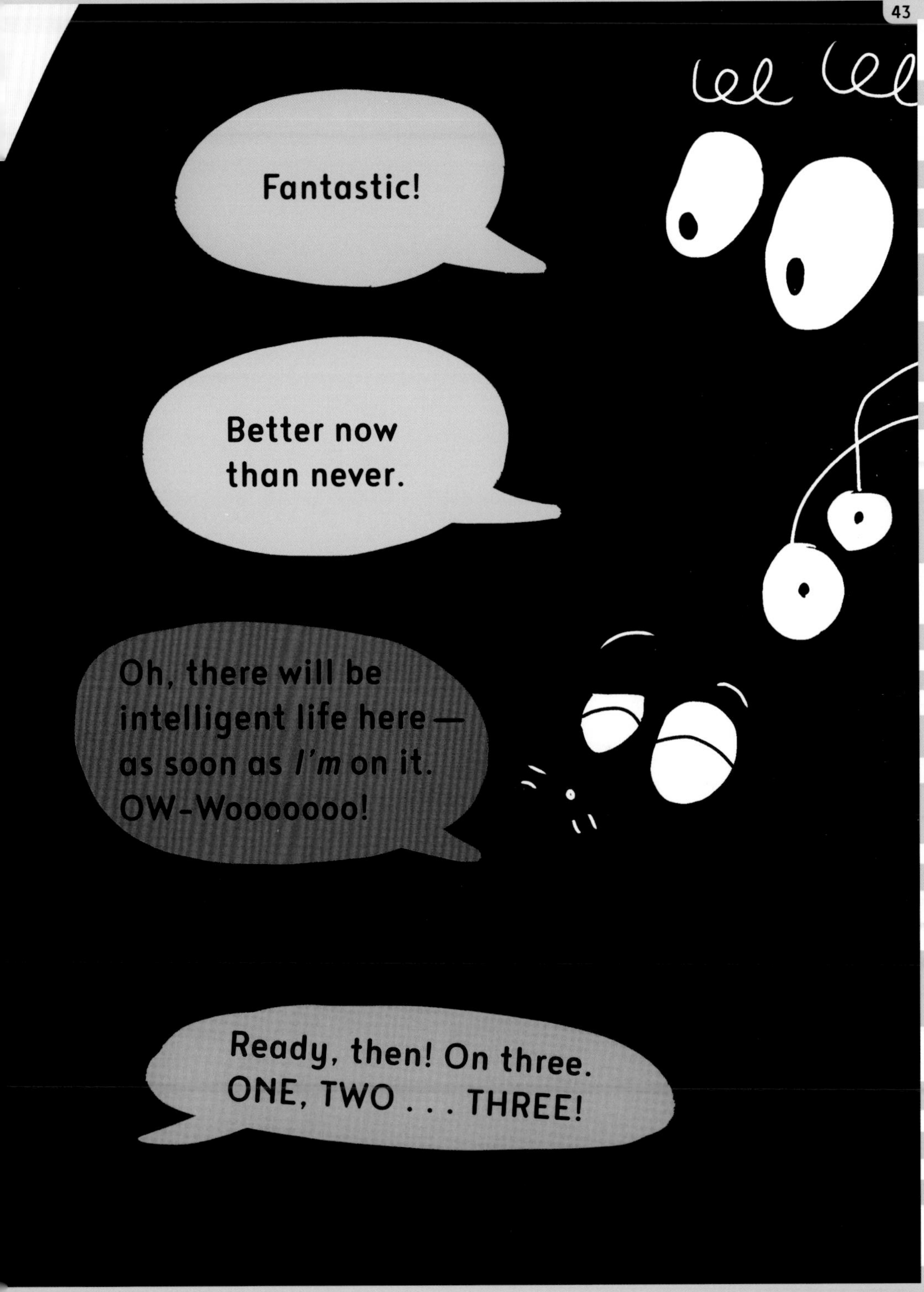
Fantastic!
Better now than never.
Oh, there will be intelligent life here— as soon as *I'm* on it. OW-Wooooooo!
Ready, then! On three. ONE, TWO . . . THREE!

StinkBug flipped the Thruster Override Switch and activated his genius exit with AP-123G (Gesundheit).

It was not exactly a door.

It was not exactly a hatch.

But if you think about it, it is the obvious way to exit a Nose.

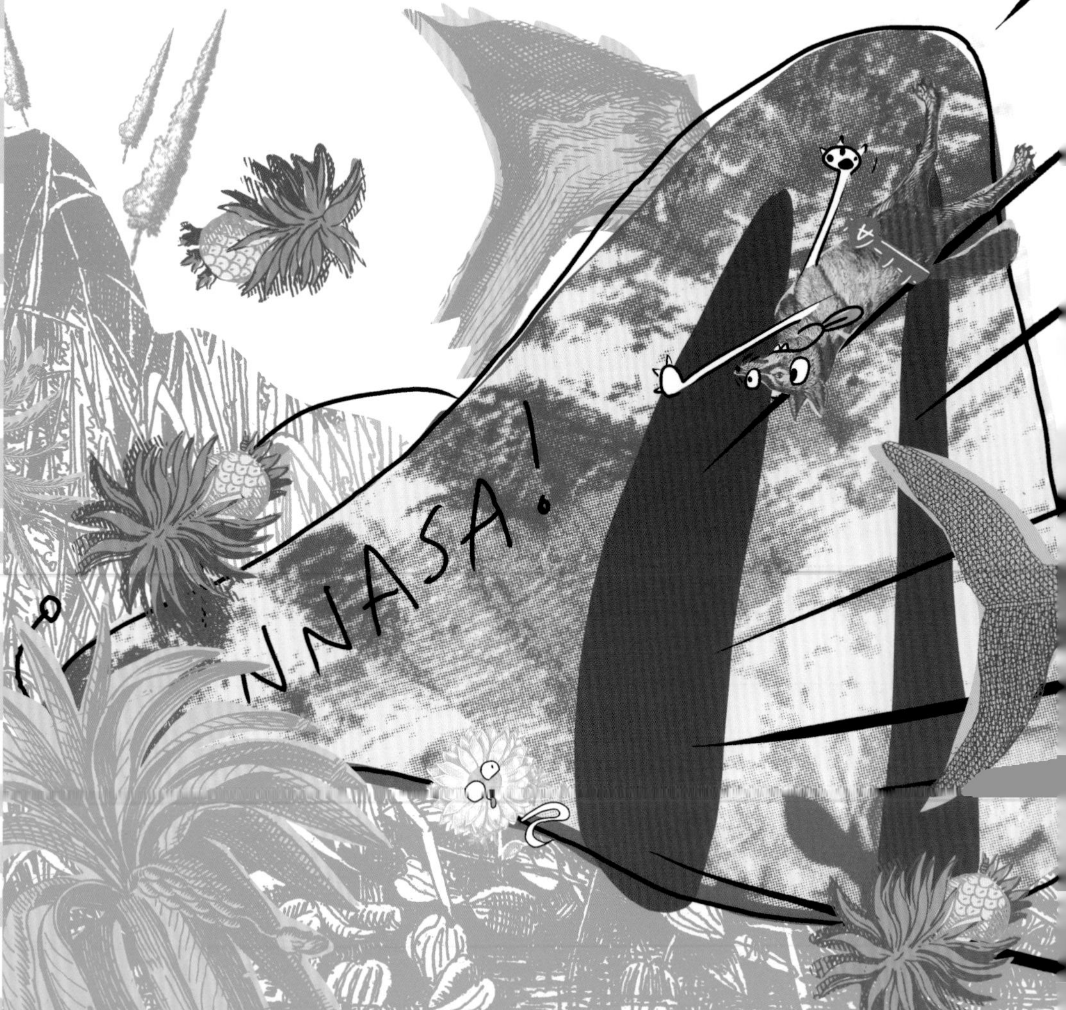

NNASA!

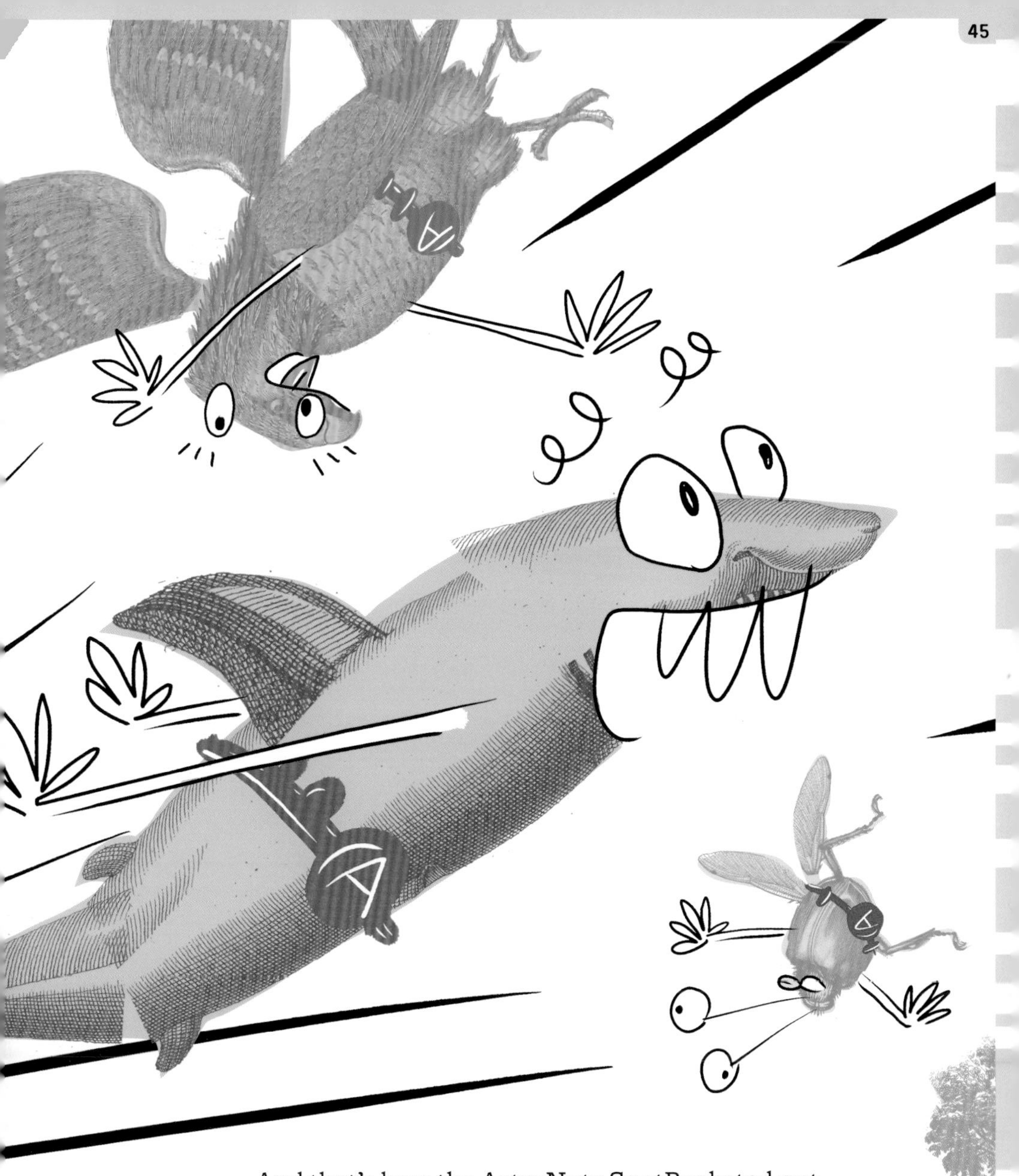

And that's how the AstroNuts SnotRocketed out of the Thomas Jefferson Nose and right into their investigation of the Plant Planet.

CHAPTER 9:

Maps, Etc.

Hitting the atmosphere, SmartHawk flew into action, using her perfect zoom vision—observing, testing, and mapping.

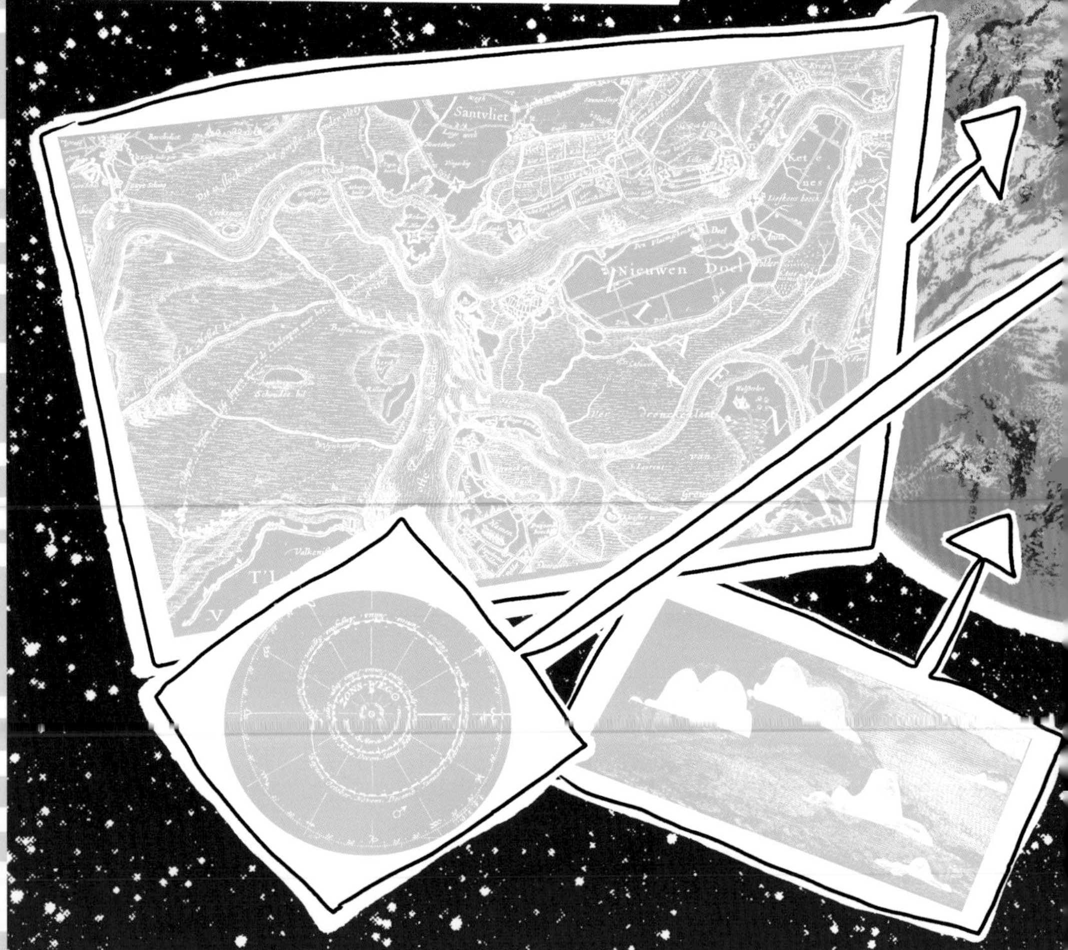
Santvliet
Nieuwen Doel

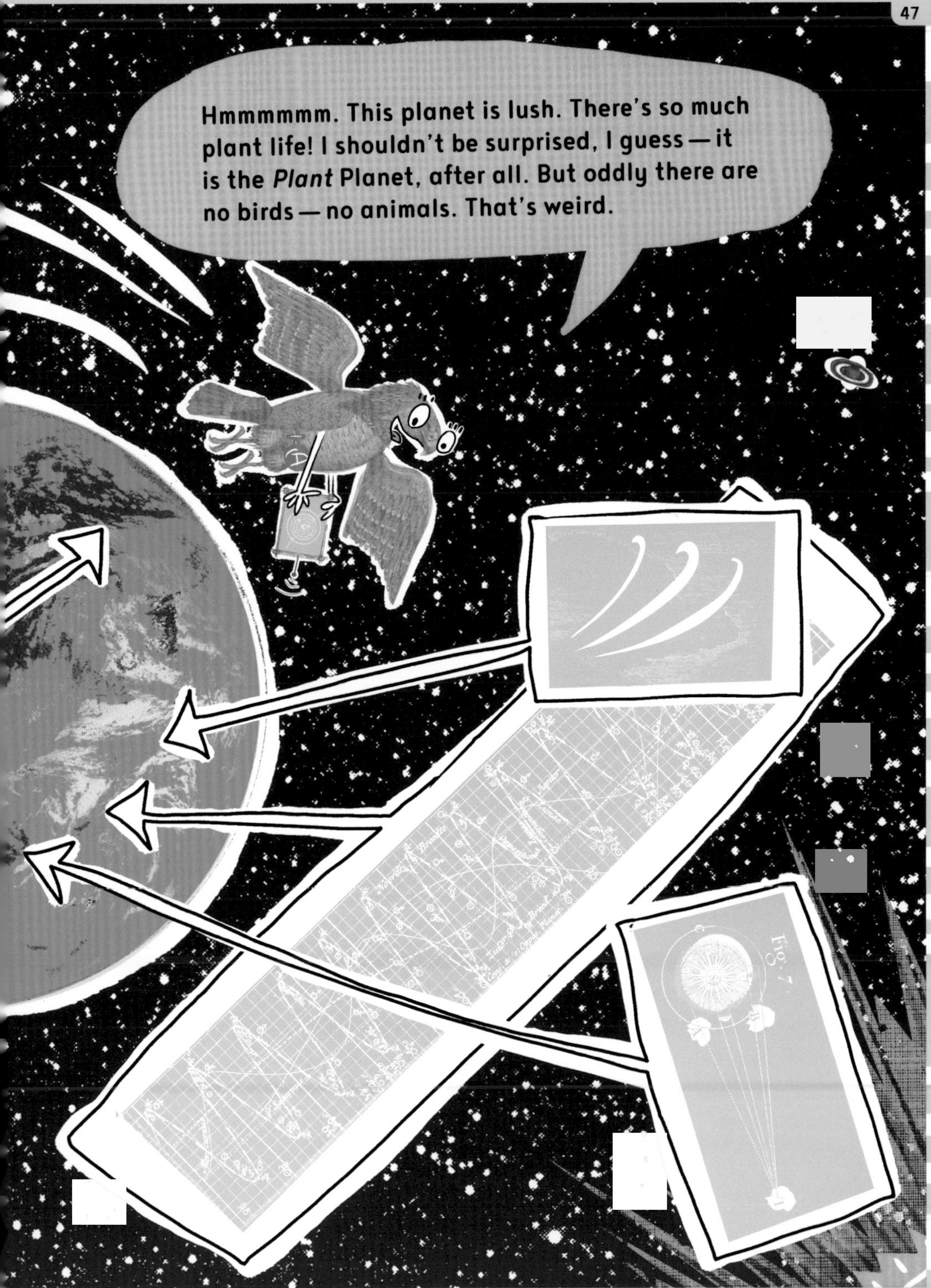
Hmmmmmm. This planet is lush. There's so much plant life! I shouldn't be surprised, I guess—it is the *Plant* Planet, after all. But oddly there are no birds—no animals. That's weird.

She input and graphed
the climate conditions.

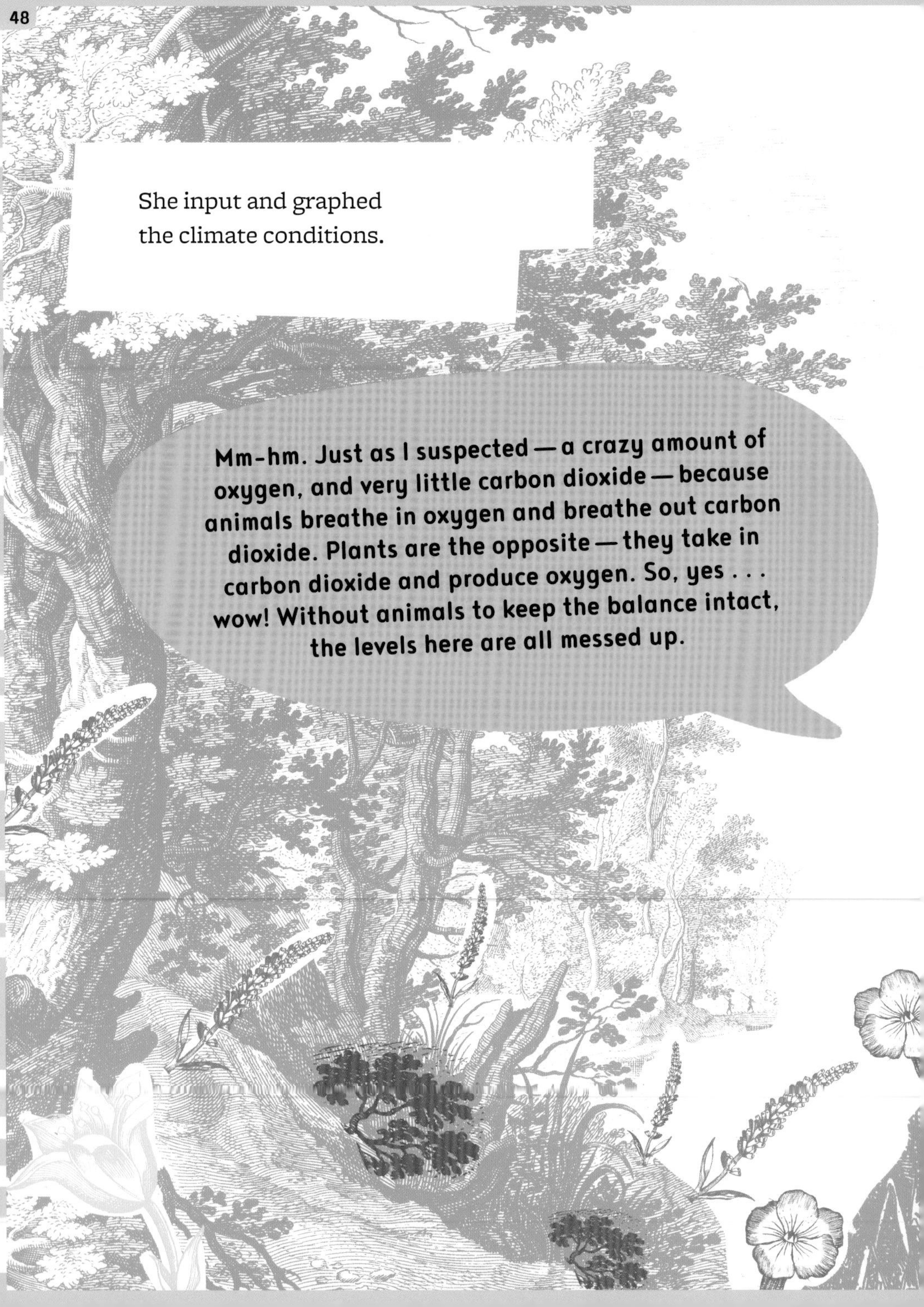
Mm-hm. Just as I suspected — a crazy amount of oxygen, and very little carbon dioxide — because animals breathe in oxygen and breathe out carbon dioxide. Plants are the opposite — they take in carbon dioxide and produce oxygen. So, yes . . . wow! Without animals to keep the balance intact, the levels here are all messed up.

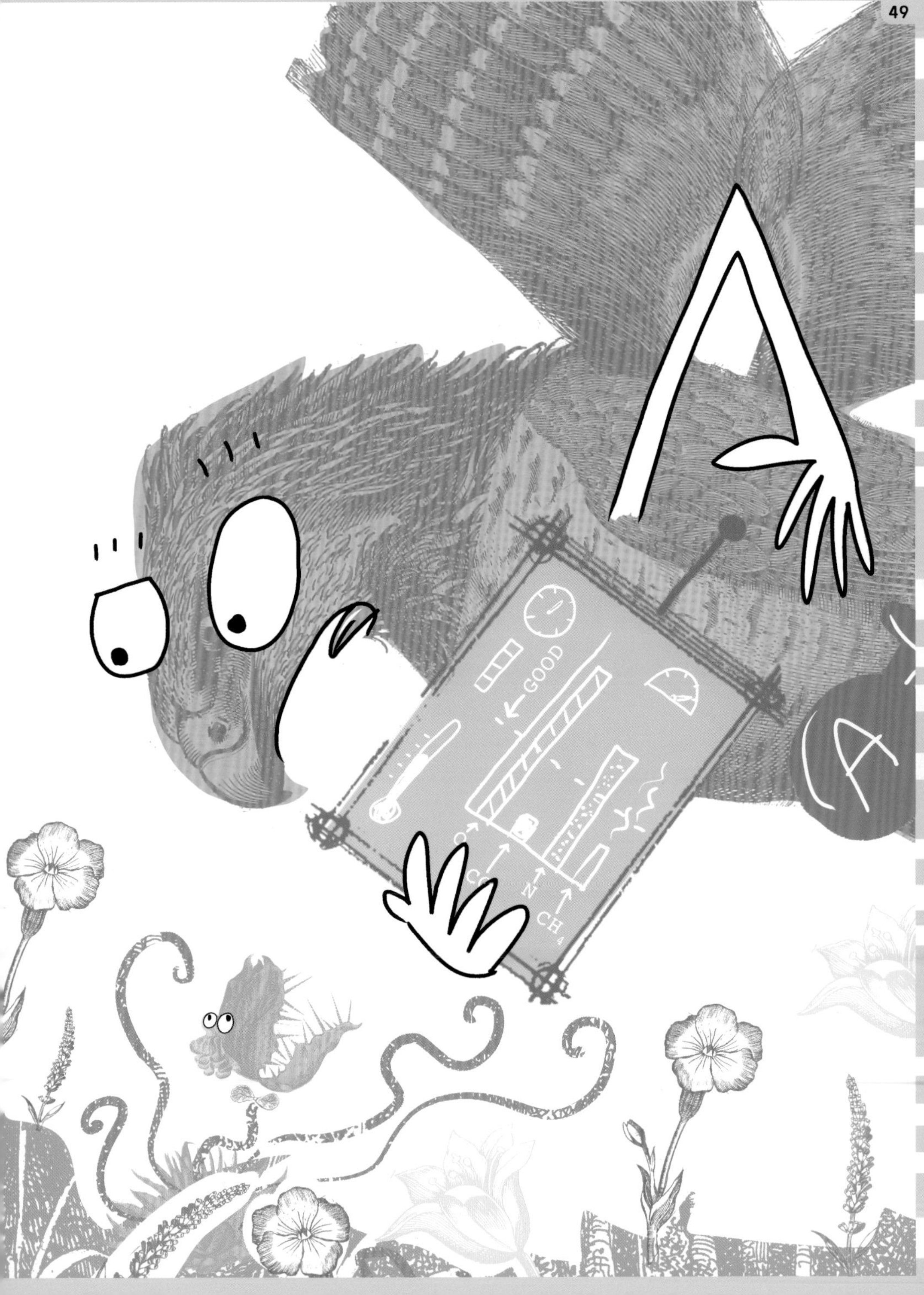
GOOD
O
CO
N
CH_4

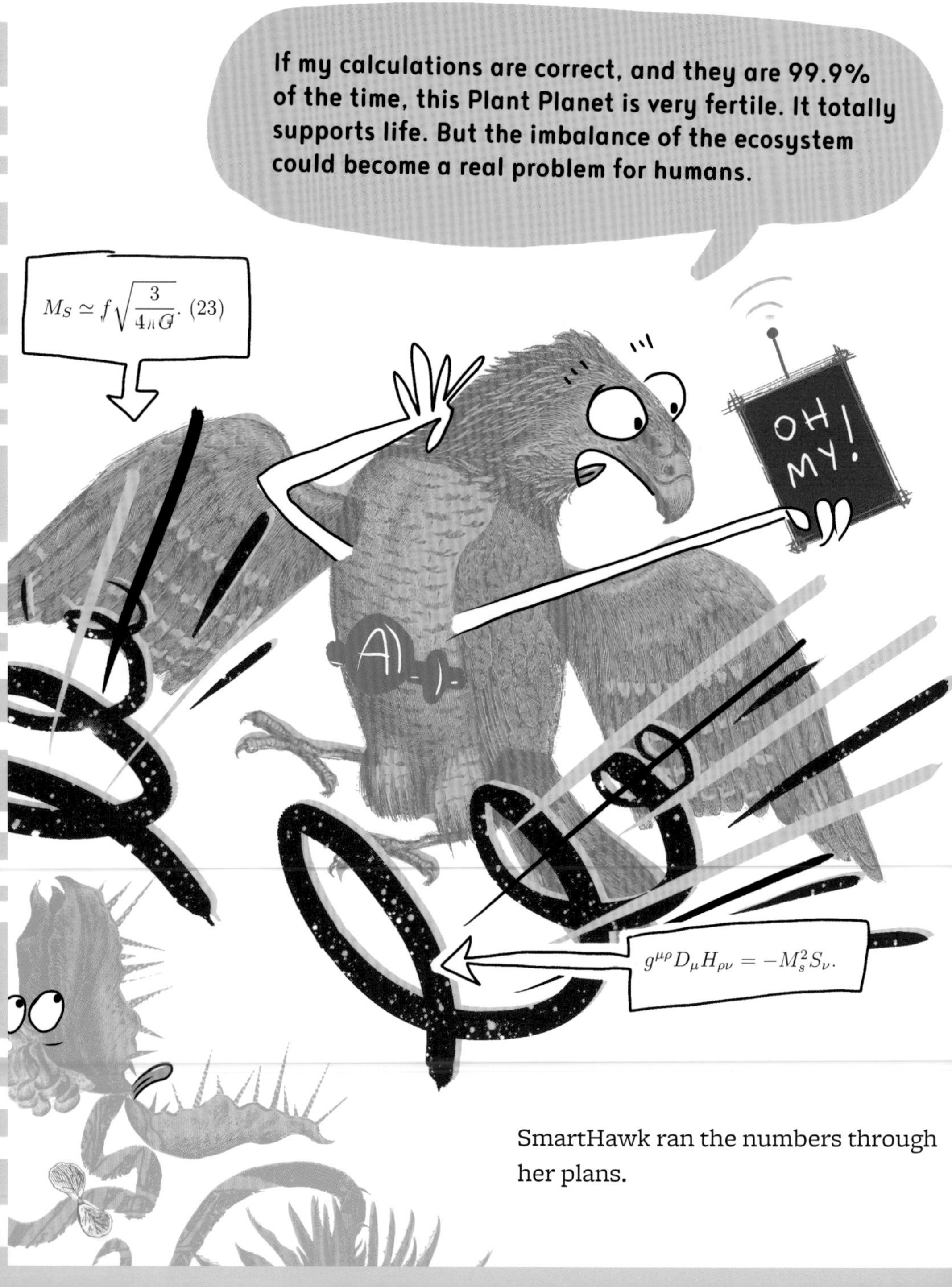
If my calculations are correct, and they are 99.9% of the time, this Plant Planet is very fertile. It totally supports life. But the imbalance of the ecosystem could become a real problem for humans.
$M_S \simeq f\sqrt{\frac{3}{4\pi G}}$. (23)
OH MY!
AI
$g^{\mu\rho} D_\mu H_{\rho\nu} = -M_s^2 S_\nu$.

SmartHawk ran the numbers through her plans.

SmartHawk was so worried by her calculations that she accidentally wing-flapped a mini Dark Energy Vortex. Then she zoomed back to the Nose Rocket to download her data.

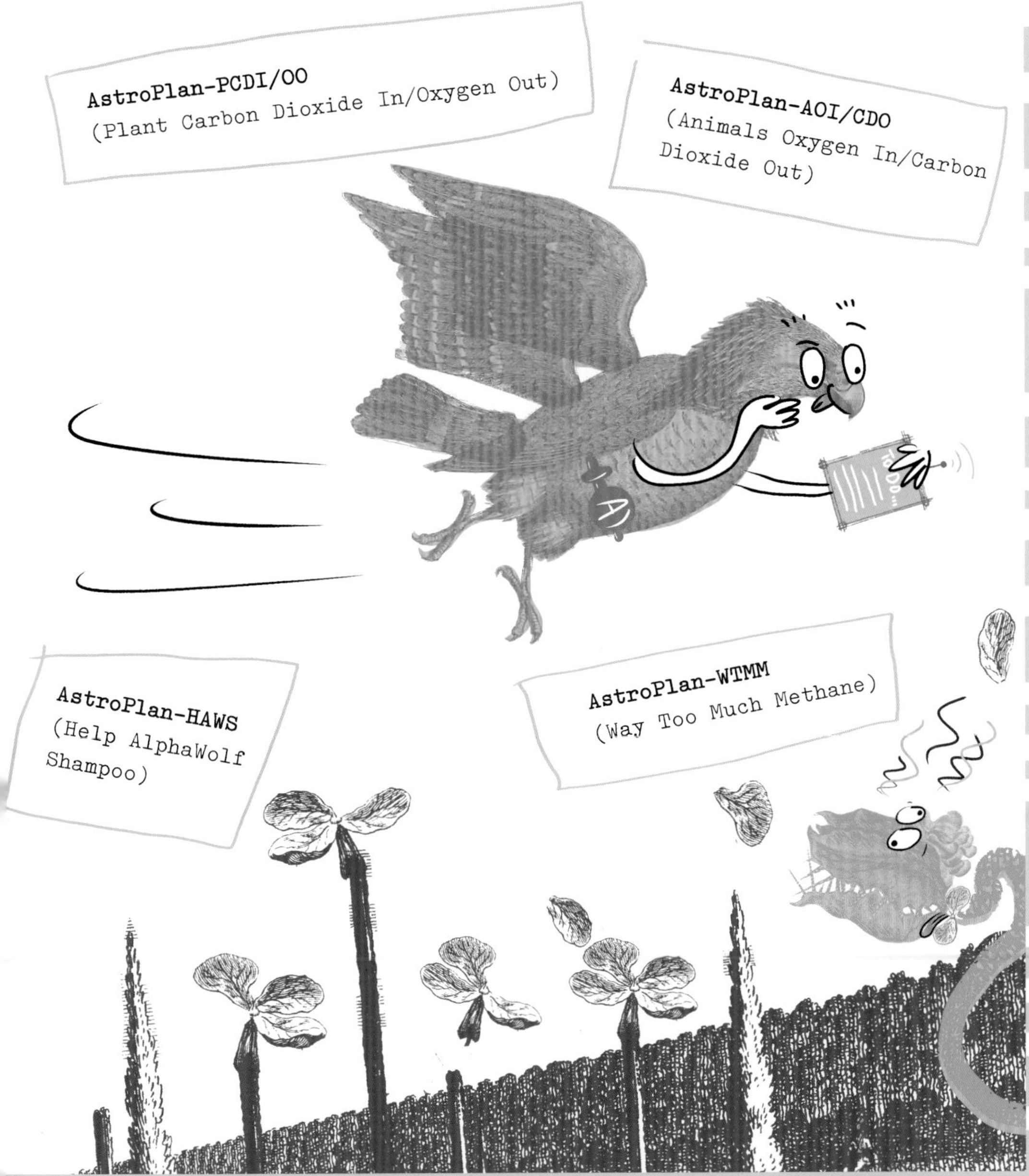
AstroPlan-PCDI/OO
(Plant Carbon Dioxide In/Oxygen Out)
AstroPlan-AOI/CDO
(Animals Oxygen In/Carbon Dioxide Out)
AstroPlan-HAWS
(Help AlphaWolf Shampoo)
AstroPlan-WTMM
(Way Too Much Methane)

CHAPTER 10:

Tay-Tay Tomatoes

Blowing out of the Nose Rocket, LaserShark, as usual, got a little distracted.

She activated her Super Electromagnetic Field. She zoomed three happy loop-de-loops. She sang a snatch of her "I Love Flying" song. And then she got down to her always-hungry, always-friendly super AstroWork.

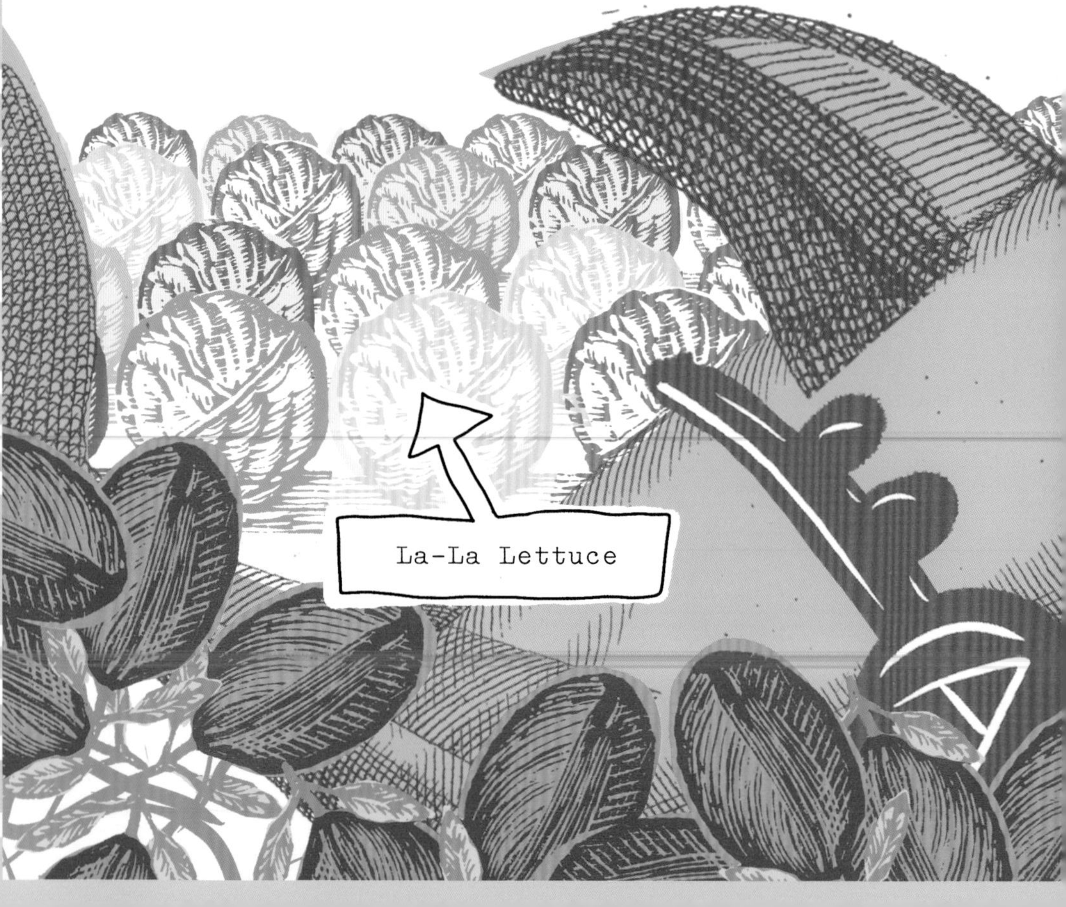
La-La Lettuce

Wooooooooooooow!!!!!!!!!!!!!!!
Look at all these plants! Look at all these salad possibilities! I think I will name and eat every one of them!
Wowza Wheatgrass
Tay-Tay Tomatoes

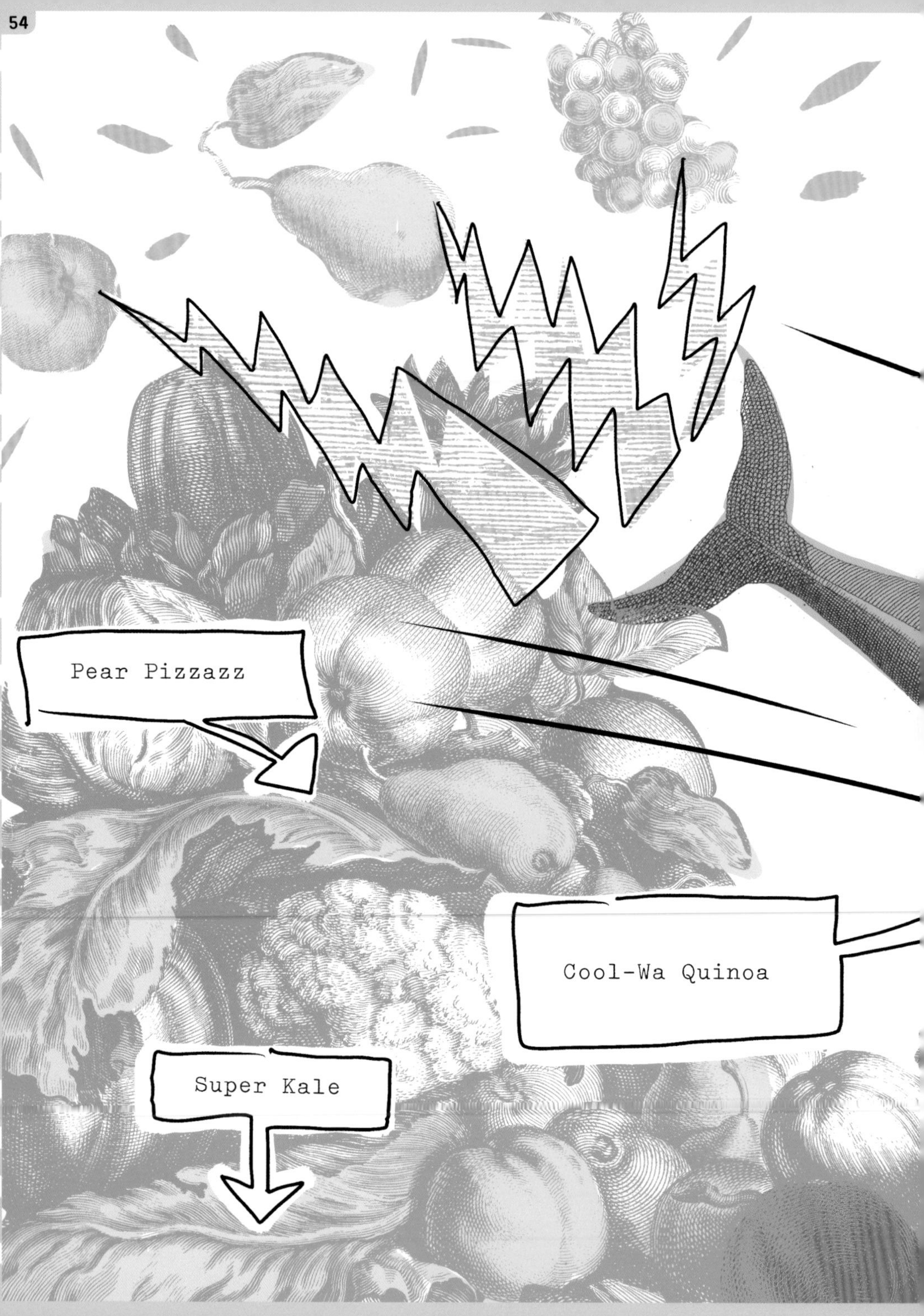
Pear Pizzazz
Cool-Wa Quinoa
Super Kale

Oh, I do love riding around on my Super Electromagnetic Waves!
And I really enjoy Super Laser-Tickling my new plant friends.
So many plant friends! I'll bet they are super glad we are here.
ASTRO tote
Familiar-Looking Venus Flytrap Kind of Plant

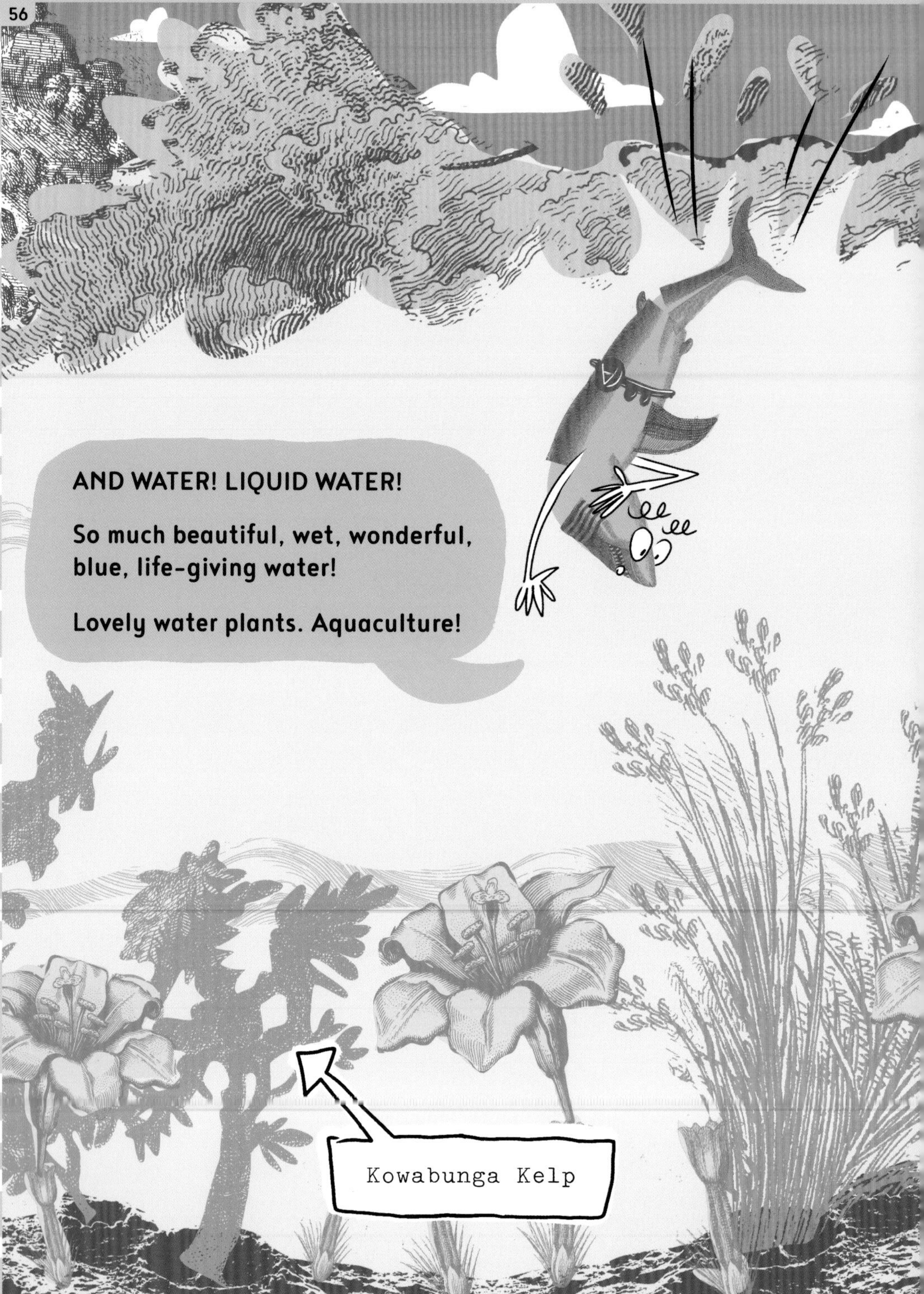
AND WATER! LIQUID WATER!
So much beautiful, wet, wonderful, blue, life-giving water!
Lovely water plants. Aquaculture!
Kowabunga Kelp

But it's odd, no fish. . . . No squid. No coral. No whale pals.

Serious Seagrass

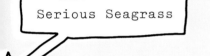

An-Amazing-Anemone

Because LaserShark loved food so much, she collected and listed almost every single plant that you could possibly eat on the whole planet. Chomping one last taste of Kowabunga Kelp in her massive jaws, she buzzed back to the Thomas Jefferson Nose Rocket.

CHAPTER 11:
Hardwood

Even though StinkBug loved science, he was not a big fan of the unknown. I don't blame him, even though the unknown is where I spend most of my time. The unknown is scary.

StinkBug tumbled out of the Nose Rocket and looked around for any giant snakes or frogs or lizards who might eat him. When that didn't happen, StinkBug kicked his serious High-Altitude Jumping legs into action and checked out the Plant Planet trees.

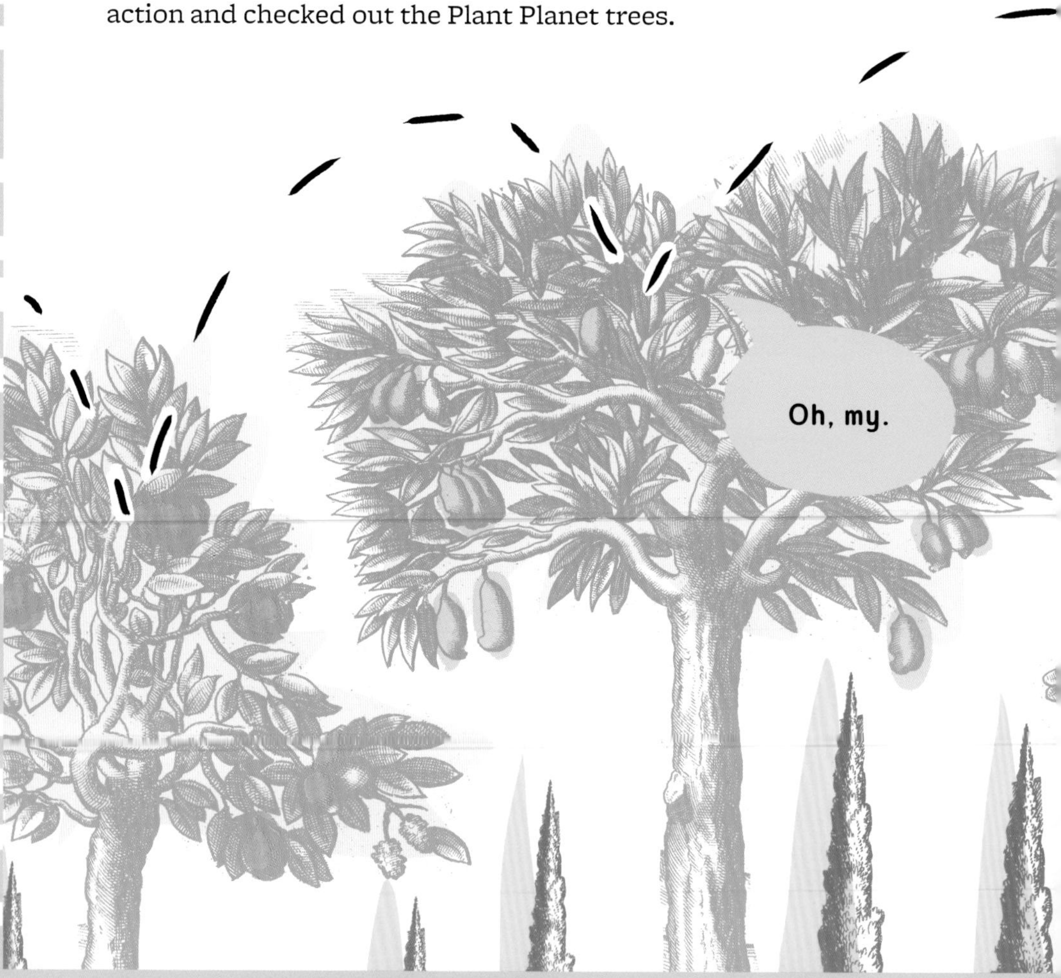
Oh, my.

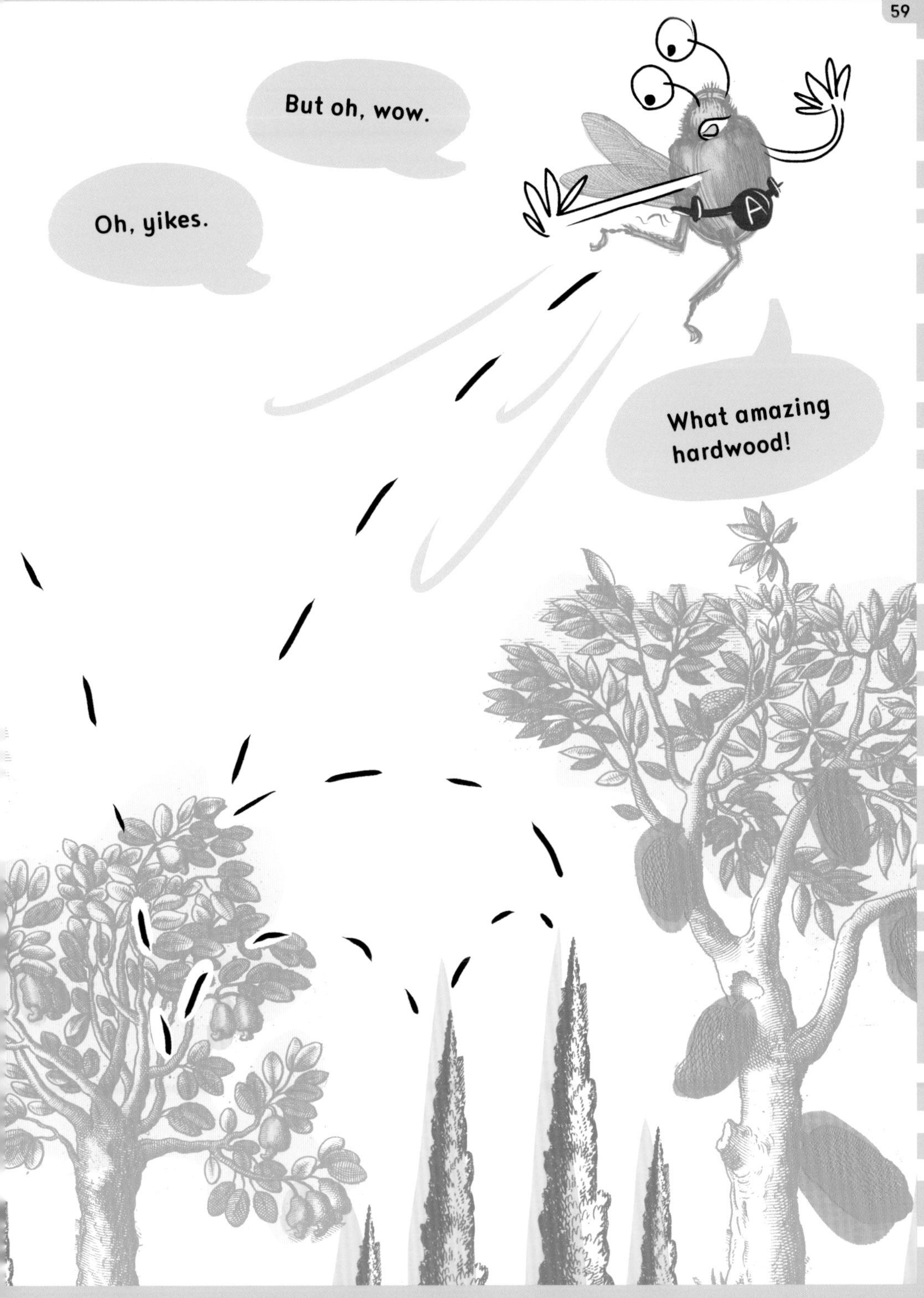
Oh, yikes.
But oh, wow.
What amazing hardwood!

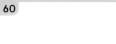

StinkBug zoomed his expert eye in on plant possibilities for building shelter on the Plant Planet.

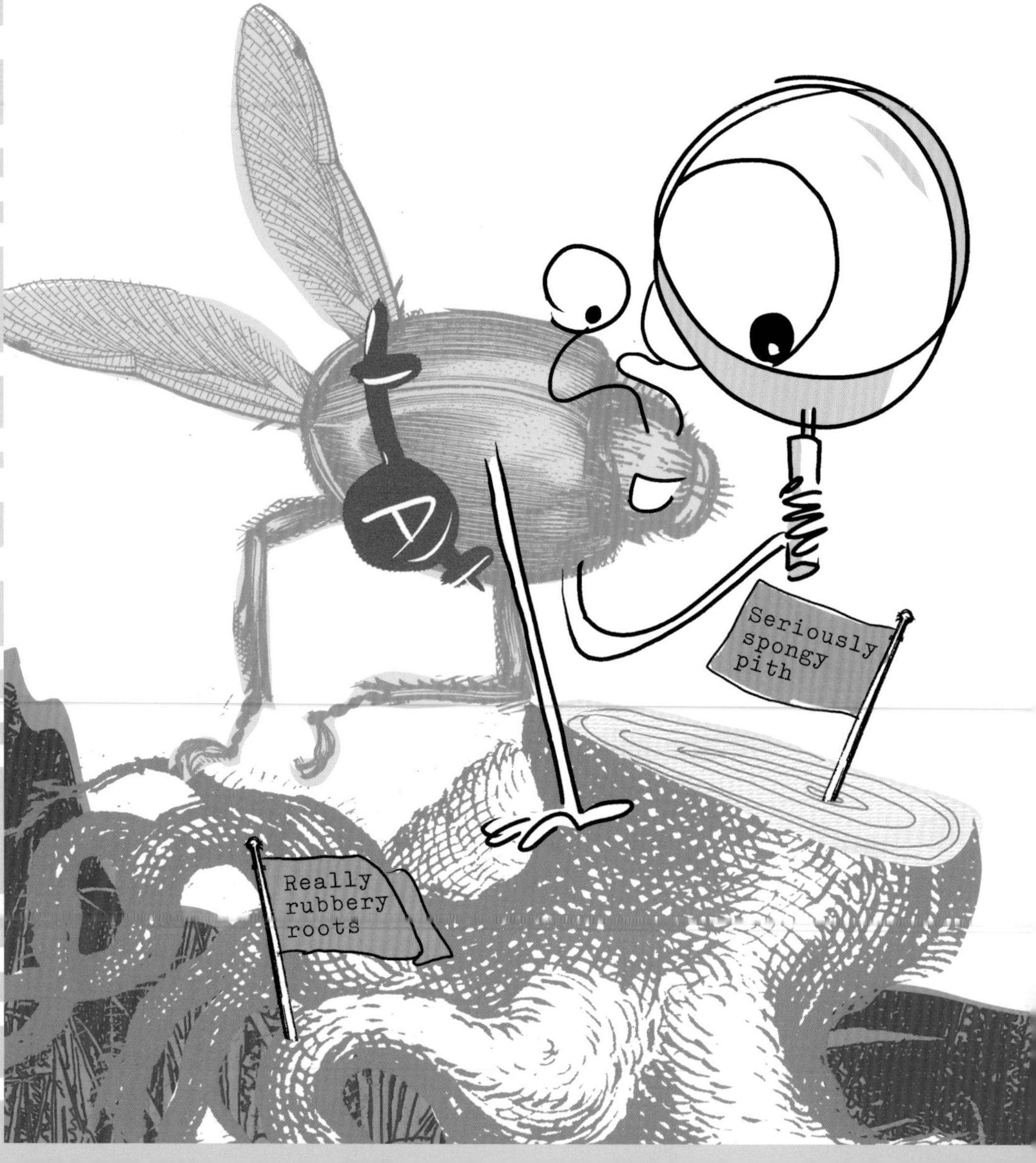
Seriously spongy pith
Really rubbery roots

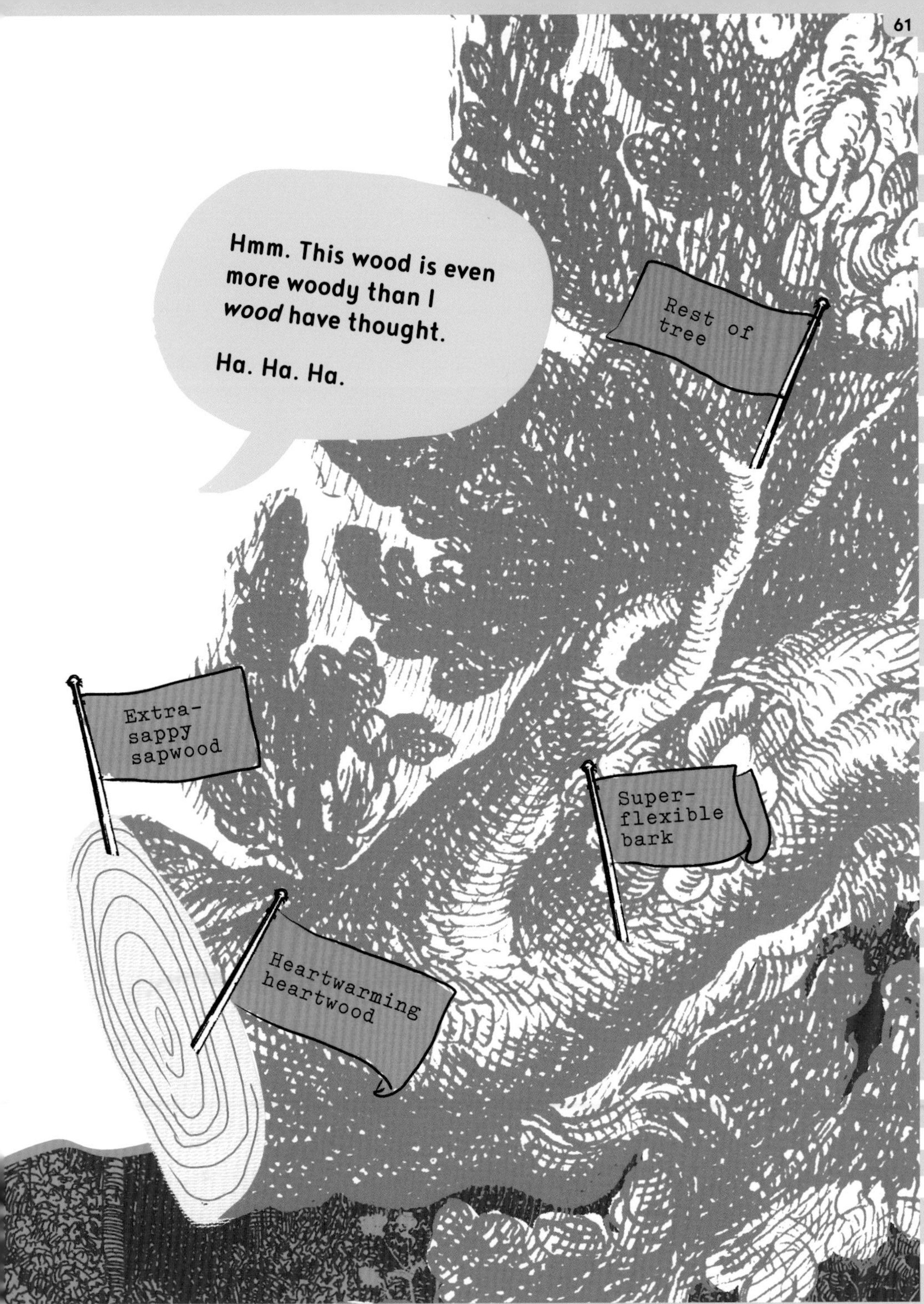
Hmm. This wood is even more woody than I *wood* have thought.
Ha. Ha. Ha.
Rest of tree
Extra-sappy sapwood
Super-flexible bark
Heartwarming heartwood

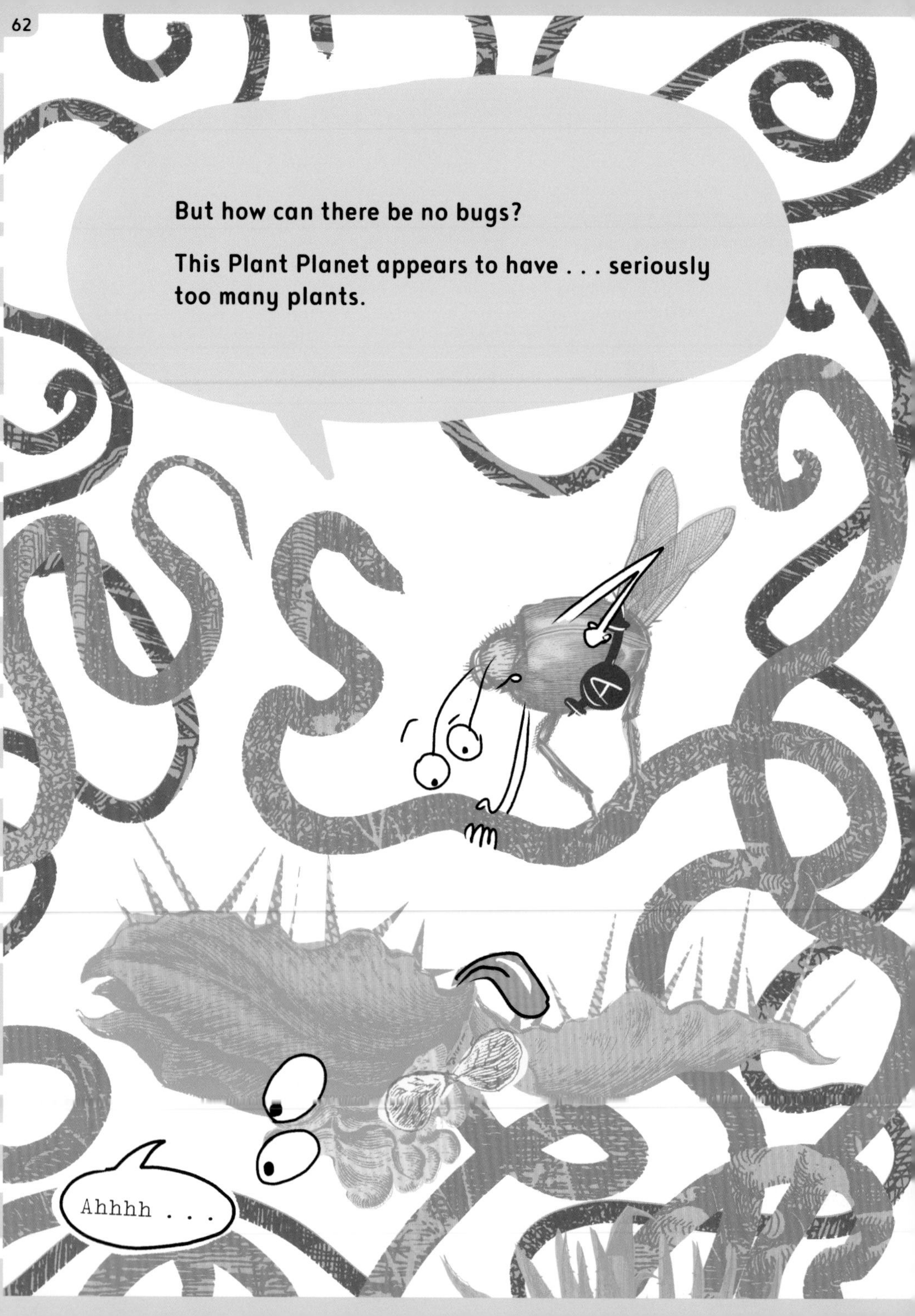
But how can there be no bugs?
This Plant Planet appears to have . . . seriously too many plants.
Ahhhh . . .

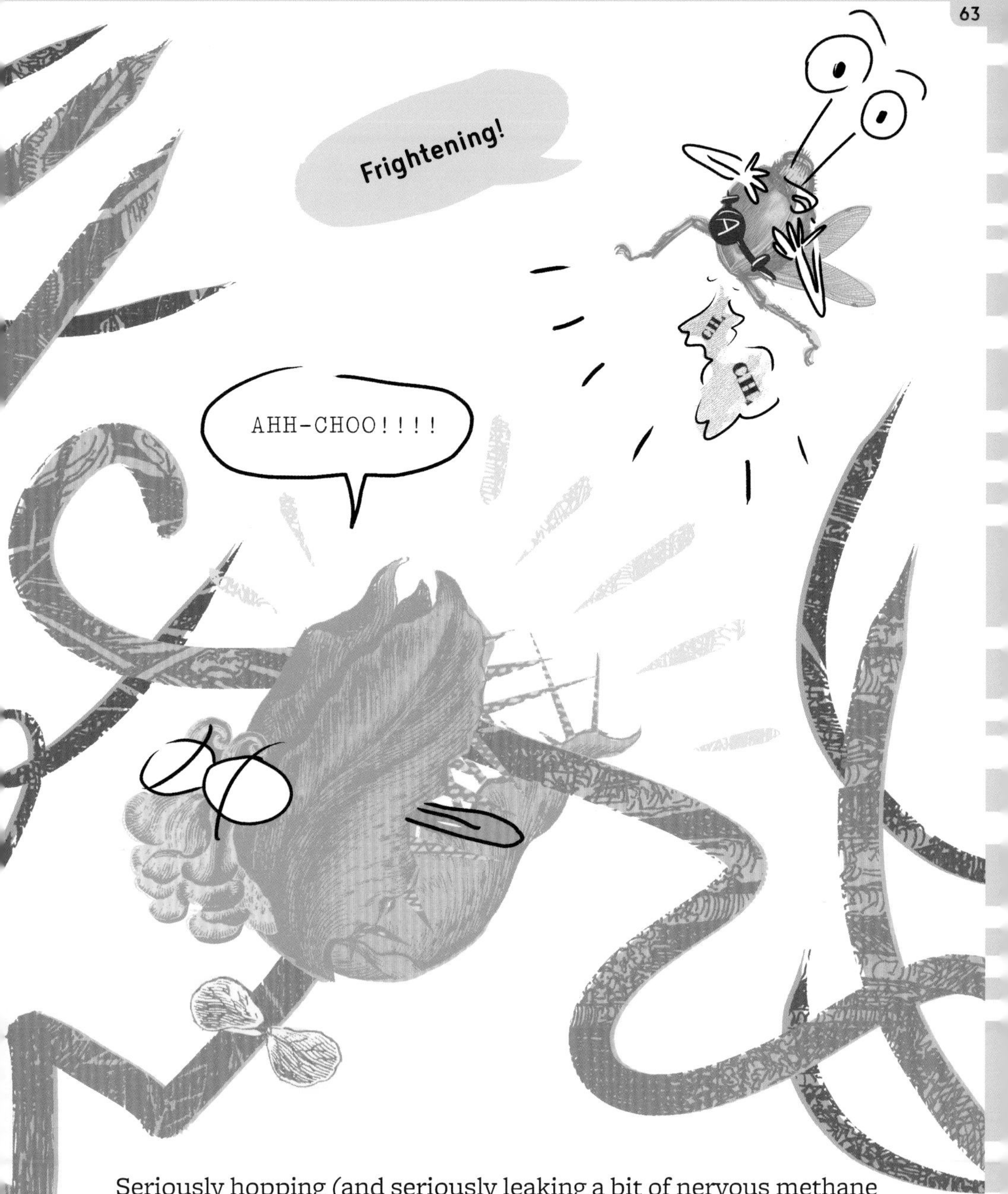
Frightening!
AHH-CHOO!!!!
CH.
CH.

Seriously hopping (and seriously leaking a bit of nervous methane gas) all the way back to the Thomas Jefferson Nose Rocket, StinkBug had no idea how right he was.

CHAPTER 12:
Inside the AlphaLounge

Meanwhile, somehow still back in the Nose Rocket: AlphaWolf, the Greatest, Bravest, and Most Amazing Mission Leader EVER, was getting ready to spring into action—just as soon as he rechecked his section of the Mission Manual.

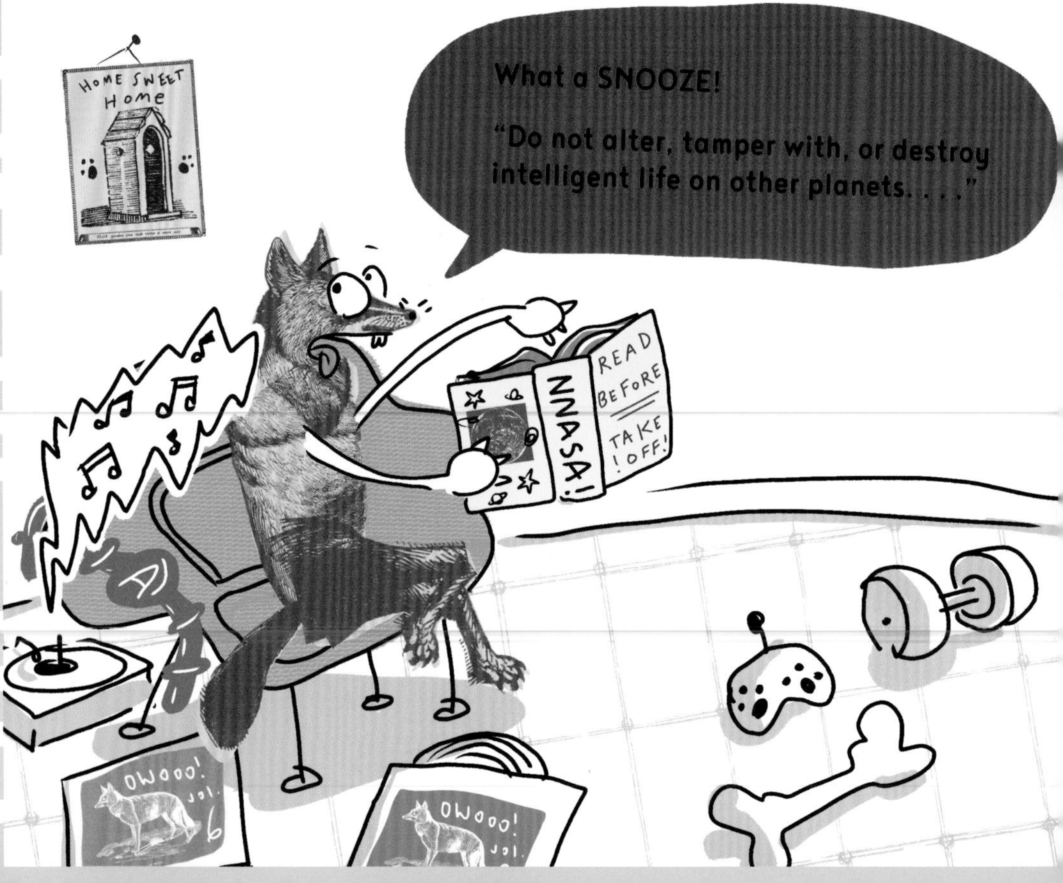

HOME SWEET Home
What a SNOOZE!
"Do not alter, tamper with, or destroy intelligent life on other planets. . . ."
NNASA!
READ BEFORE TAKE OFF!
OWOOO! vol. 6
OWOOO! vol.

It was a shame he thought this was boring, because really, this is pretty serious stuff. Trust me, if there is one thing I know, it's this: The balance of a planet is key to its survival. And existing life is key to its balance. So if you are ever exploring an unknown planet, it would be smart of you to be very careful about not messing up existing life on that planet.

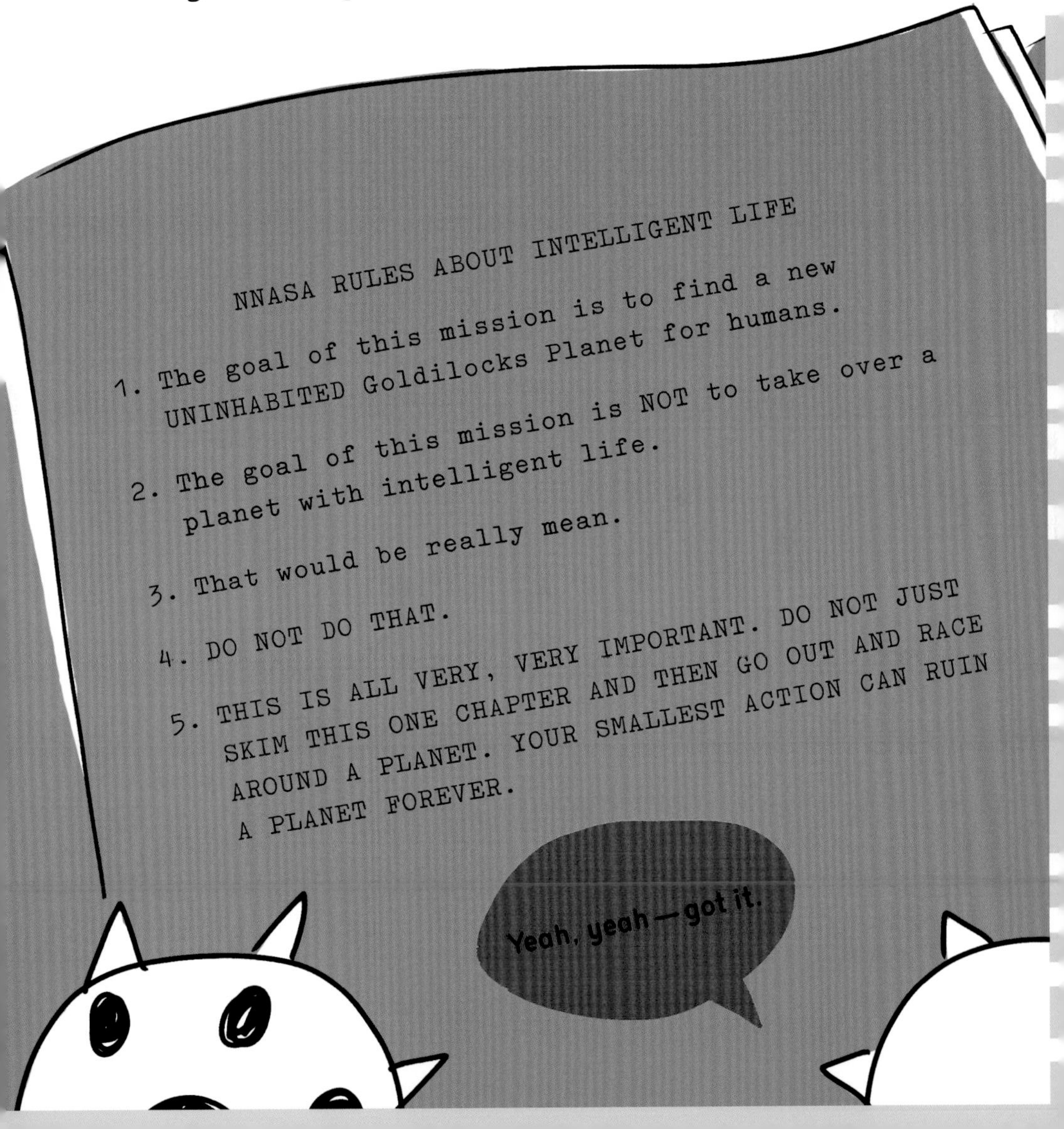
NNASA RULES ABOUT INTELLIGENT LIFE

1. The goal of this mission is to find a new UNINHABITED Goldilocks Planet for humans.
2. The goal of this mission is NOT to take over a planet with intelligent life.
3. That would be really mean.
4. DO NOT DO THAT.
5. THIS IS ALL VERY, VERY IMPORTANT. DO NOT JUST SKIM THIS ONE CHAPTER AND THEN GO OUT AND RACE AROUND A PLANET. YOUR SMALLEST ACTION CAN RUIN A PLANET FOREVER.

Yeah, yeah—got it.

AlphaWolf trimmed his claws. He brushed his fur (twice). He gave himself one of his Positive Attitude pep talks. Then he realized it wasn't very exciting in the ship without anyone to boss around.

Maybe it was time to do his job.

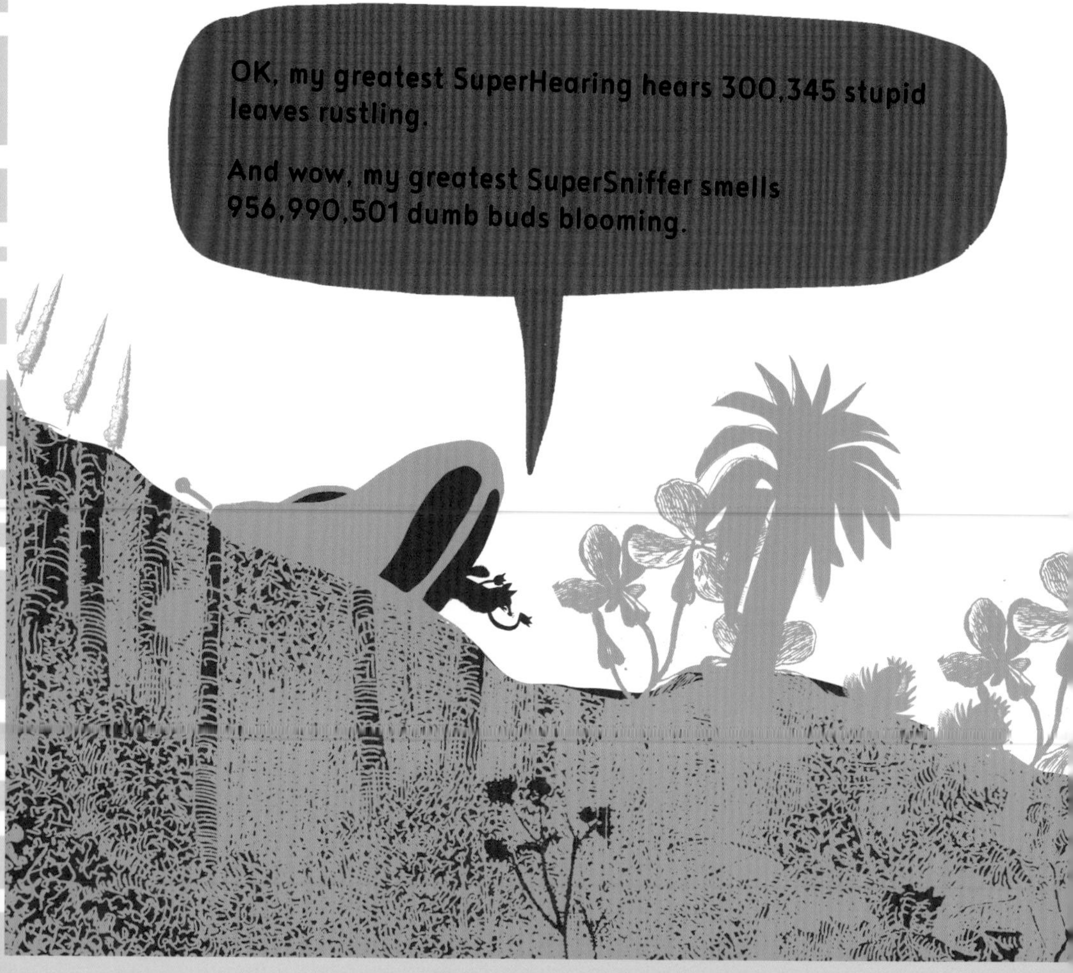
OK, my greatest SuperHearing hears 300,345 stupid leaves rustling.
And wow, my greatest SuperSniffer smells 956,990,501 dumb buds blooming.

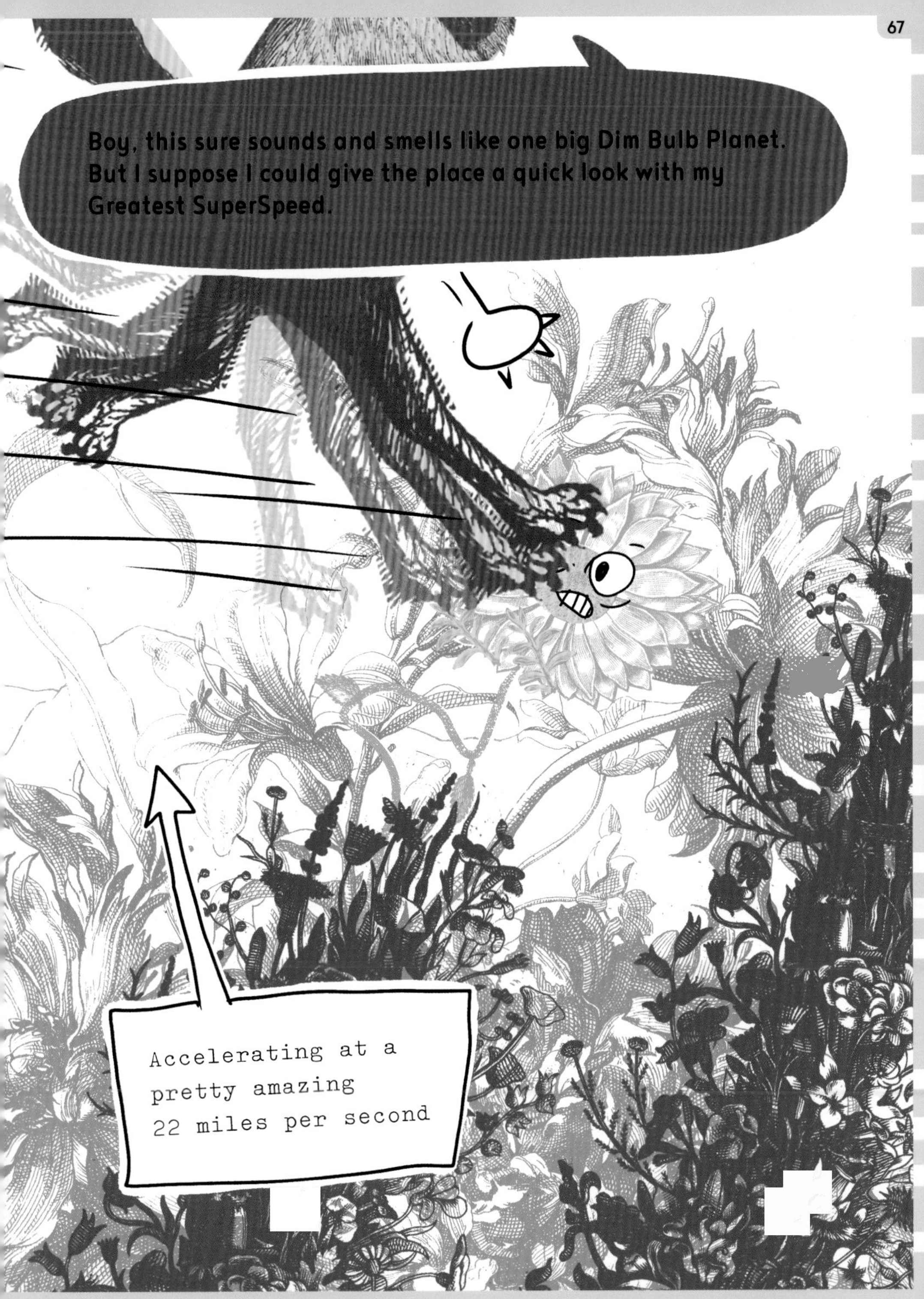
Boy, this sure sounds and smells like one big Dim Bulb Planet. But I suppose I could give the place a quick look with my Greatest SuperSpeed.
Accelerating at a pretty amazing 22 miles per second

Have you ever heard the saying "Stop and smell the roses"? It's a good piece of advice I've learned in my experience spinning through space.

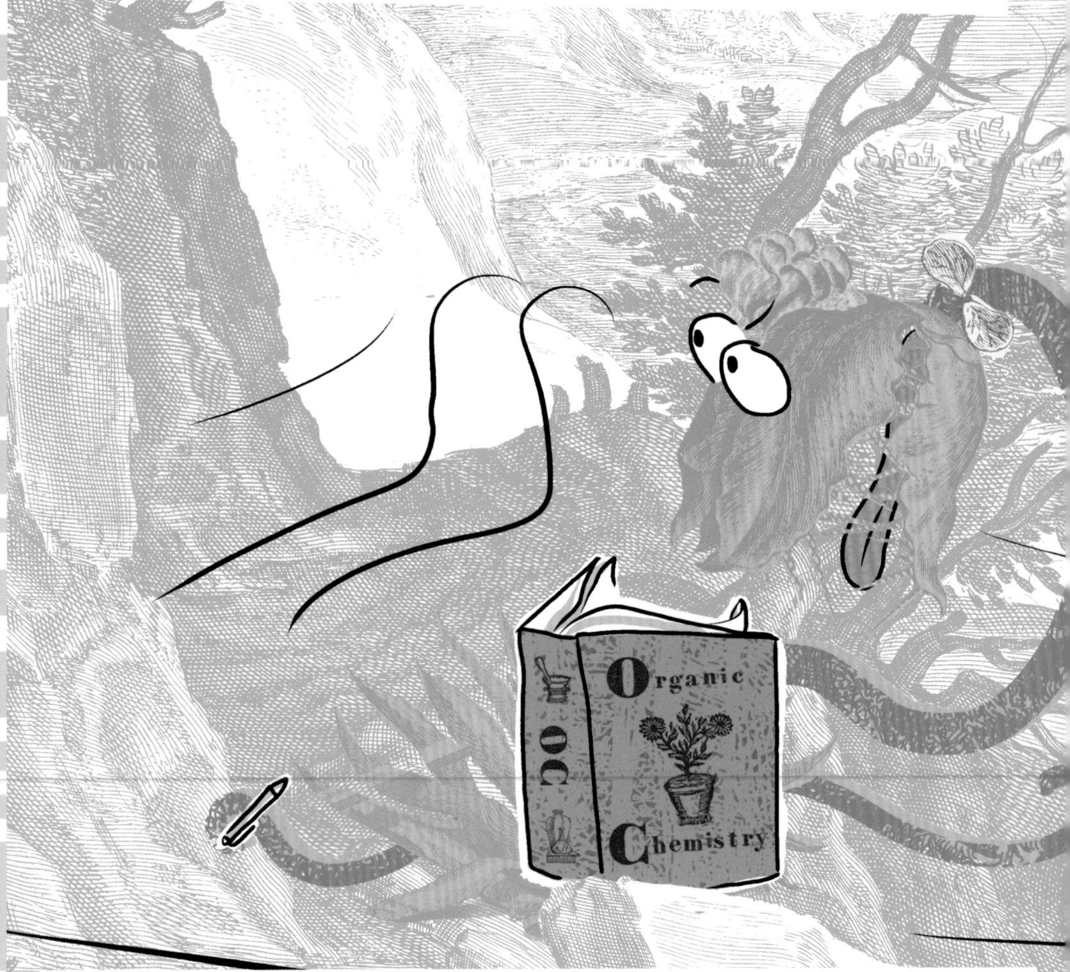
Organic Chemistry
OC

And if you were an overpowered experimental astronaut wolf looking for intelligent life on a Goldilocks Planet, I might also add, "Stop and look at the Giant Venus Flytrap reading a chemistry textbook."

And I would further add, “You might spot an entire advanced civilization hiding right under your greatest superpowered nose.”

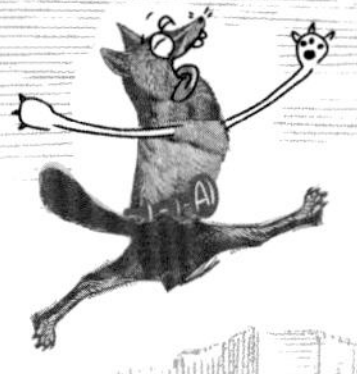

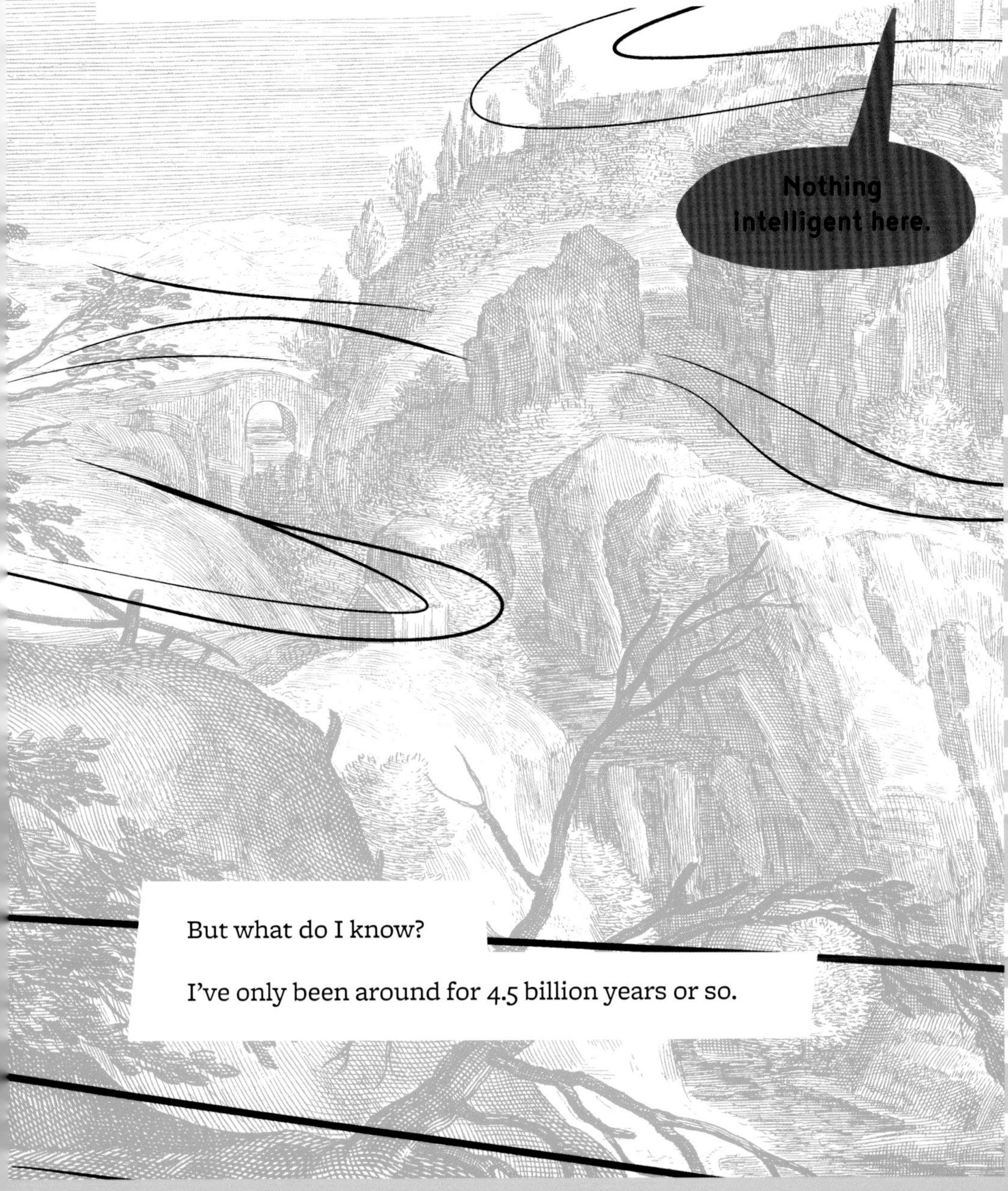
Nothing intelligent here.

But what do I know?

I’ve only been around for 4.5 billion years or so.

CHAPTER 13:

Lunchtime

Just between you and me, I never thought the Plant Planet was all that great. But the AstroNuts were pretty pleased with themselves for completing their first scientific look at a planet.

And they were just starting to reward themselves with LaserShark's delicious AstroPicnic when the voice of Command Escape snorted out of the Thomas Jefferson Left Nostril Port.

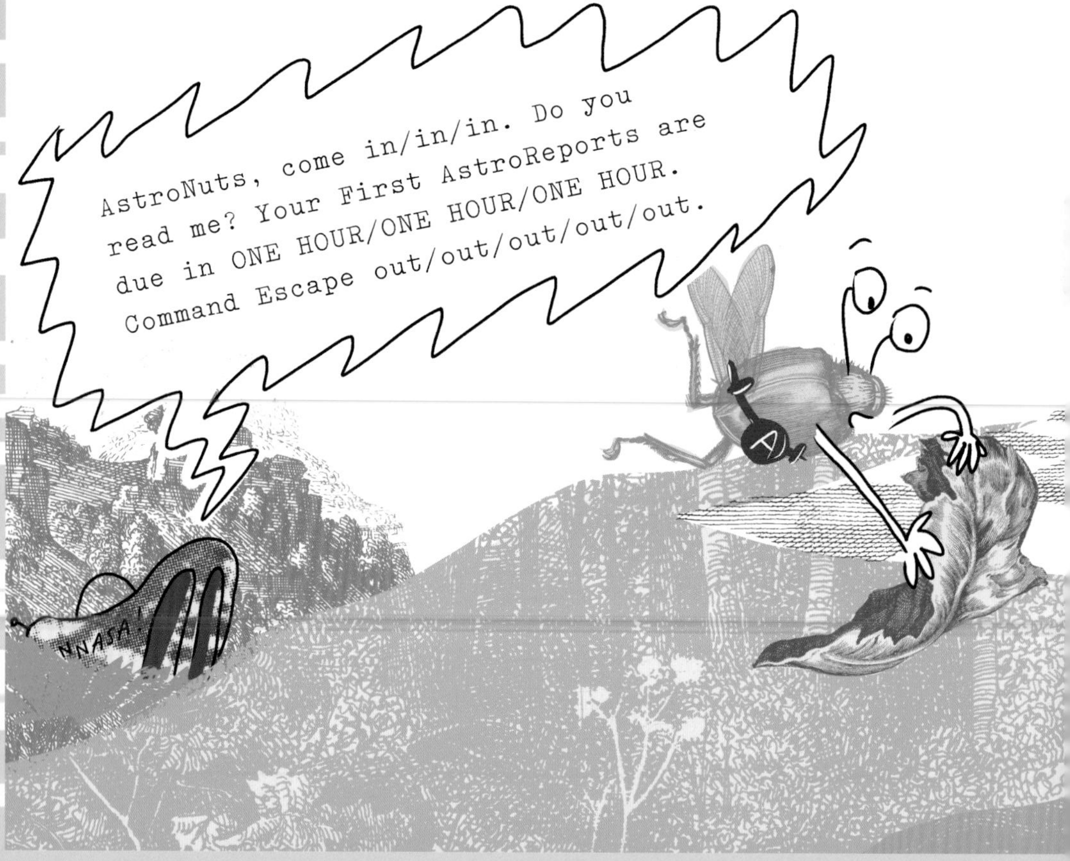
AstroNuts, come in/in/in. Do you read me? Your First AstroReports are due in ONE HOUR/ONE HOUR/ONE HOUR. Command Escape out/out/out/out/out.
NNASA!

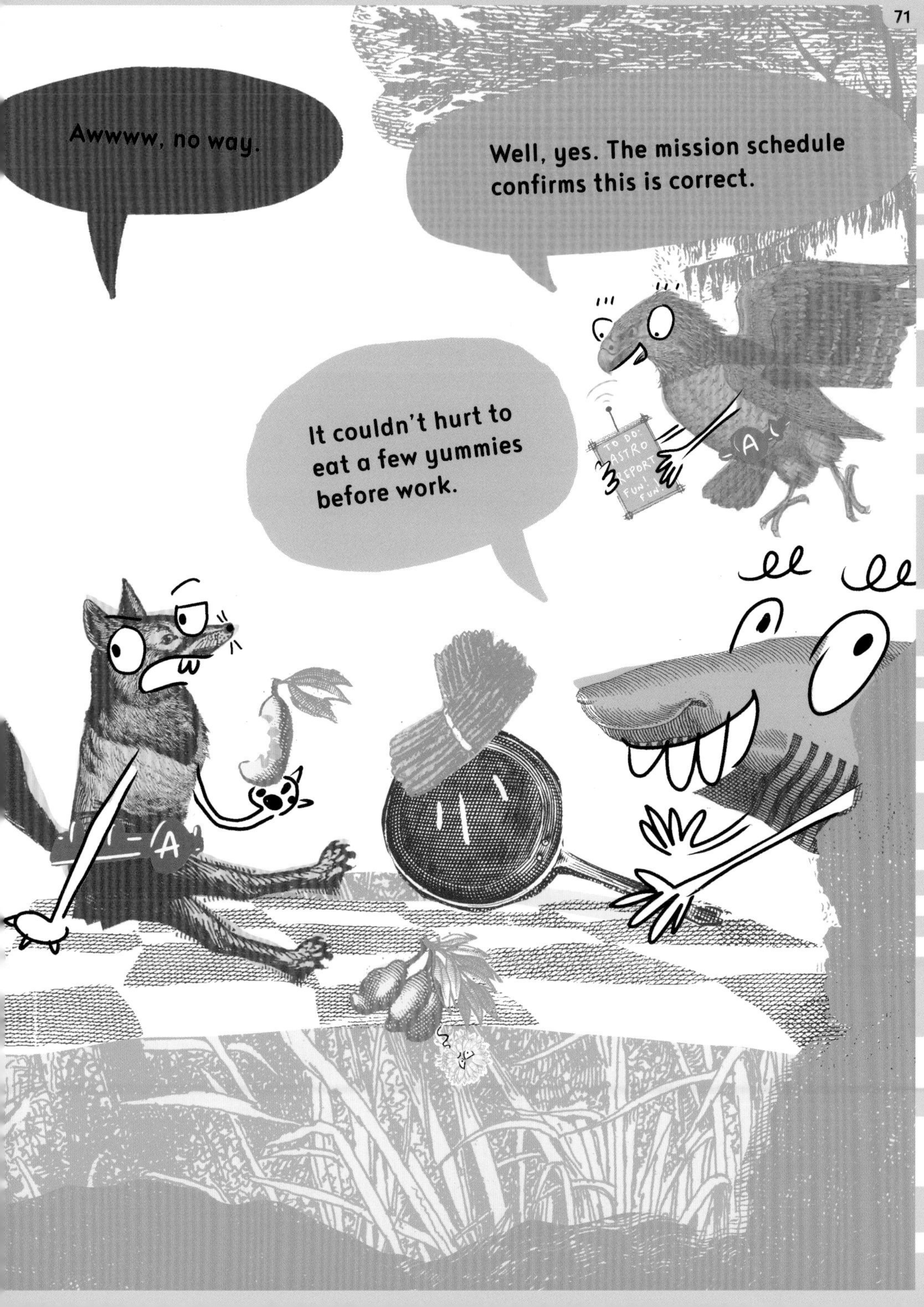
Awwww, no way.
Well, yes. The mission schedule confirms this is correct.
It couldn't hurt to eat a few yummies before work.
TO DO: ASTRO REPORT FUN! FUN!

The AstroNuts decided to pretend they didn't hear Command Escape, and kept eating their picnic. But Command Escape had a trick up his Nose Rocket. Using the Nose Remote Control back on Earth, Command Escape activated the Xtreme Intake and . . .

. . . sucked the AstroNuts into the Nostril Ports and all the way down to the AstroWorkLab.

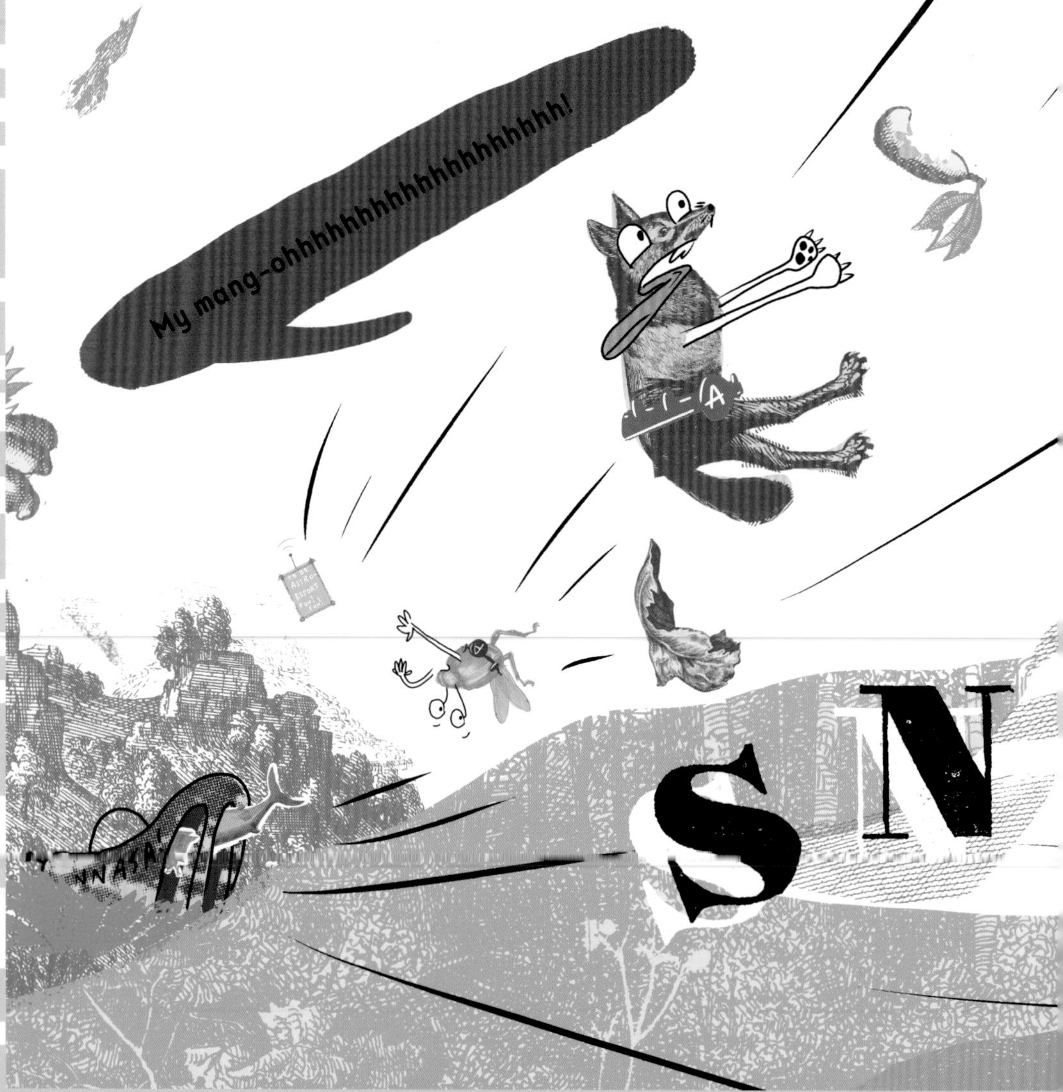
My mang-ohhhhhhhhhhhhhhhhh!
SN

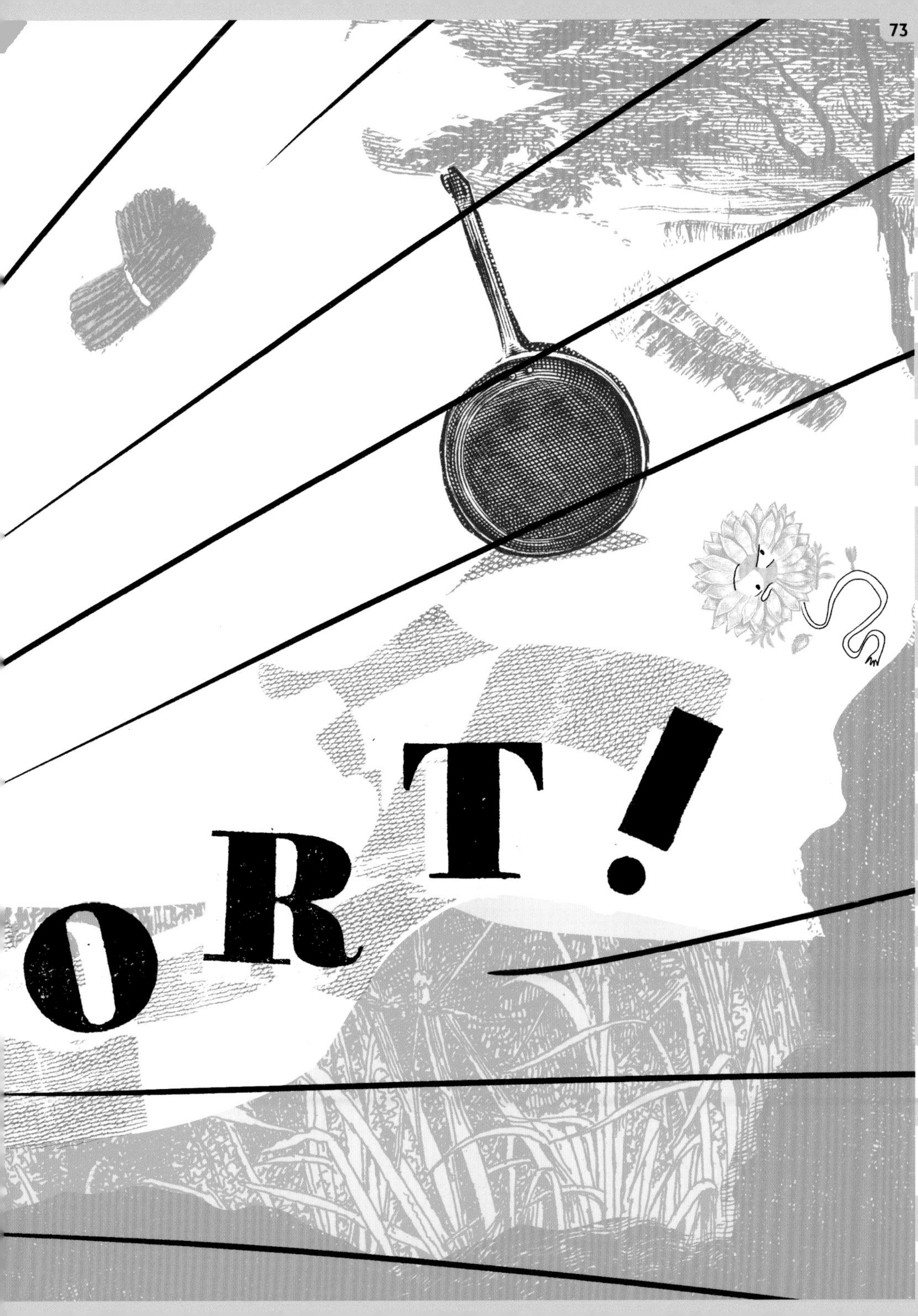
ORT!

The AstroNuts got to work in the AstroWorkLab.

Well, some of them did.

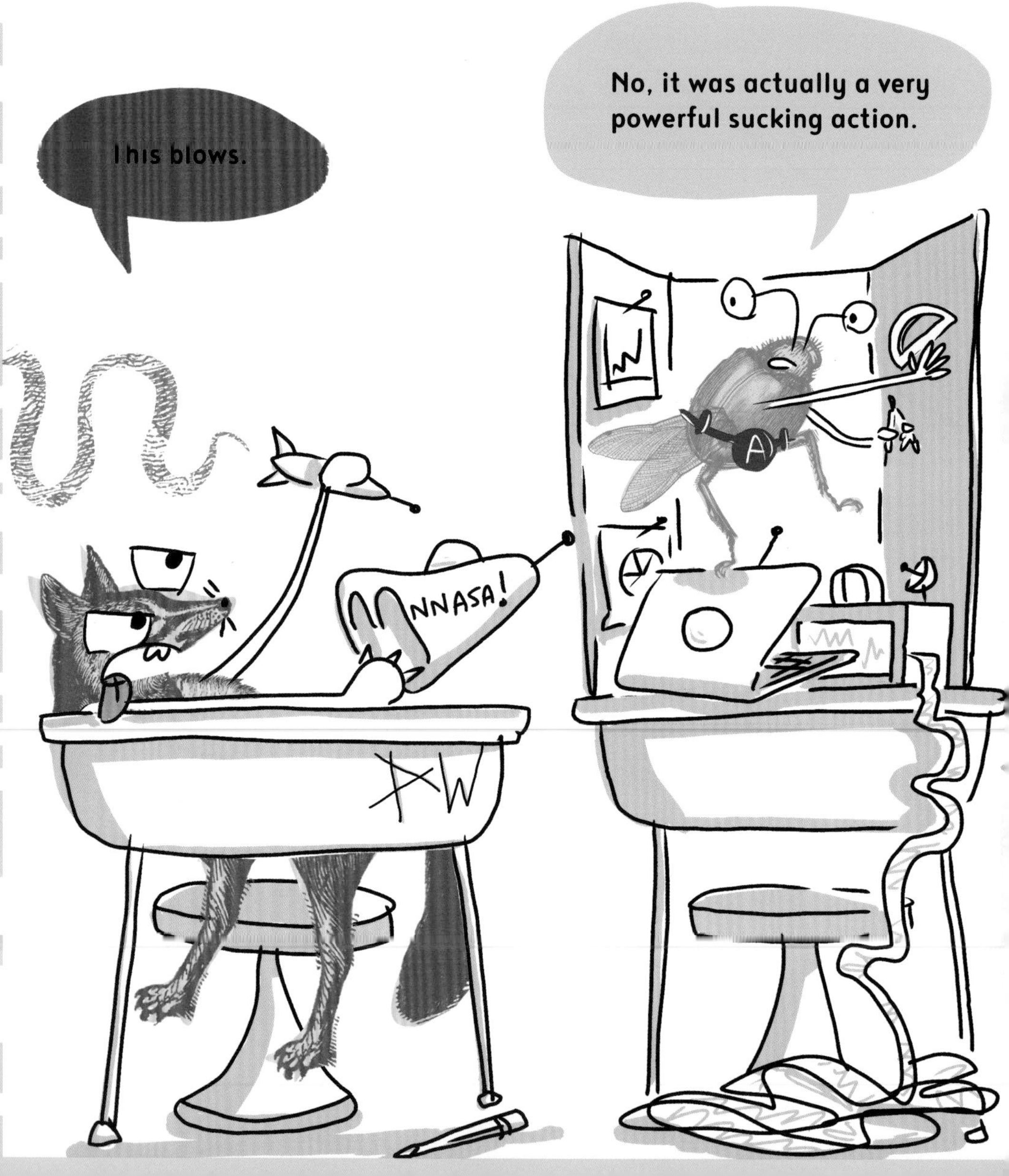
This blows.
No, it was actually a very powerful sucking action.
NNASA!

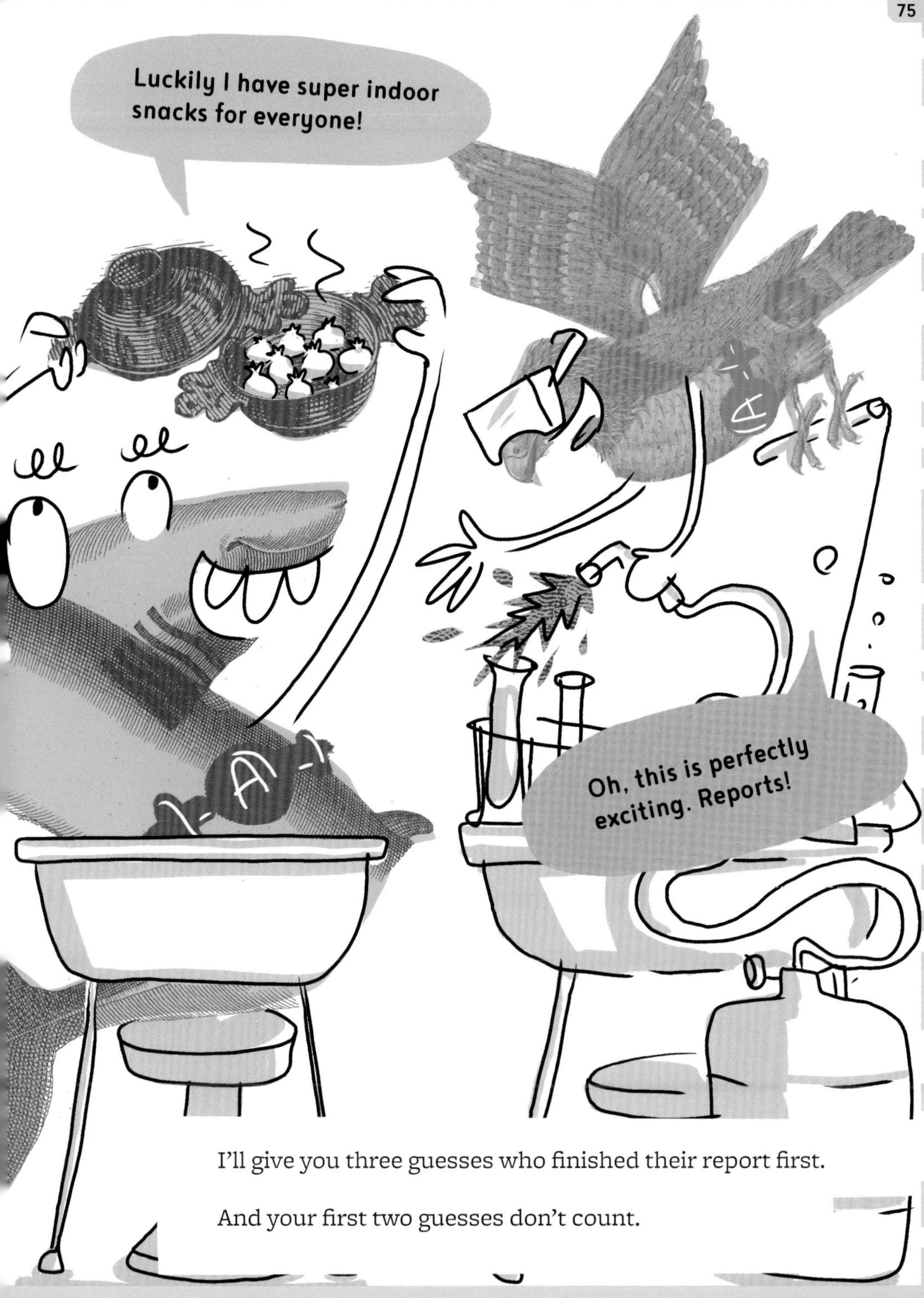
Luckily I have super indoor snacks for everyone!
Oh, this is perfectly exciting. Reports!

I'll give you three guesses who finished their report first.

And your first two guesses don't count.

AstroNut Report

AstroName: SmartHawk
AstroTitle: Planning and rules officer
Investigating: climate and ecosystem

Earth Atmosphere:

21%
0.1%
78%
.44%
O_2 CO_2 N CH_4

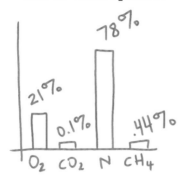

Plant Planet Atmosphere:

51%
0.001%
20%
21%
O_2 CO_2 N CH_4

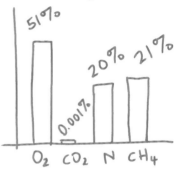

Earth Temperatures:

AVG. 61°F
JFMAMJJASOND

Plant Planet Temperatures:

AVG. 89.6°F
JFMAMJJASOND

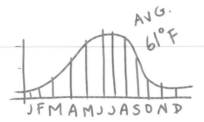

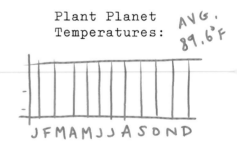

Earth Ecosystem:

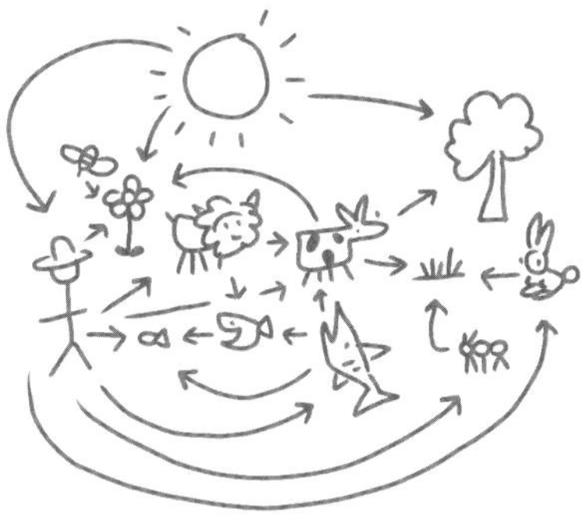

Plant Planet Ecosystem:

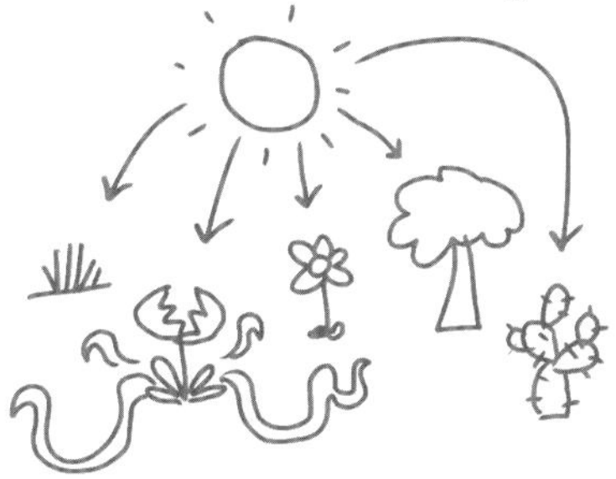

Conclusion:

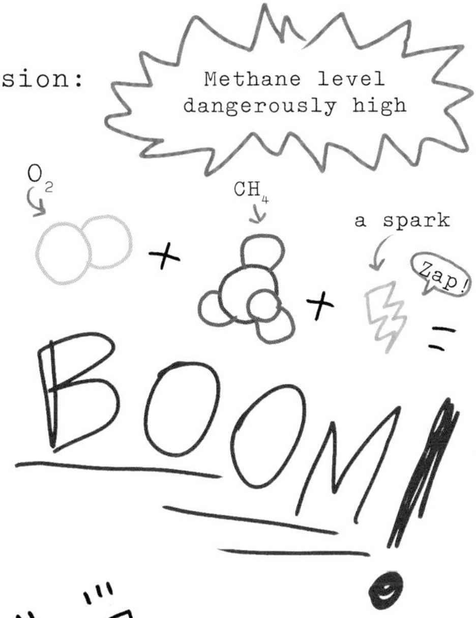
Methane level dangerously high
O_2
CH_4
a spark
Zap!
BOOM!

Temperature and Atmosphere composition are good, Plant Life is a bit overgrown.

I'm puzzled. I haven't seen any animal, bird, or insect life. This is a very unbalanced ecosystem.

High levels of methane plus oxygen could be a perfectly explosive climate problem.

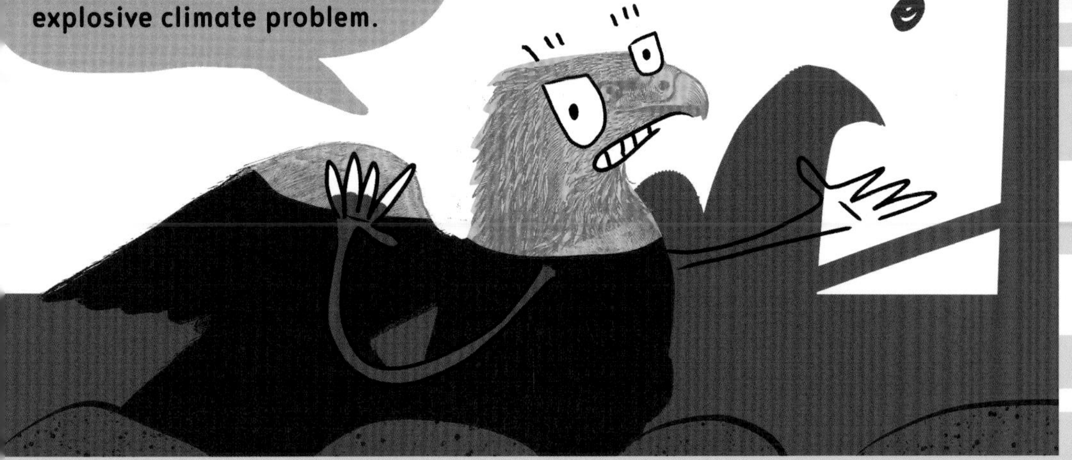

AstroNut Report

AstroName: Laser Shark

AstroTitle: nurse, cook, and security

Investigating: food

Plants-I-Saw-Today Menu:

Starter

Salad of Super Kale and Tay-Tay Tomatoes

Silly Seaweed Tempura

Pastas

Ho-Ho-Whole Wheat Fusilli

Sonic Spaghetti

yum!

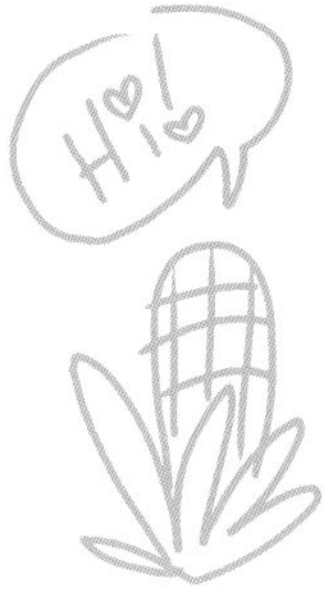
Hi!

Mains

Big Old Butternut Squash

Colossal Piece of Corn

Roasts/Chicken/Fish

(None Here)

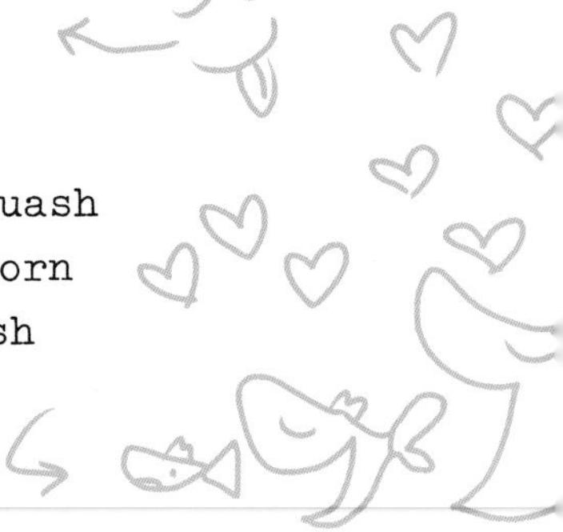

Desserts

Cool-Wa Quinoa à la Mode

Pear Pizzazz Tart

Mmmm!

Dangerous Earth Things:

- Grizzly Bears
- Rattlesnakes
- Mean Sharks
- African Honeybees
- Hippos
- Box Jellyfish
- Cholera
- Tummy Aches
- Humans
- Poison Dart Frogs
- Scorpions
- Komodo Dragons
- Tsetse Fly
- Mosquitos
- Brazilian Wandering Spider
- Blue-Ringed Octopus

Dangerous Plant Planet Things:

- This is weird.
- I know it's the Plant Planet.
- But there is nothing BUT plants here!!!
- No dangerous fish or animals or bugs or reptiles.

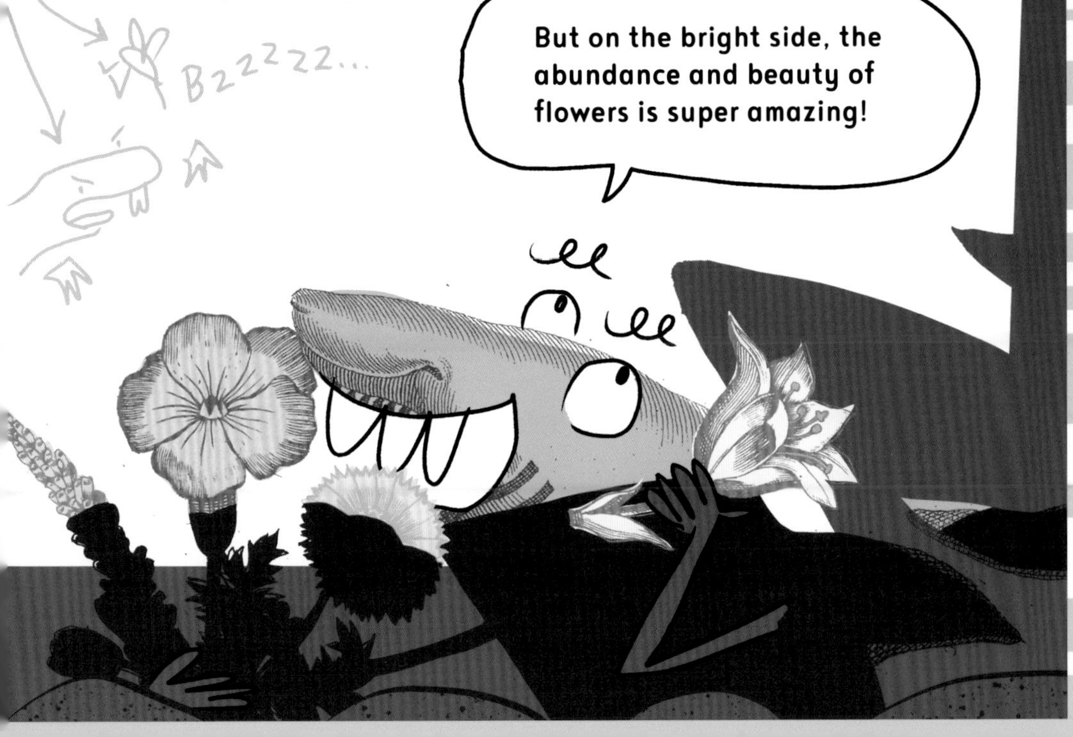
But on the bright side, the abundance and beauty of flowers is super amazing!

AstroNut Report

AstroName: STINKBUG
AstroTitle: PILOT AND TECH OFFICER
Investigating: SHELTER

Available Building Materials:

WOOD

BAMBOO

GRASSES

DIRT

ME →
MONDO PEAPODS

ME↓
GIANT SQUASH

ME↓
SUPERSIZED FLOWERS

CACTI

BIG APPLE
← ME

Earth Plant Cell:

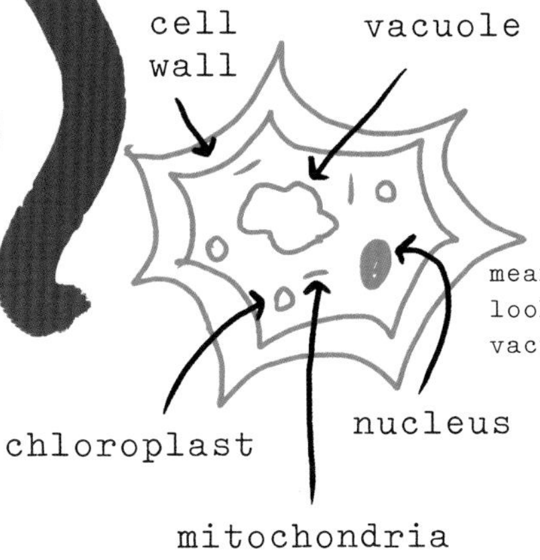
cell wall
vacuole
chloroplast
nucleus
mitochondria

Plant Planet Plant Cell:

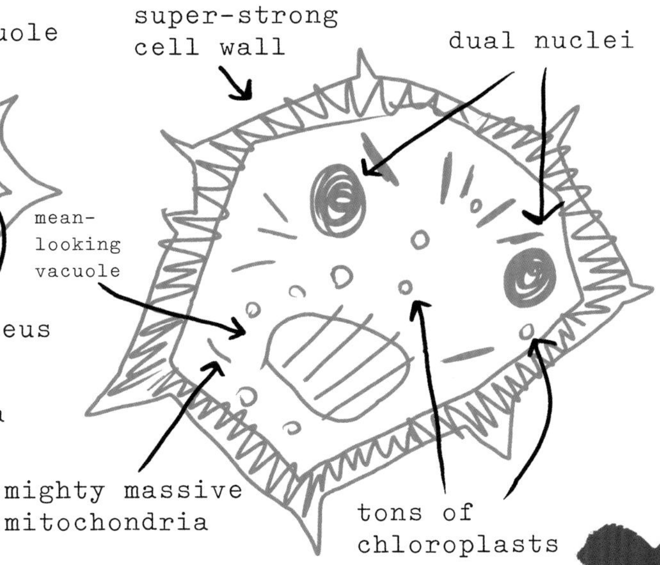
super-strong cell wall
dual nuclei
mean-looking vacuole
mighty massive mitochondria
tons of chloroplasts

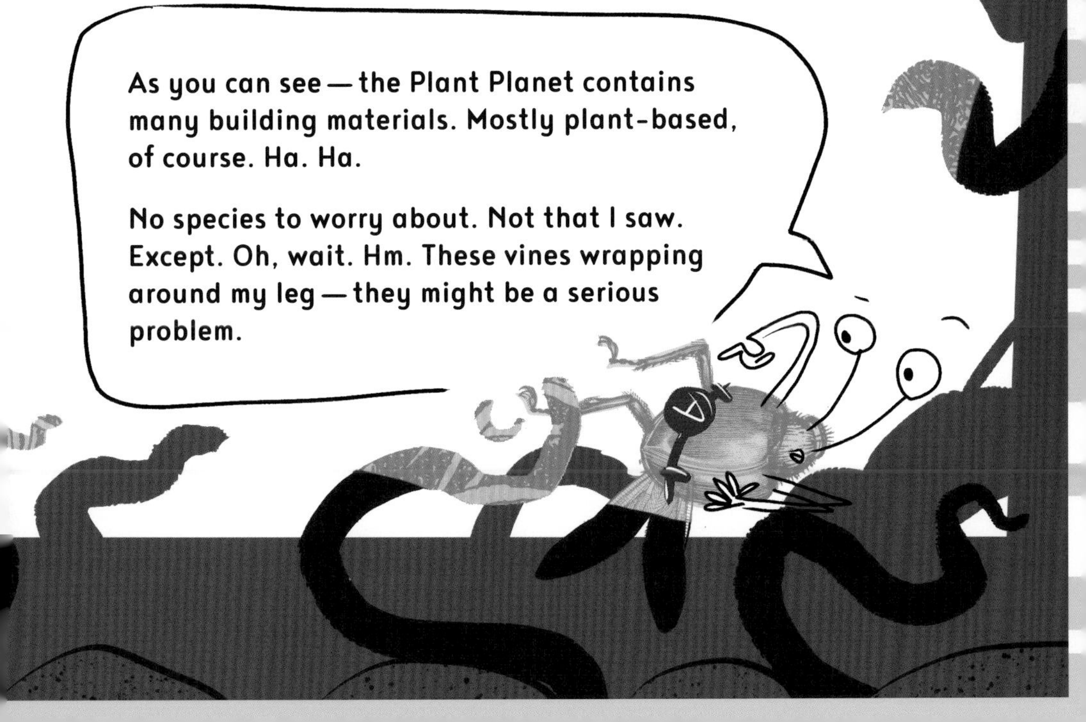
As you can see — the Plant Planet contains many building materials. Mostly plant-based, of course. Ha. Ha.
No species to worry about. Not that I saw. Except. Oh, wait. Hm. These vines wrapping around my leg — they might be a serious problem.

AstroNut Report

AstroName:
AstroTitle:
Investigating:

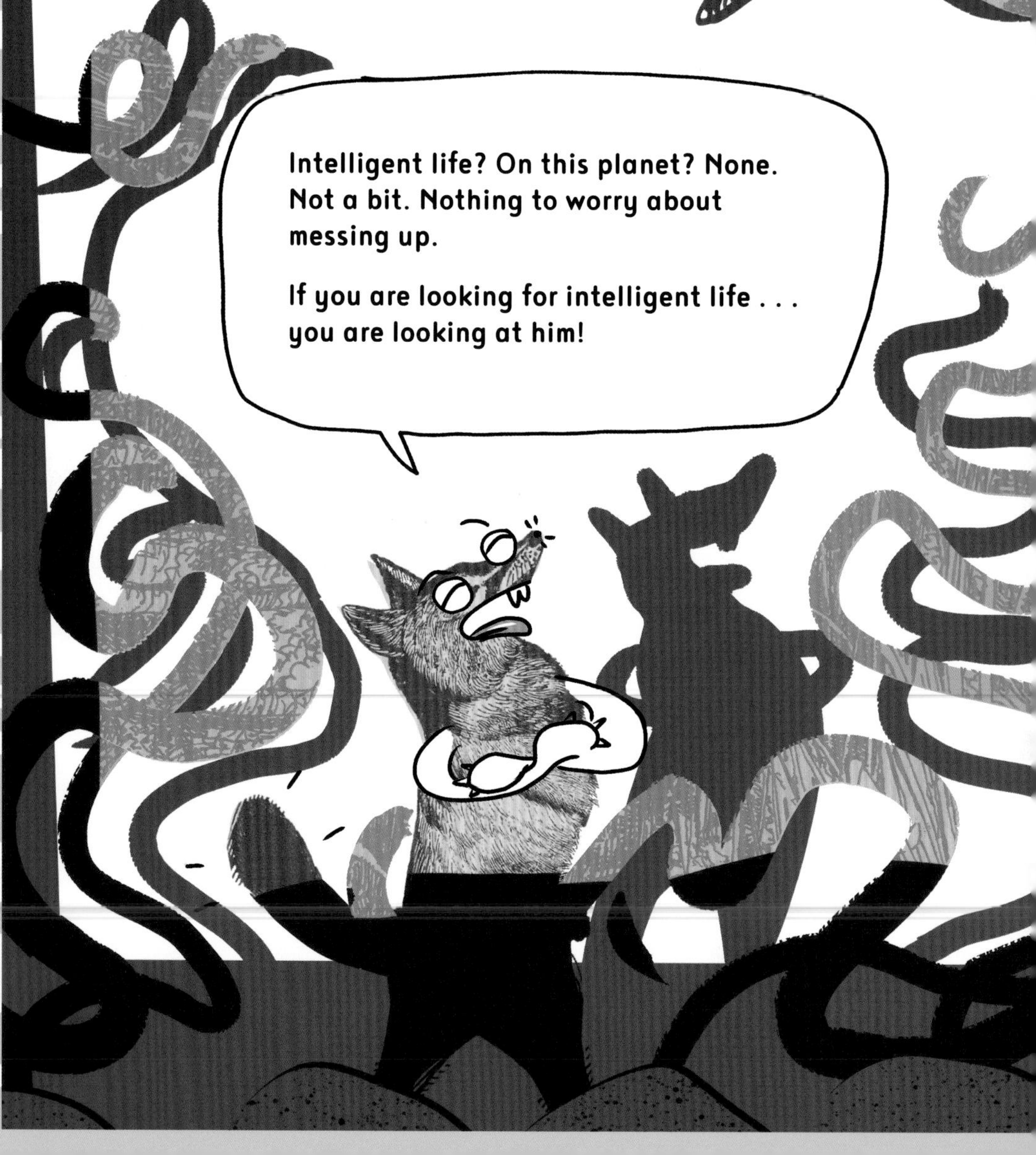
Intelligent life? On this planet? None. Not a bit. Nothing to worry about messing up.
If you are looking for intelligent life . . . you are looking at him!

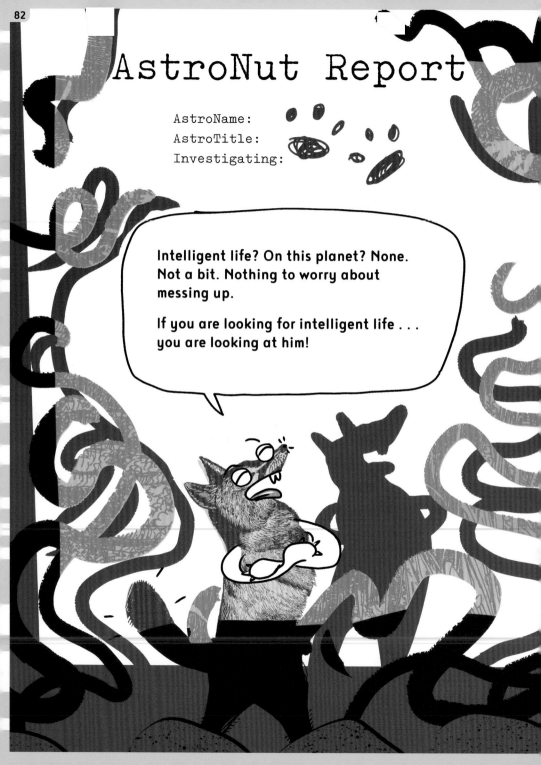

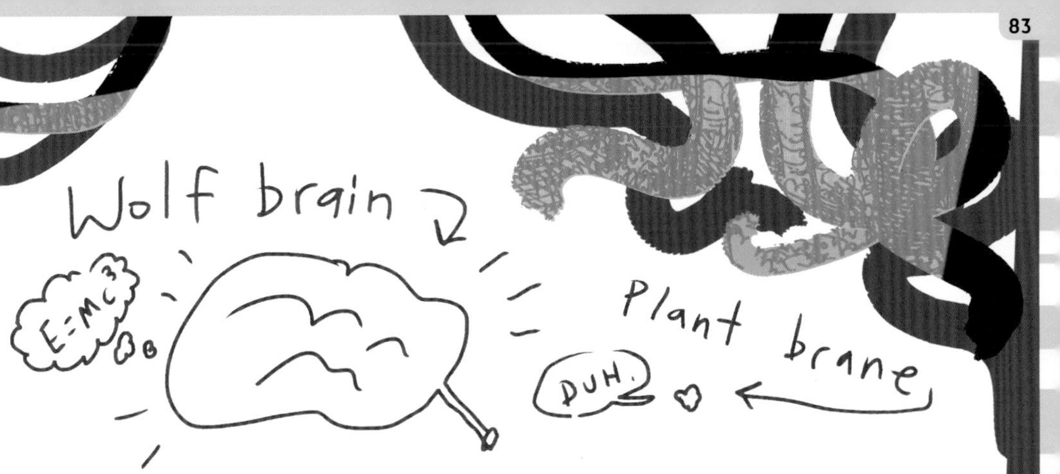
Wolf brain
E=MC3
Plant brane
DUH.

Characteristics of Intelligent Life:

- Self-awareness / Thought / Memory = ME
- Communication abilities - check!
- Tool-making abilities

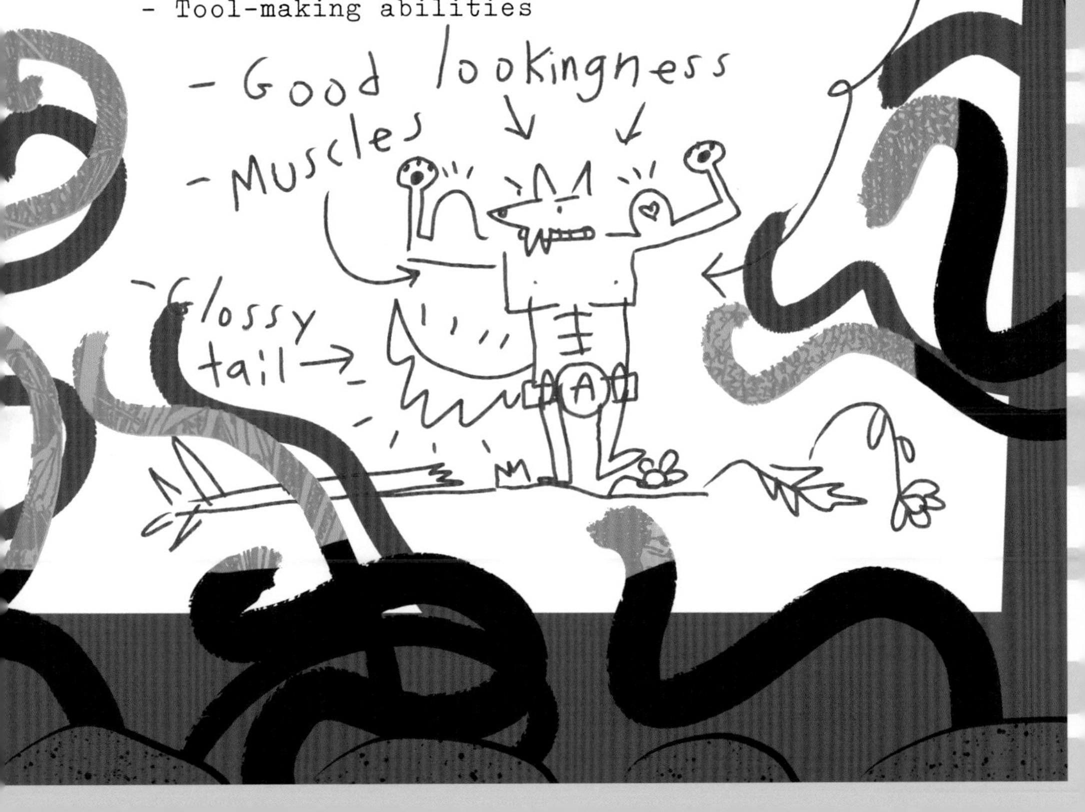
- Good lookingness
- Muscles
- Glossy tail

You know that feeling after you've turned in your homework? When you are so glad you are finished that you don't notice anything around you? Not even really bad things really near to you?

Well, that's exactly how the AstroNuts were feeling.

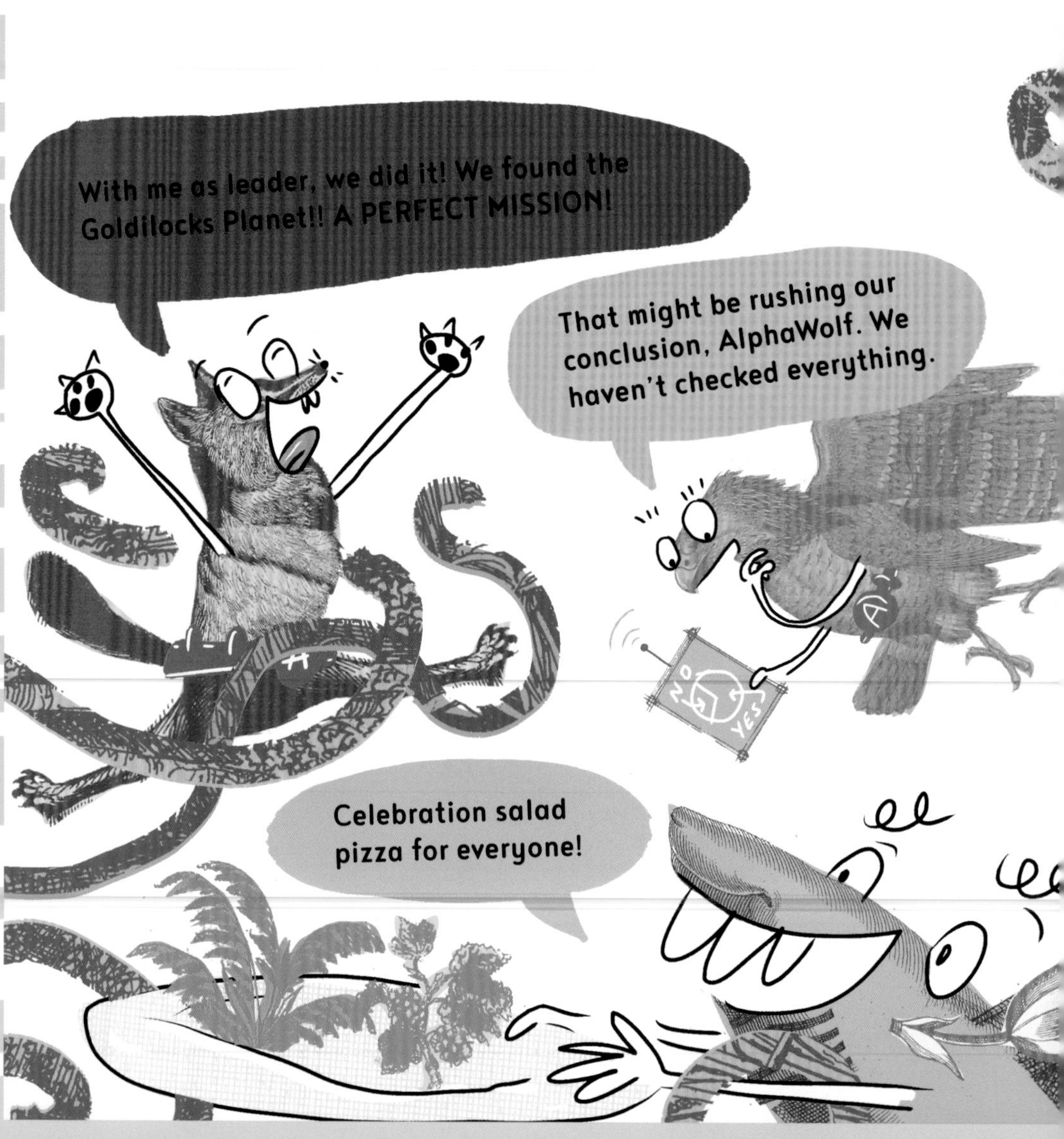
With me as leader, we did it! We found the Goldilocks Planet!! A PERFECT MISSION!
That might be rushing our conclusion, AlphaWolf. We haven't checked everything.
NO
YES
Celebration salad pizza for everyone!

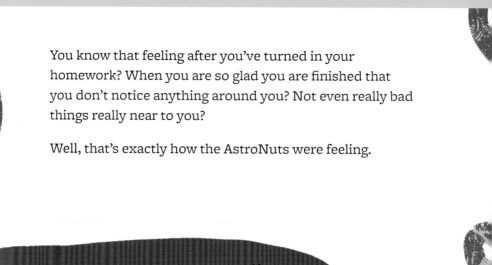

But fortunately for the AstroNuts, back at NNASA HQ, Command Escape was paying attention.

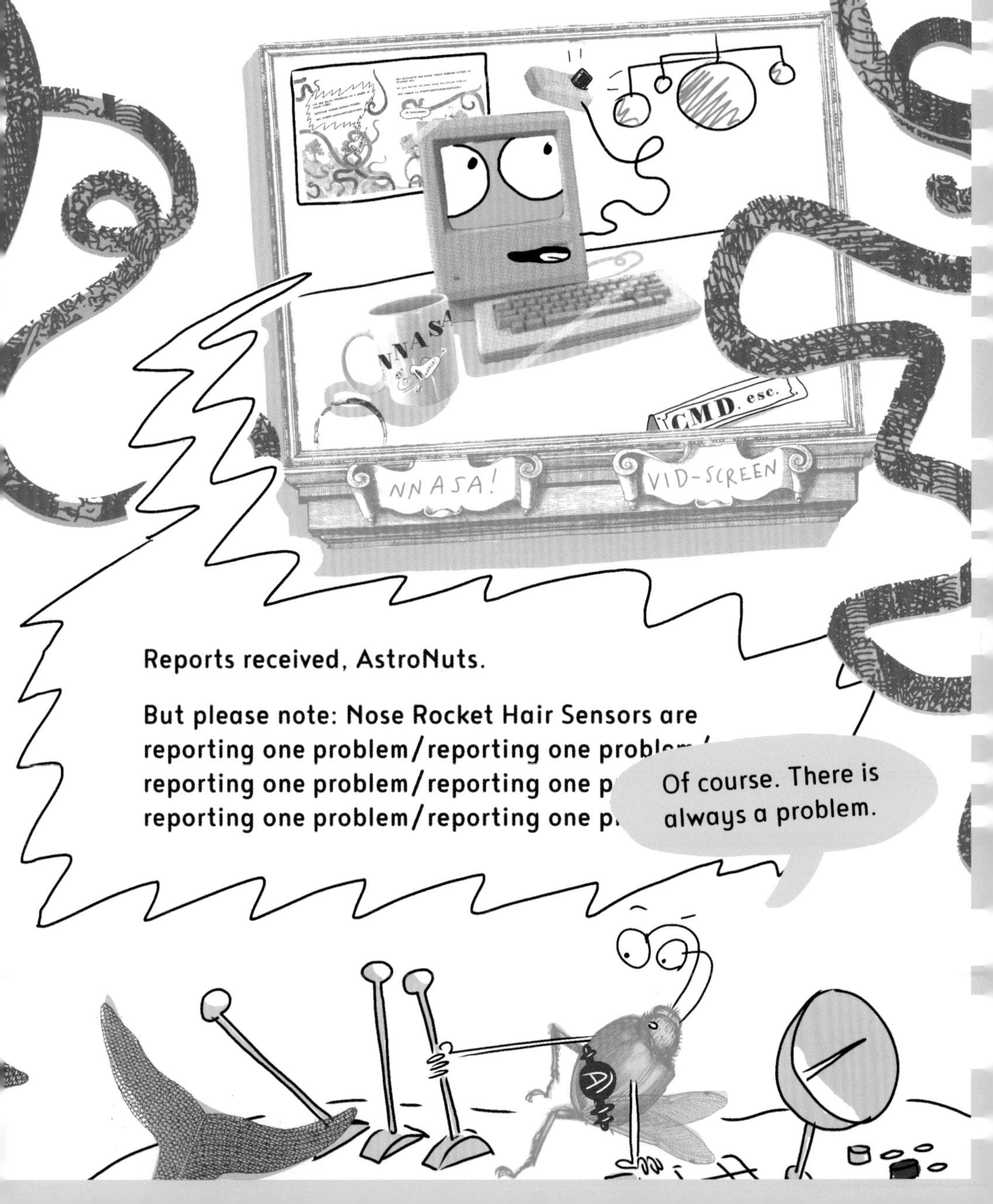
NNASA
CMD. esc.
NNASA!
VID-SCREEN
Reports received, AstroNuts.
But please note: Nose Rocket Hair Sensors are reporting one problem/reporting one probl
reporting one problem/reporting one p
reporting one problem/reporting one p
Of course. There is always a problem.

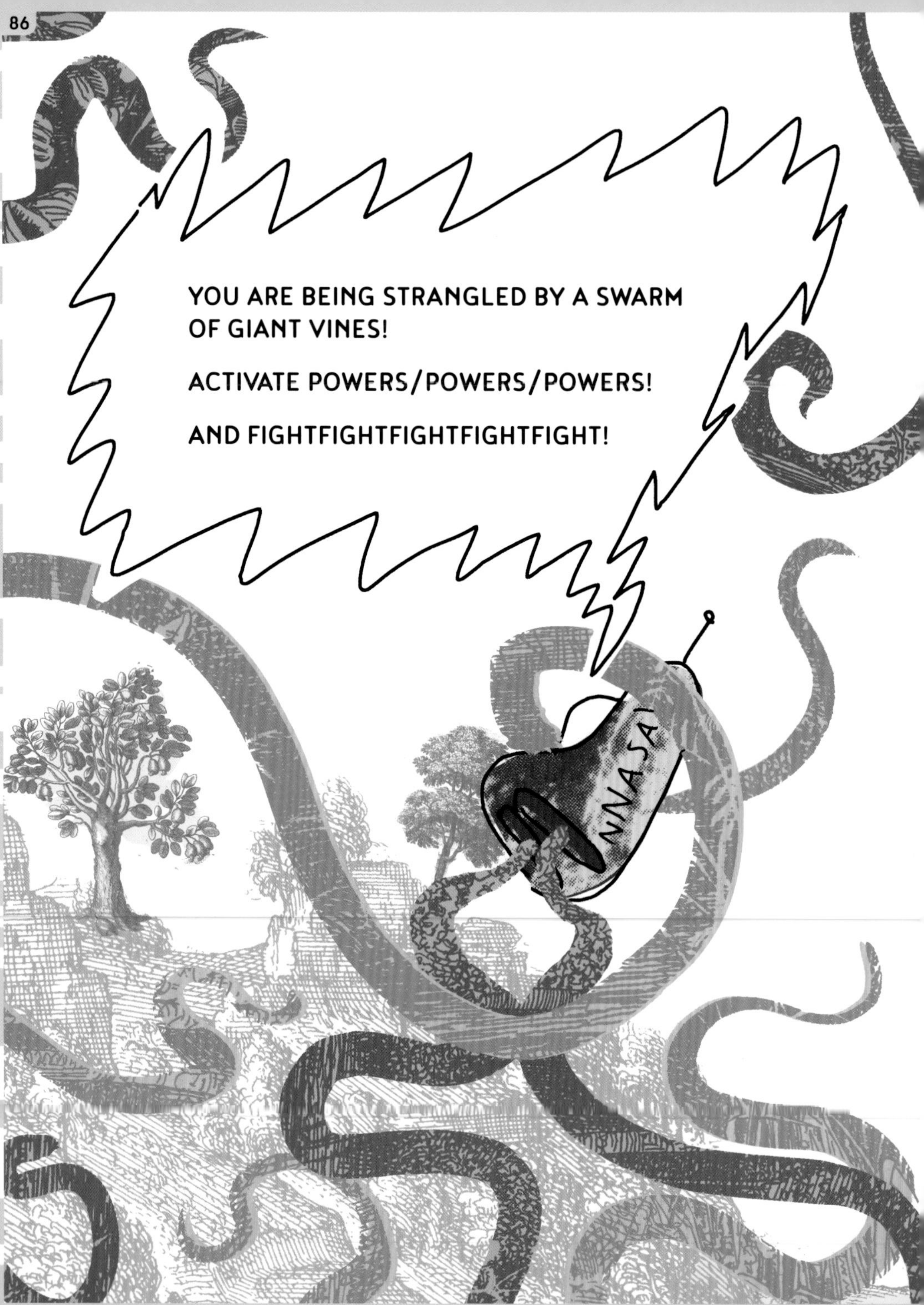
YOU ARE BEING STRANGLED BY A SWARM OF GIANT VINES!
ACTIVATE POWERS/POWERS/POWERS!
AND FIGHTFIGHTFIGHTFIGHTFIGHT!

The AstroNuts had never heard Command Escape so freaked out.

So you better believe they Activated Powers.

And jumped to FIGHTFIGHTFIGHTFIGHTFIGHT!

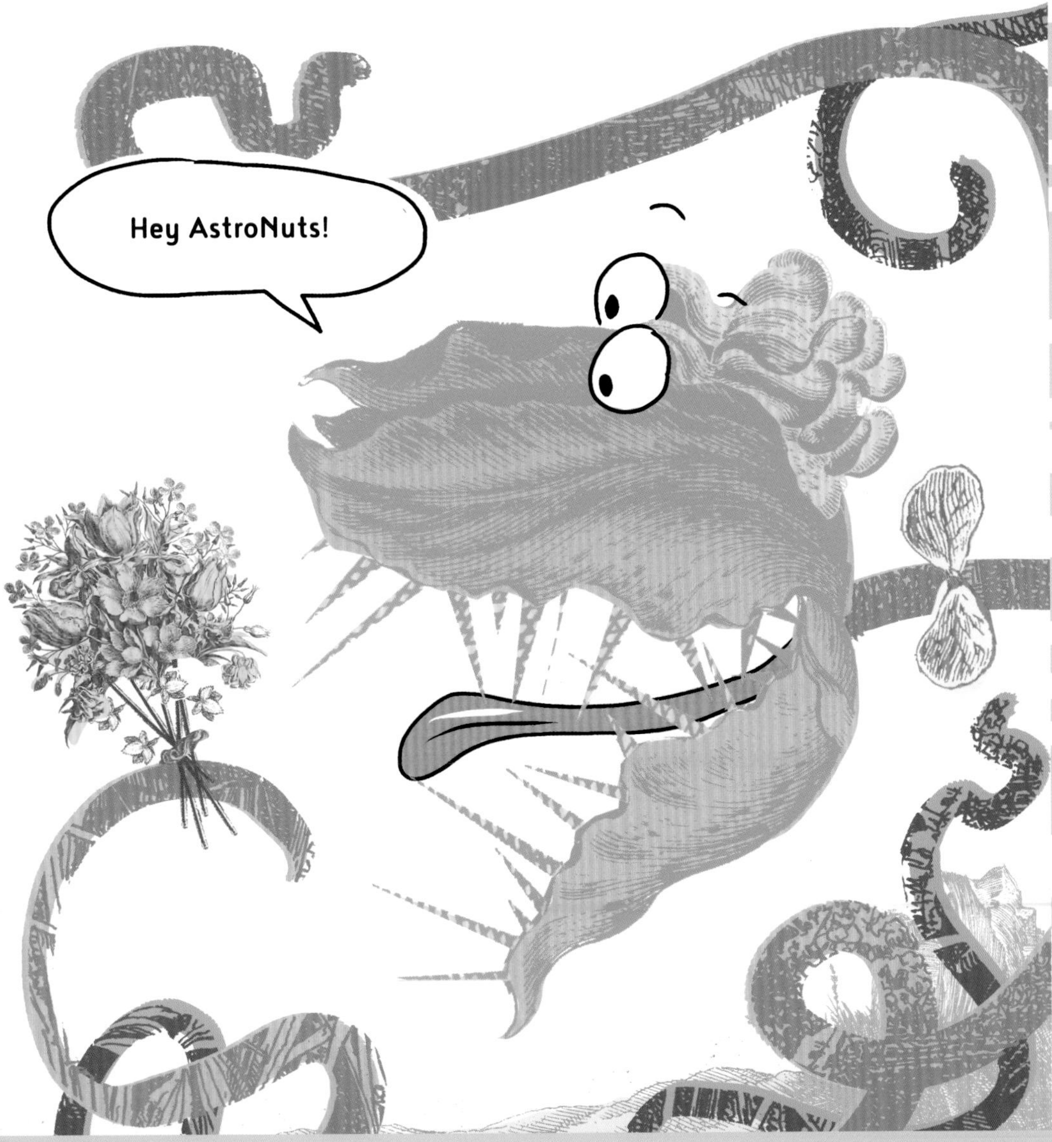
Hey AstroNuts!

CHAPTER 14:
The Battle

I've seen a lot of fights, a lot of battles, a lot of wars in my time. Like *T. rex* vs. Triceratops. Orca vs. Giant Squid. Army Ants vs. Fire Ants. So believe me when I tell you—the AstroNuts used their superpowers to put up a rousing good fight.

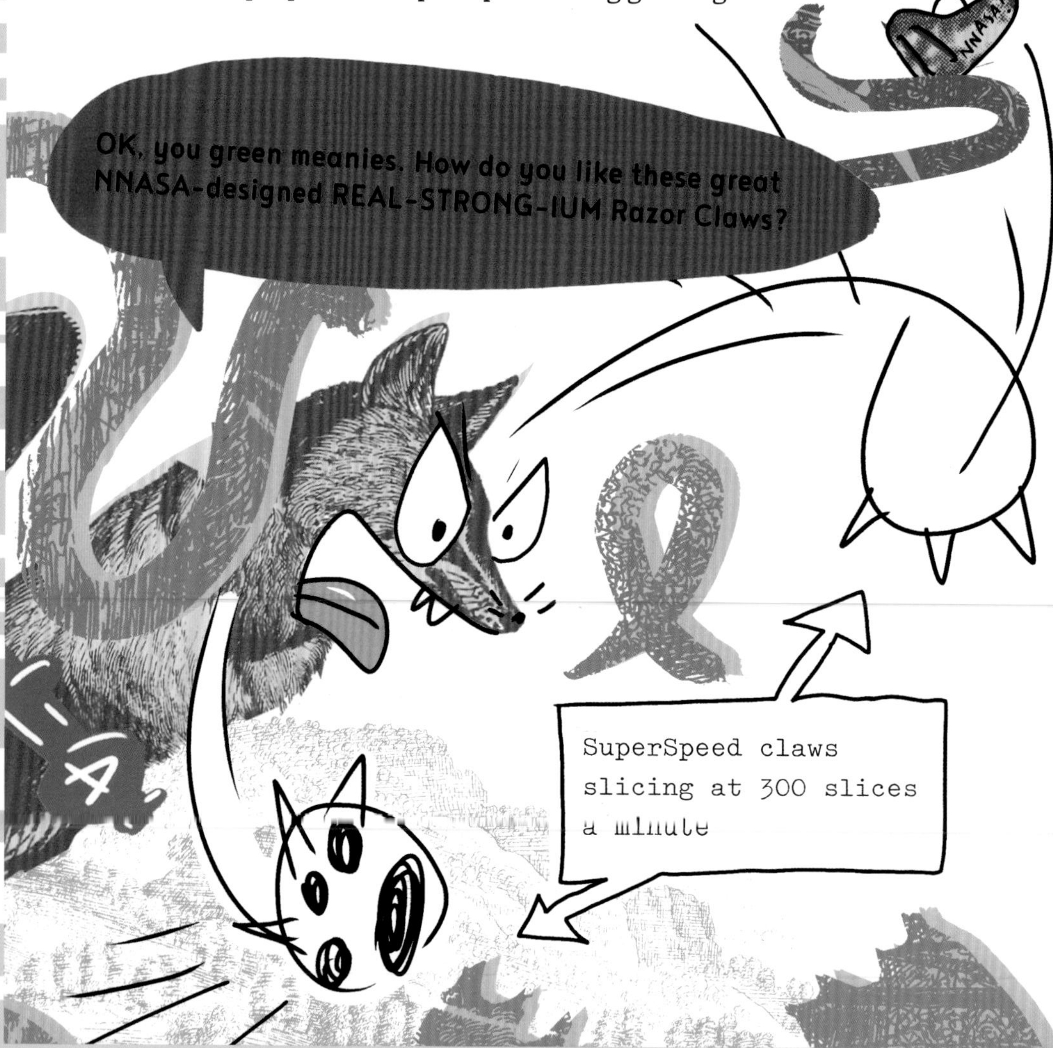
NNASA
OK, you green meanies. How do you like these great NNASA-designed REAL-STRONG-IUM Razor Claws?
SuperSpeed claws slicing at 300 slices a minute

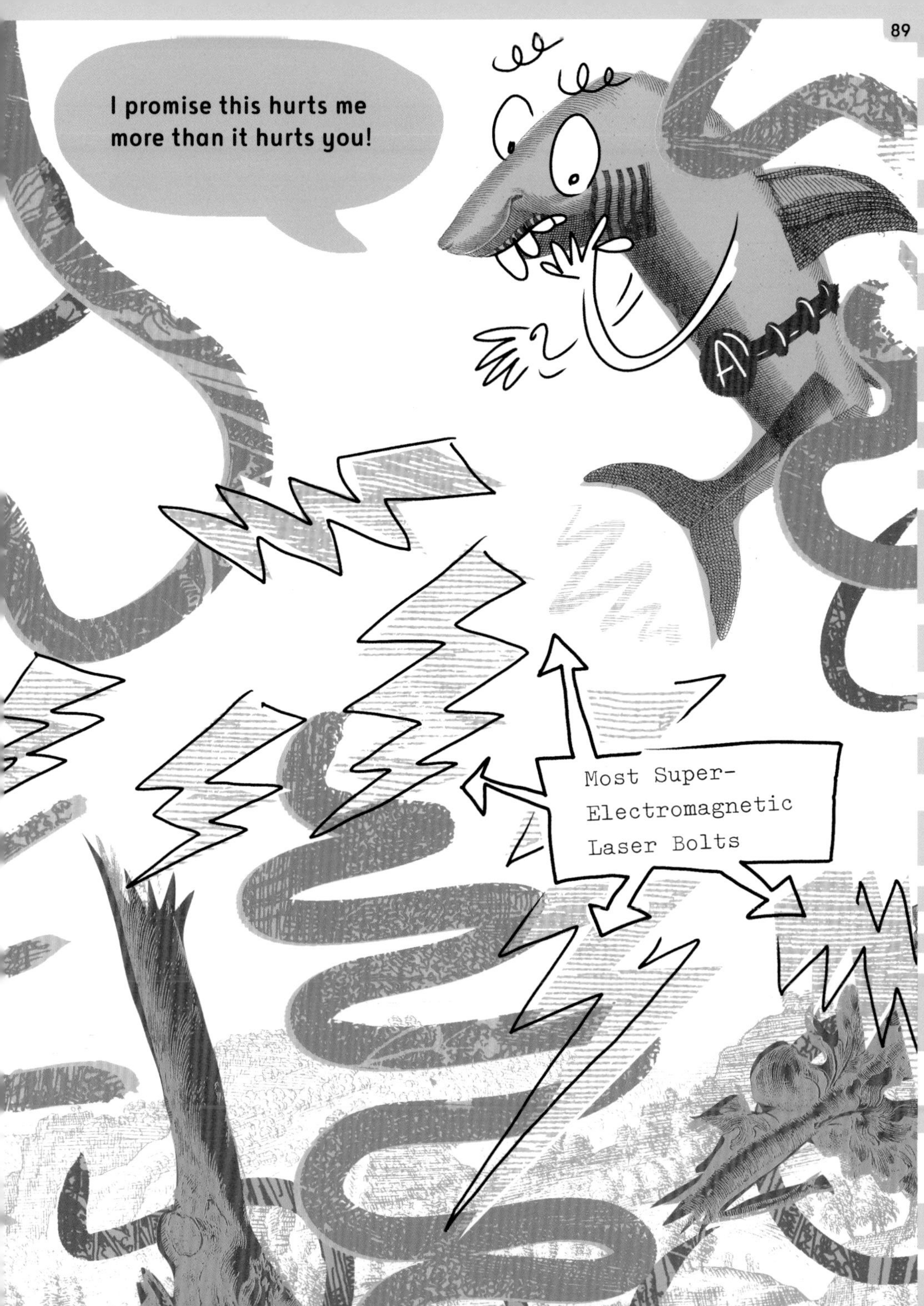
I promise this hurts me more than it hurts you!
Most Super-Electromagnetic Laser Bolts

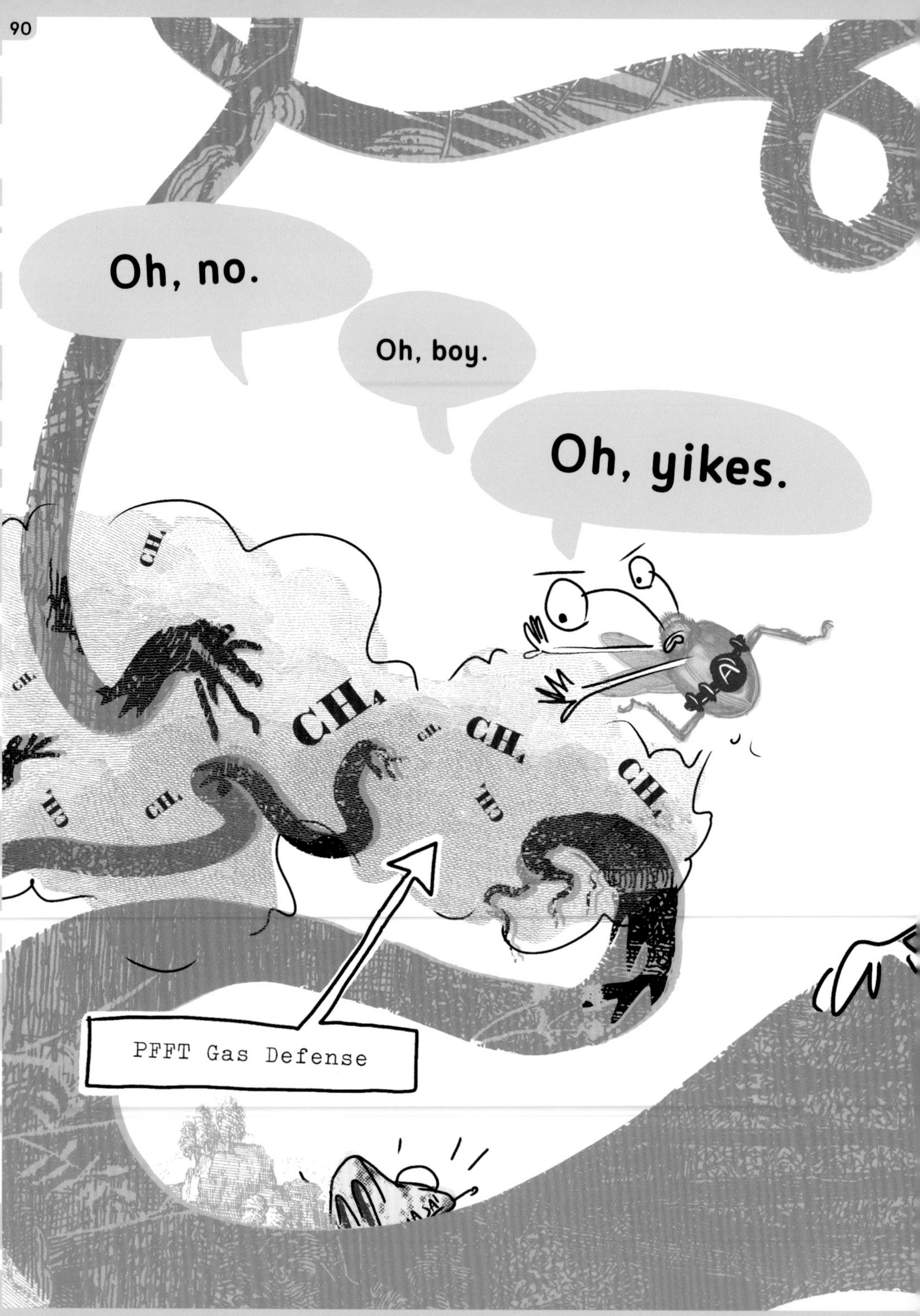
Oh, no.
Oh, boy.
Oh, yikes.
CH_4
PFFT Gas Defense

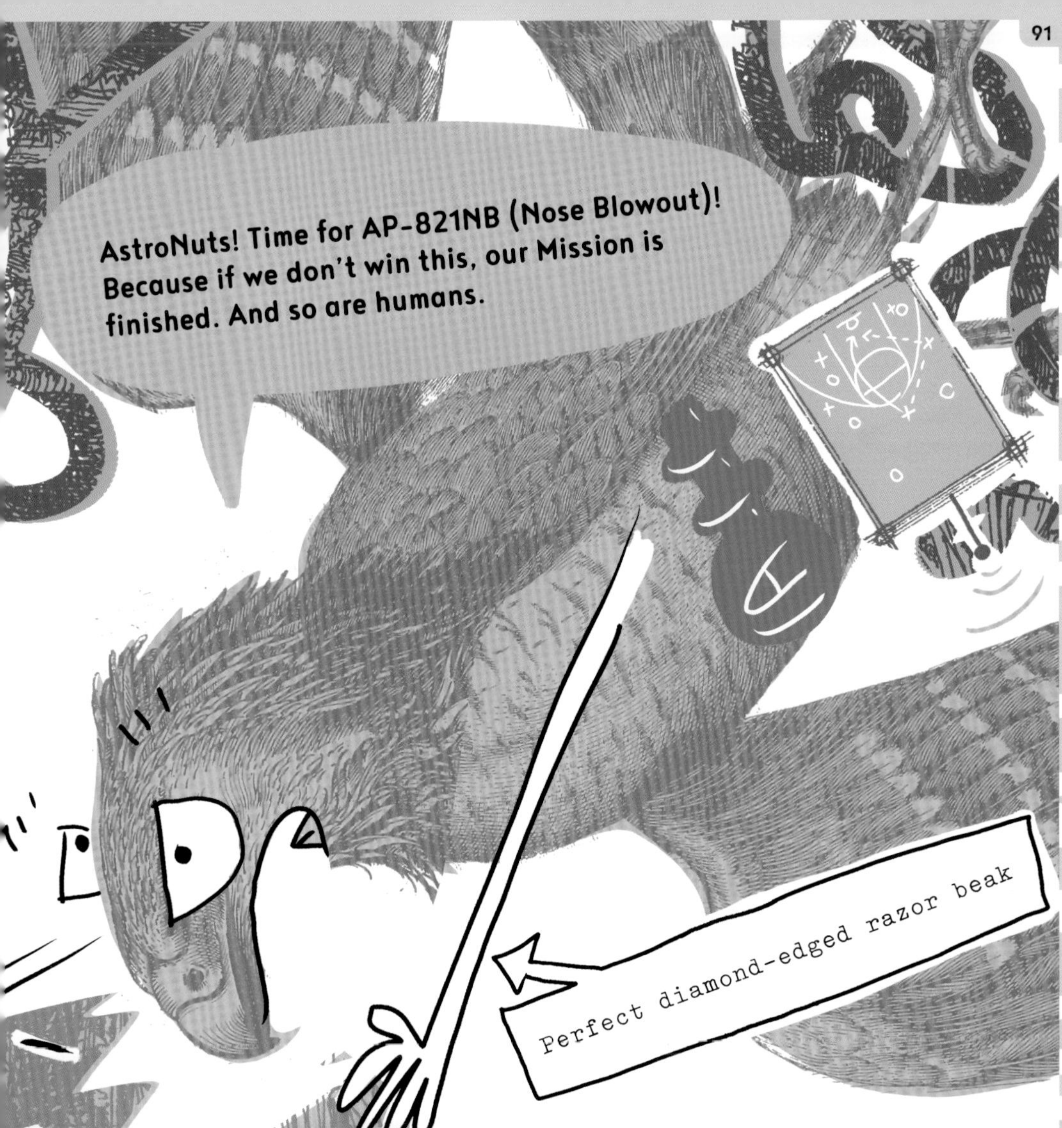
AstroNuts! Time for AP-821NB (Nose Blowout)! Because if we don't win this, our Mission is finished. And so are humans.
Perfect diamond-edged razor beak

As usual, SmartHawk was exactly right. AstroPlan-821NB was a perfect plan for this precise situation.

Until AlphaWolf decided he needed to make Plan 821NB even greater.

He howled a crazy howl, and . . .

I am so sorry to interrupt this fierce AstroNut vs. Plant Battle. But you may remember I promised you the Straight Science on how humans got into this problem of needing to look for another planet in the first place.

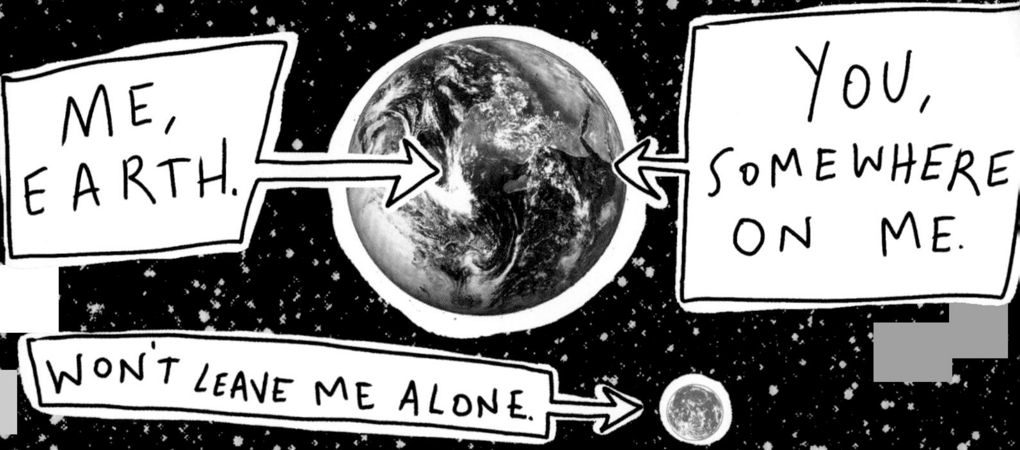
ME, EARTH.
YOU, SOMEWHERE ON ME.
WON'T LEAVE ME ALONE.

Well, here are five important facts for you:

1. My climate is getting warmer.
2. This is because of humans. → YOU
3. This is seriously true.
4. This is seriously bad.
5. If you don't do something, you are cooked.

And here is the Straight Science:

1.

In the last 100 years, my average temperature has gone steadily up—2013, 2014, 2015, 2016, 2017, and 2018 were the 6 hottest years ever recorded.

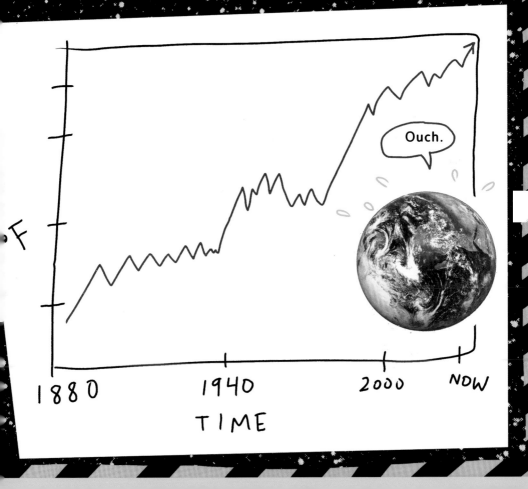

2.

My rising temperature has been caused by you clever humans inventing things that burn coal and oil and gas.

Burning these fossil fuels puts crazy amounts of CO_2 (carbon dioxide) into my atmosphere.

More CO_2 in my atmosphere produces the Greenhouse Effect, trapping heat from the sun close to me.

The Greenhouse Effect heats me up.

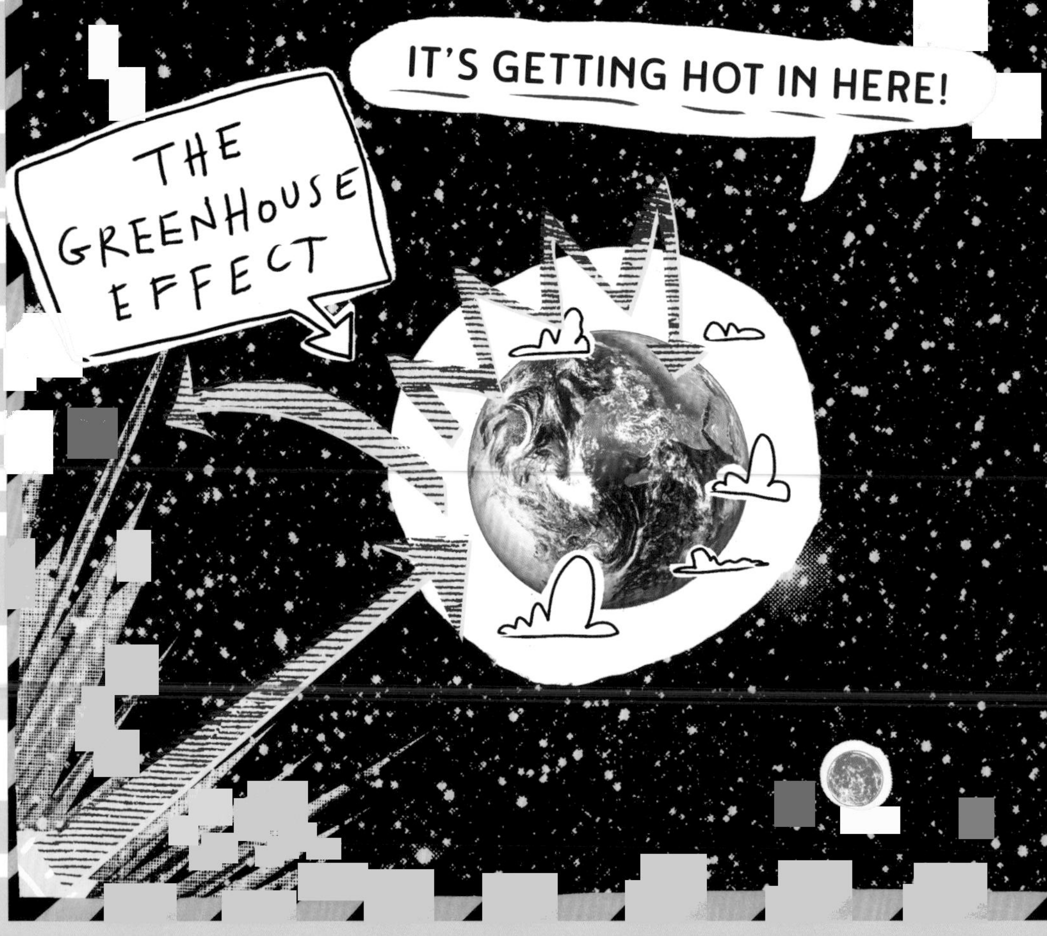
IT'S GETTING HOT IN HERE!
THE GREENHOUSE EFFECT

3.

Now, you don't have to believe any of this is true just because I am Earth—your very own planet—and I wouldn't lie to you.

No, you can believe my climate change is true because 97% of your own human scientists who have studied this agree:

MY CLIMATE CHANGE IS BEING CAUSED BY HUMAN ACTIVITY.

Cough!
Cough!

The humans who disagree seem to be mostly humans who are making money by making climate change worse. Doesn't that seem a bit suspicious?

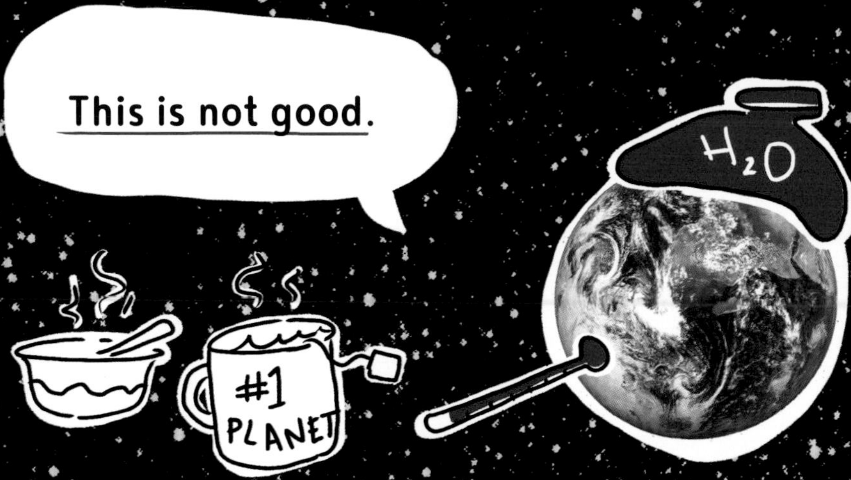
This is not good.
H_2O
#1
PLANET

4.

Because a hotter me is bad news for everything living on me.

My rising temperature means a lot worse than you just getting a little warmer.

It means:

- my ice caps melting
- my oceans rising over your cities
- more violent storms, fires, and droughts
- all kinds of plant, animal, and bug life being extinguished

And I can’t help it.

This climate fever of mine is like a very bad flu.
A Humans-Burning-Fossil-Fuels Flu.

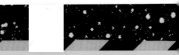

5.

You humans burning fossil fuels, wasting water, and not paying attention to the signs I've been giving you—that's what got us both into this mess. All those hot years, all those ice caps melting, all that ocean rise—those were my signals to you! But you ignored them.

So now it's up to you to figure a way out. You can:

a) Burn less fossil fuels or b) Find another planet with air and water and plants and animals, just like Me. And transport all 7.7 billion humans there to live.

It doesn't really matter to me what you decide. I'm a planet. I think in millions of years. If your species decides to temporarily wreck my finely balanced climate and ecosystems by ending all human existence—I'll be sad. I'll miss you.

But I will also, in a few thousand or million years, be just fine.

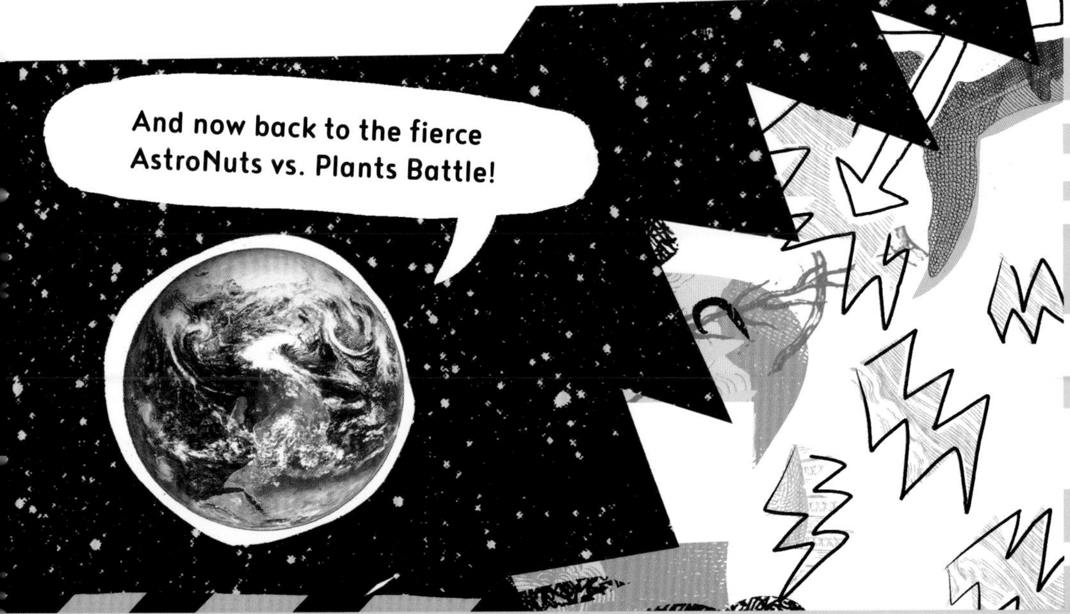
And now back to the fierce AstroNuts vs. Plants Battle!

. . . added his special touch to SmartHawk’s AstroPlan-821NB, by putting on a show-off burst of his Greatest SuperSpeed.

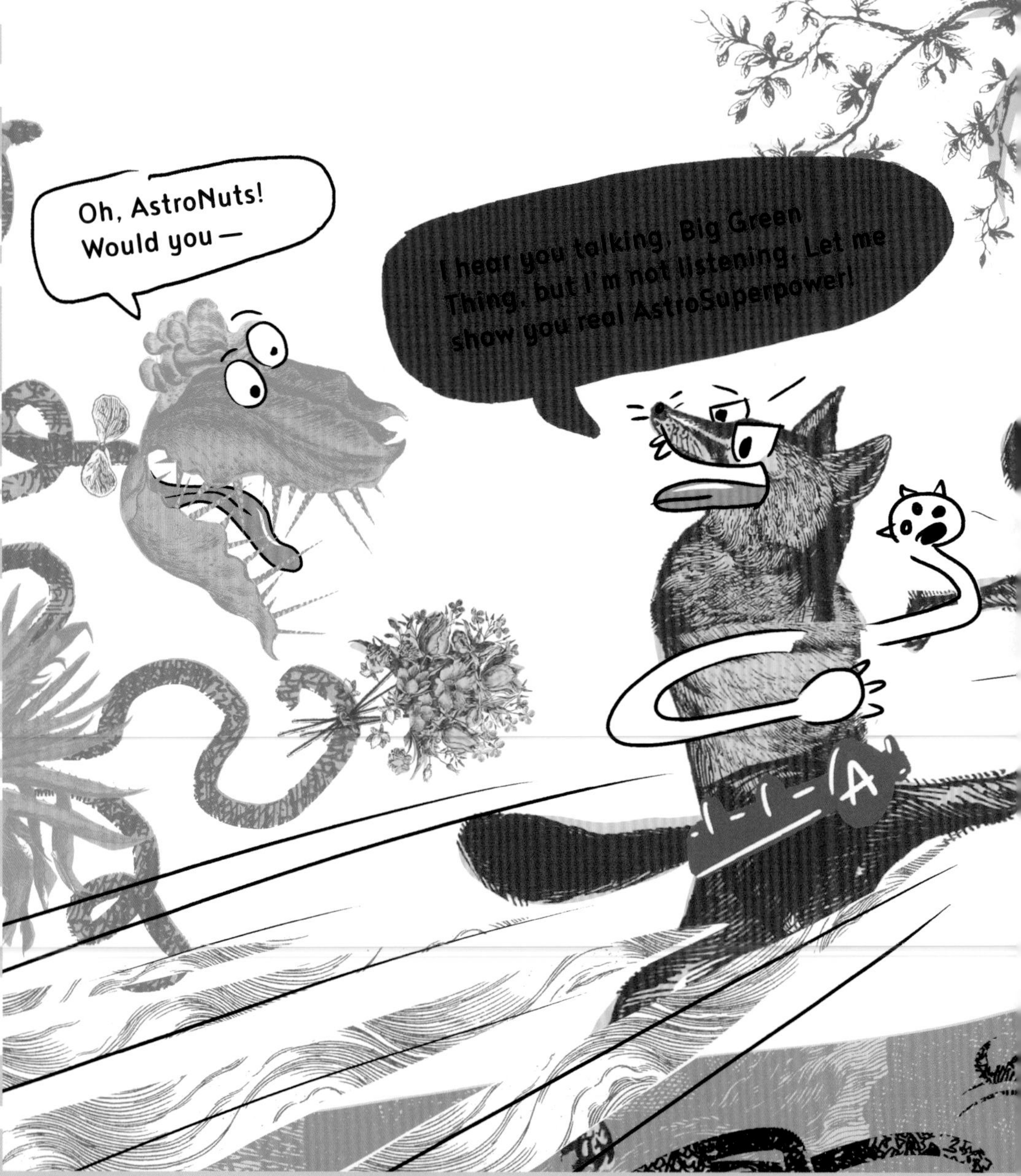
Oh, AstroNuts! Would you—
I hear you talking, Big Green Thing, but I’m not listening. Let me show you real AstroSuperpower!

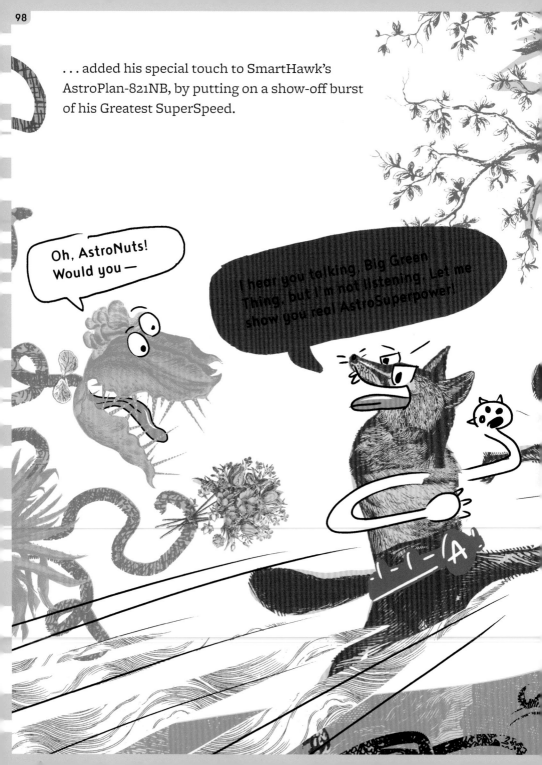

AlphaWolf SuperSpeed ran. He SuperSpeed tripped. And SuperSpeed fell smack into LaserShark . . .

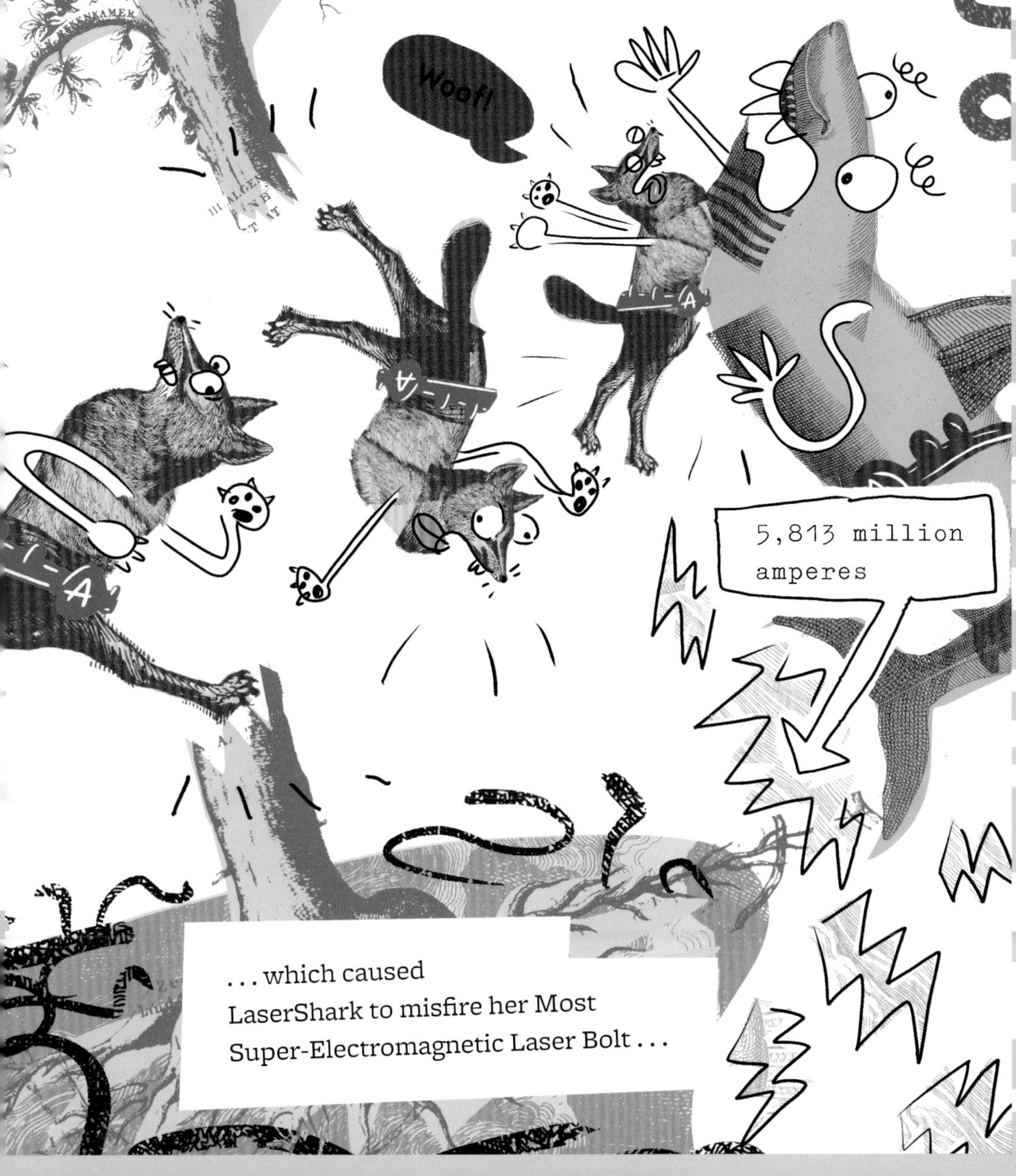
Woof!
5,813 million amperes

. . . which caused LaserShark to misfire her Most Super-Electromagnetic Laser Bolt . . .

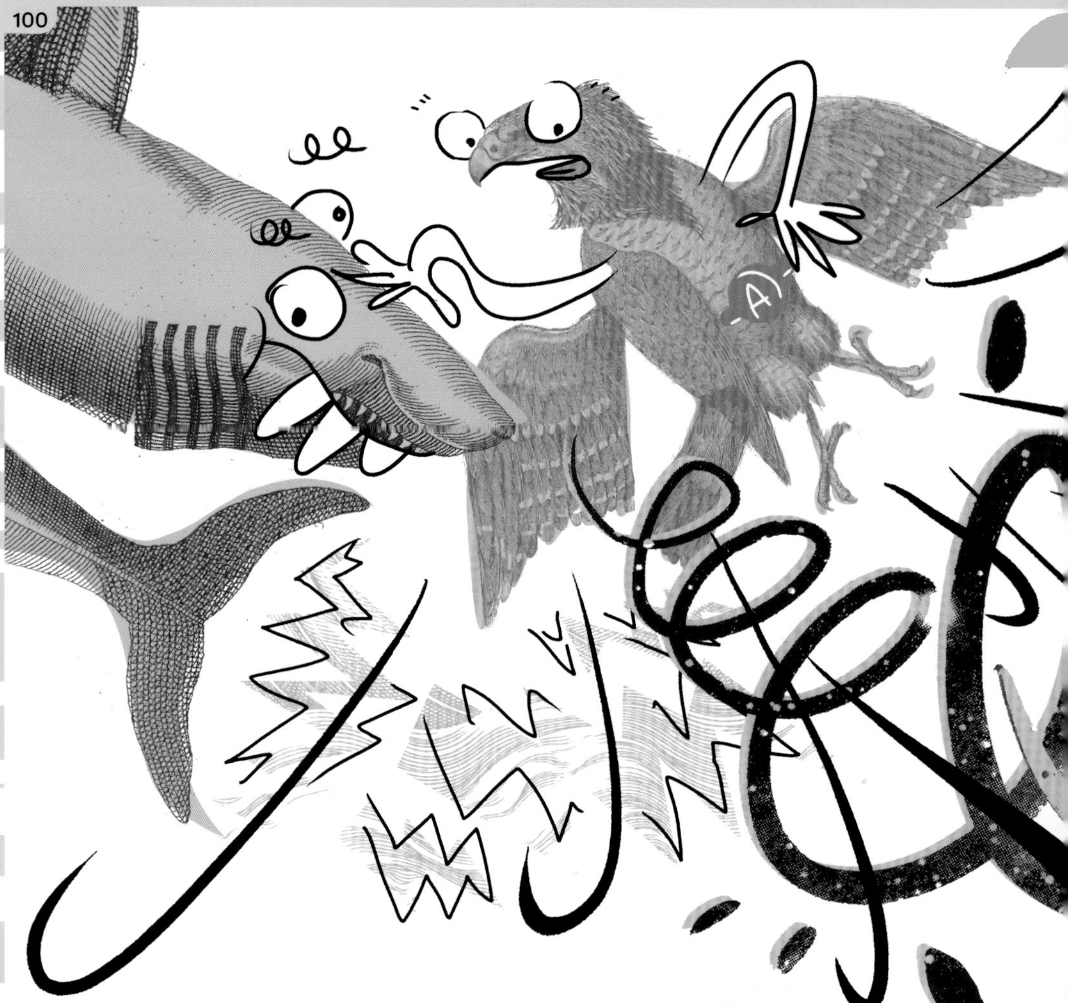

. . . which fused with SmartHawk's
Most Perfect Dark Energy Tornado . . .

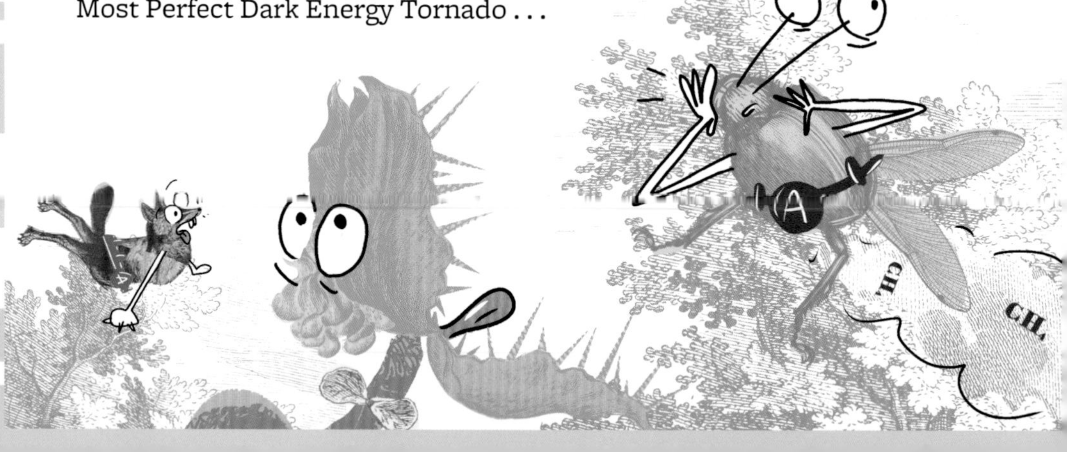

. . . and formed a terrible Electrified Dark Energy Super Vortex . . .

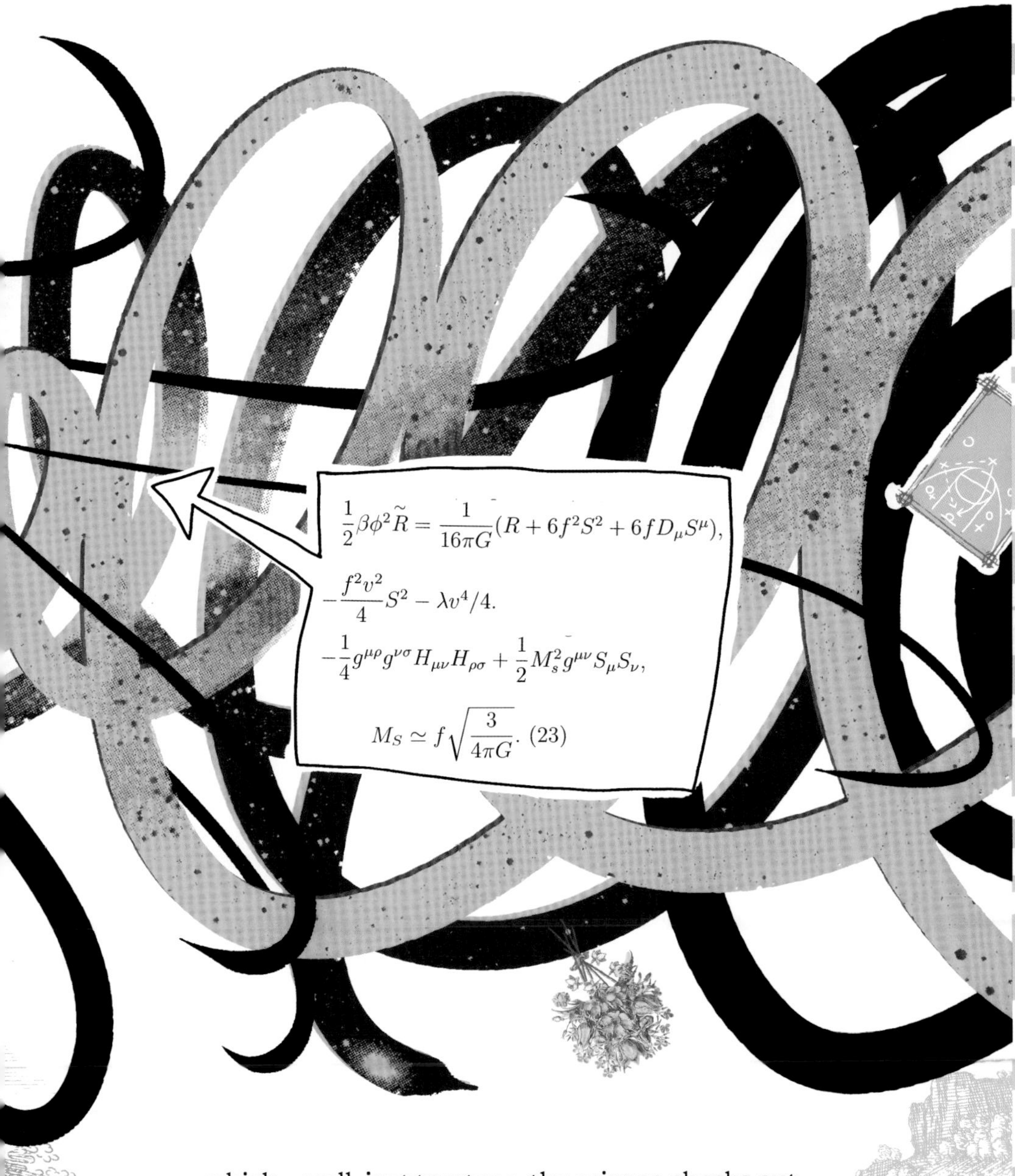
$\frac{1}{2}\beta\phi^2\tilde{R} = \frac{1}{16\pi G}(R + 6f^2S^2 + 6fD_\mu S^\mu),$
$-\frac{f^2v^2}{4}S^2 - \lambda v^4/4.$
$-\frac{1}{4}g^{\mu\rho}g^{\nu\sigma}H_{\mu\nu}H_{\rho\sigma} + \frac{1}{2}M_s^2 g^{\mu\nu}S_\mu S_\nu,$
$M_S \simeq f\sqrt{\frac{3}{4\pi G}}.$ (23)

. . . which—well, just trust me, the science checks out—

. . . knocked them all out—

so they could be quite easily wrapped up by the Giant Vines . . .

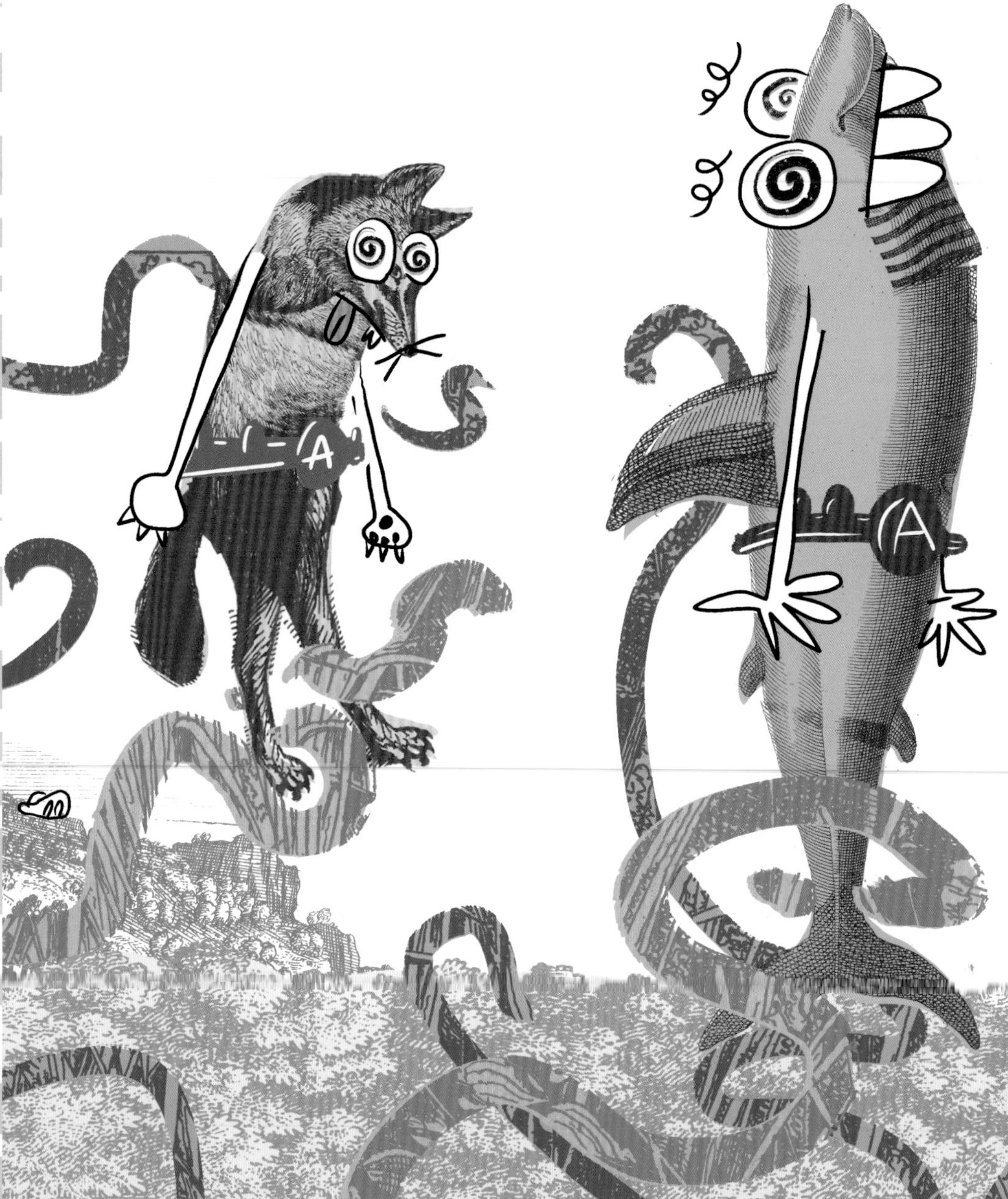

. . . and carried off to meet their fate at Plant Planet Headquarters.

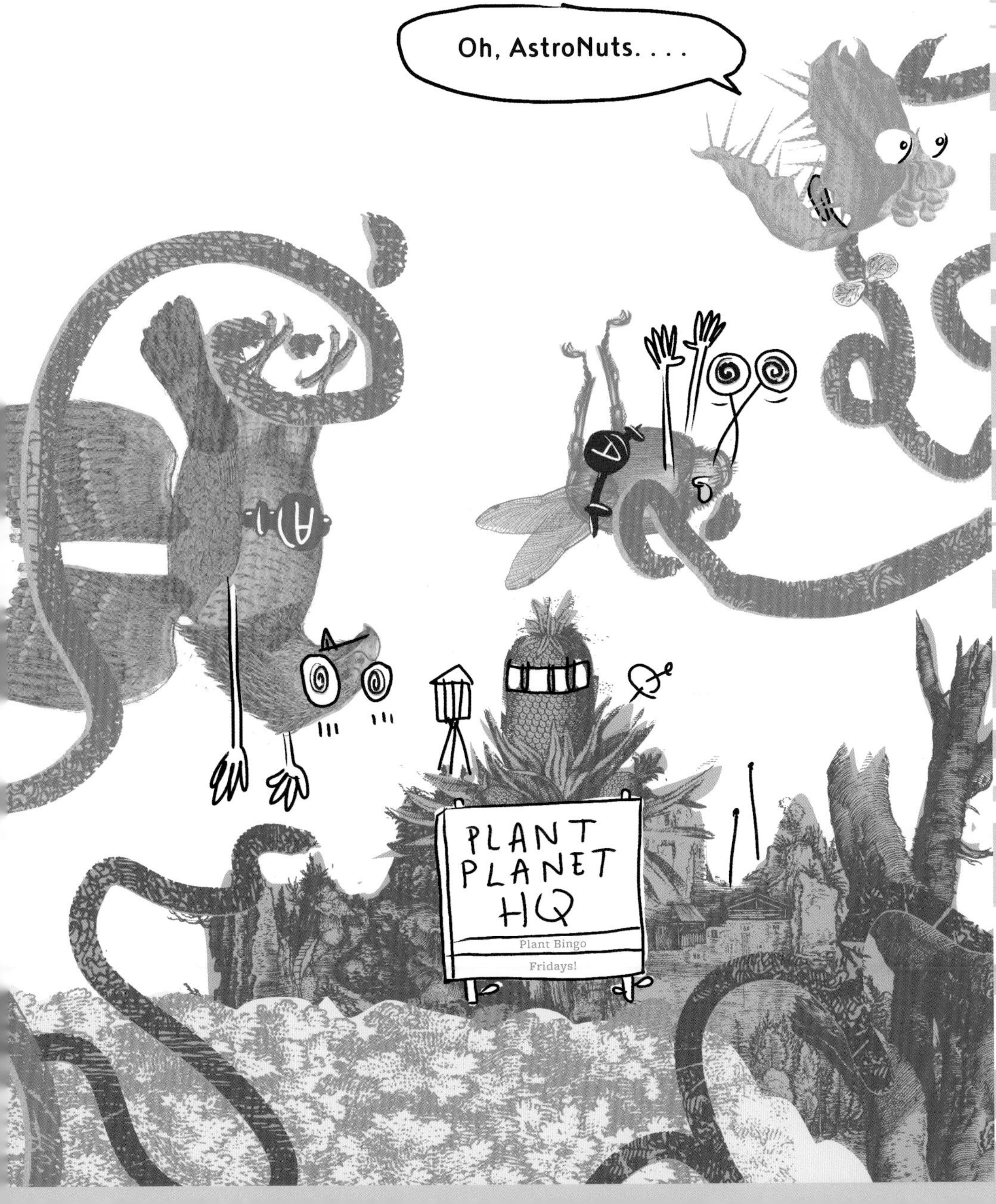
Oh, AstroNuts. . . .
PLANT PLANET HQ
Plant Bingo
Fridays!

CHAPTER 15:

Inside PPHQ

When the AstroNuts finally woke up from being conked out by their own accidental Electrified Dark Energy Super Vortex, they could not believe they had somehow been captured by a bunch of plants! But really—how did they not see that coming?

That's a question for another time.

For the moment, the most pressing question was probably *Are we about to get eaten alive by a giant plant?*

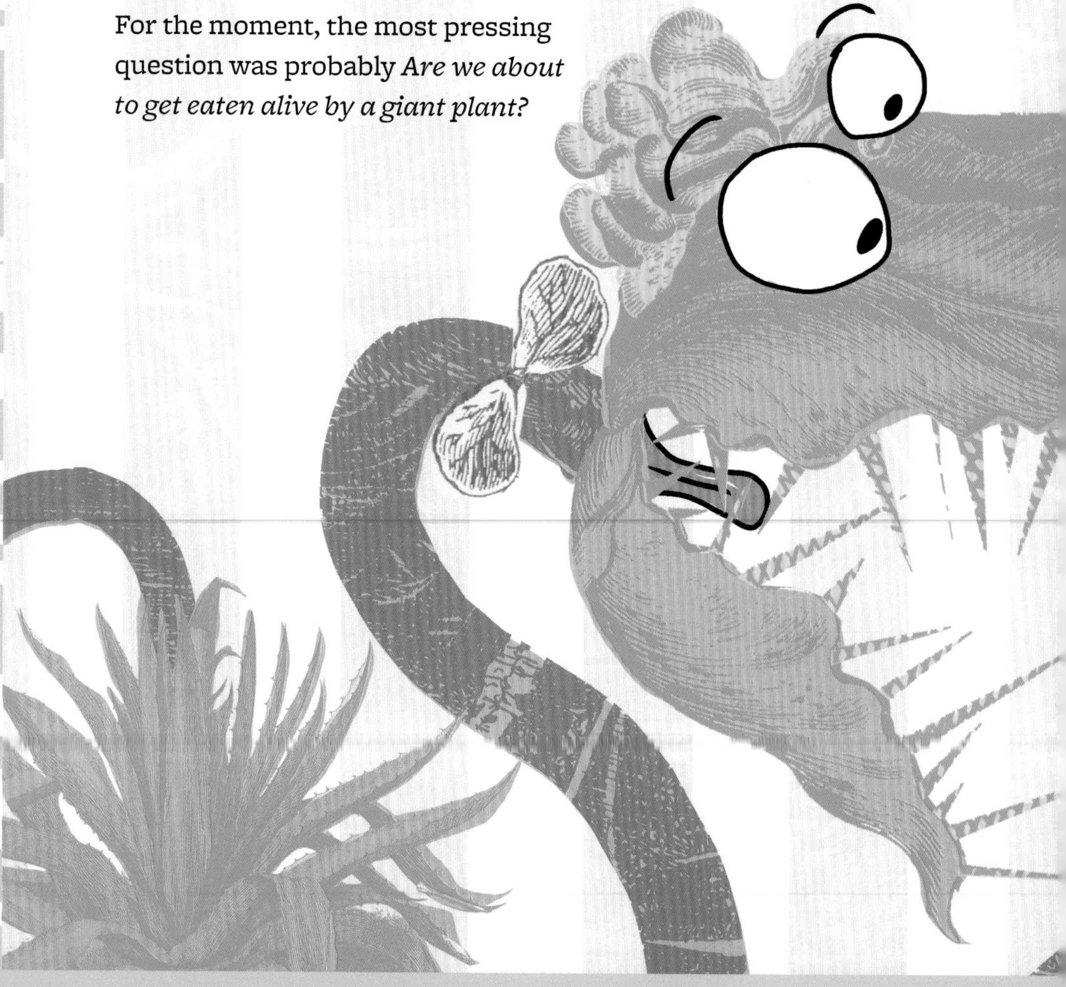

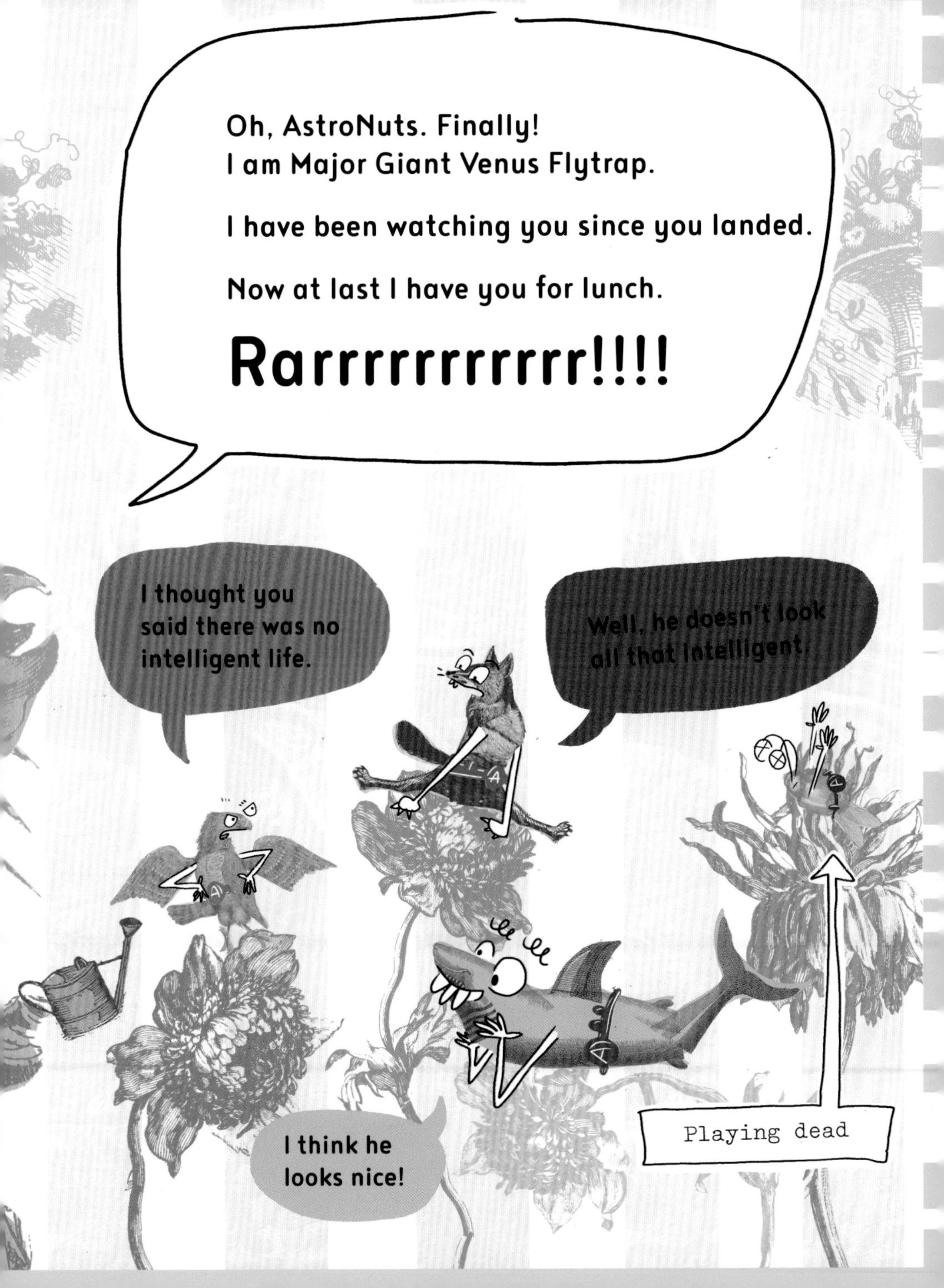
Oh, AstroNuts. Finally!
I am Major Giant Venus Flytrap.
I have been watching you since you landed.
Now at last I have you for lunch.
Rarrrrrrrrrrr!!!!
I thought you said there was no intelligent life.
Well, he doesn't look all that intelligent.
I think he looks nice!
Playing dead

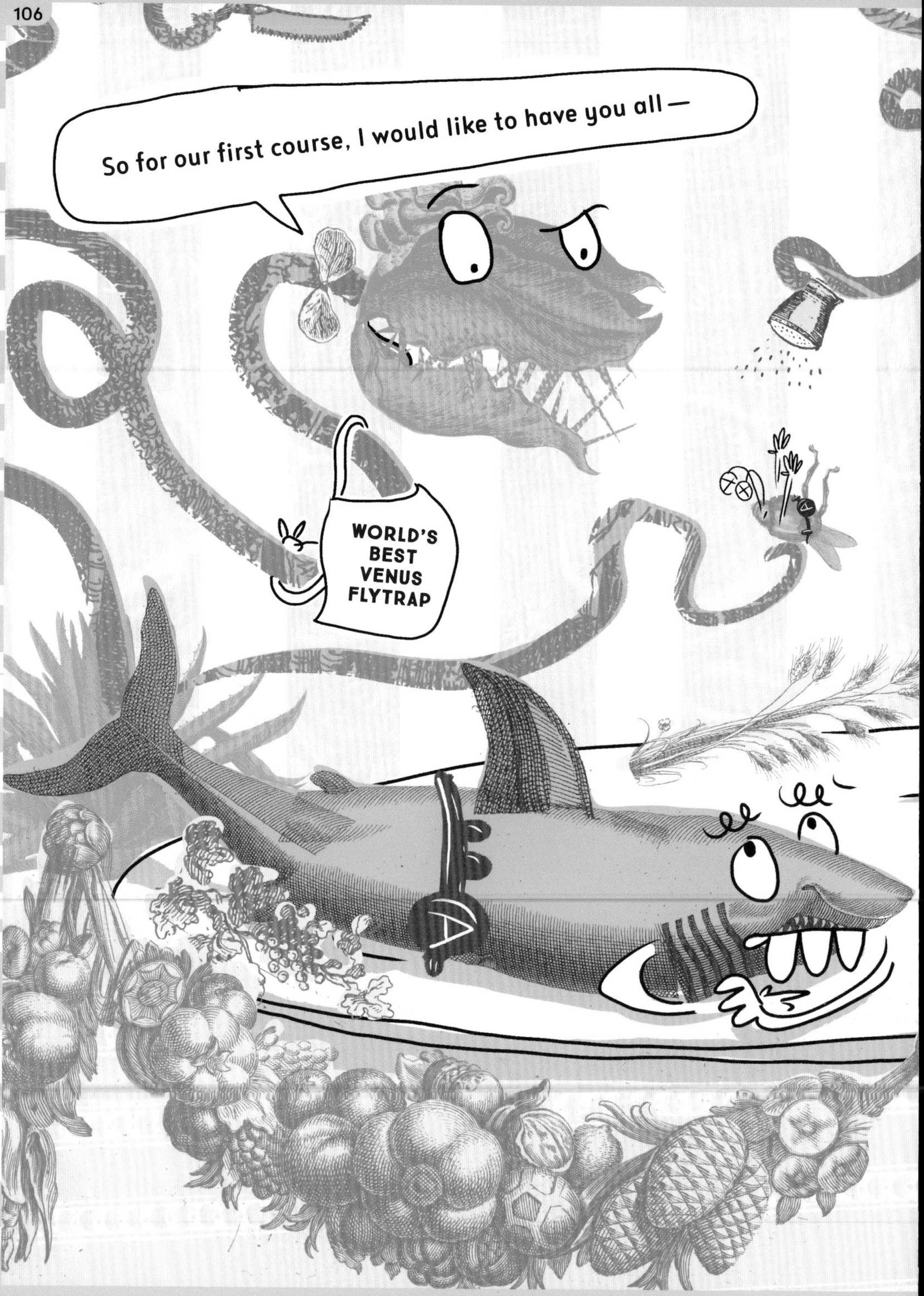
So for our first course, I would like to have you all—
WORLD'S BEST VENUS FLYTRAP

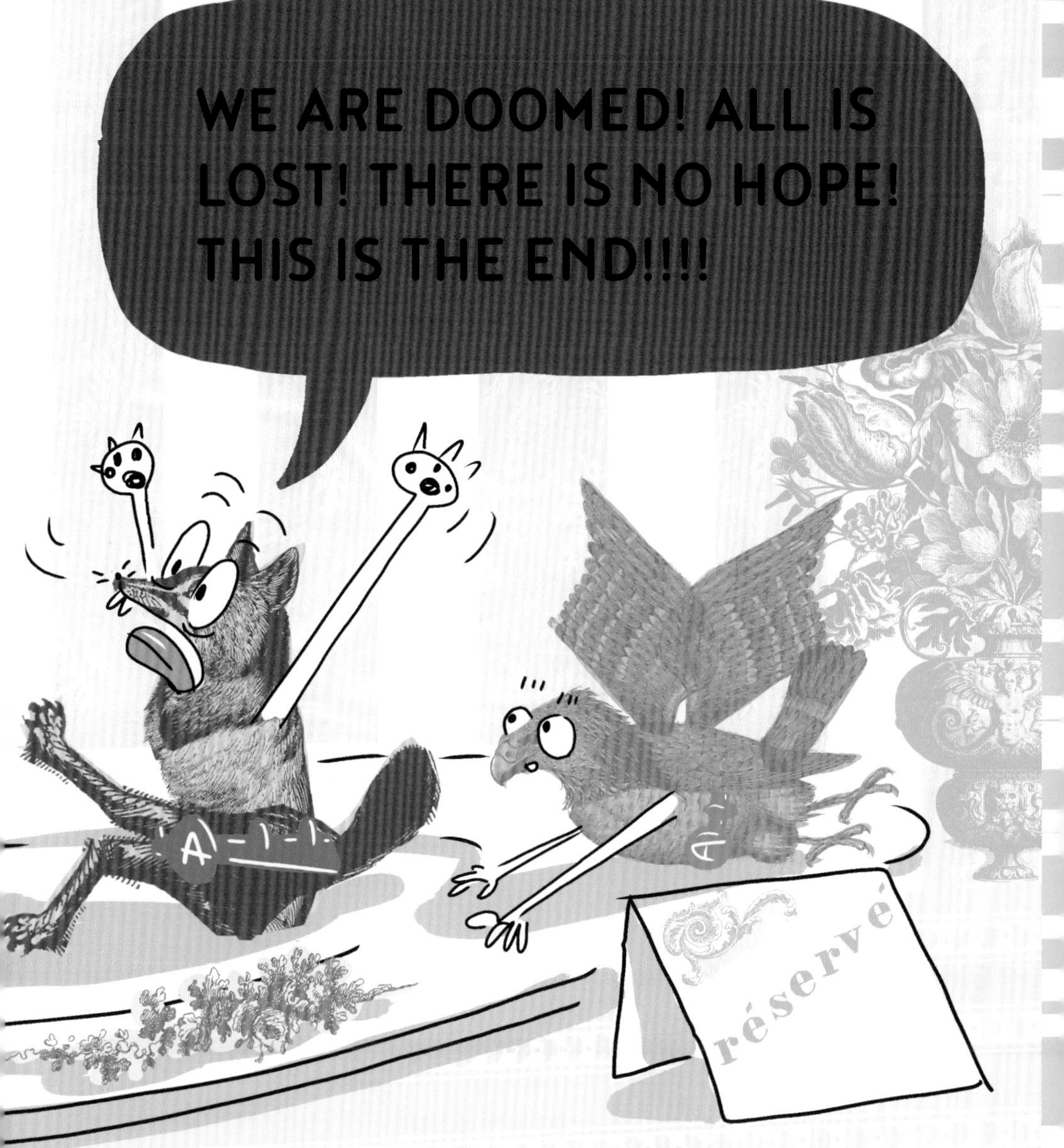
WE ARE DOOMED! ALL IS LOST! THERE IS NO HOPE! THIS IS THE END!!!!
réservé

It really did seem like all was lost. They were on a plate, after all. What were they supposed to think? But thank goodness AlphaWolf, as usual, was completely mistaken.

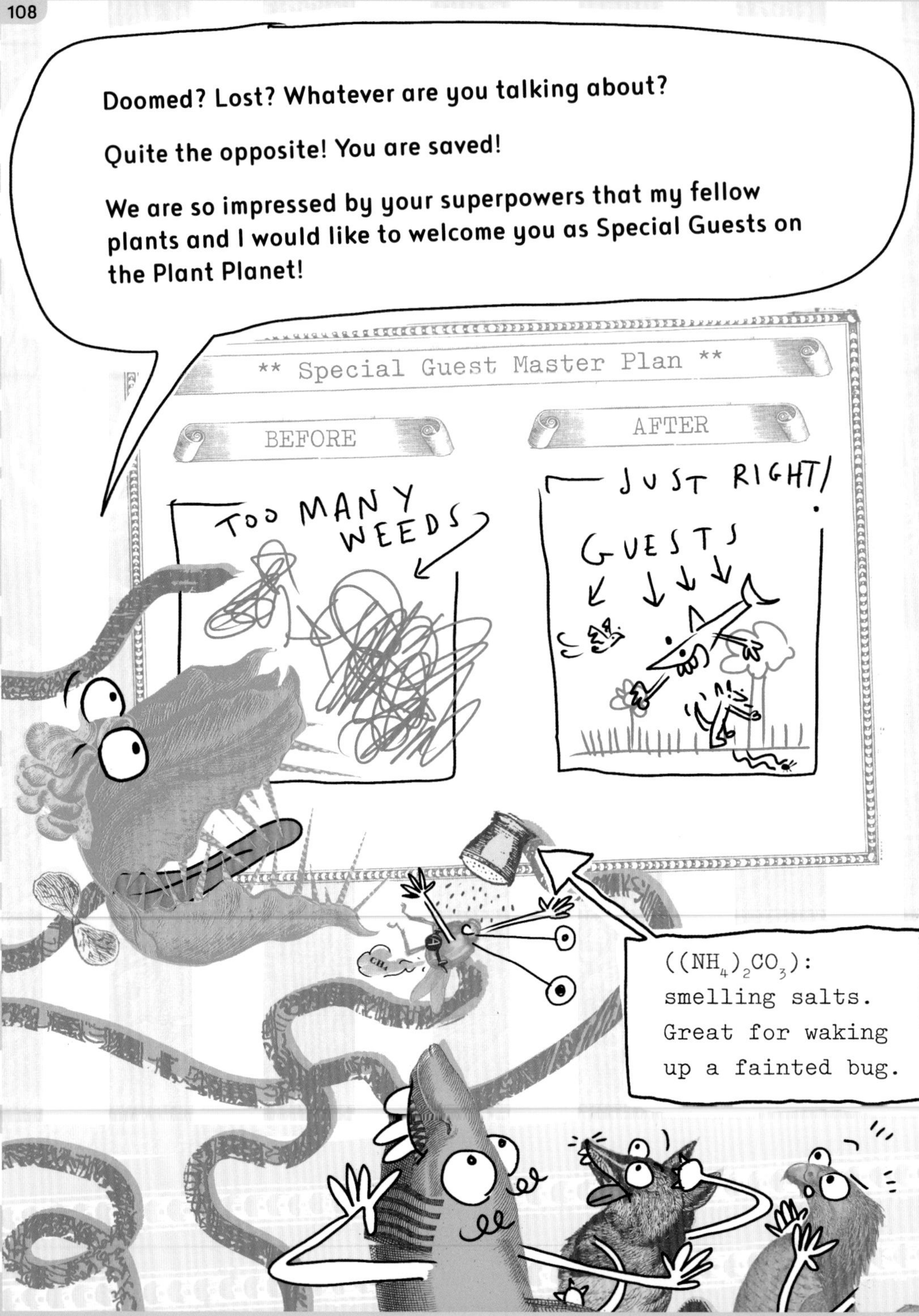
Doomed? Lost? Whatever are you talking about?
Quite the opposite! You are saved!
We are so impressed by your superpowers that my fellow plants and I would like to welcome you as Special Guests on the Plant Planet!
** Special Guest Master Plan **
BEFORE
AFTER
TOO MANY WEEDS
JUST RIGHT!
GUESTS
$((NH_4)_2CO_3)$: smelling salts. Great for waking up a fainted bug.

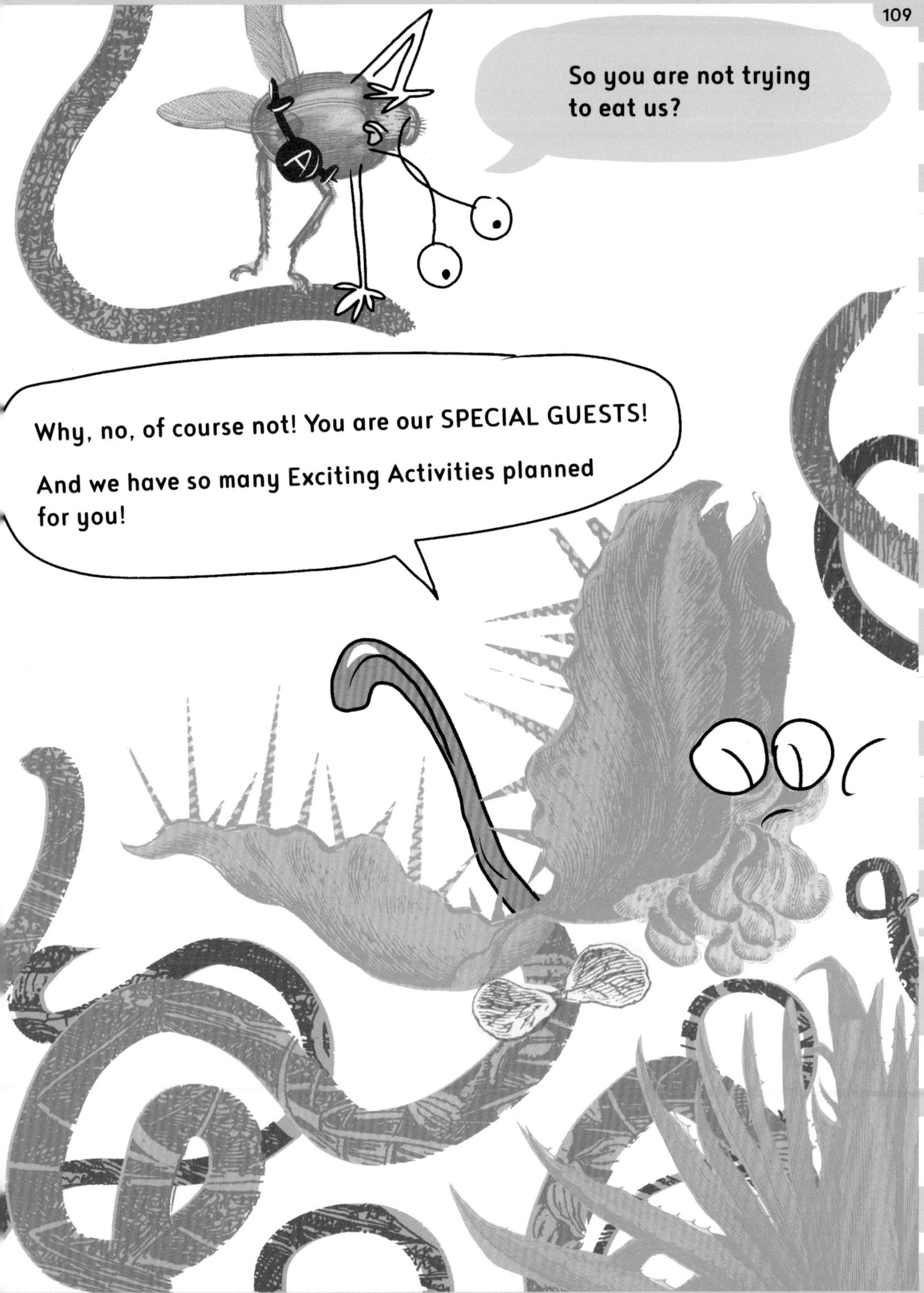
So you are not trying to eat us?
Why, no, of course not! You are our SPECIAL GUESTS! And we have so many Exciting Activities planned for you!

Looking out across the Plant Planet, Major Giant Venus Flytrap launched into a very beautiful speech about how wonderful the AstroNuts were, how lucky the Plant Planet was to have them visit, how perfect this was all going to be, how he'd forgotten to call his mom the night before, the last really good book he read, even his favorite color.

(It's green.)

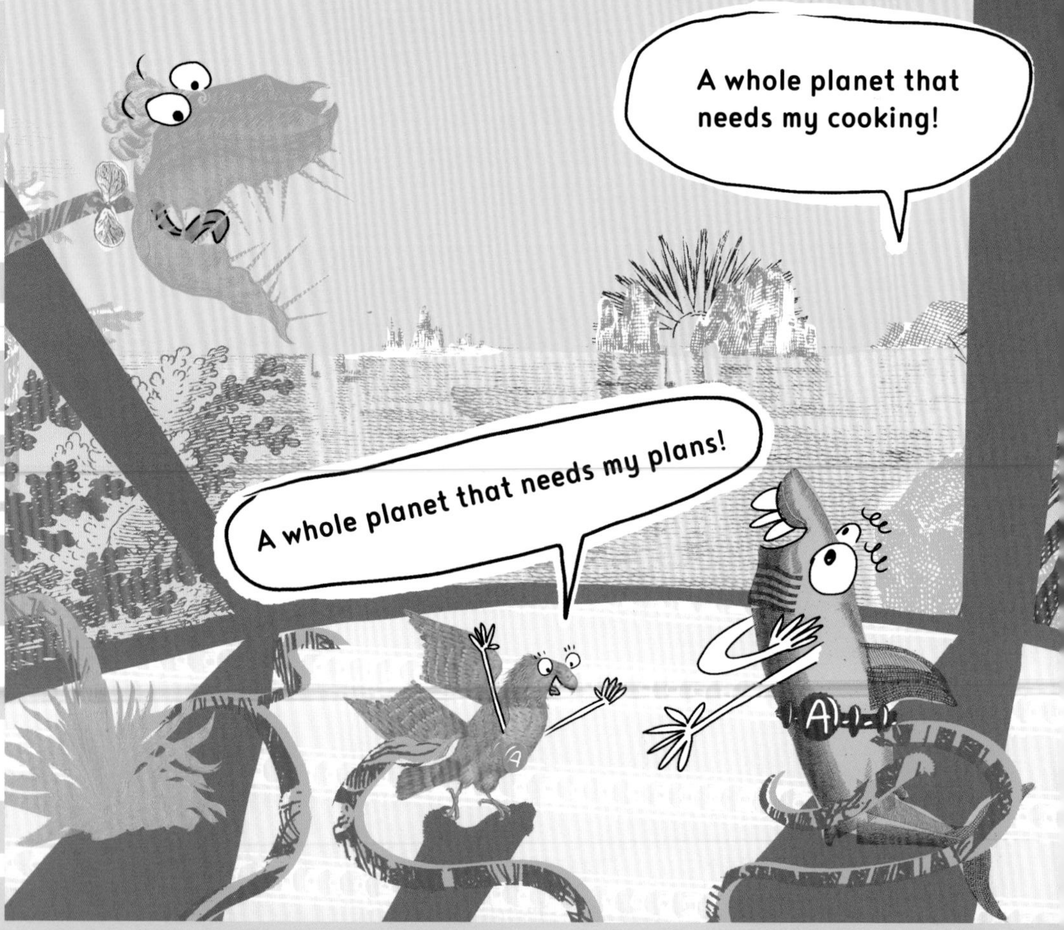
A whole planet that needs my cooking!
A whole planet that needs my plans!

The whole thing really went on and on much too long. It was very confusing, but it was very nice, and it made our AstroNuts feel very wanted.

It's nice to feel wanted in a new place, sometimes.

But trust the experience of a planet who has been around for 4.5 billion years—not always.

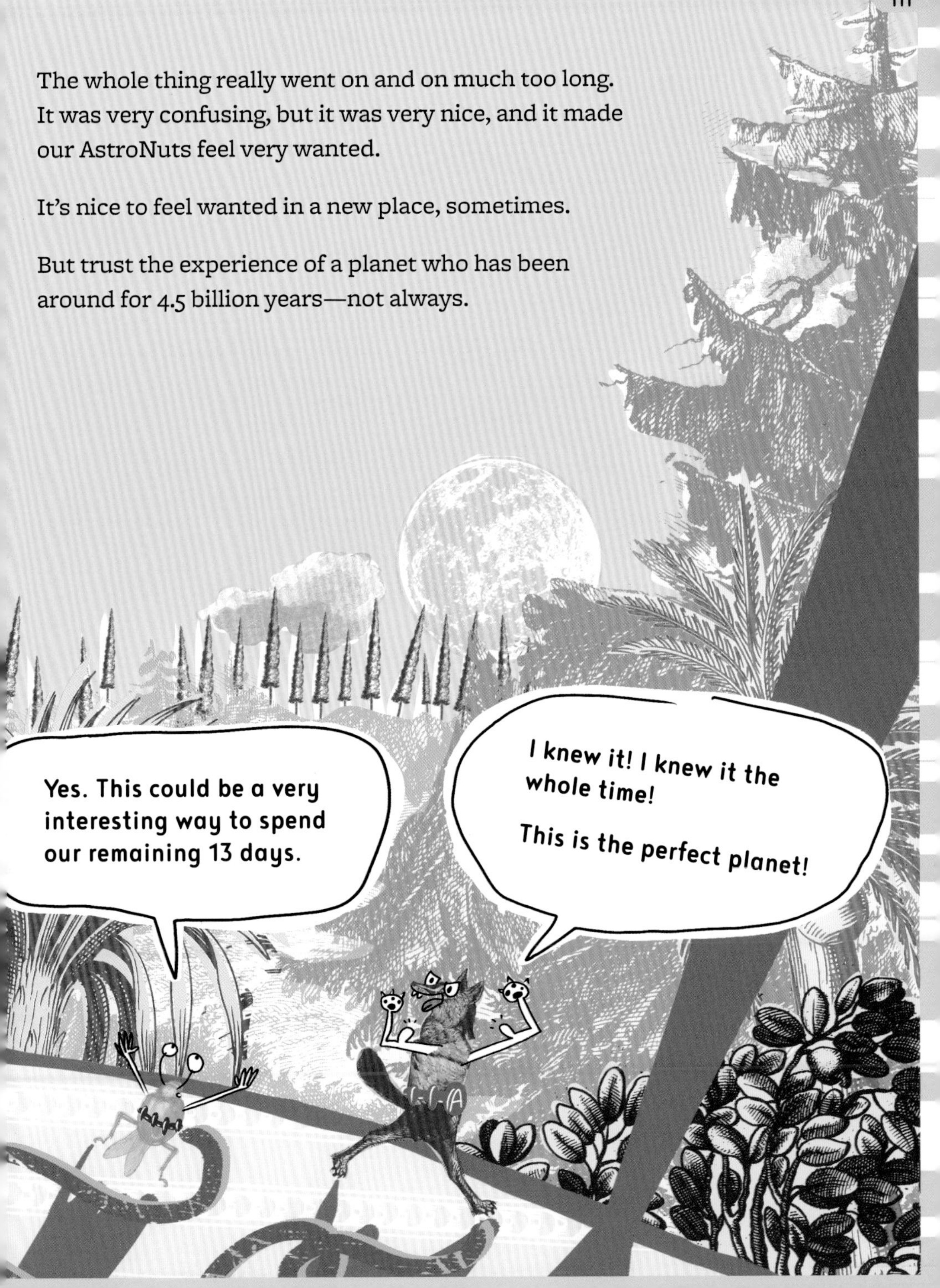
Yes. This could be a very interesting way to spend our remaining 13 days.
I knew it! I knew it the whole time!
This is the perfect planet!

CHAPTER 16:
Exciting Activities

The AstroNuts were so glad that both the Nose Rocket fight and the Getting Eaten for Lunch mix-up were just misunderstandings. Even as an innocent bystander millions of miles away, I was glad those tense moments were behind us.

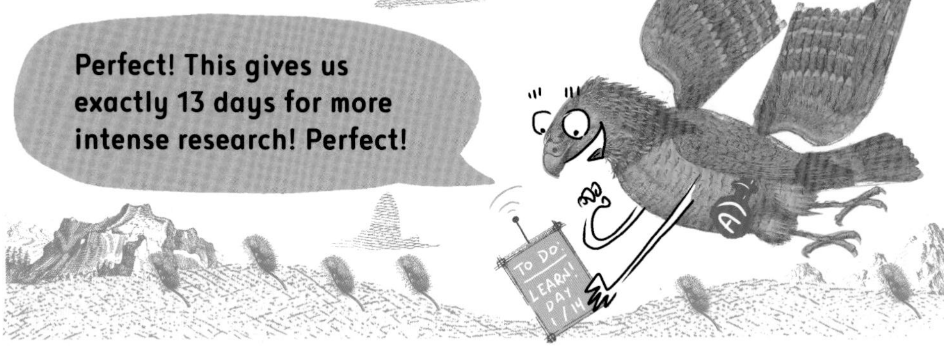
Perfect! This gives us exactly 13 days for more intense research! Perfect!
TO DO: LEARN! DAY 1/14

They were also pretty excited by the Exciting Activities Major Giant Venus Flytrap invited them to participate in.

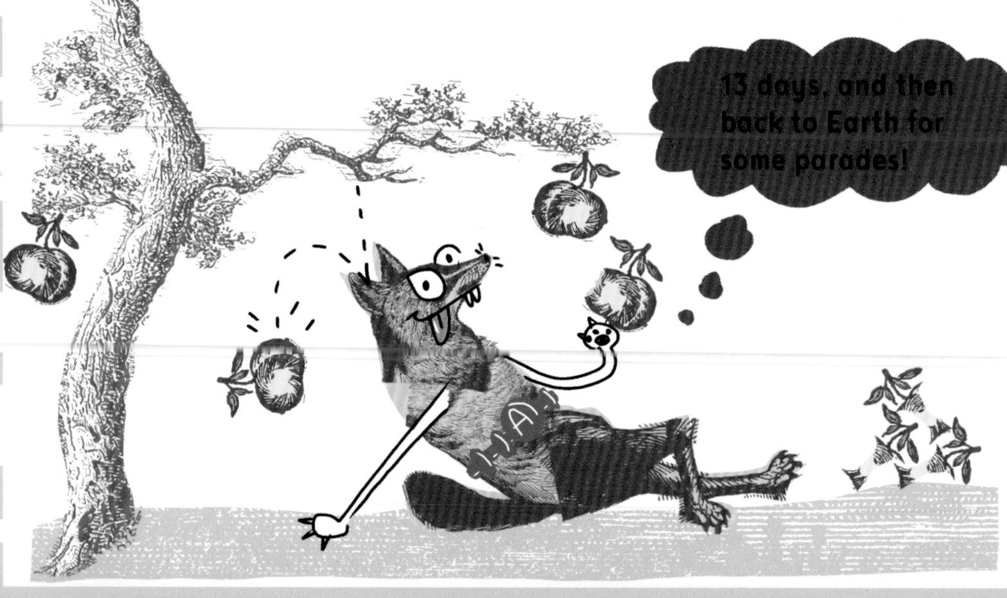
13 days, and then back to Earth for some parades!

Because the activities were exactly like research—

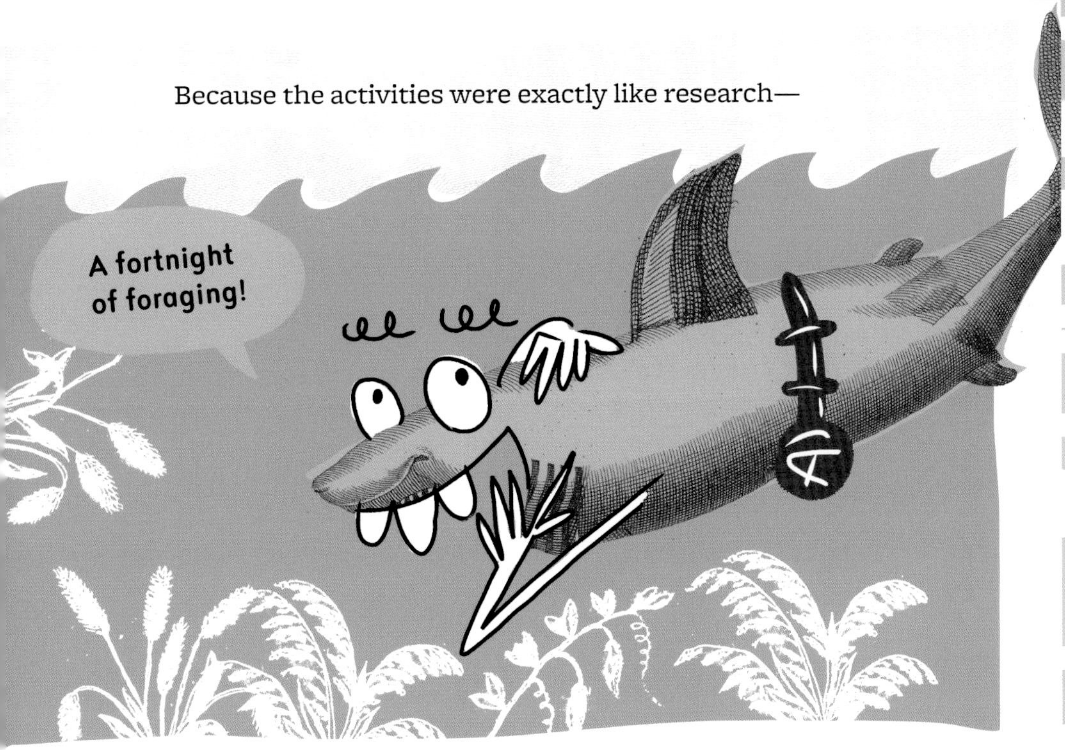
A fortnight of foraging!

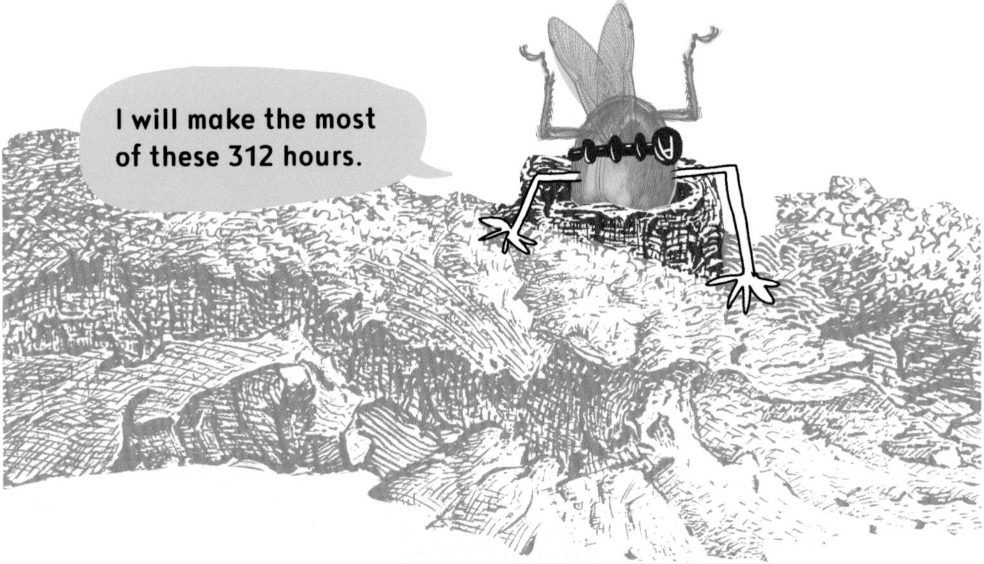
I will make the most of these 312 hours.

—the exact Goldilocks Planet research they were there to do in the first place. It was almost too convenient to believe.

Special Guest StinkBug got invited to enjoy checking, trimming, and repairing the massive Plant Planet's root systems.

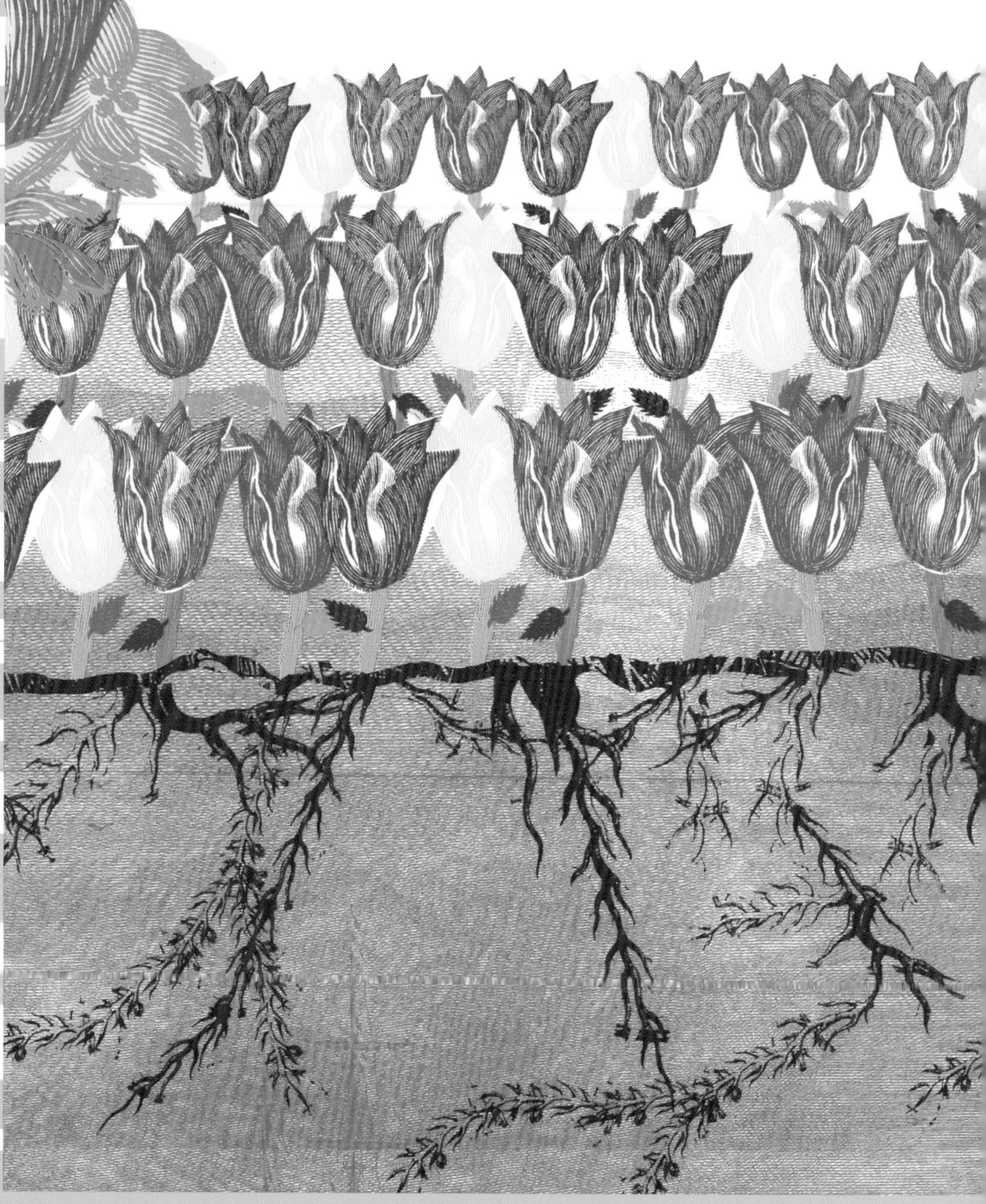

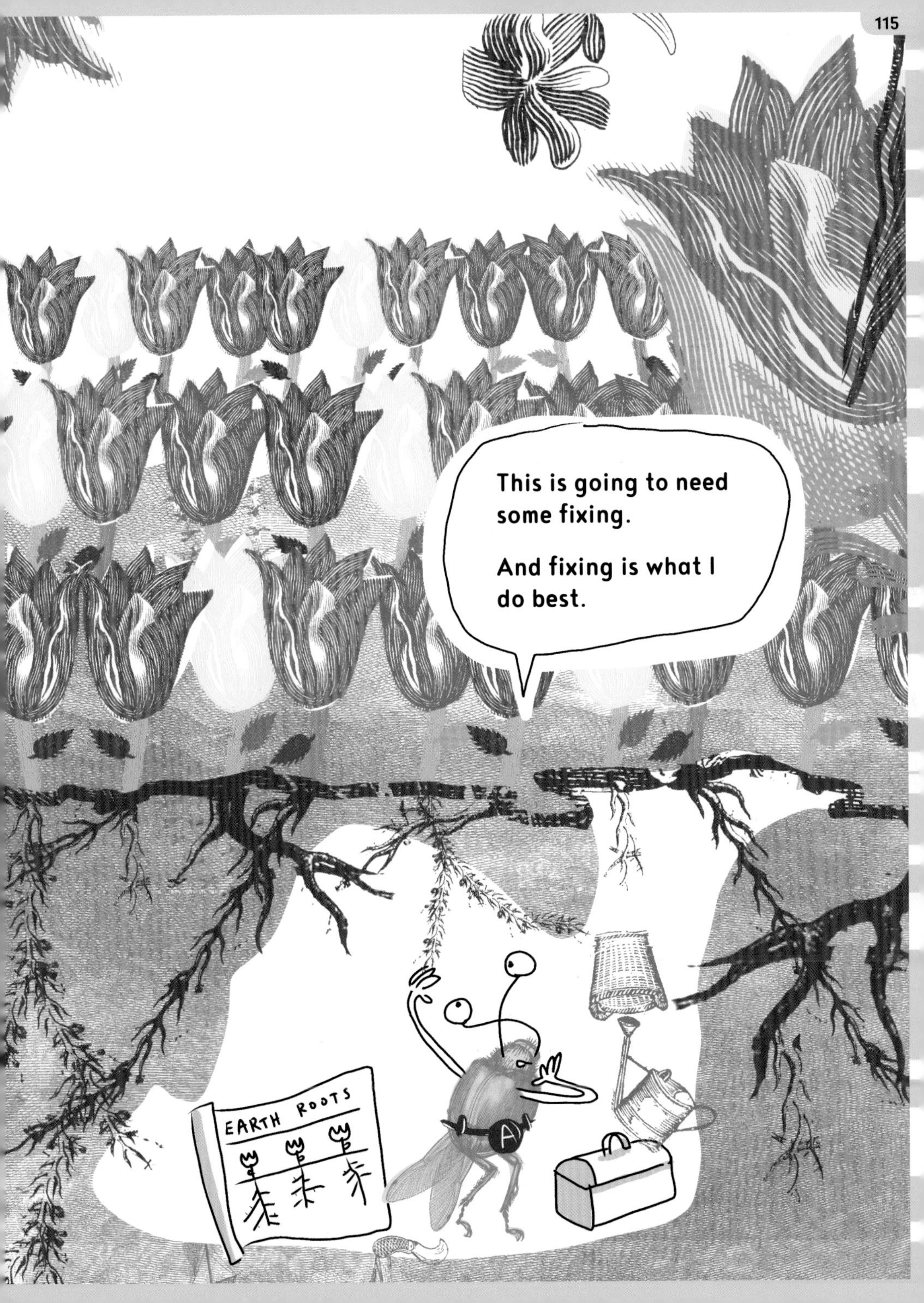
This is going to need some fixing.
And fixing is what I do best.
EARTH ROOTS
A

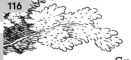

Special Guest AlphaWolf got invited to enjoy clearing, cutting, weeding, chopping, stacking, shaping, shearing, snipping, and clipping the endless Plant Planet forests.

And he was, as always, absolutely sure he was the greatest at it.

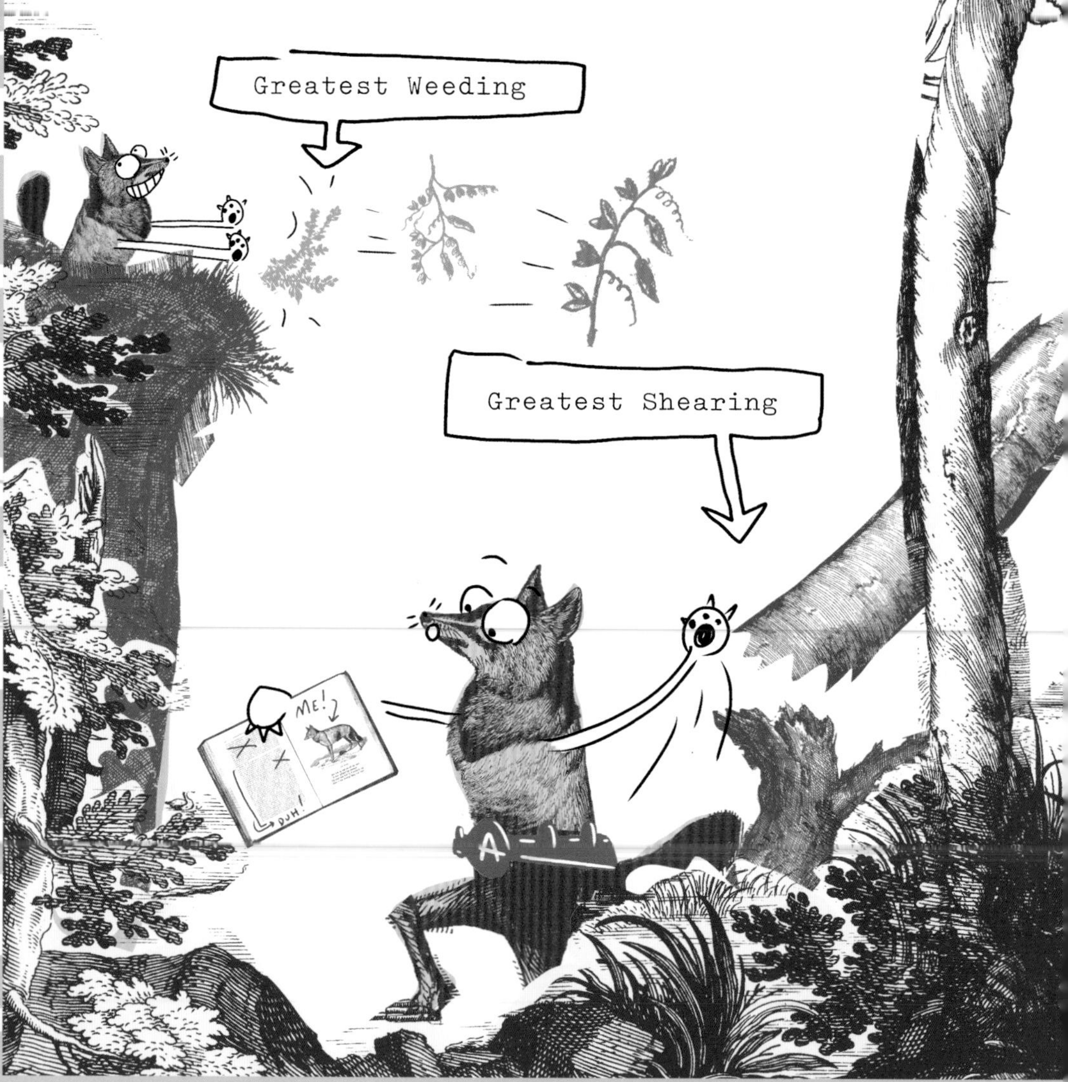
Greatest Weeding
Greatest Shearing
ME!
DUH!
A

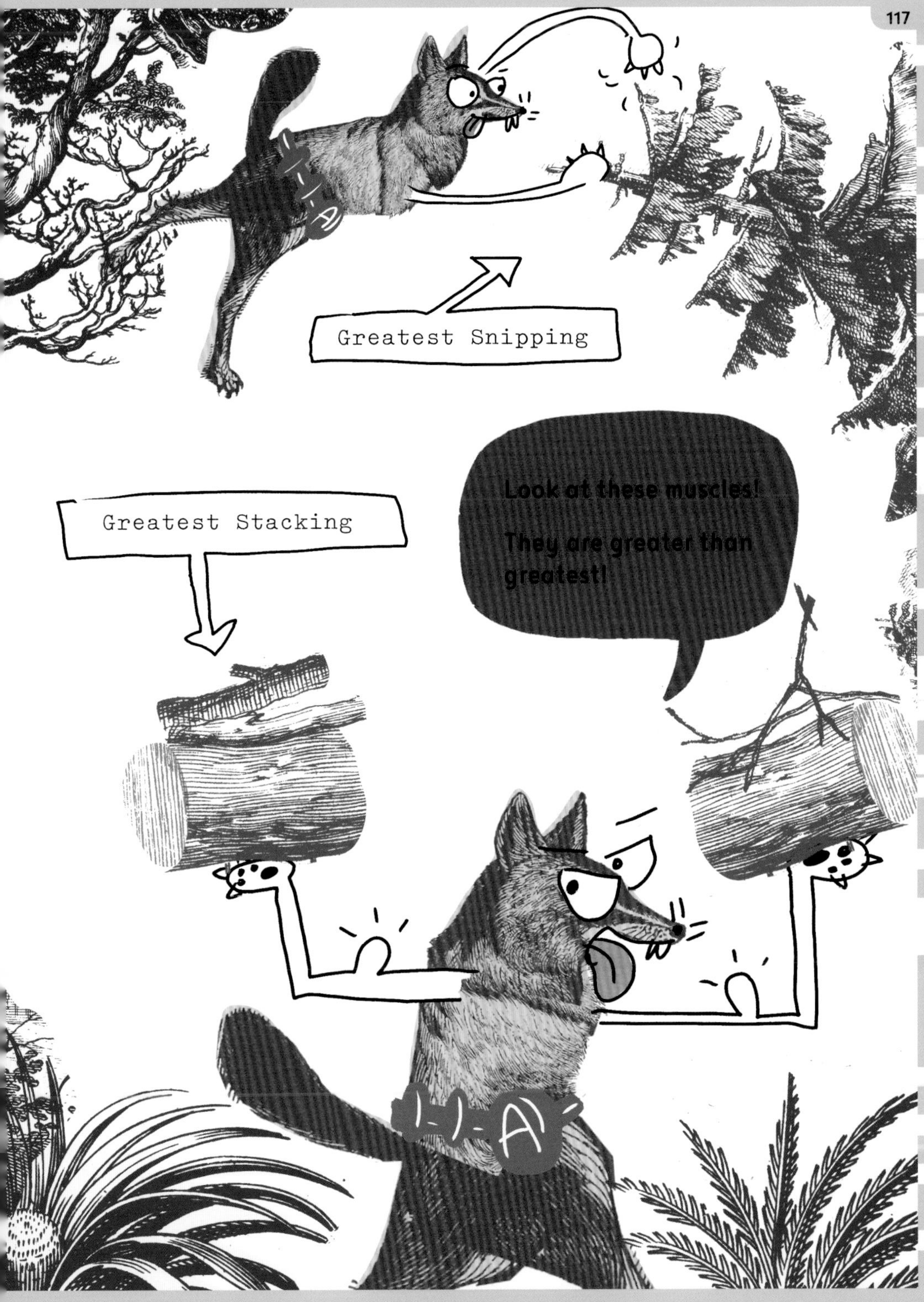
Greatest Snipping
Greatest Stacking
Look at these muscles!
They are greater than greatest!

Special Guest LaserShark got invited to enjoy picking, plucking, and gathering truckloads of monster-sized fruits, vegetables, nuts, berries, and tubers from the terribly overgrown Plant Planet gardens.

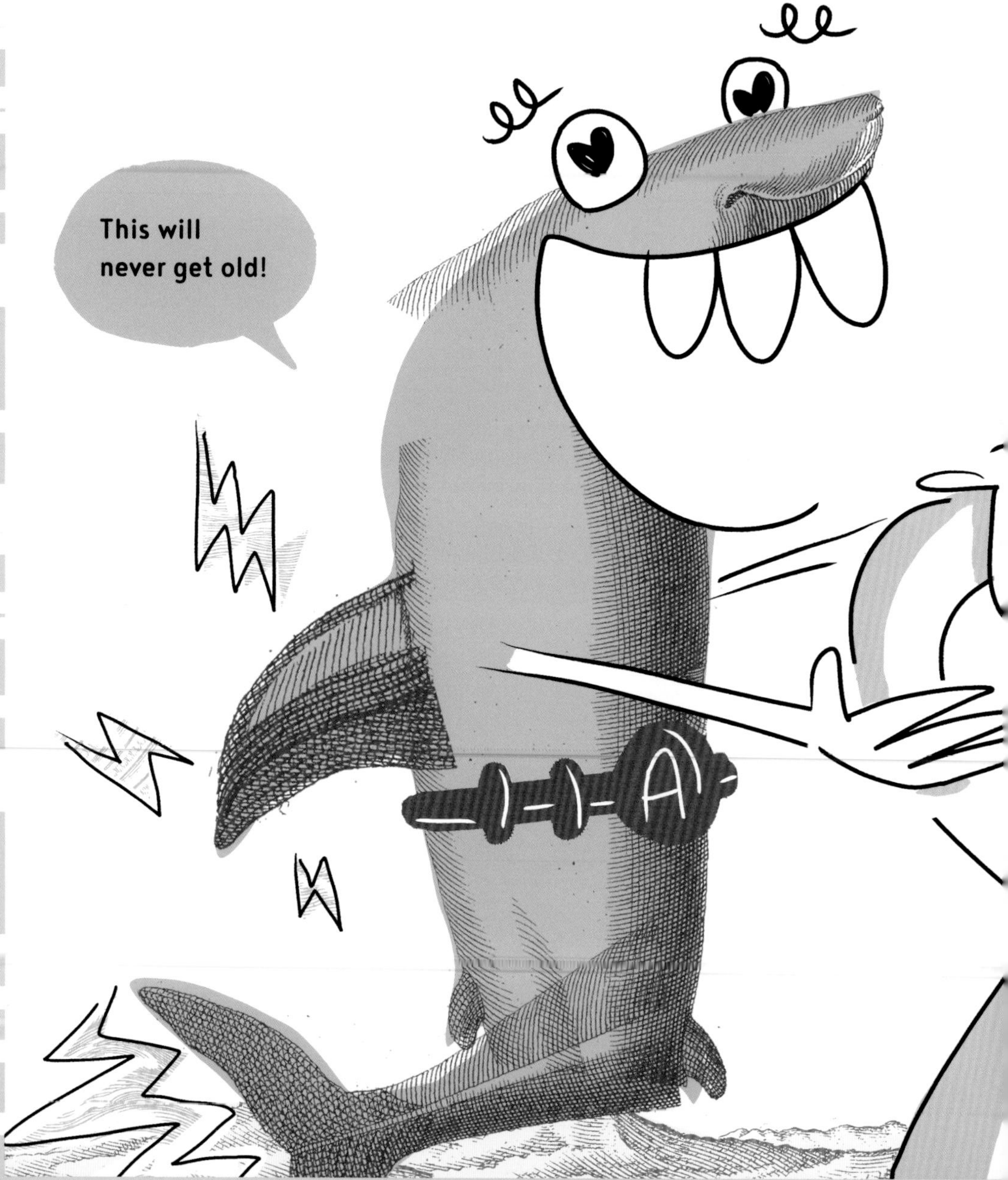
This will never get old!

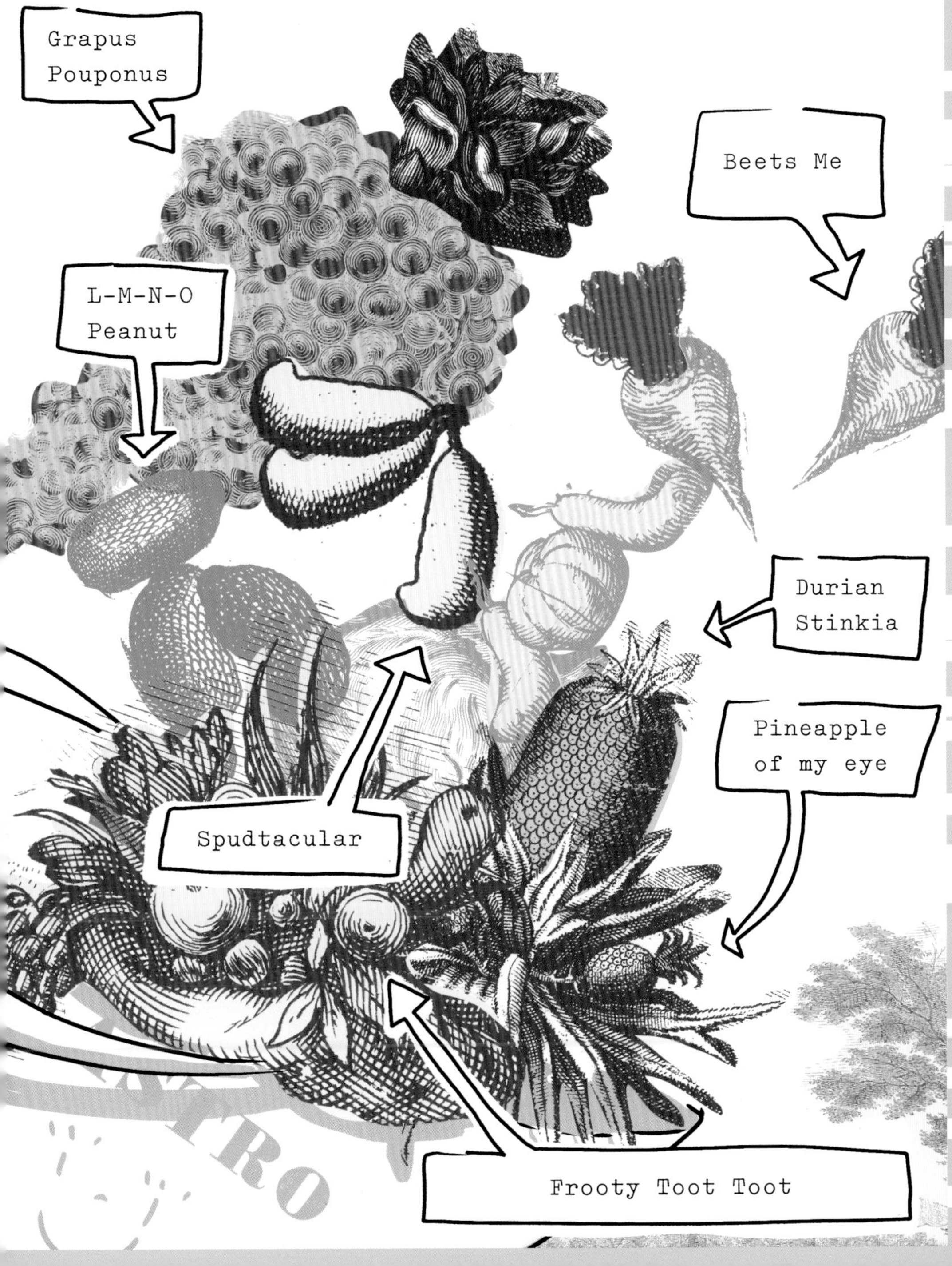
Grapus Pouponus
Beets Me
L-M-N-O Peanut
Durian Stinkia
Pineapple of my eye
Spudtacular
Frooty Toot Toot

Special Guest SmartHawk got invited to plot out the ideal growth schedule for all plants.

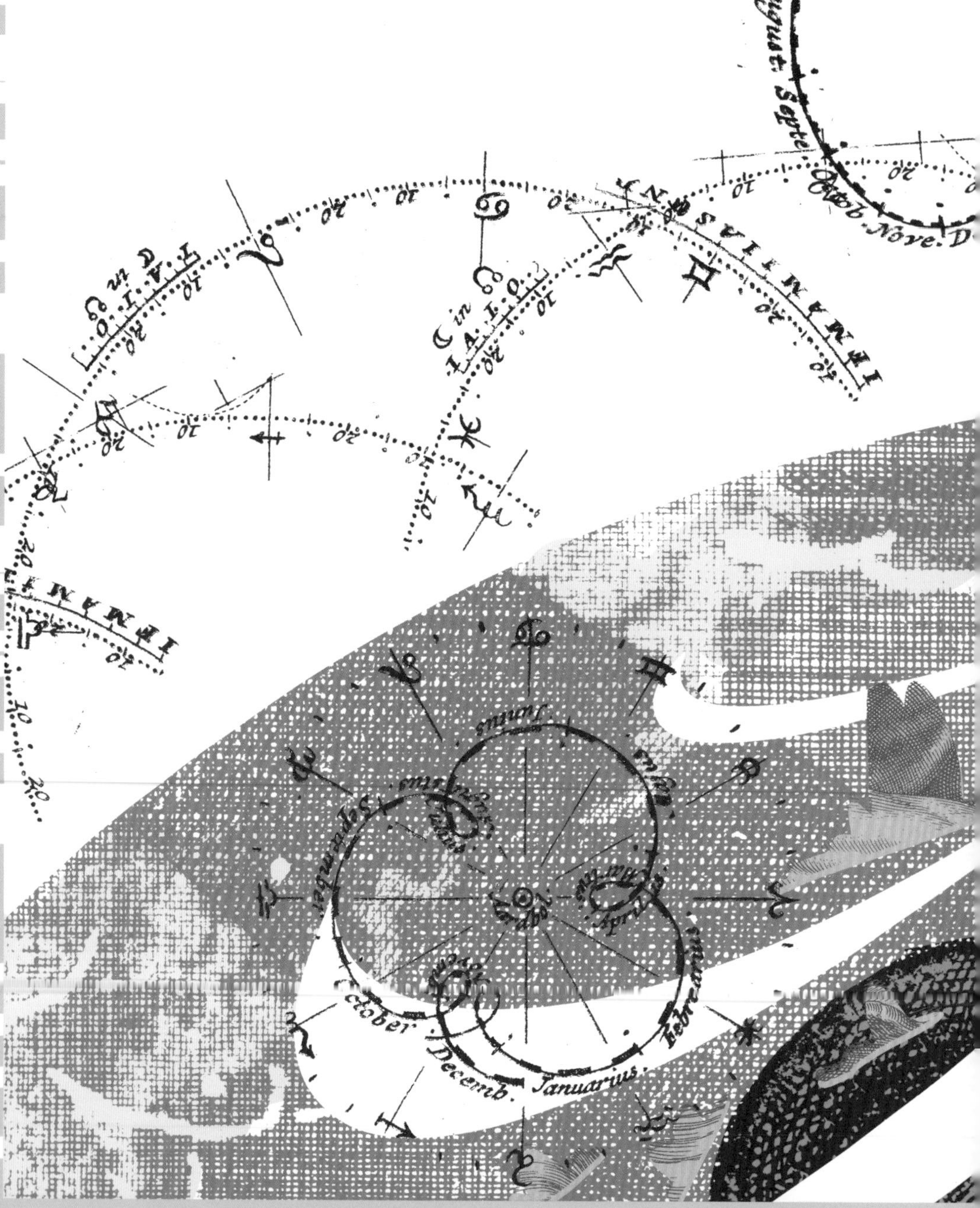
August
Nove.
Decemb.
Januarius

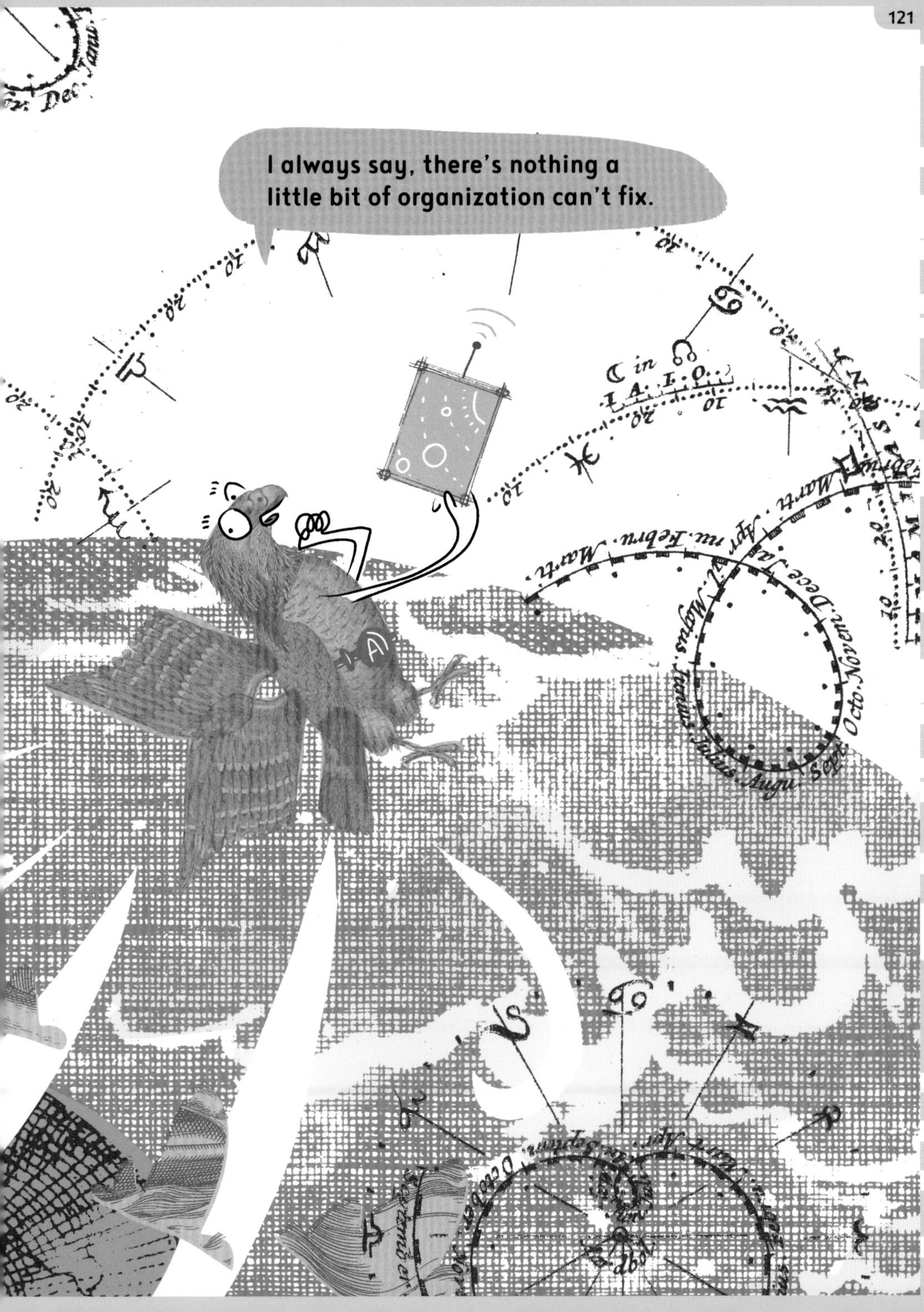
I always say, there's nothing a little bit of organization can't fix.

At the end of that long day of Exciting Activities, Major Giant Venus Flytrap tucked the Special Guests into bed.

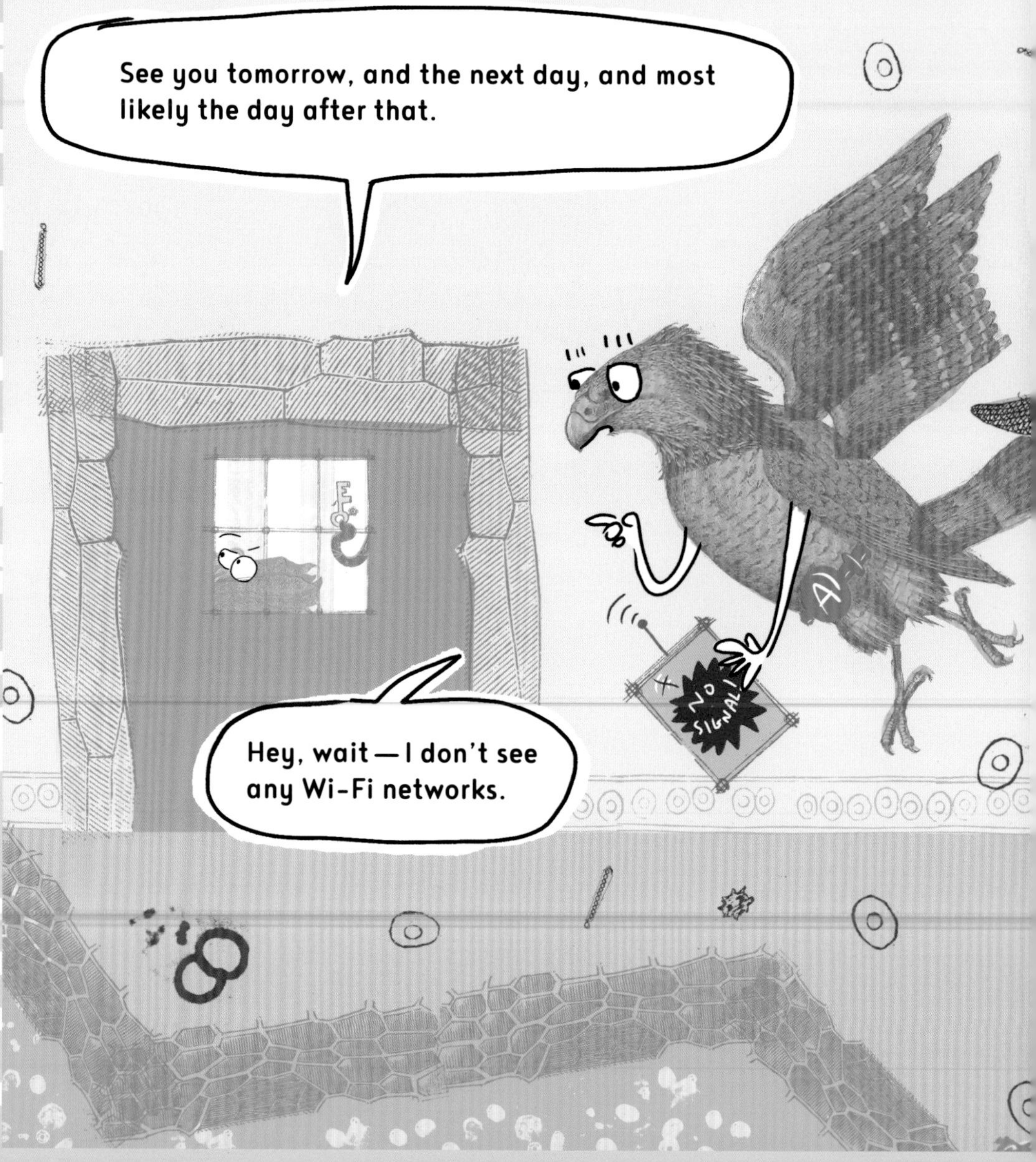
See you tomorrow, and the next day, and most likely the day after that.
NO SIGNAL!
Hey, wait — I don't see any Wi-Fi networks.

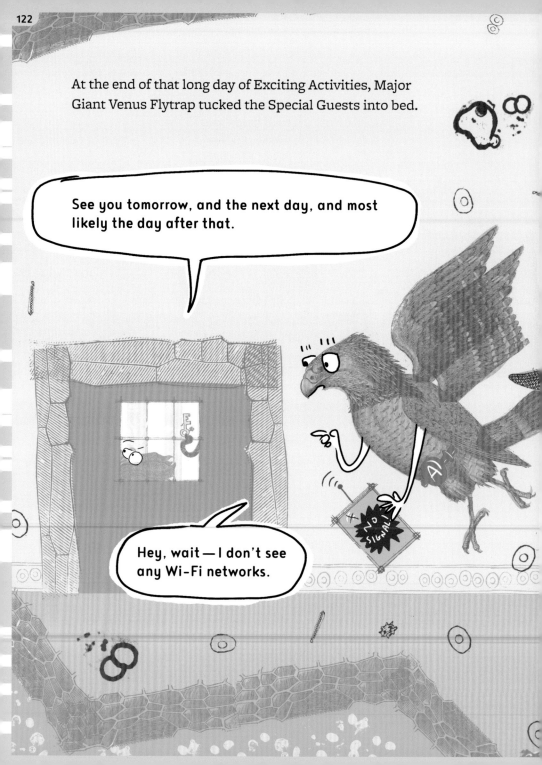

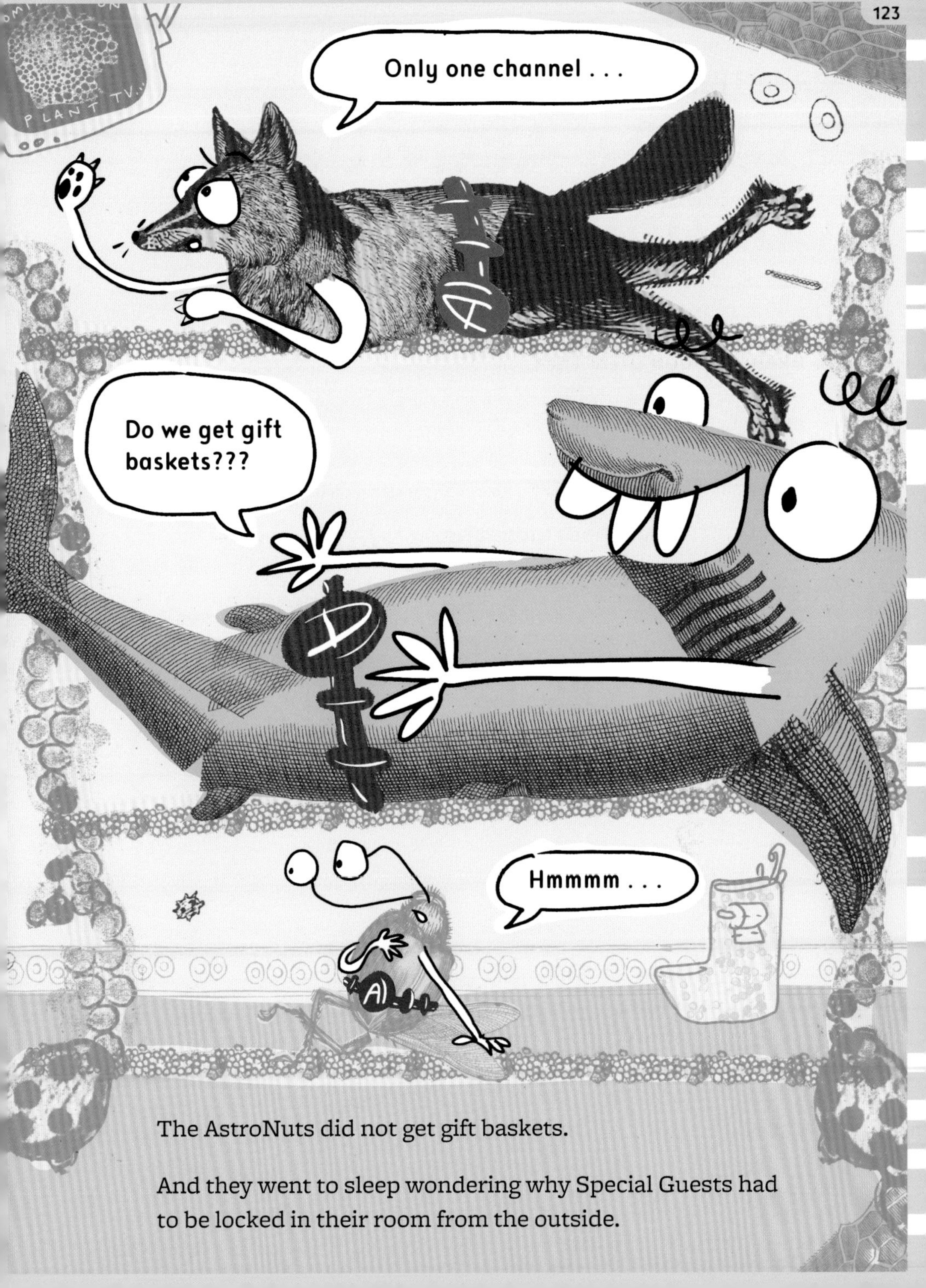
PLANT TV
Only one channel . . .
Do we get gift baskets???
Hmmmm . . .

The AstroNuts did not get gift baskets.

And they went to sleep wondering why Special Guests had to be locked in their room from the outside.

CHAPTER 17:

Exciting Activities, Continued

The next morning, **DAY 2** on the Plant Planet, Major Giant Venus Flytrap told his Special Guests to please enjoy another day of Exciting Activities.

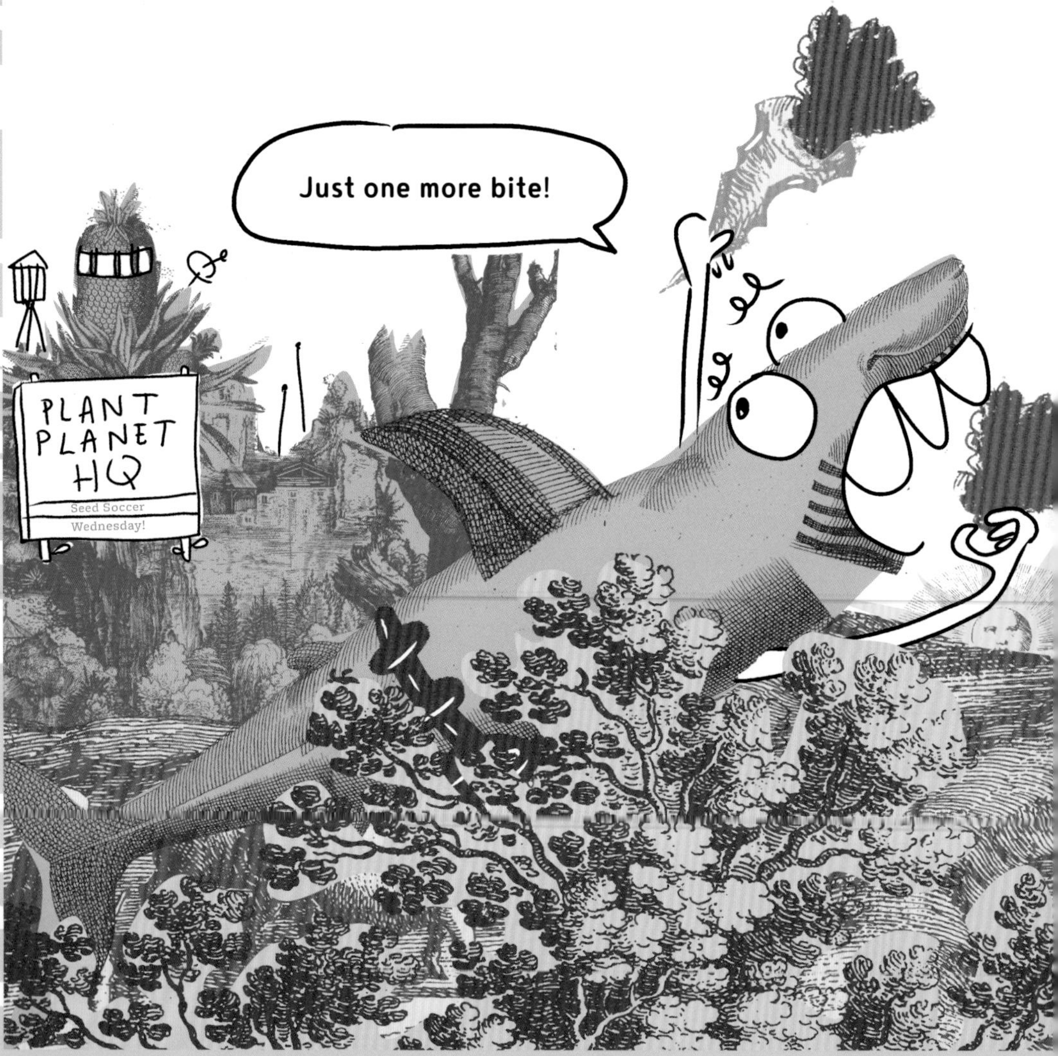

Just one more bite!
PLANT PLANET HQ
Seed Soccer Wednesday!

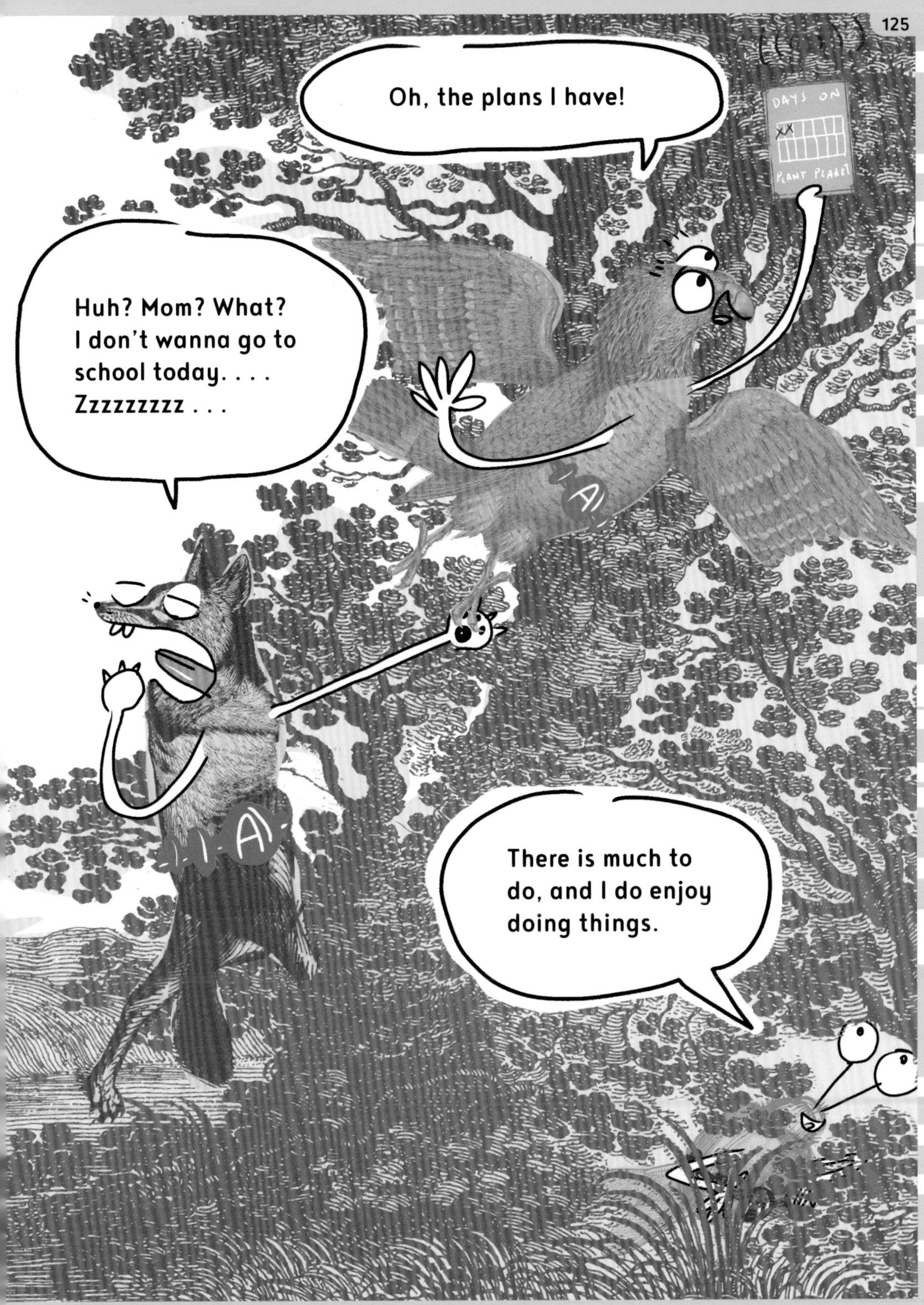
Oh, the plans I have!
DAYS ON
PLANT PLANET
Huh? Mom? What? I don't wanna go to school today. . . . Zzzzzzzzz . . .
There is much to do, and I do enjoy doing things.

On **DAY 3** of Exciting Activities, StinkBug secretly thought this day seemed an awful lot like Day 2. But he did enjoy finding the strange new Plant Planet root vegetables. So he figured the day wasn't a total waste.

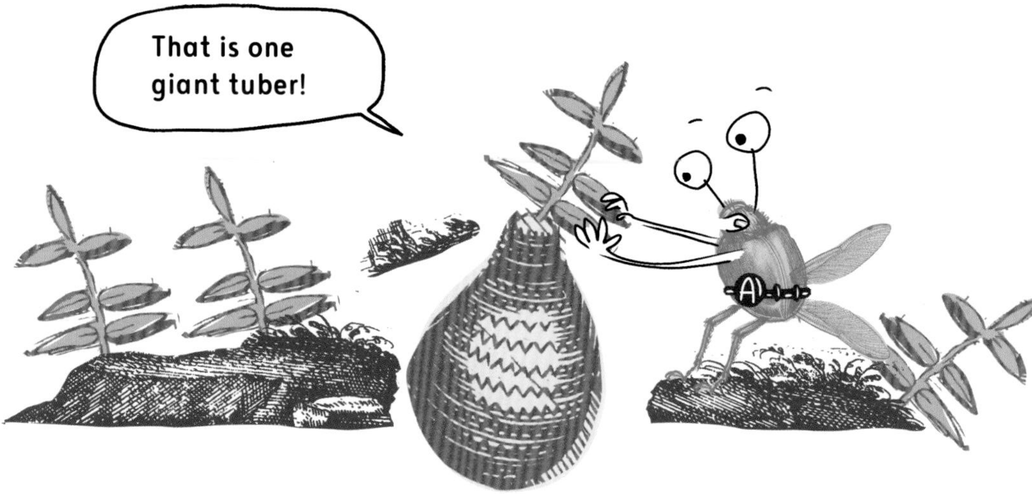
That is one giant tuber!

On **DAY 4**'s More Exciting Activities, SmartHawk began to worry—after looking closer at the whole planet—when she still could not find any bird, or animal, or bug life. At all. But she was very glad to chart this discovery.

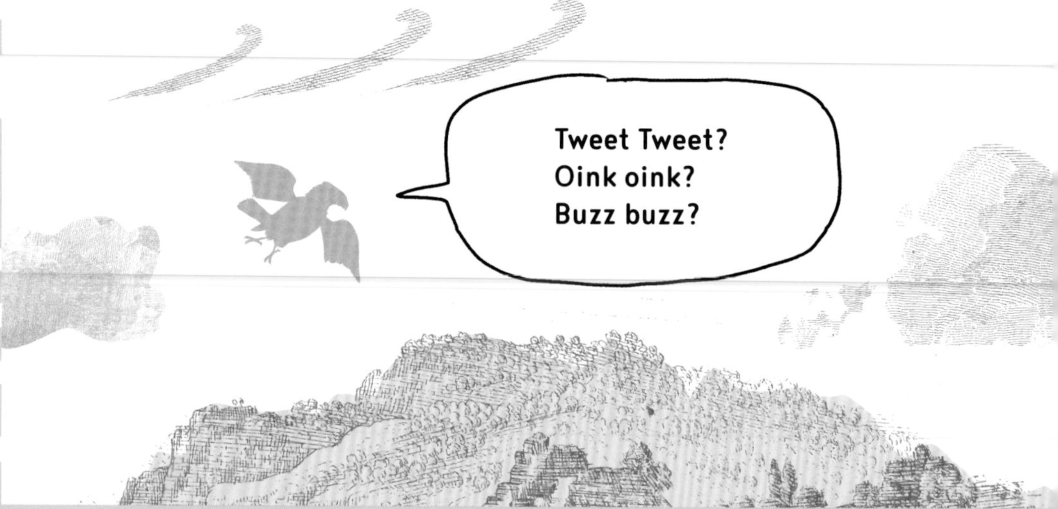
Tweet Tweet?
Oink oink?
Buzz buzz?

By **DAY 5** of Required Exciting Activities, LaserShark quit caring that she couldn't find any fishy friends, because she was now in charge of compost for the whole planet.

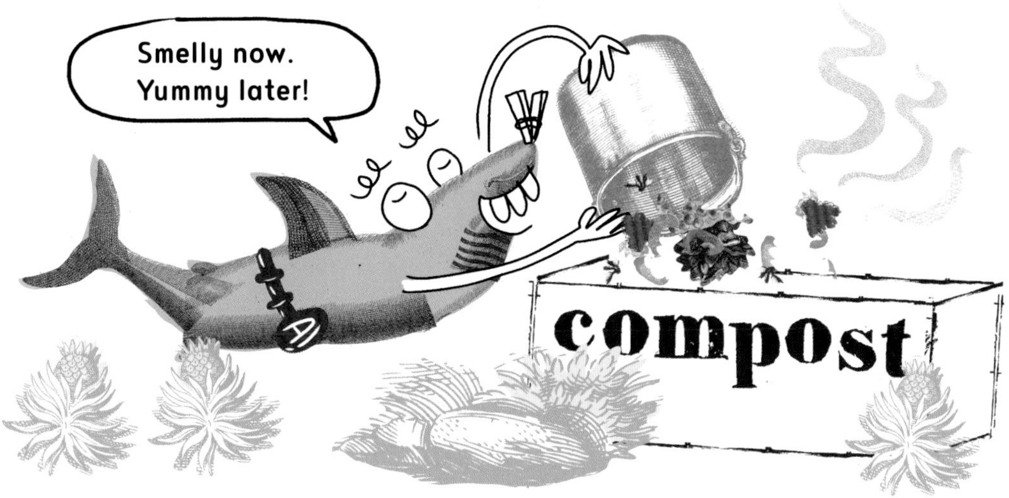
Smelly now.
Yummy later!
compost

By **DAY 6**'s Yes, Even More Exciting Activities, AlphaWolf couldn't take it anymore.

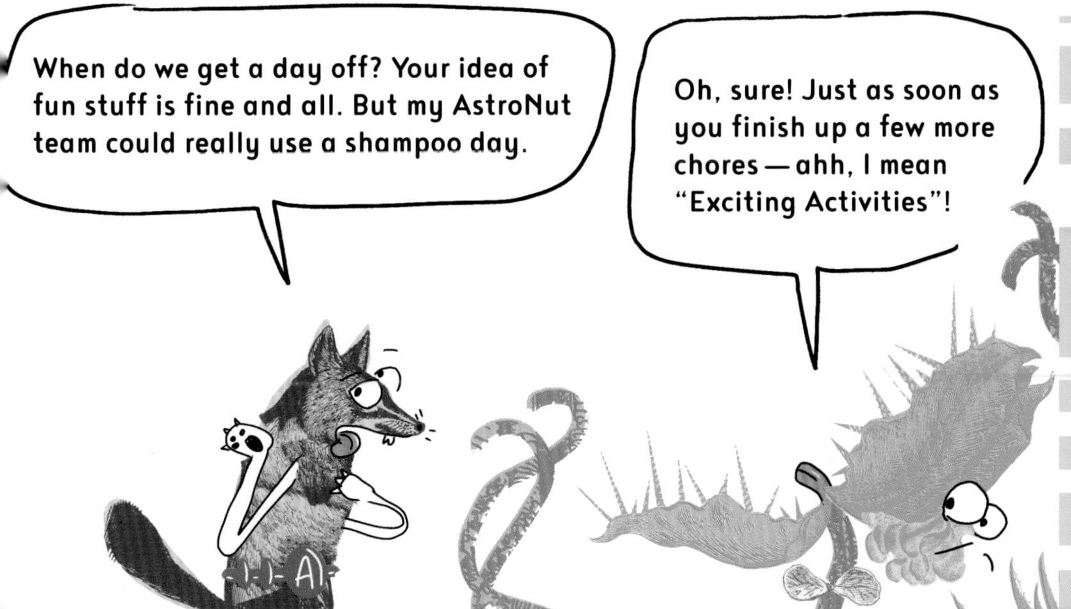
When do we get a day off? Your idea of fun stuff is fine and all. But my AstroNut team could really use a shampoo day.
Oh, sure! Just as soon as you finish up a few more chores—ahh, I mean "Exciting Activities"!

So AlphaWolf got back to his Exciting Activity of clearing more and more and more and more and more trees.

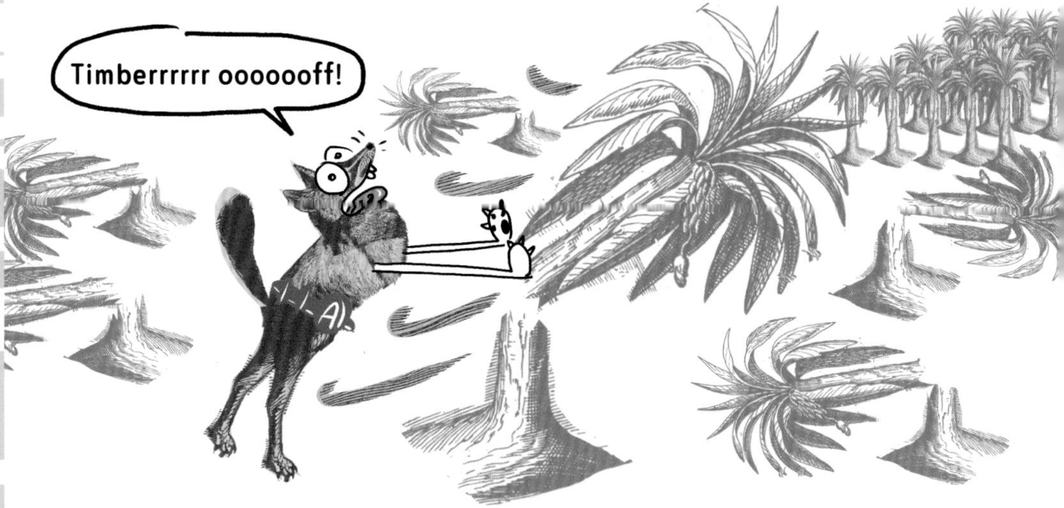
Timberrrrrr ooooooff!

DAY 7 found SmartHawk starting to hate even the words "Exciting Activities." She diagrammed the different kinds of Plant Planet photosynthesis she had observed in various places on the planet. She was really starting to worry about the lopsided Plant Planet ecosystem.

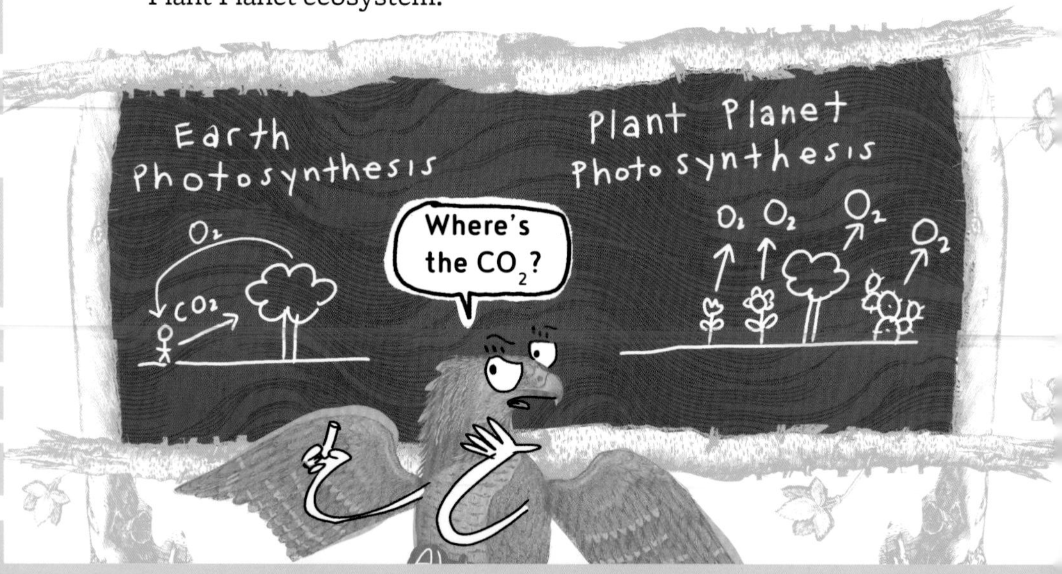
Earth Photosynthesis
O_2
CO_2
Where's the CO_2?
Plant Planet Photosynthesis
O_2 O_2 O_2 O_2

On **DAY 8**, even LaserShark felt less than enthusiastic.

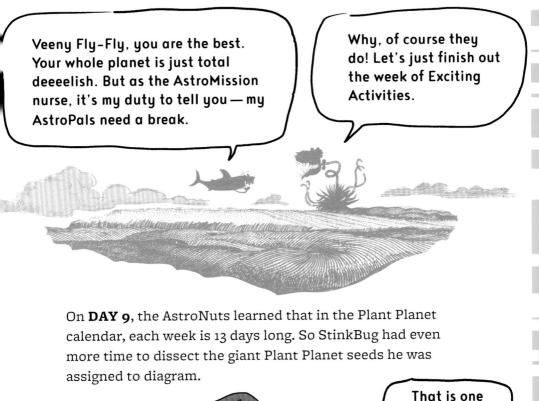

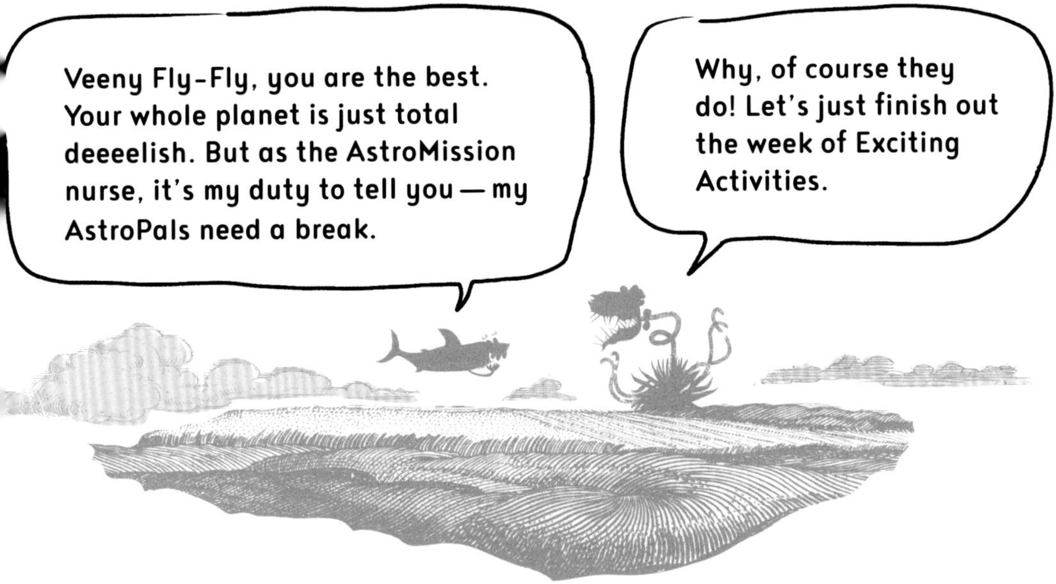
Veeny Fly-Fly, you are the best. Your whole planet is just total deeeelish. But as the AstroMission nurse, it's my duty to tell you — my AstroPals need a break.
Why, of course they do! Let's just finish out the week of Exciting Activities.

On **DAY 9**, the AstroNuts learned that in the Plant Planet calendar, each week is 13 days long. So StinkBug had even more time to dissect the giant Plant Planet seeds he was assigned to diagram.

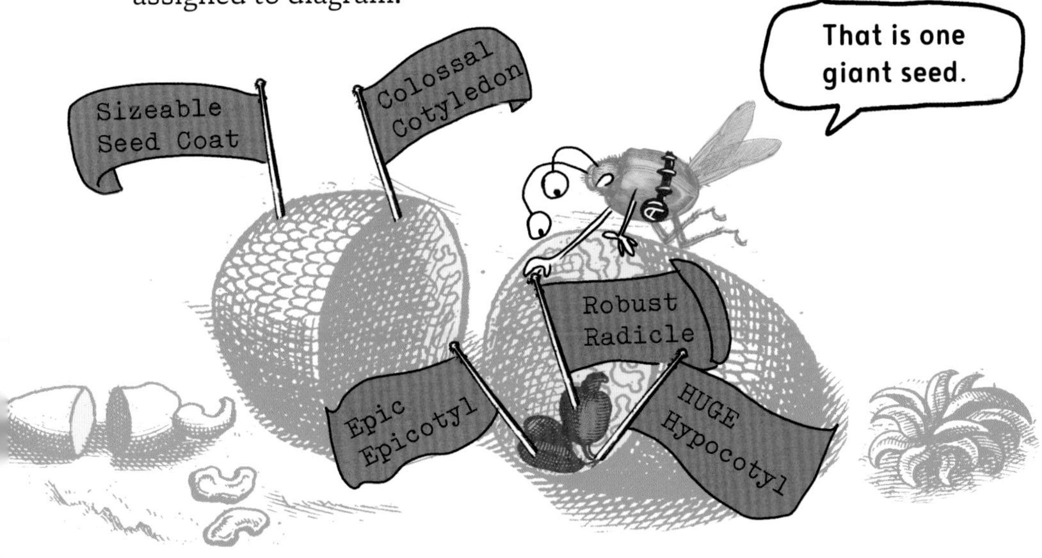
That is one giant seed.
Sizeable Seed Coat
Colossal Cotyledon
Robust Radicle
Epic Epicotyl
HUGE Hypocotyl

On **DAY 10**, LaserShark got super buried in her Exciting Activities, which now only felt like the same stinky chores. Over and over again.

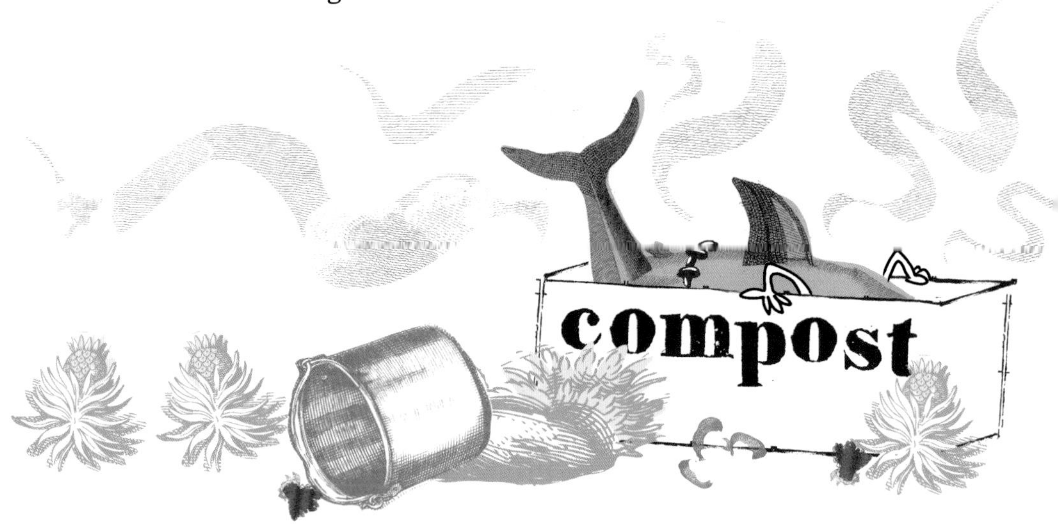
compost

So on **DAY 11**, it was SmartHawk's turn to try the direct approach.

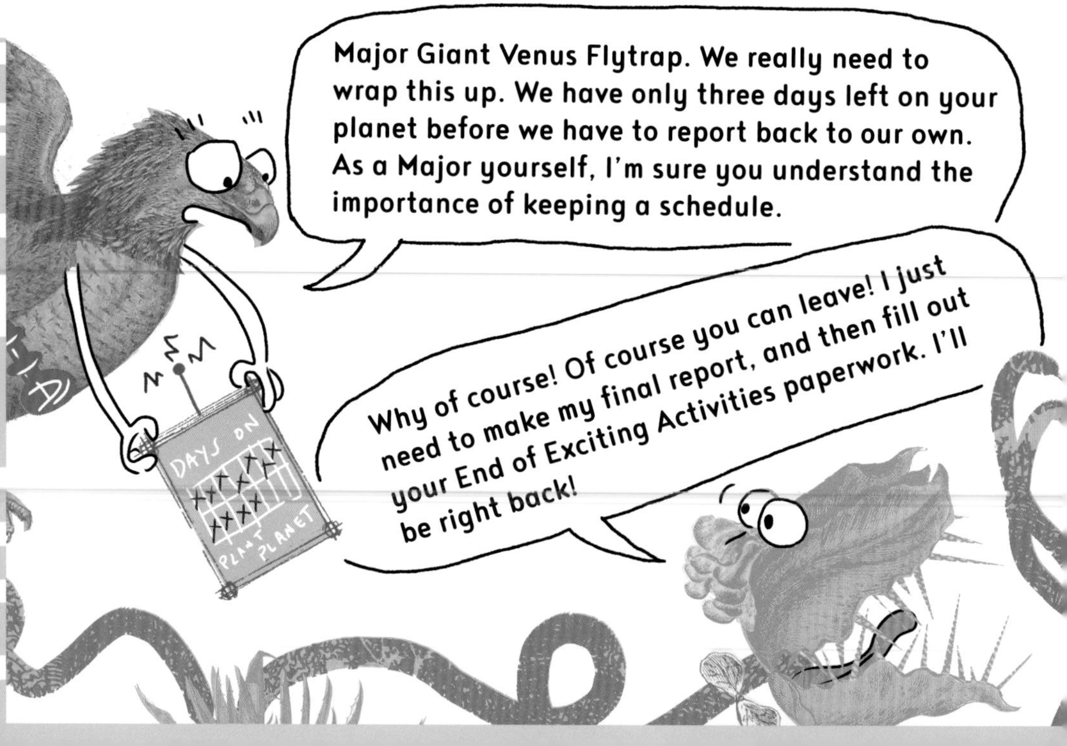
Major Giant Venus Flytrap. We really need to wrap this up. We have only three days left on your planet before we have to report back to our own. As a Major yourself, I'm sure you understand the importance of keeping a schedule.
DAYS ON PLANT PLANET
Why of course! Of course you can leave! I just need to make my final report, and then fill out your End of Exciting Activities paperwork. I'll be right back!

But Major Giant Venus Flytrap didn't come right back. And on **DAY 12**, AstroWolf was back to clearing trees.

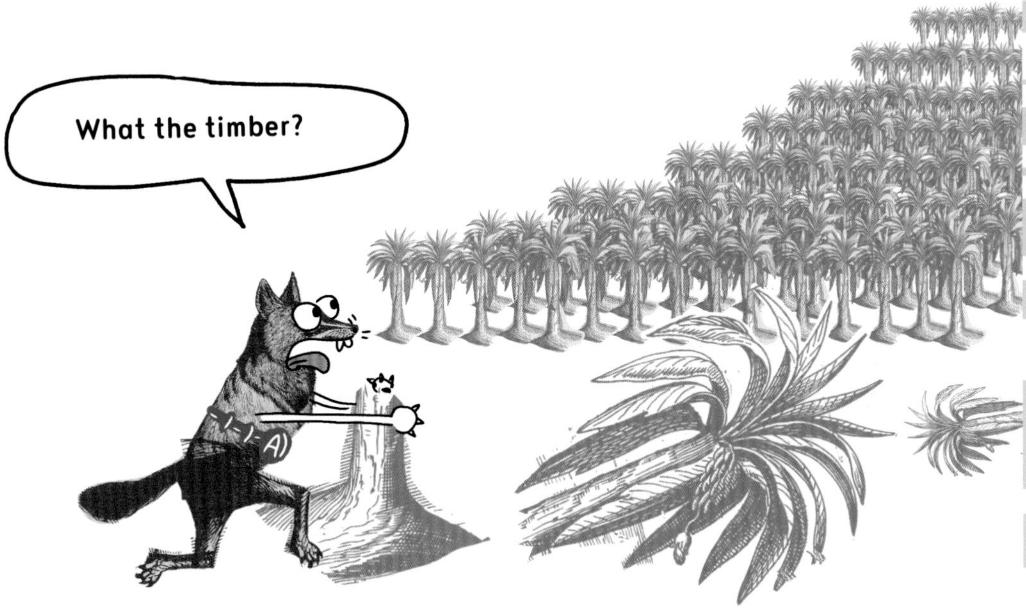
What the timber?

And on **DAY 13**, StinkBug was back to digging up roots.

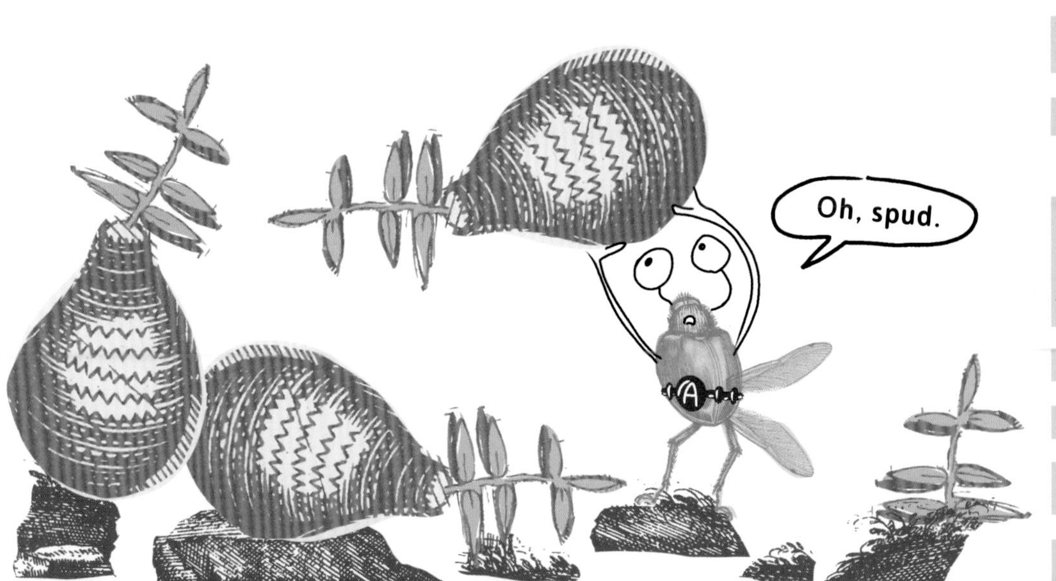
Oh, spud.

Finally, on the morning of **DAY 14**, the last day on the Plant Planet, all of the AstroNuts, back in their Special Guest Room, realized something.

Something that was actually pretty obvious. Something they probably should have realized on about, oh, **DAY 2.**

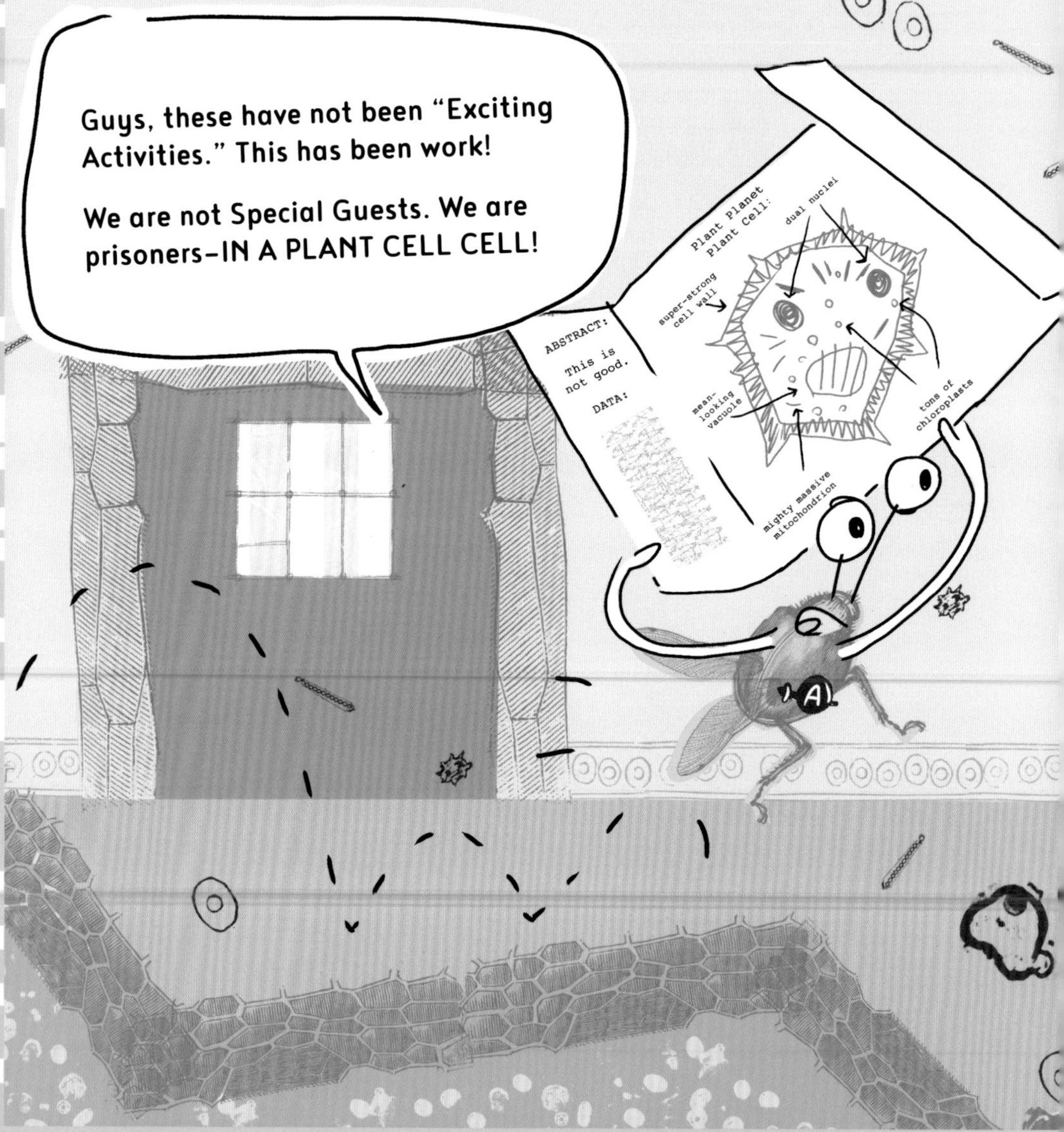
Guys, these have not been "Exciting Activities." This has been work!
We are not Special Guests. We are prisoners—IN A PLANT CELL CELL!
Plant Planet Plant Cell:
dual nuclei
super-strong cell wall
ABSTRACT:
This is not good.
DATA:
mean-looking vacuole
tons of chloroplasts
mighty massive mitochondrion

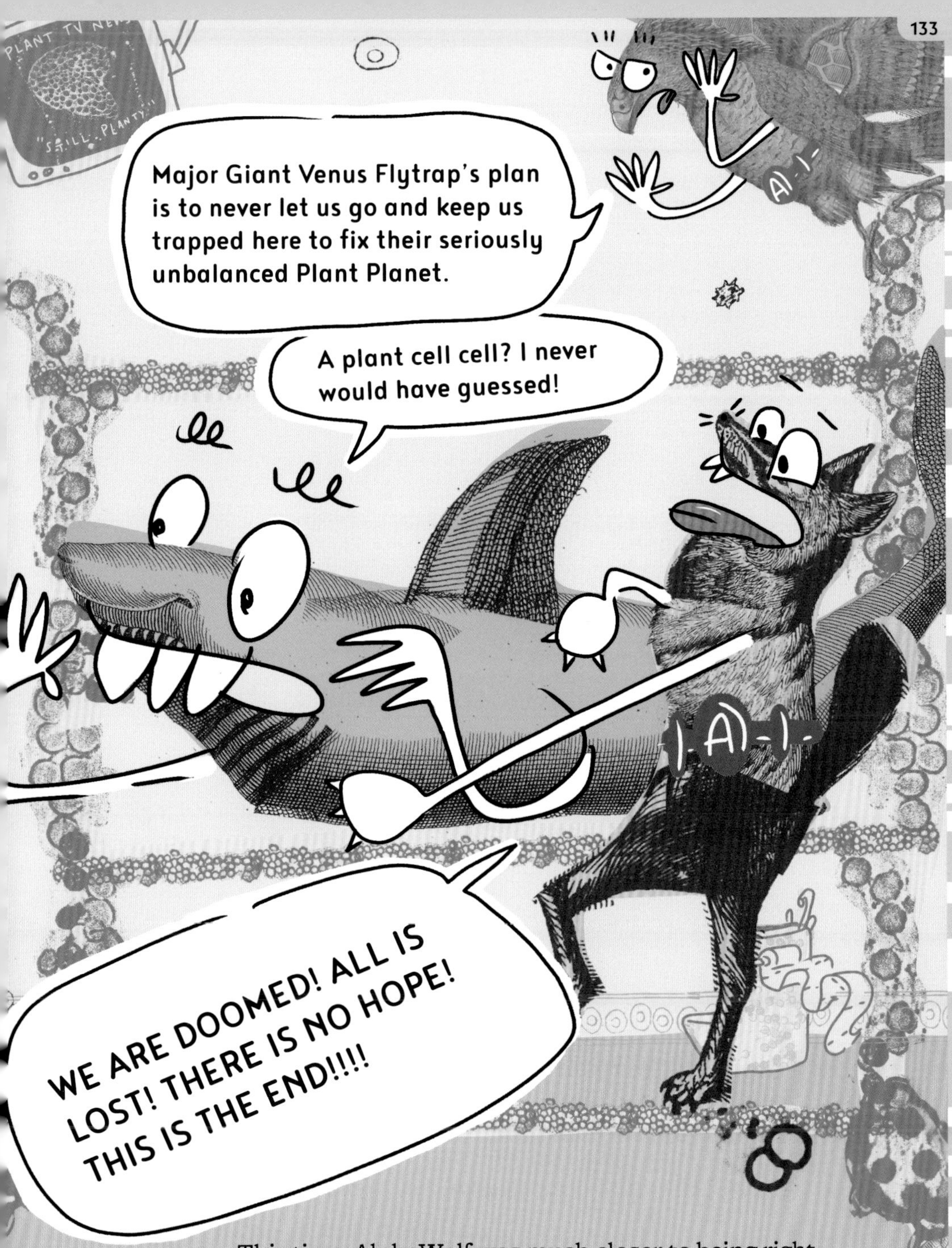
Major Giant Venus Flytrap's plan is to never let us go and keep us trapped here to fix their seriously unbalanced Plant Planet.
A plant cell cell? I never would have guessed!
WE ARE DOOMED! ALL IS LOST! THERE IS NO HOPE! THIS IS THE END!!!!

This time, AlphaWolf was much closer to being right.

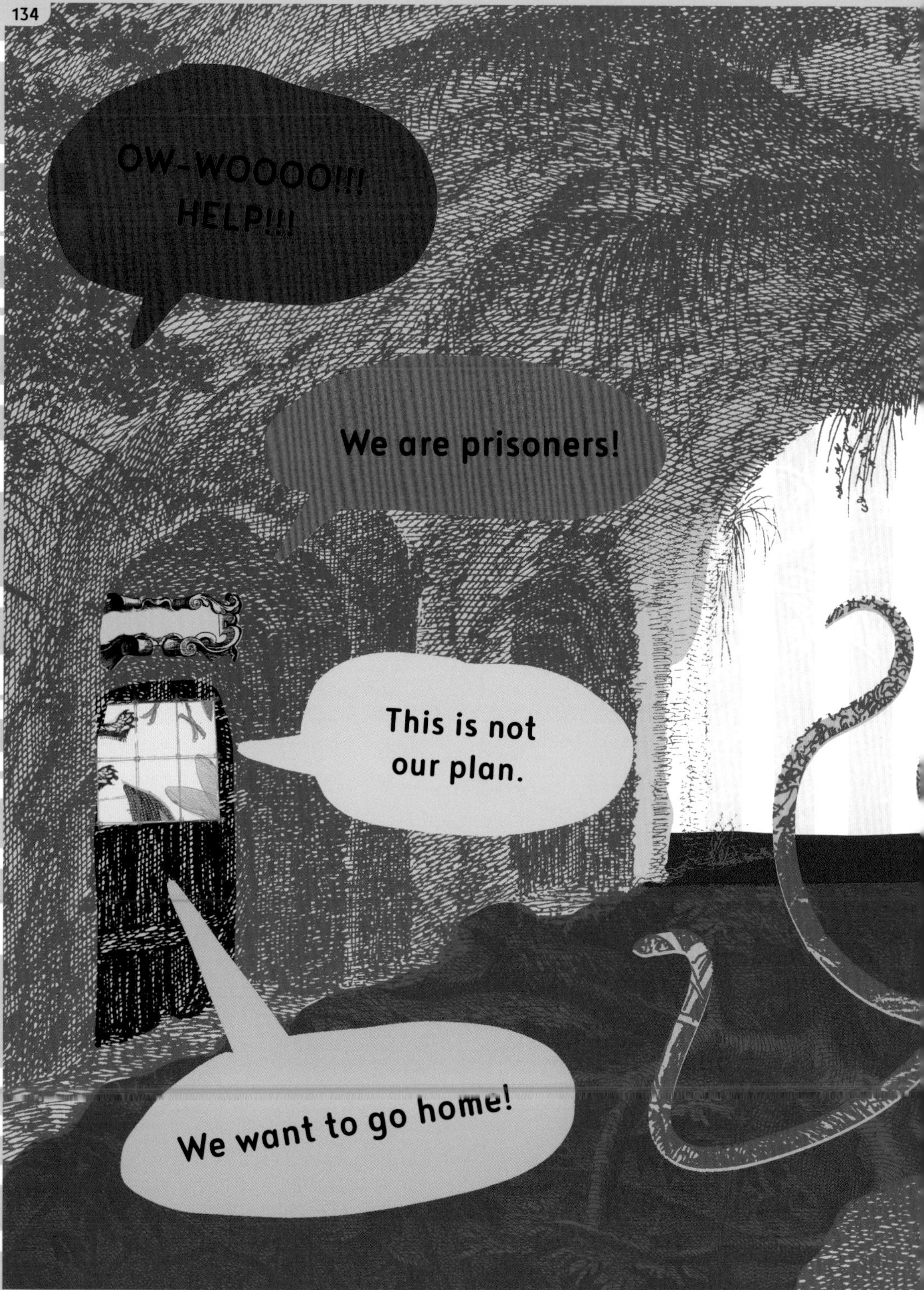
OW-WOOOO!!! HELP!!!
We are prisoners!
This is not our plan.
We want to go home!

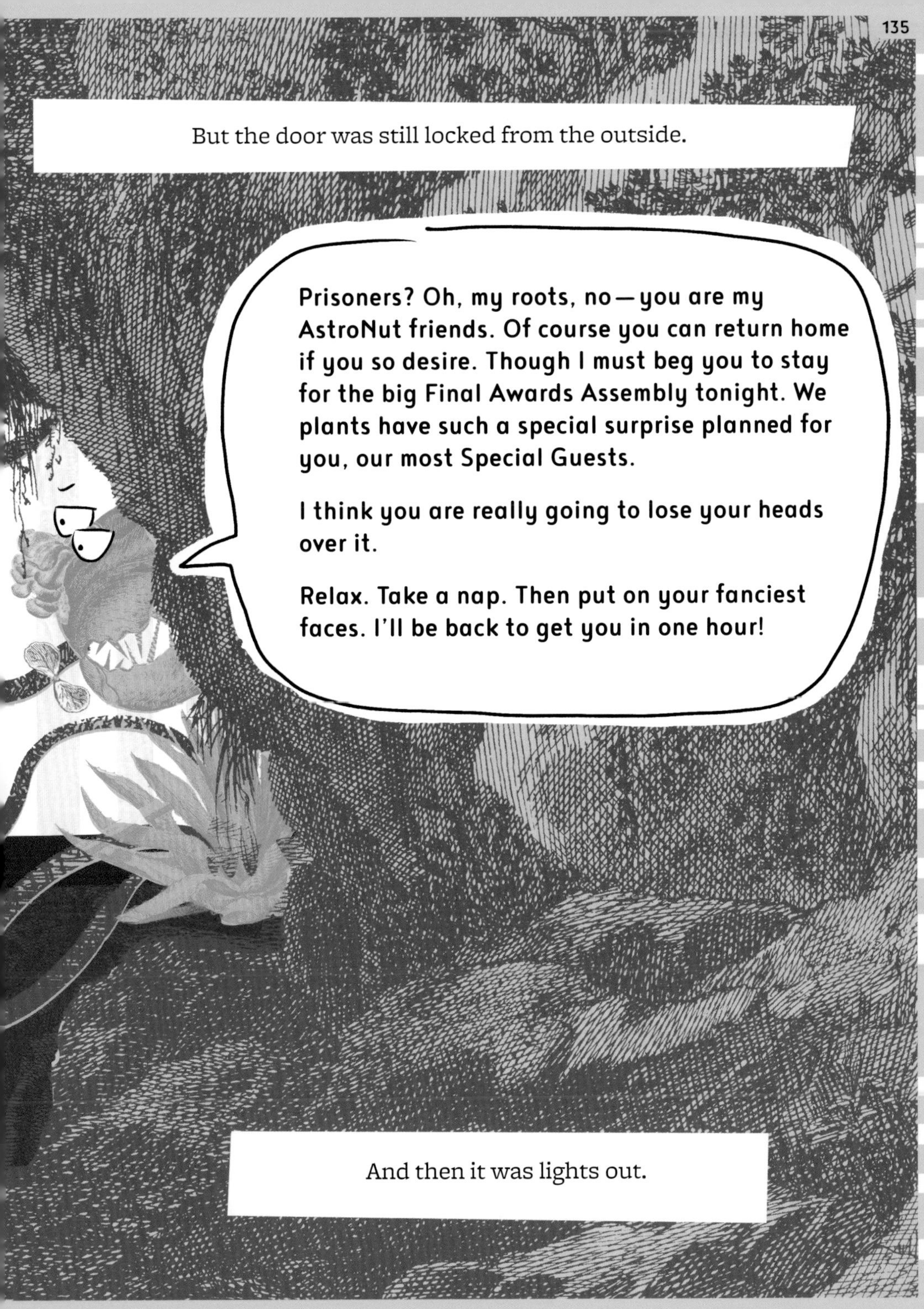
But the door was still locked from the outside.
Prisoners? Oh, my roots, no—you are my AstroNut friends. Of course you can return home if you so desire. Though I must beg you to stay for the big Final Awards Assembly tonight. We plants have such a special surprise planned for you, our most Special Guests.
I think you are really going to lose your heads over it.
Relax. Take a nap. Then put on your fanciest faces. I'll be back to get you in one hour!
And then it was lights out.

CHAPTER 18:
ZAP!

///// Official NNASA transcript /////
//// of ASTRONUT MISSION 1 ////

SmartHawk: I think we really ARE prisoners. It's all been lies. We are not taking a nap. There is no final awards assembly.

AlphaWolf: But there might be. So here's the plan: We break out. We steal the awards. We Nose Rocket home. LaserShark, use your Super-Electromagnetic Laser Bolt to blast us out of here!

LaserShark: Maybe this is just another misunderstanding? The Major keeps calling us his Special Guests. And he seems so nice.

AlphaWolf: This is an order, LaserShark. From your mission leader. Show me the sparks. NOW!!!

LaserShark: I really don't like to resort to violence.

SmartHawk: AlphaWolf's plan does have a 49.95% chance of working. LaserShark, for the mission's sake, I think you should try to blast us out of here.

LaserShark: Oh, all right. . . .

—loud electromagnetic ZAP! sound—

AlphaWolf: OW-WOOOOOOOOOO!!! MY TAIL! MY TAIL! MY AWESOME SILKY TAIL IS ON FIRE!!!! YOU DIDN'T HIT THE PLANT CELL. YOU HIT MEEEEE!!!!!

StinkBug: This gives me an idea. I might be able to use LaserShark's laser to build exactly what we need.

—strange construction noises—

StinkBug: LaserShark, direct your electro-blast over here.

—ZAP!—

StinkBug: And here.

—ZAP!—

StinkBug: And here. Here. Here. And there.

—ZAP!—ZAP!—ZAP!—ZAP!—

CHAPTER 19:
Jailbreak

StinkBug hotwired the lights back on and revealed his idea. I've known several geniuses in my day (though fewer than you might think), and this was a truly genius invention.

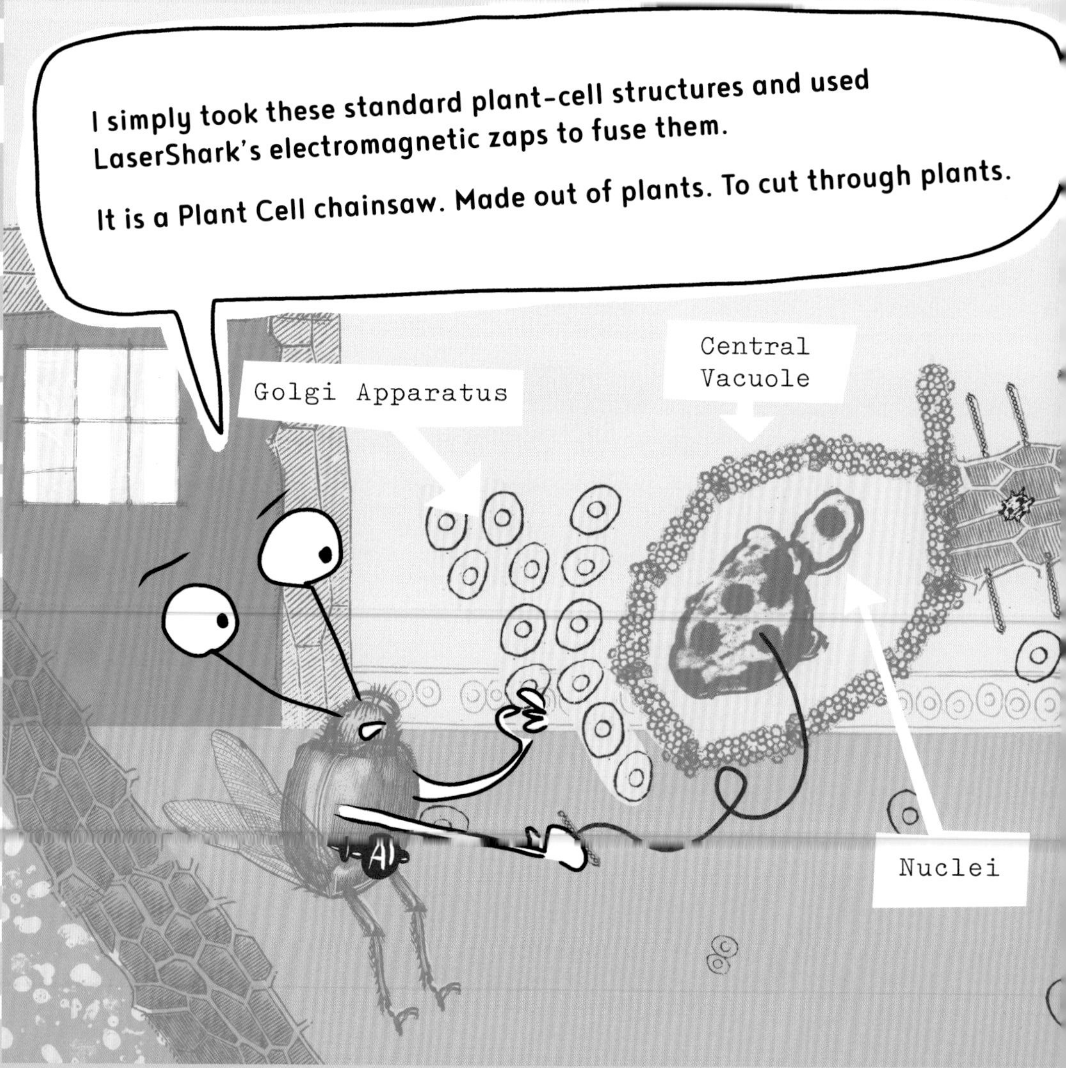
I simply took these standard plant-cell structures and used LaserShark's electromagnetic zaps to fuse them.
It is a Plant Cell chainsaw. Made out of plants. To cut through plants.
Golgi Apparatus
Central Vacuole
Nuclei
AI

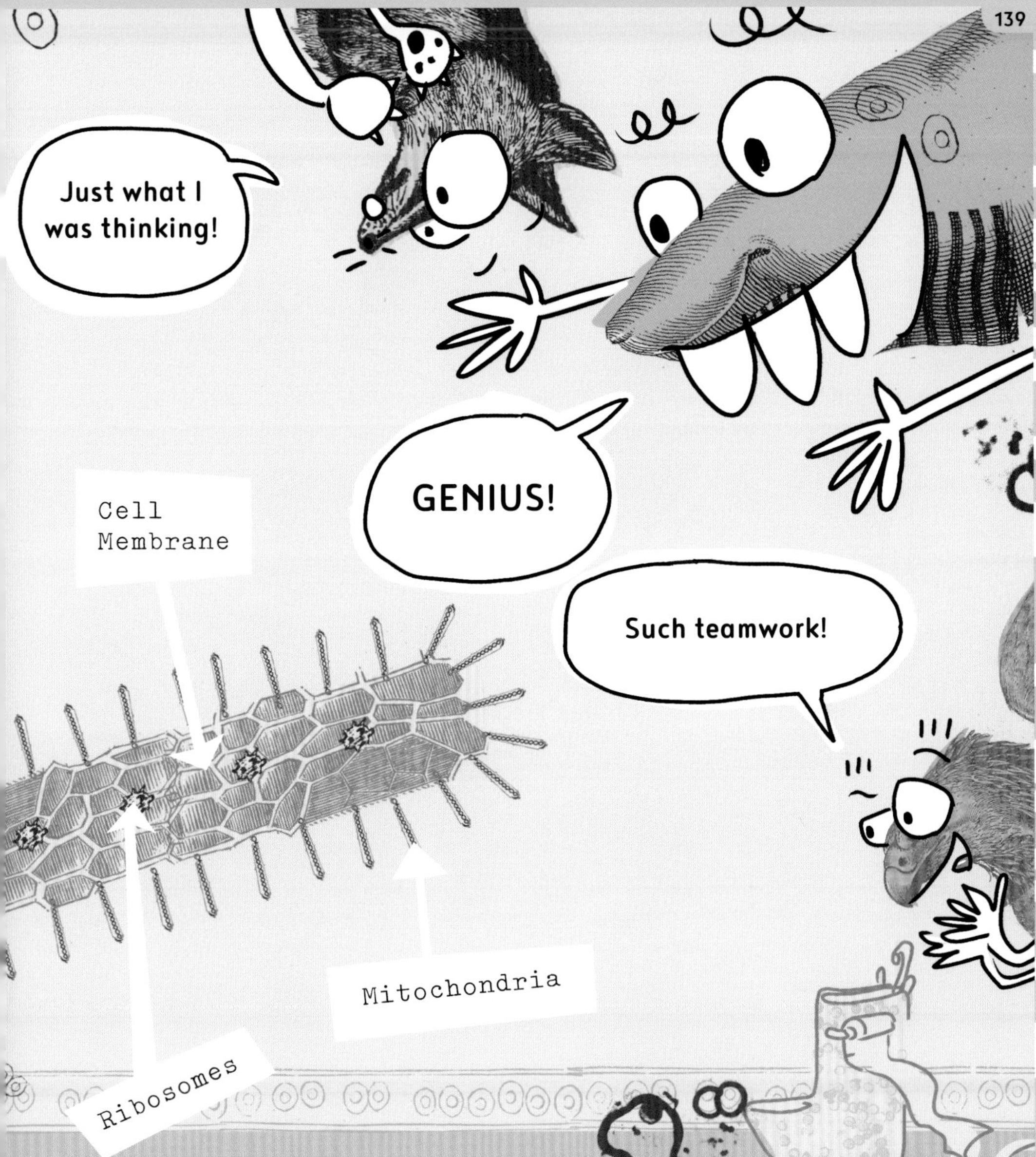
Just what I was thinking!
GENIUS!
Such teamwork!
Cell Membrane
Mitochondria
Ribosomes

StinkBug flipped the Golgi Apparatus switch ON. He revved the Nuclei to HIGH.

Then he jammed the whirling Mitochondria chain into the Plant Cell wall (with a truly sickening squishy sound).

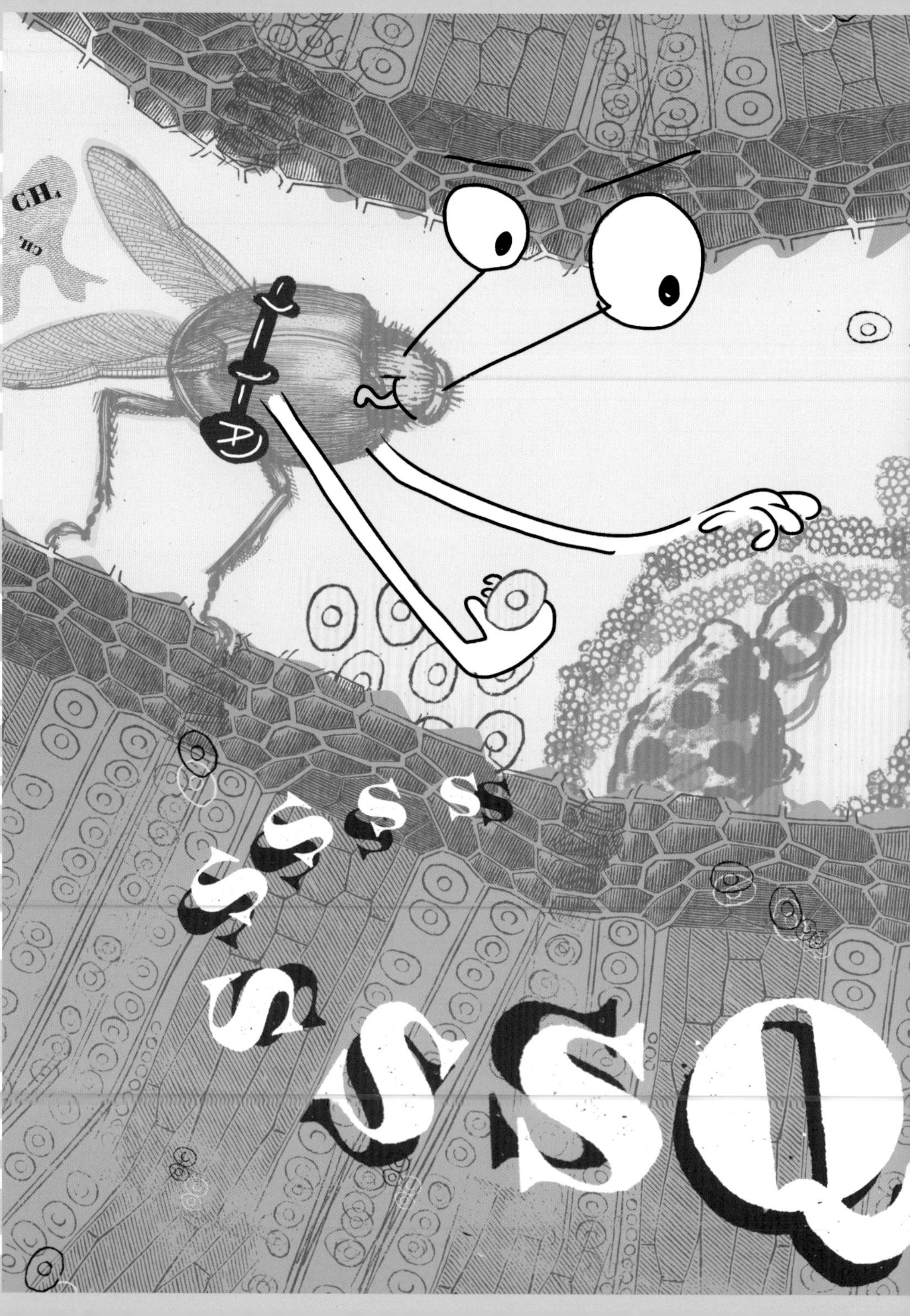
SSSSSSSSQ

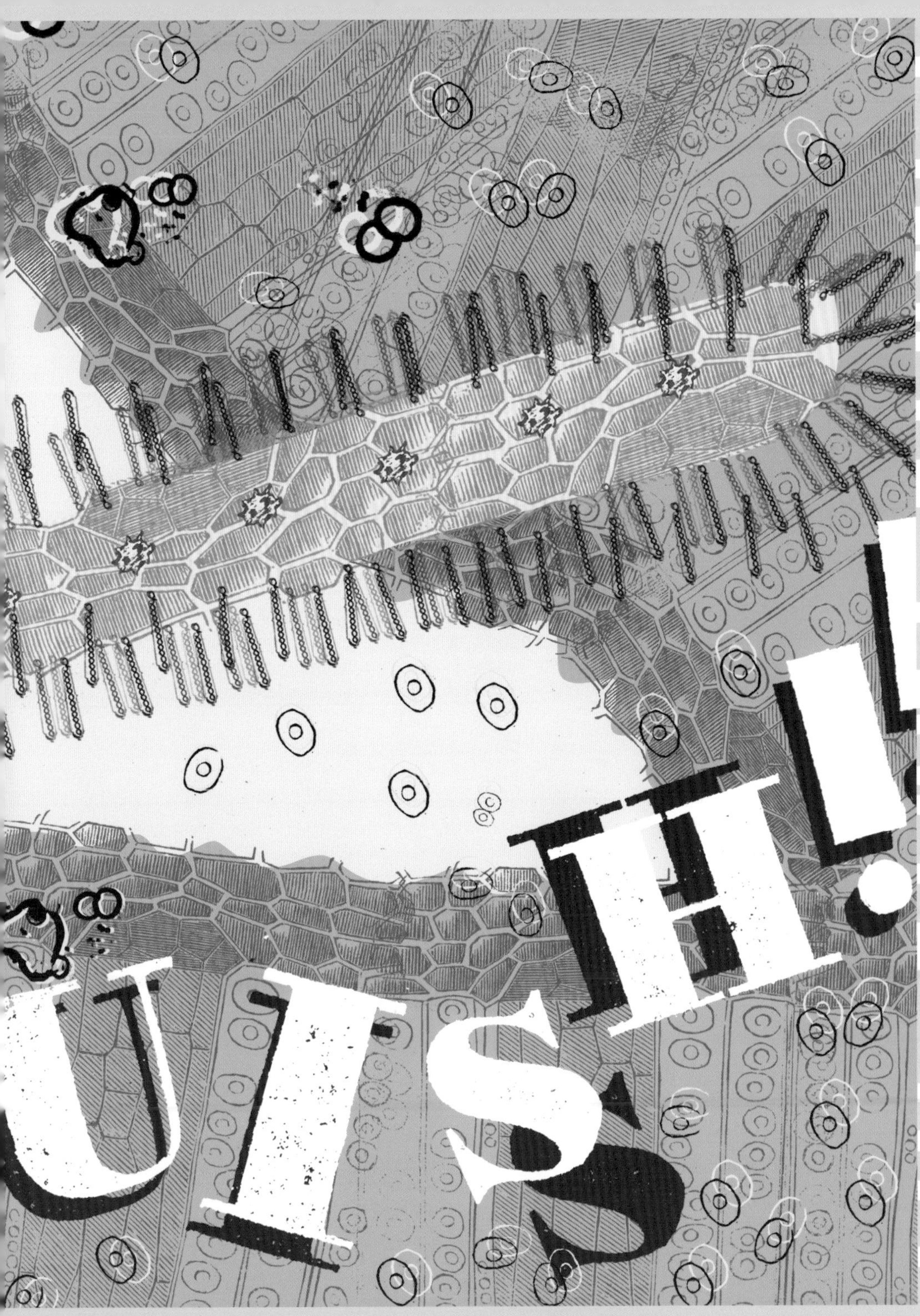
UISH!

The AstroNuts blasted out of the Plant Cell.

They were free! Free! FREE!

The AstroNuts had come to the Plant Planet hoping for the just-right planet. But they discovered a planet seriously imbalanced, overrun by just one kind of life—plant life—at the expense of all others.

And you humans don't need me to tell you how much can go wrong when one species dominates all of the others and completely wrecks the balance of a perfectly good planet that has been doing fine for millions and millions and millions of years!

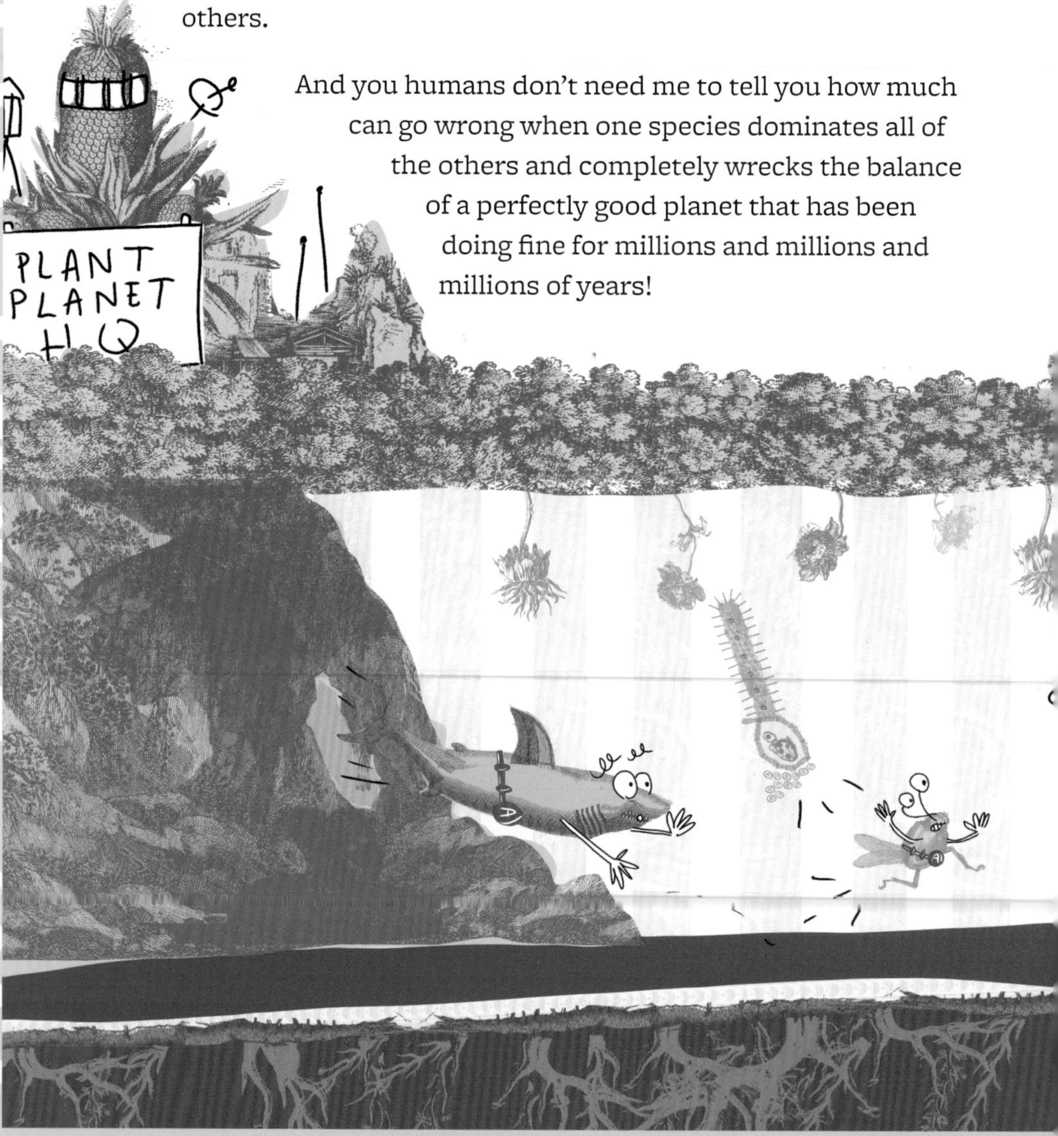
PLANT PLANET HQ

Sorry. Sorry to go off on a rant like that.

But I'm sure you can understand why I might be a little ticked off these days.

So anyway, the AstroNuts took off back to their Thomas Jefferson Nose Rocket. They were feeling good. They were feeling like . . .

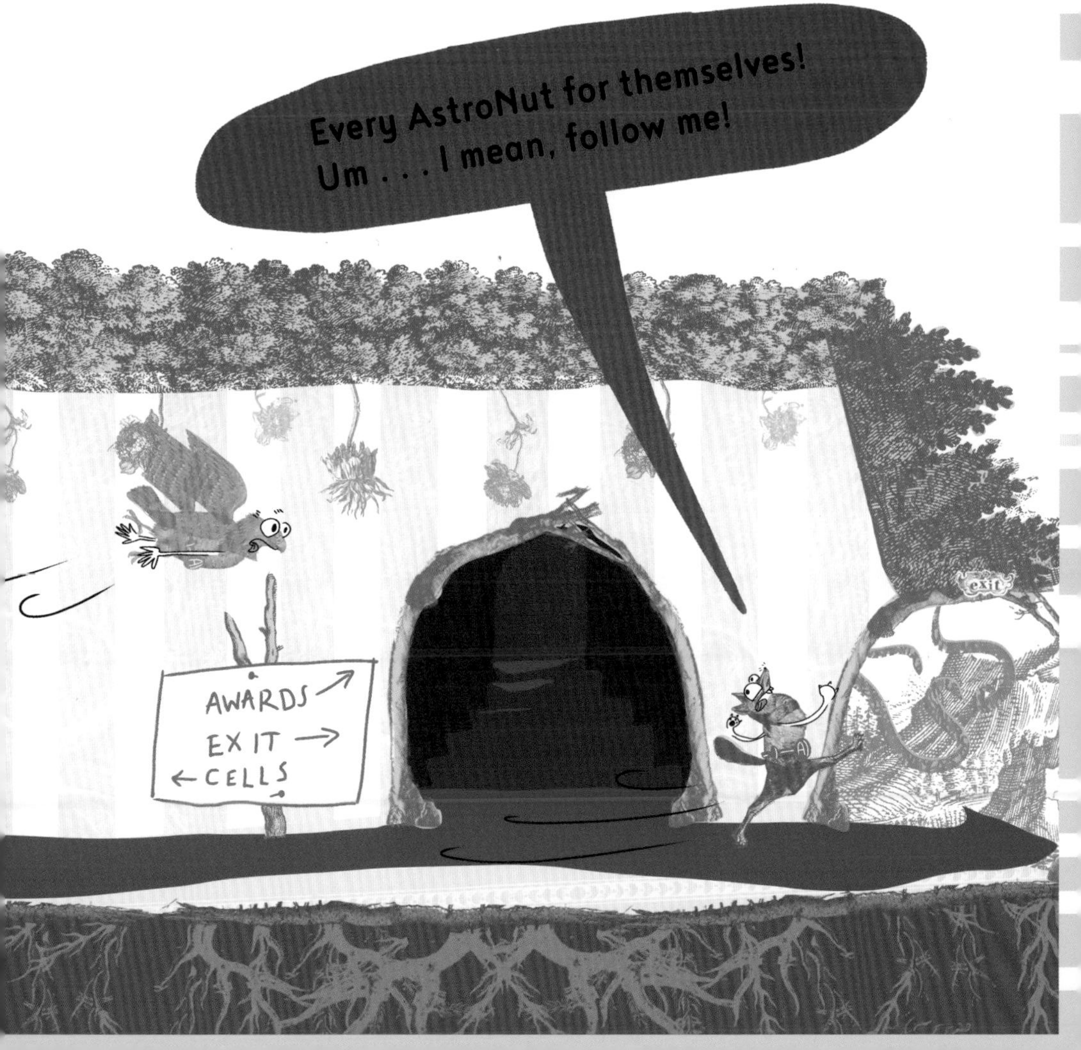
Every AstroNut for themselves!
Um . . . I mean, follow me!
AWARDS
EXIT
CELLS
exit

WE ARE THE ASTRONUTS!

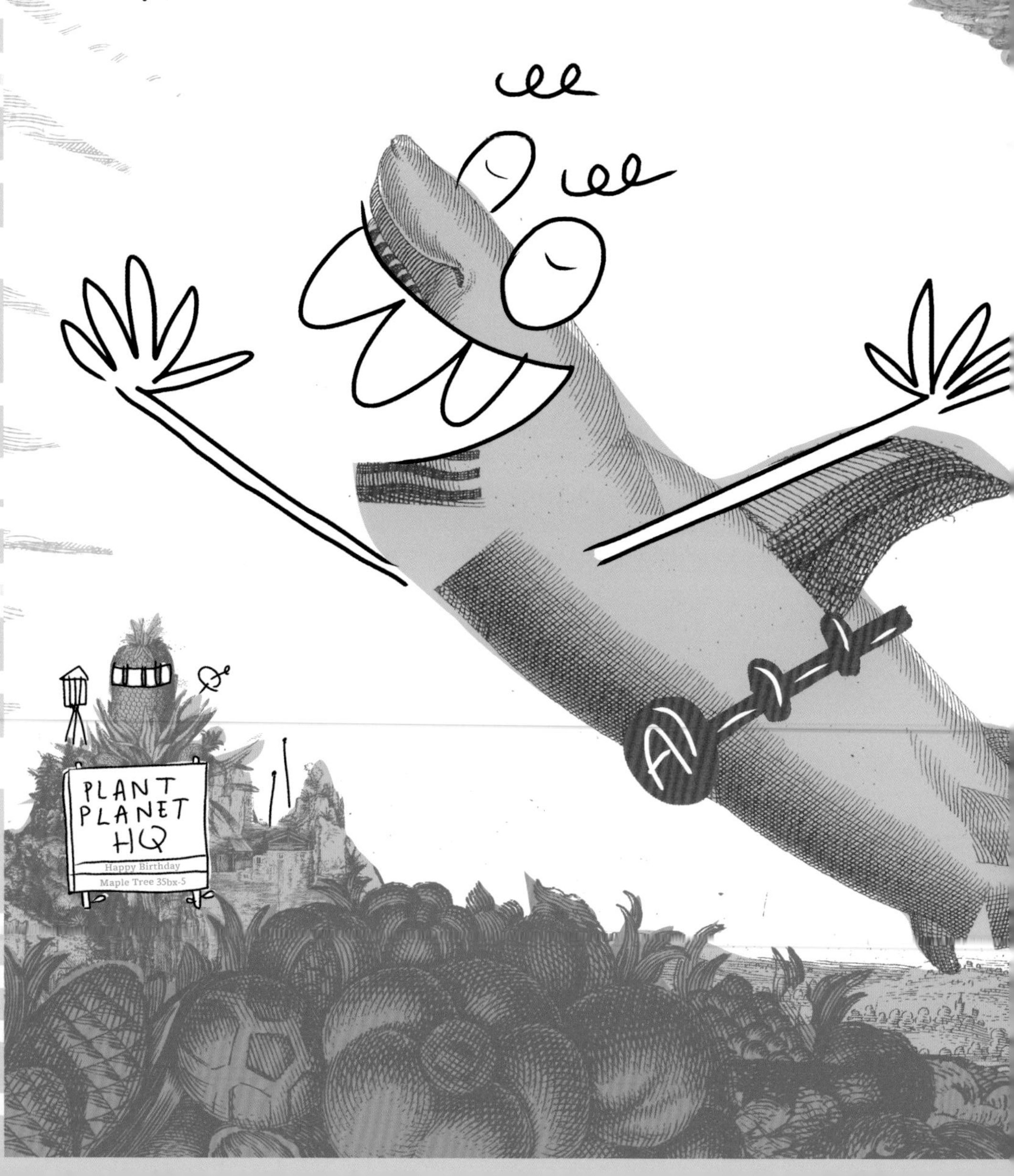
PLANT PLANET HQ
Happy Birthday
Maple Tree 35bx-5

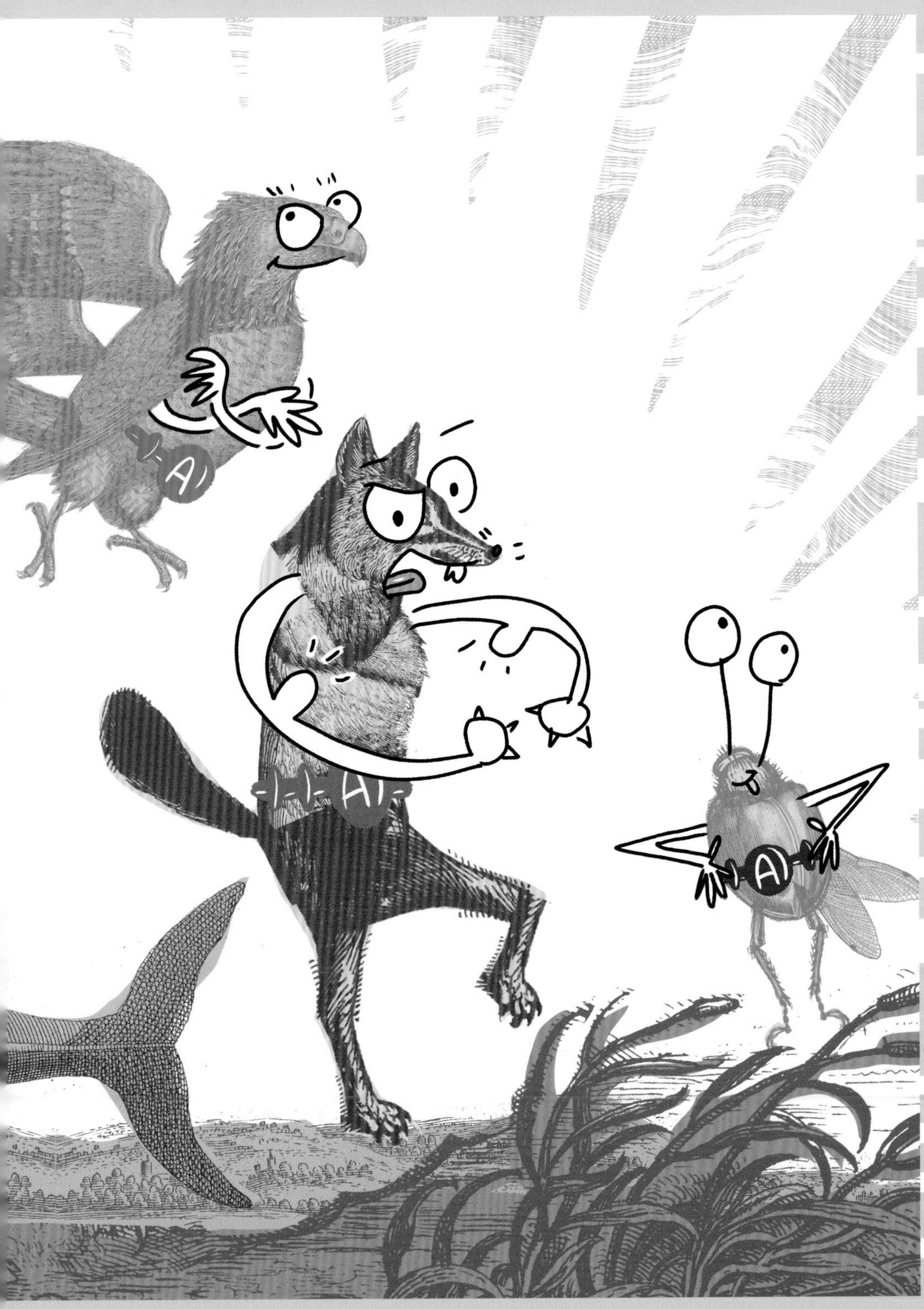

CHAPTER 20:
An Invitation

The AstroNuts walked to the Thomas Jefferson Nose Rocket in slow motion, like you humans always do when you are feeling heroic, and being cool. The AstroNuts had escaped the maybe-dangerous, maybe-just-chorelike plant life of the Plant Planet. They had completed their mission. And now it was time to go home.

But just then, keen-eyed Mission Leader AlphaWolf spotted something on the nose of the Nose Rocket.

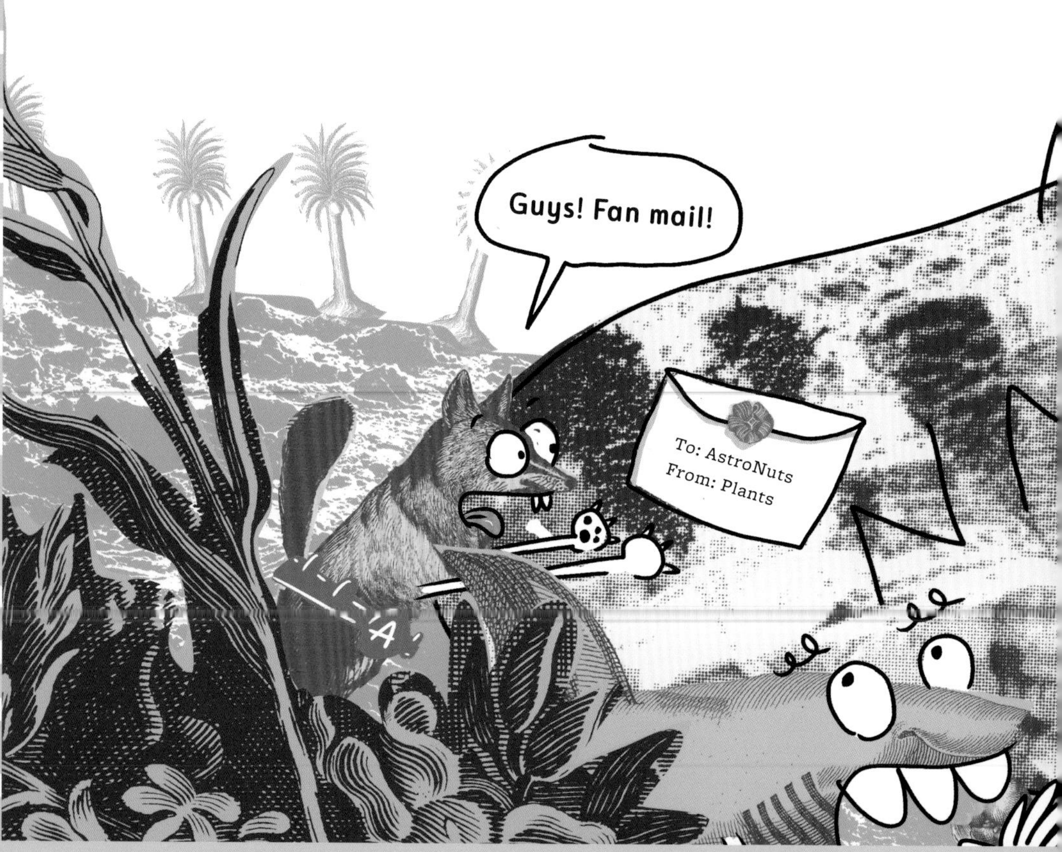
Guys! Fan mail!
To: AstroNuts
From: Plants

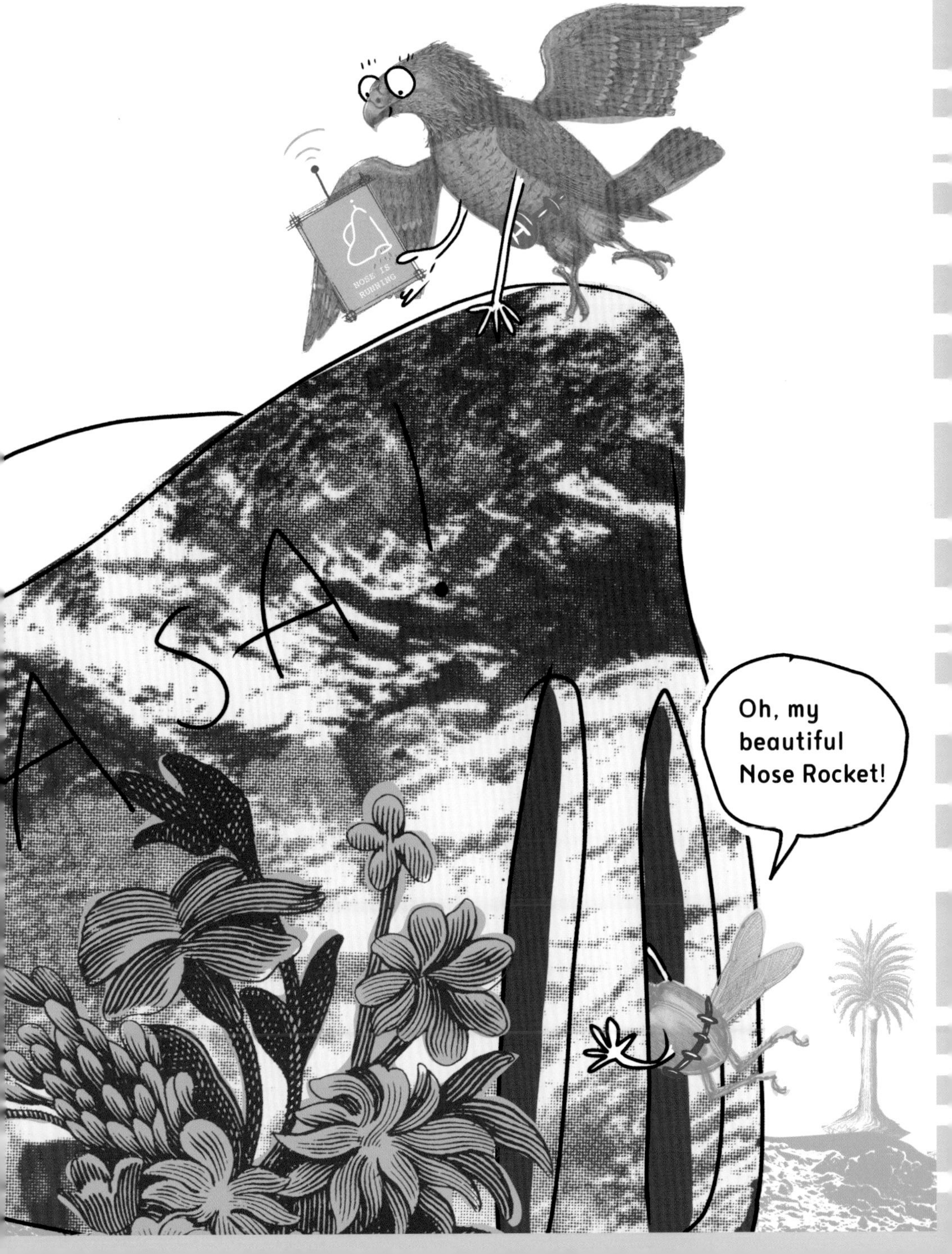
NOSE IS RUNNING
ASAI
Oh, my beautiful Nose Rocket!

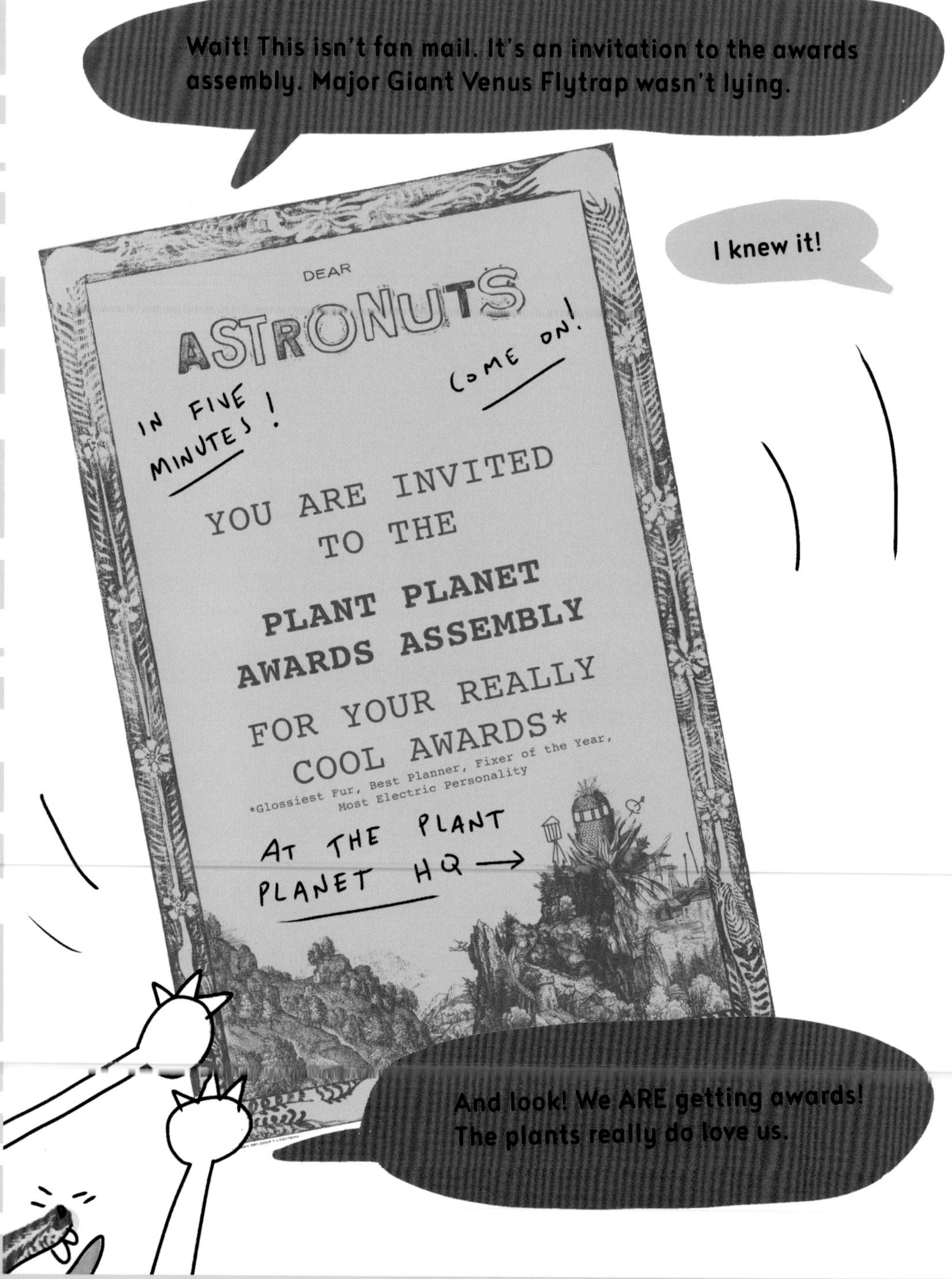
Wait! This isn't fan mail. It's an invitation to the awards assembly. Major Giant Venus Flytrap wasn't lying.
I knew it!
DEAR
ASTRONUTS
COME ON!
IN FIVE MINUTES!
YOU ARE INVITED TO THE
PLANT PLANET AWARDS ASSEMBLY
FOR YOUR REALLY COOL AWARDS*
*Glossiest Fur, Best Planner, Fixer of the Year, Most Electric Personality
AT THE PLANT PLANET HQ →
And look! We ARE getting awards! The plants really do love us.

Oh, feathers. Now I'm not so sure. Maybe the plants were just happy we were helping them. Maybe they think different things are exciting than we do.

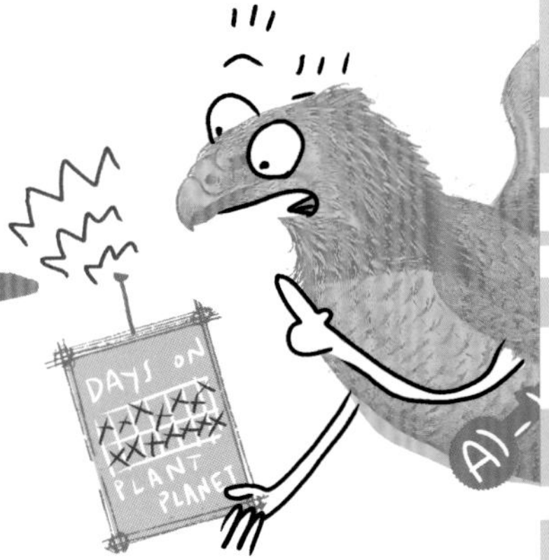
DAYS ON
PLANT PLANET

Oh, don't we feel just terrible. I knew it was a misunderstanding. The plants were trying to be so nice to us. And we just attacked them. Again.

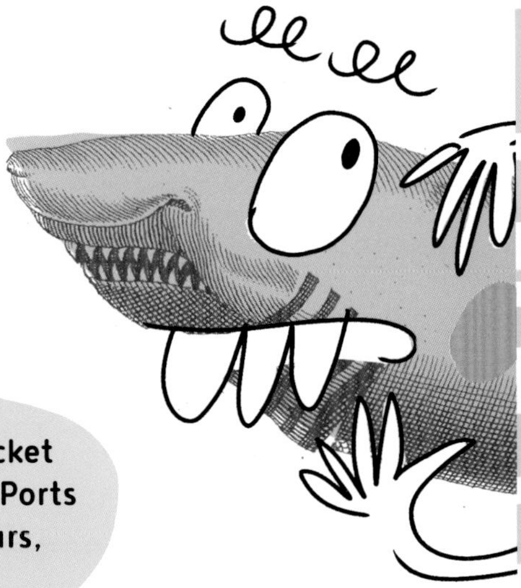

Yes, it is possible we were mean. But our Rocket Propulsion Systems are ready to go. Nostril Ports have been picked clear. Blastoff is in six hours, whether we're on the Nose Rocket or not.

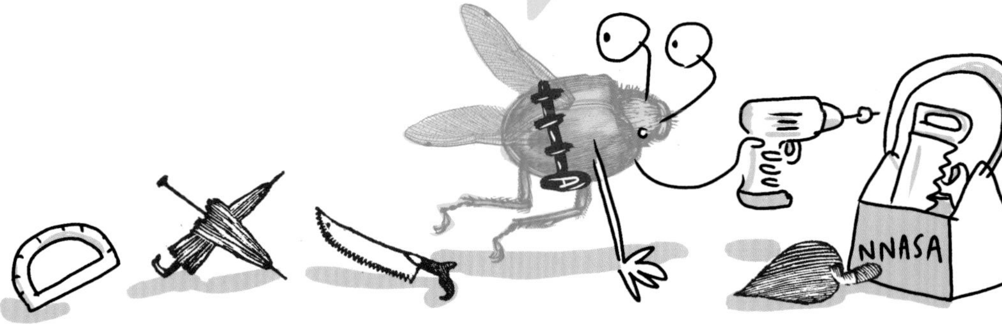
NNASA

Have you ever accepted an invitation to something you thought was going to be amazing? But it turned out to be truly terrible?

Have you ever accepted an invitation to something you thought was going to be terrible? But it turned out to be truly amazing?

The AstroNuts were not sure which kind of invitation this was. The AstroNuts thought about what they should do. The two choices were pretty clear.

1. Get in the Nose Rocket and go home.

or

2. Go to the Plant Planet awards assembly and see what it was all about.

AlphaWolf decided for them.

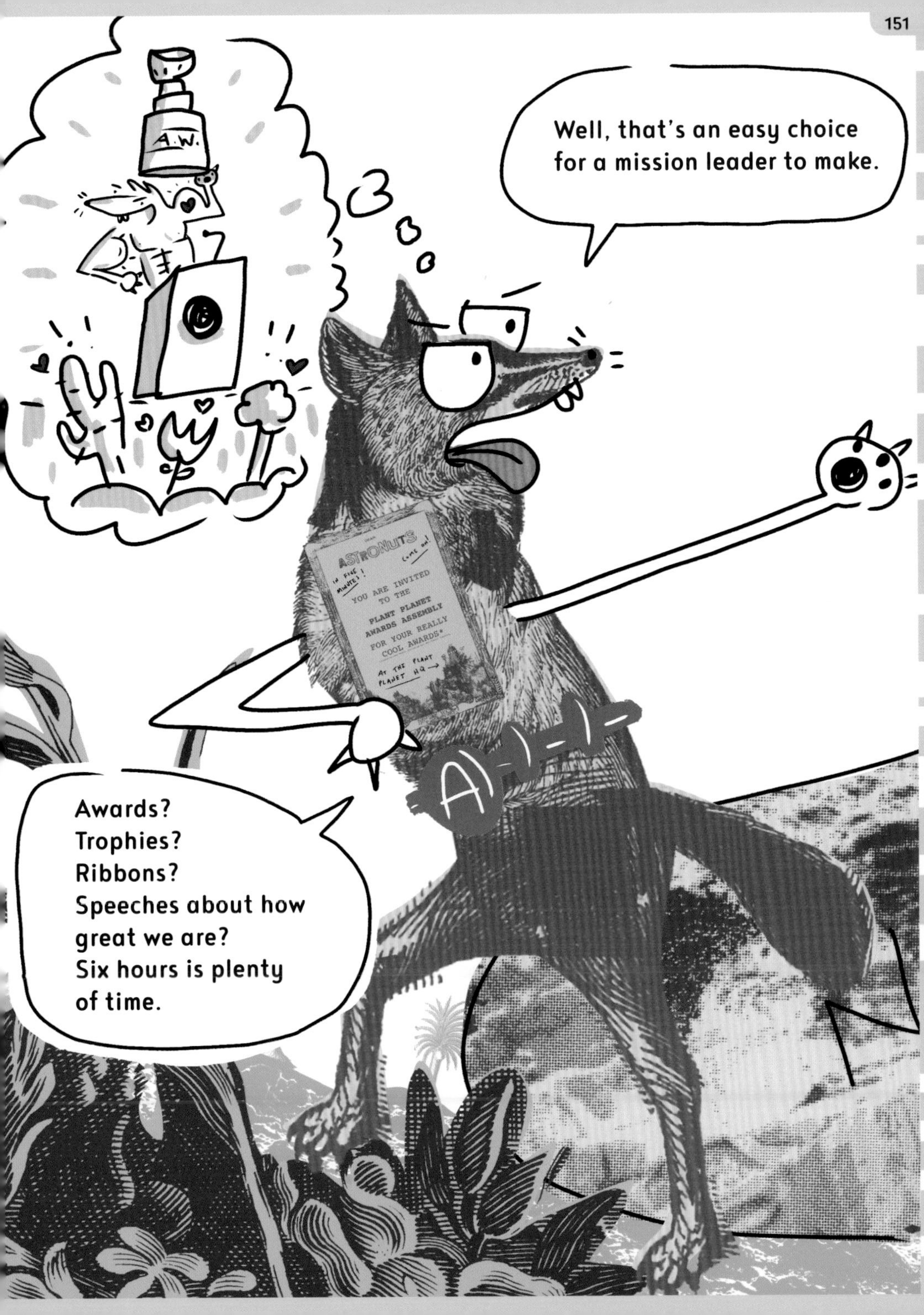
Well, that's an easy choice for a mission leader to make.
A.W.
ASTRONUTS
IN FIVE MINUTES!
COME ON!
YOU ARE INVITED TO THE PLANT PLANET AWARDS ASSEMBLY FOR YOUR REALLY COOL AWARDS*
AT THE PLANT PLANET HQ →
Awards? Trophies? Ribbons? Speeches about how great we are? Six hours is plenty of time.

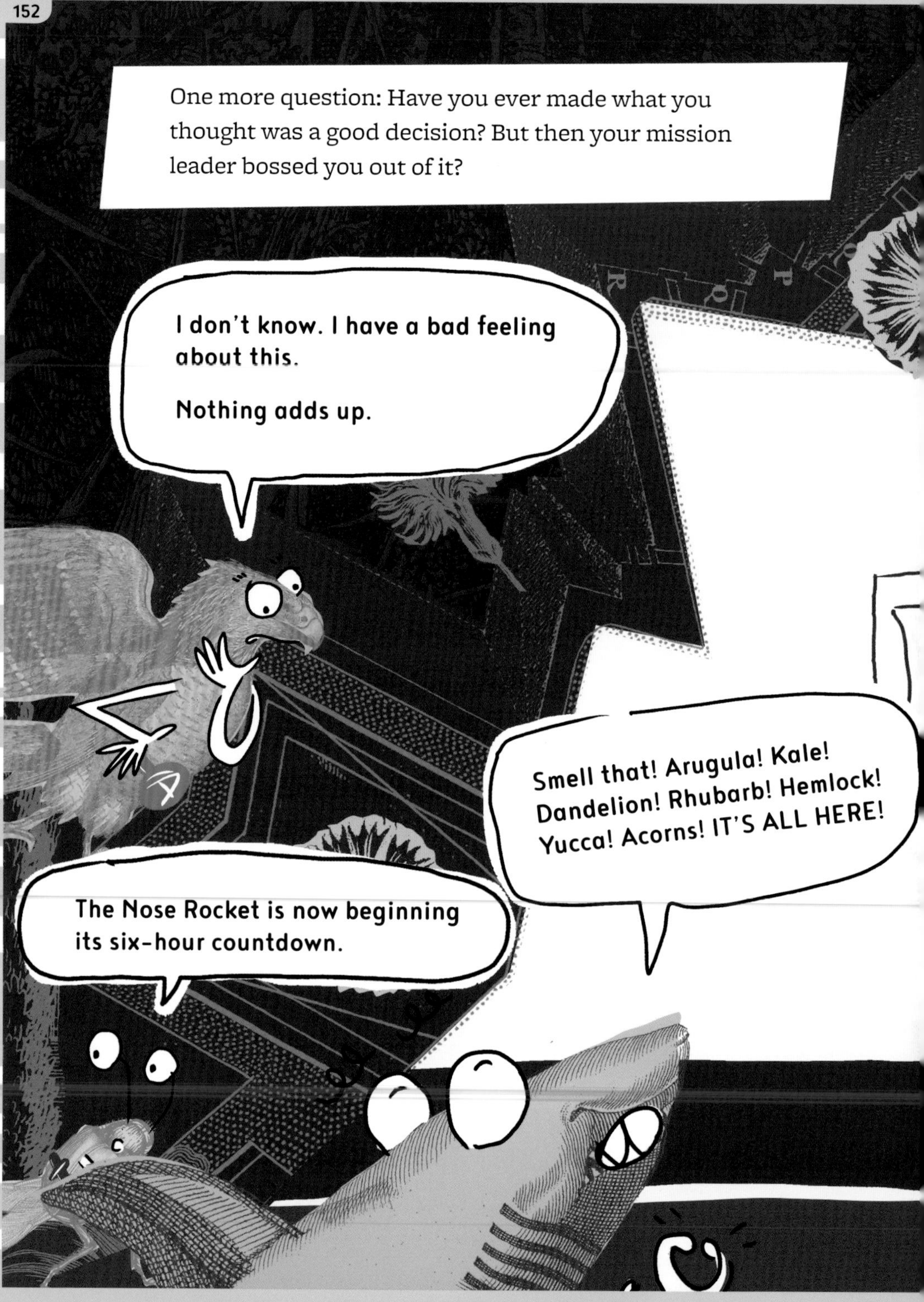
One more question: Have you ever made what you thought was a good decision? But then your mission leader bossed you out of it?
I don't know. I have a bad feeling about this.
Nothing adds up.
Smell that! Arugula! Kale! Dandelion! Rhubarb! Hemlock! Yucca! Acorns! IT'S ALL HERE!
The Nose Rocket is now beginning its six-hour countdown.

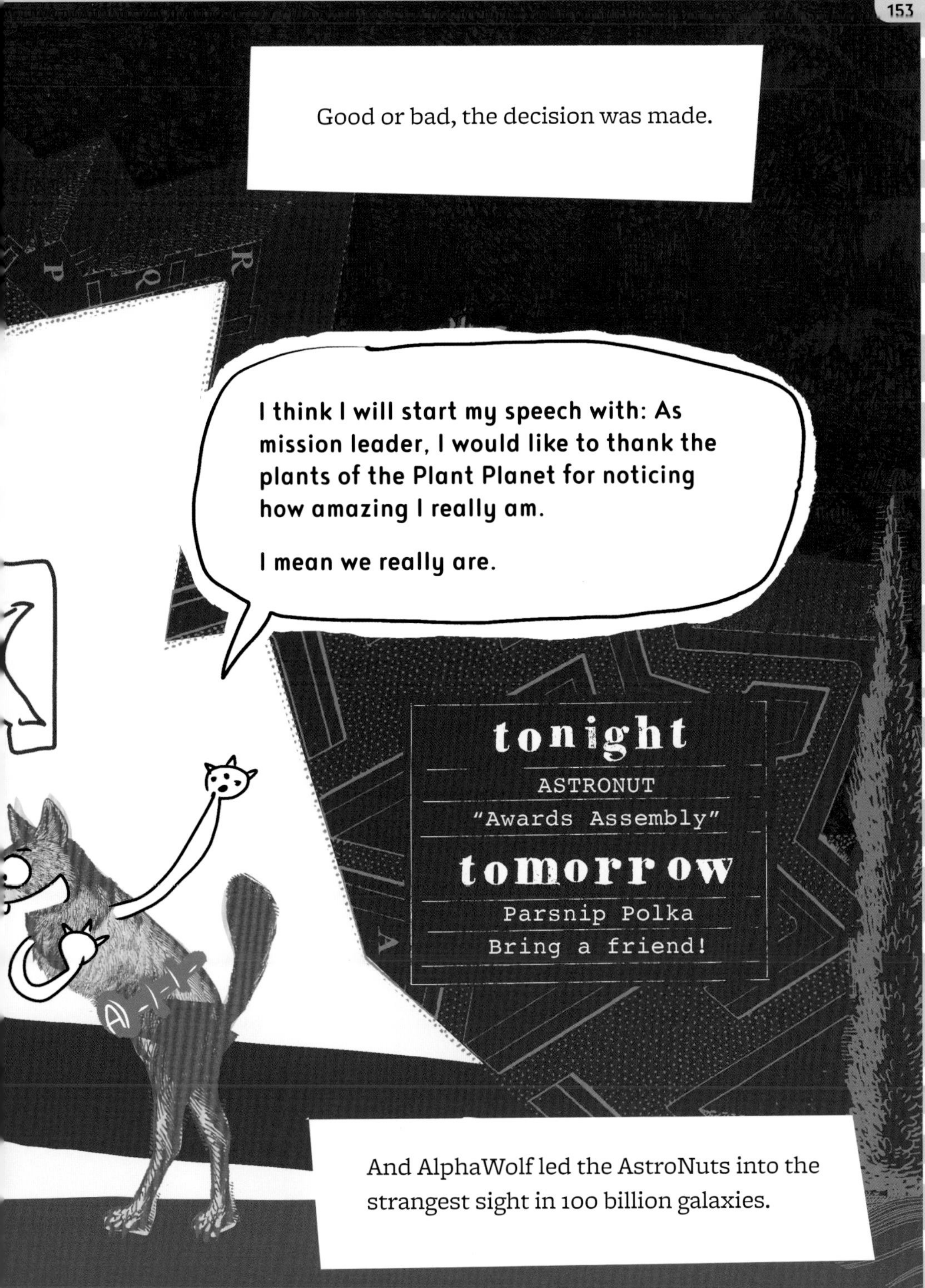
Good or bad, the decision was made.
I think I will start my speech with: As mission leader, I would like to thank the plants of the Plant Planet for noticing how amazing I really am.
I mean we really are.
tonight
ASTRONUT
"Awards Assembly"
tomorrow
Parsnip Polka
Bring a friend!
And AlphaWolf led the AstroNuts into the strangest sight in 100 billion galaxies.

CHAPTER 21:
The Assembly

The AstroNuts stepped into a gigantic greenhouse auditorium filled with thousands of plants, maybe millions of plants.

On the stage, a tiny daisy led all the plants in reciting the Plant Planet Pledge of Allegiance.

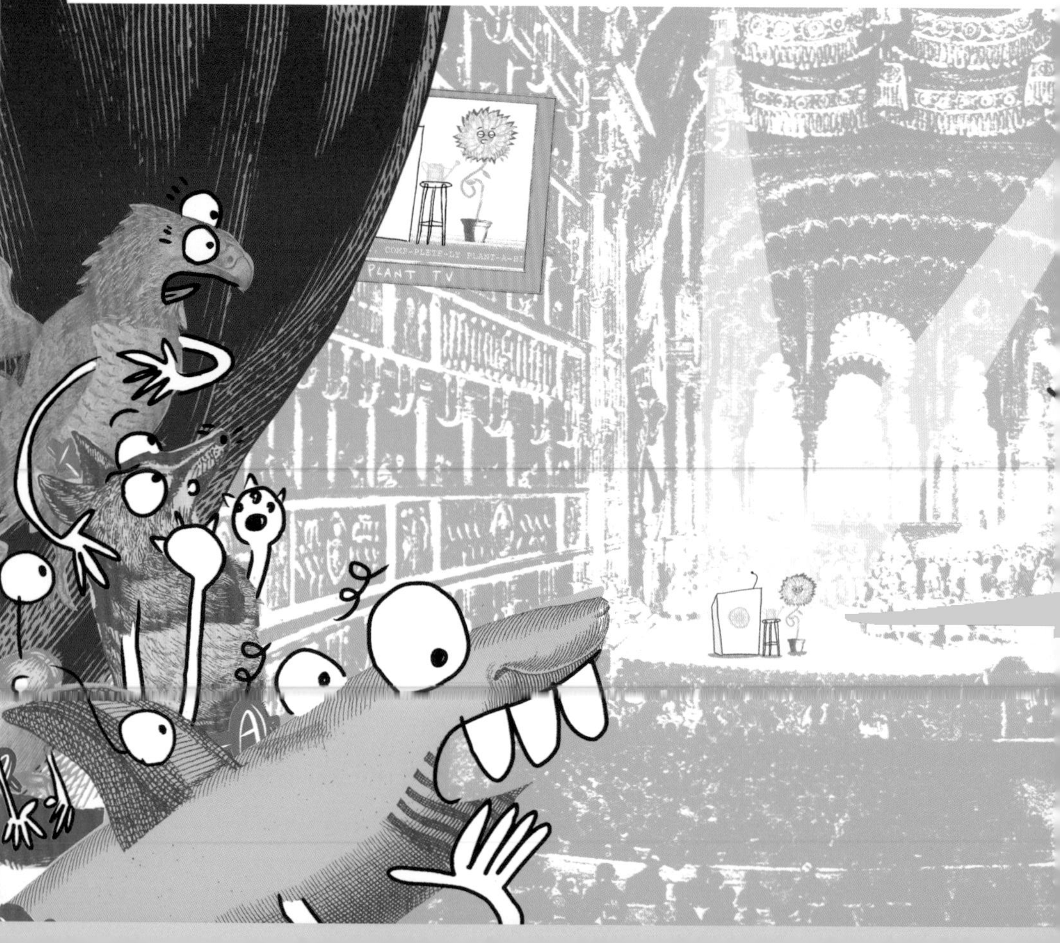
PLANT TV

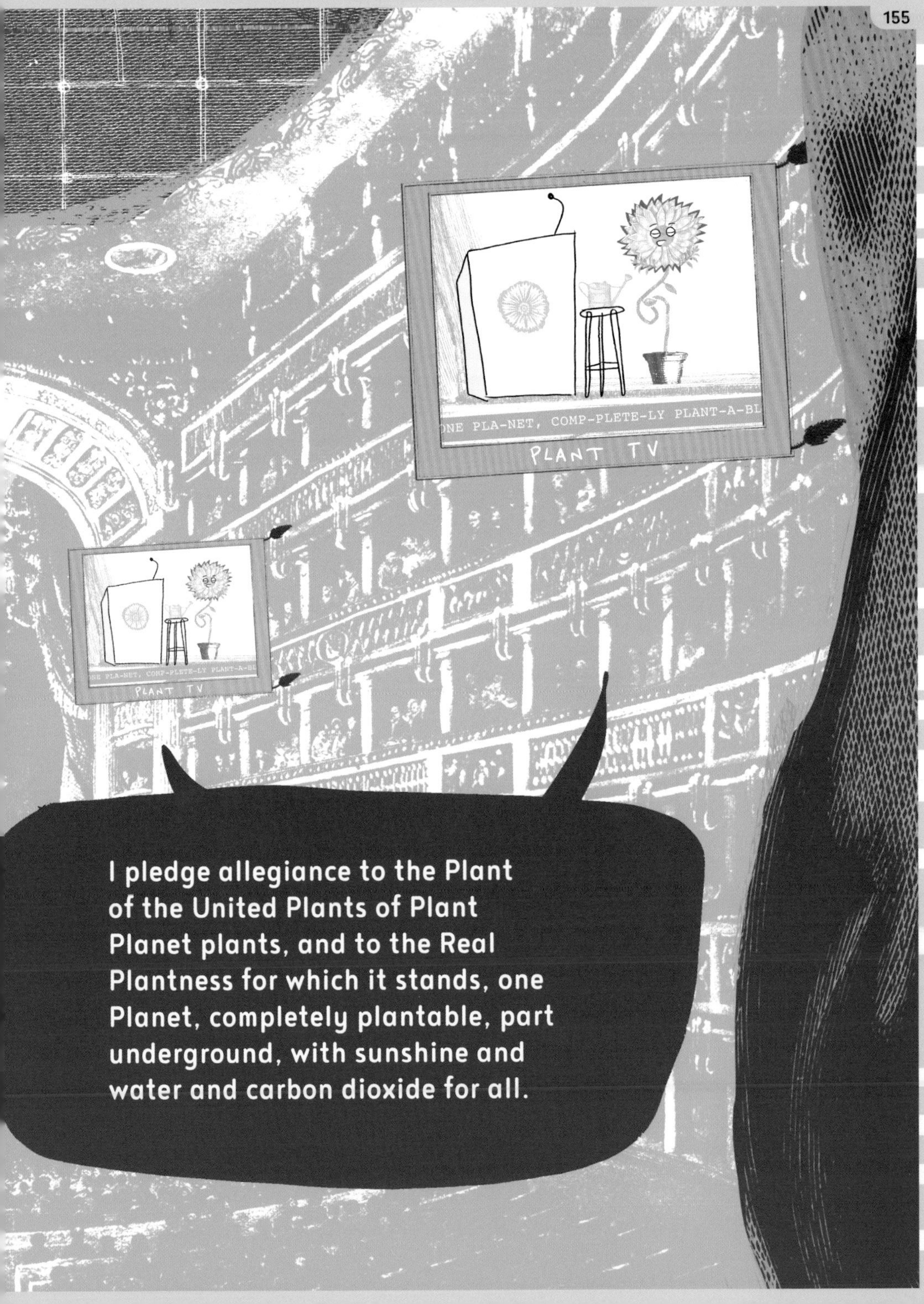
ONE PLA-NET, COMP-PLETE-LY PLANT-A-BL
PLANT TV
I pledge allegiance to the Plant of the United Plants of Plant Planet plants, and to the Real Plantness for which it stands, one Planet, completely plantable, part underground, with sunshine and water and carbon dioxide for all.

The daisy seemed suspiciously excited to see them.

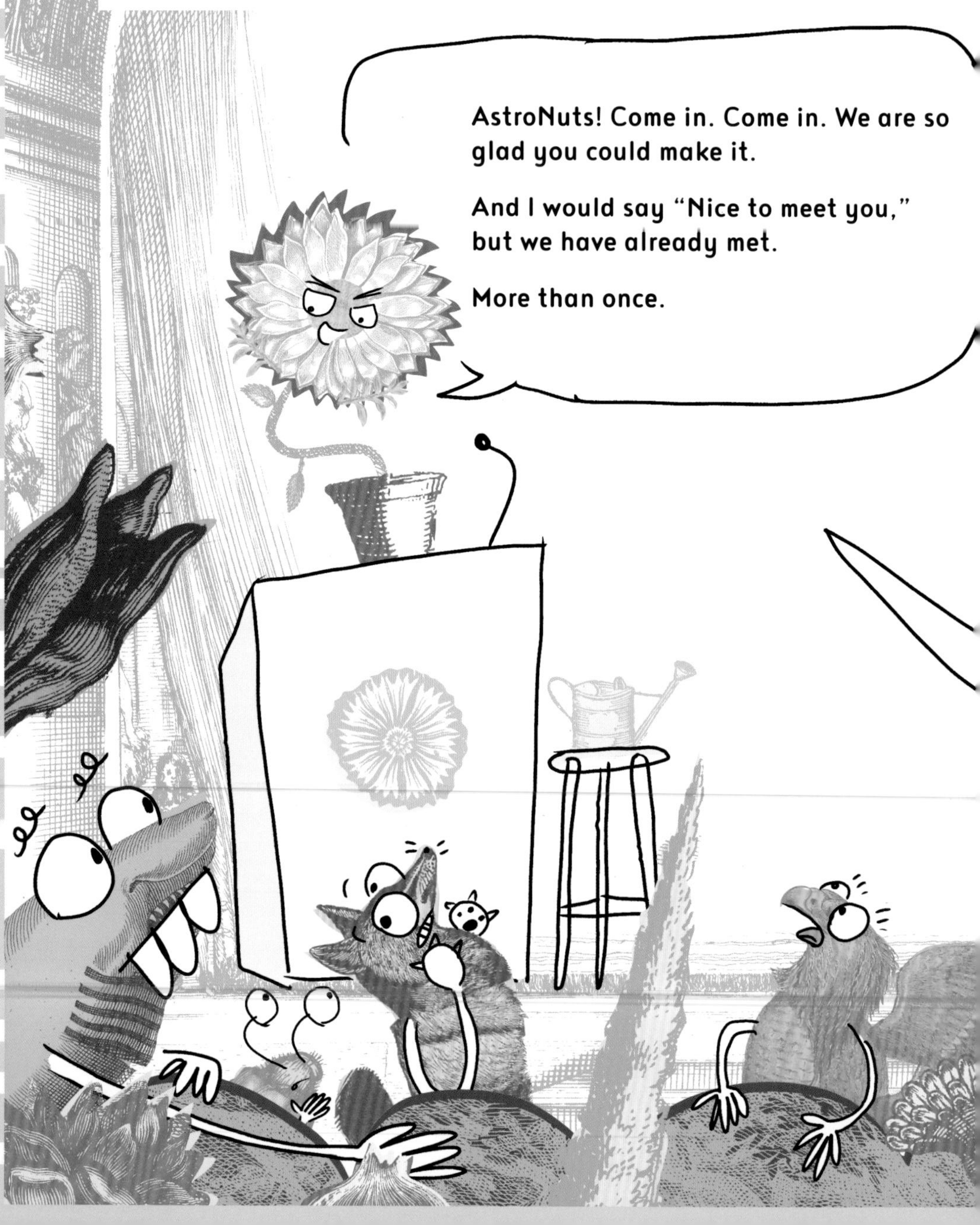
AstroNuts! Come in. Come in. We are so glad you could make it.
And I would say "Nice to meet you," but we have already met.
More than once.

First, when you crashed your Nose Rocket right into me.

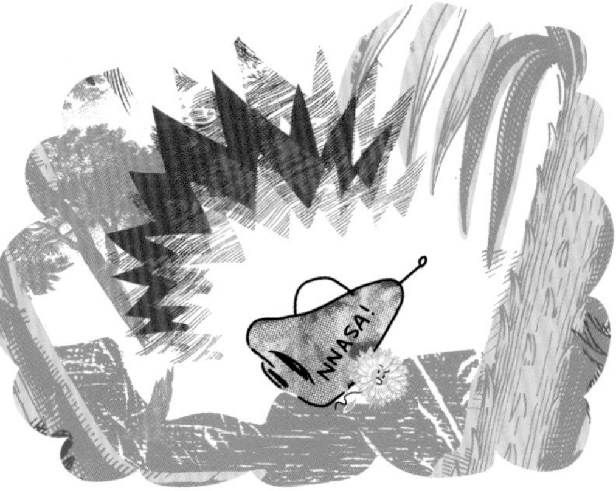
NNASA!

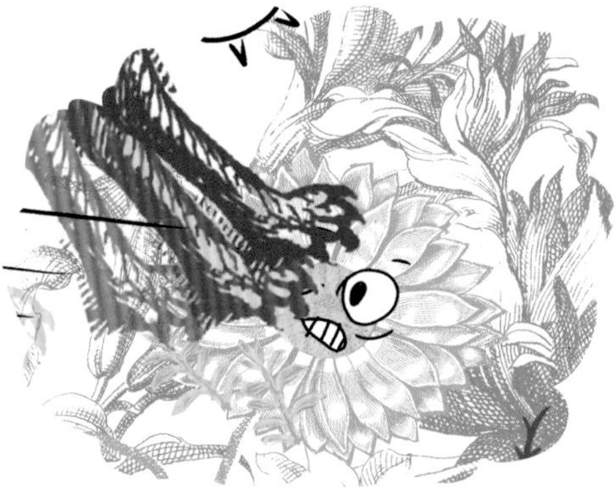

Again, when the hairy one stepped on me.

And finally, when all four of you picnicked right on top of me.

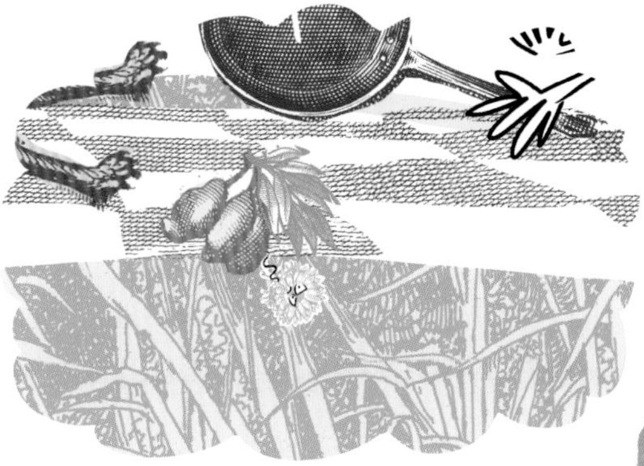

So it's about time to introduce myself.

I am Daisy. I am the Supreme Leader of the Plant Planet.

And I am . . .

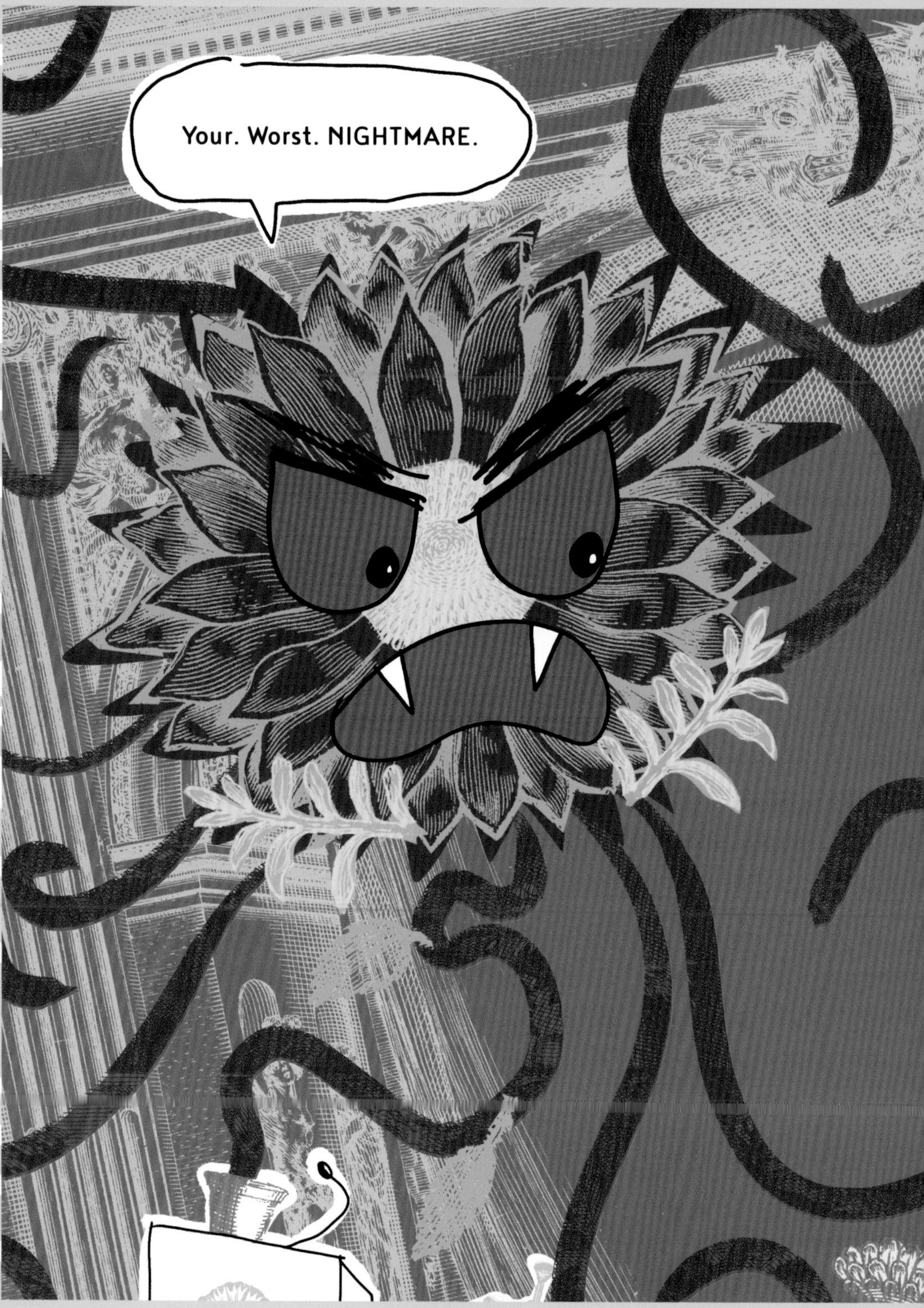
Your. Worst. NIGHTMARE.

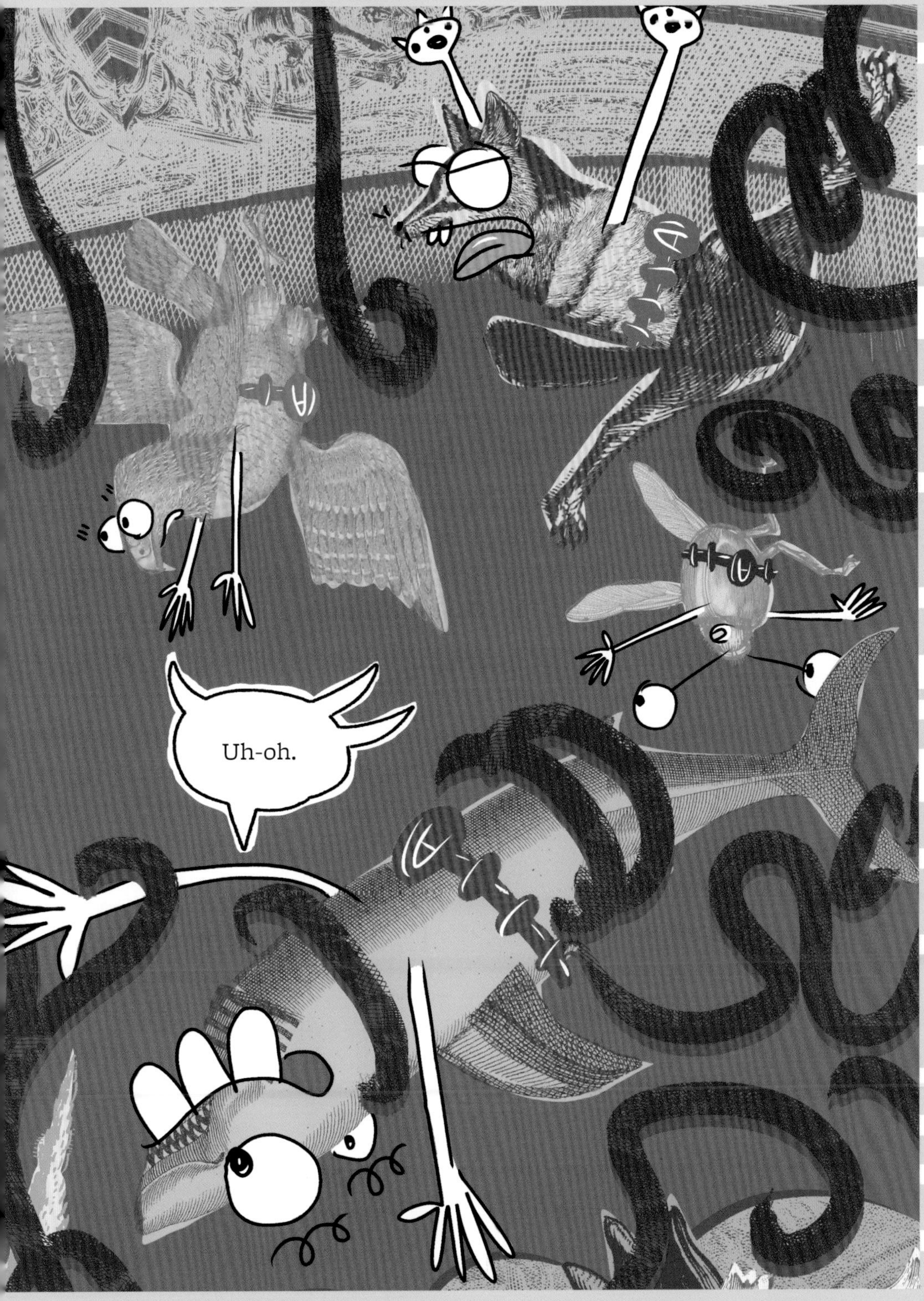
Uh-oh.

The AstroNuts were a bit surprised to find out that this little flower, Daisy, and not Major Giant Venus Flytrap, was the leader of the Plant Planet.

And they were completely shocked to get pushed onstage and dumped in a cage that clearly had no awards in it.

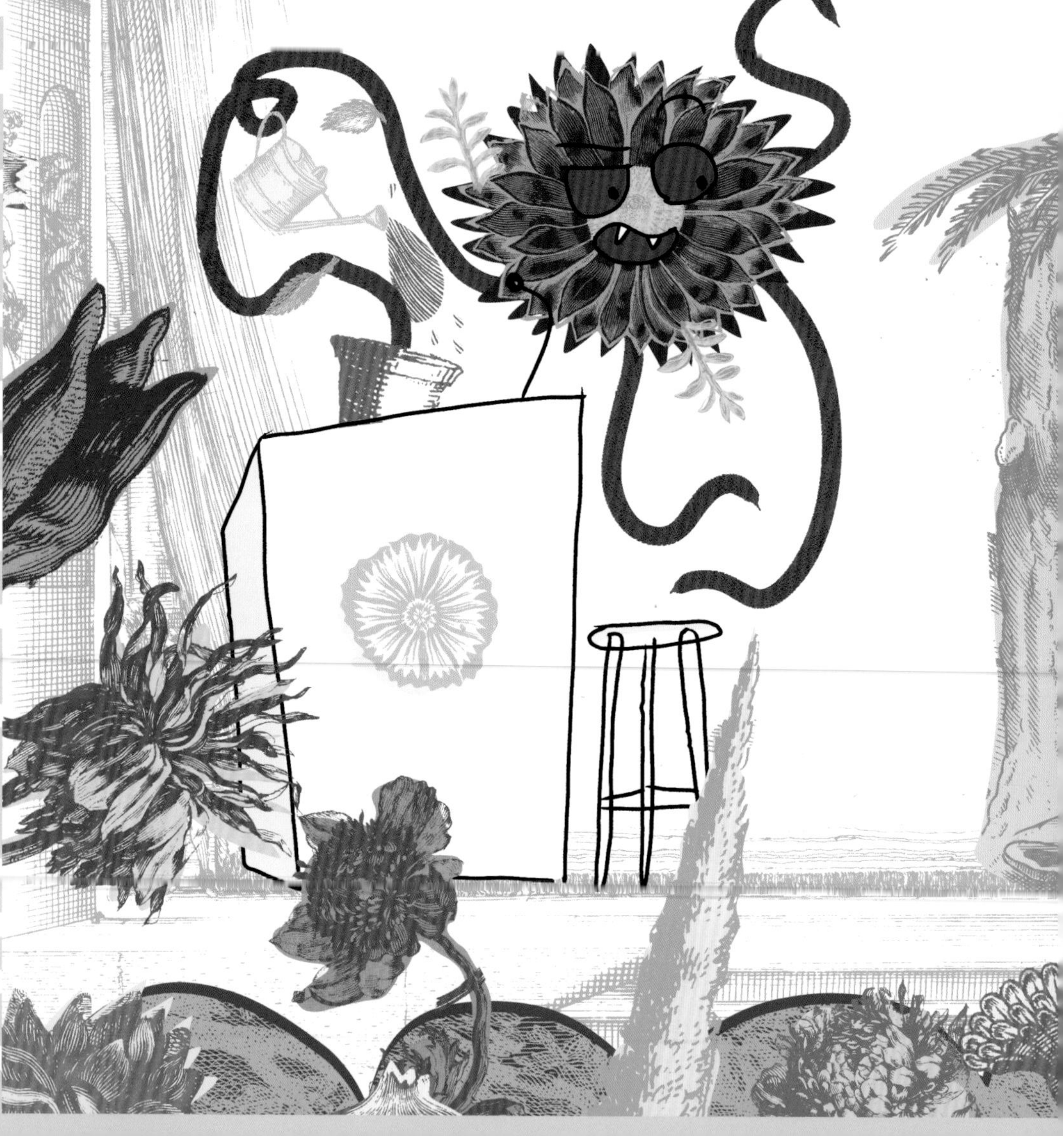

You know that part in stories where the Bad Guy captures the Good Guys, and then starts explaining everything that has happened, and all of the Bad Things that are going to happen next, which, for some terrible reason, always seems to include the total destruction of me?

Well, that's exactly what happened next.

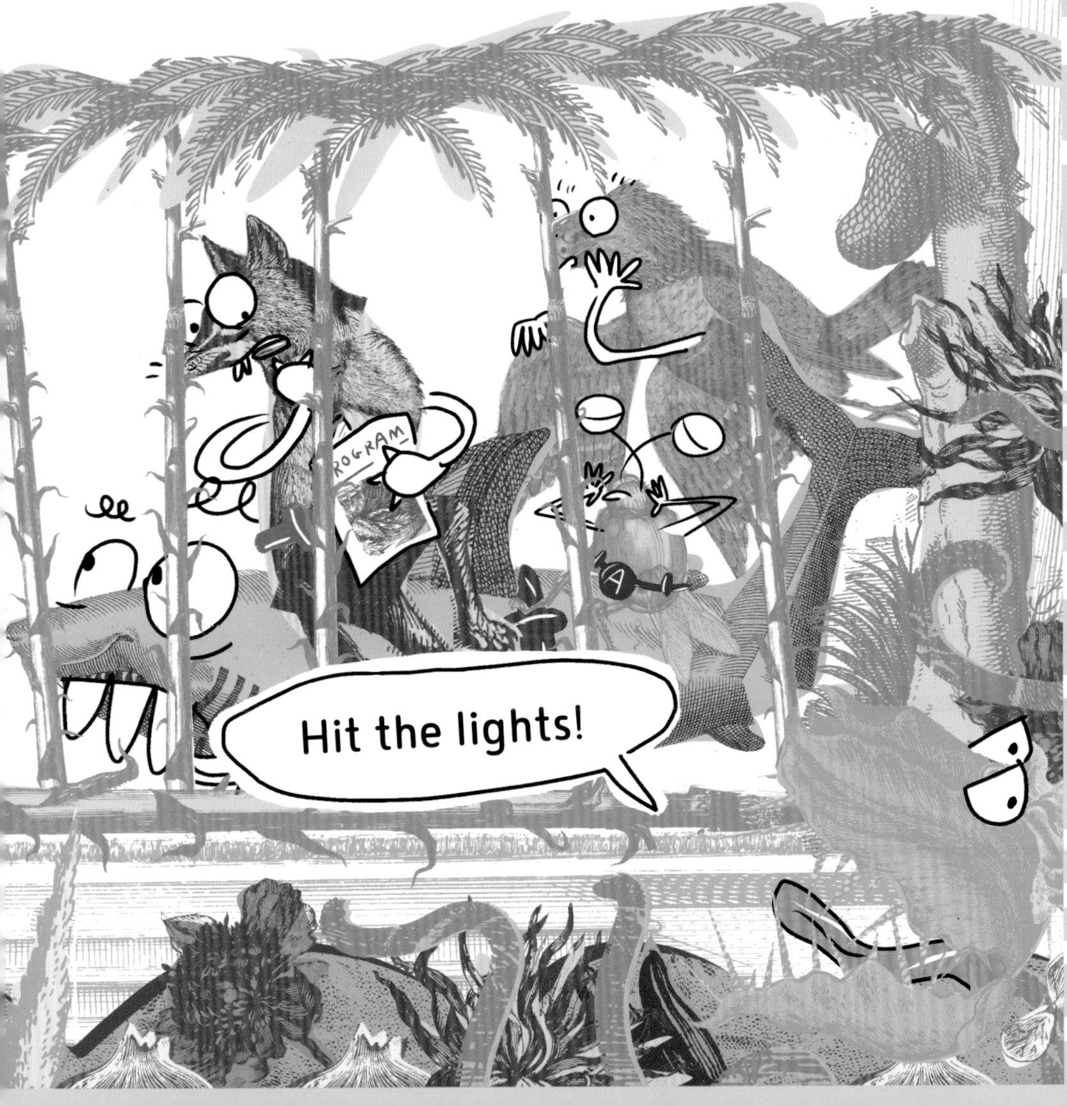
ROGRAM
Hit the lights!

CHAPTER 22:
Welcome?

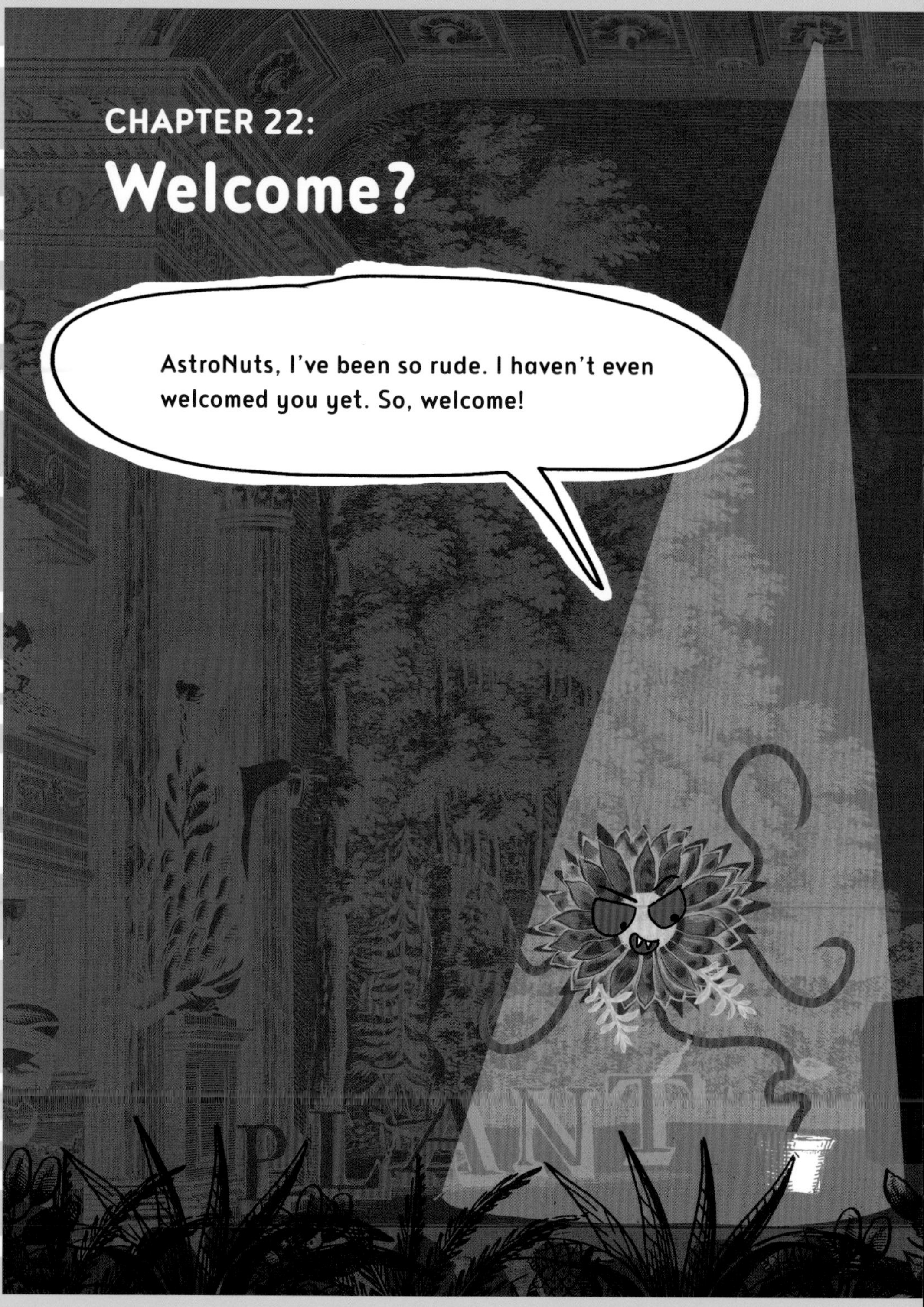
AstroNuts, I've been so rude. I haven't even welcomed you yet. So, welcome!
PLANT

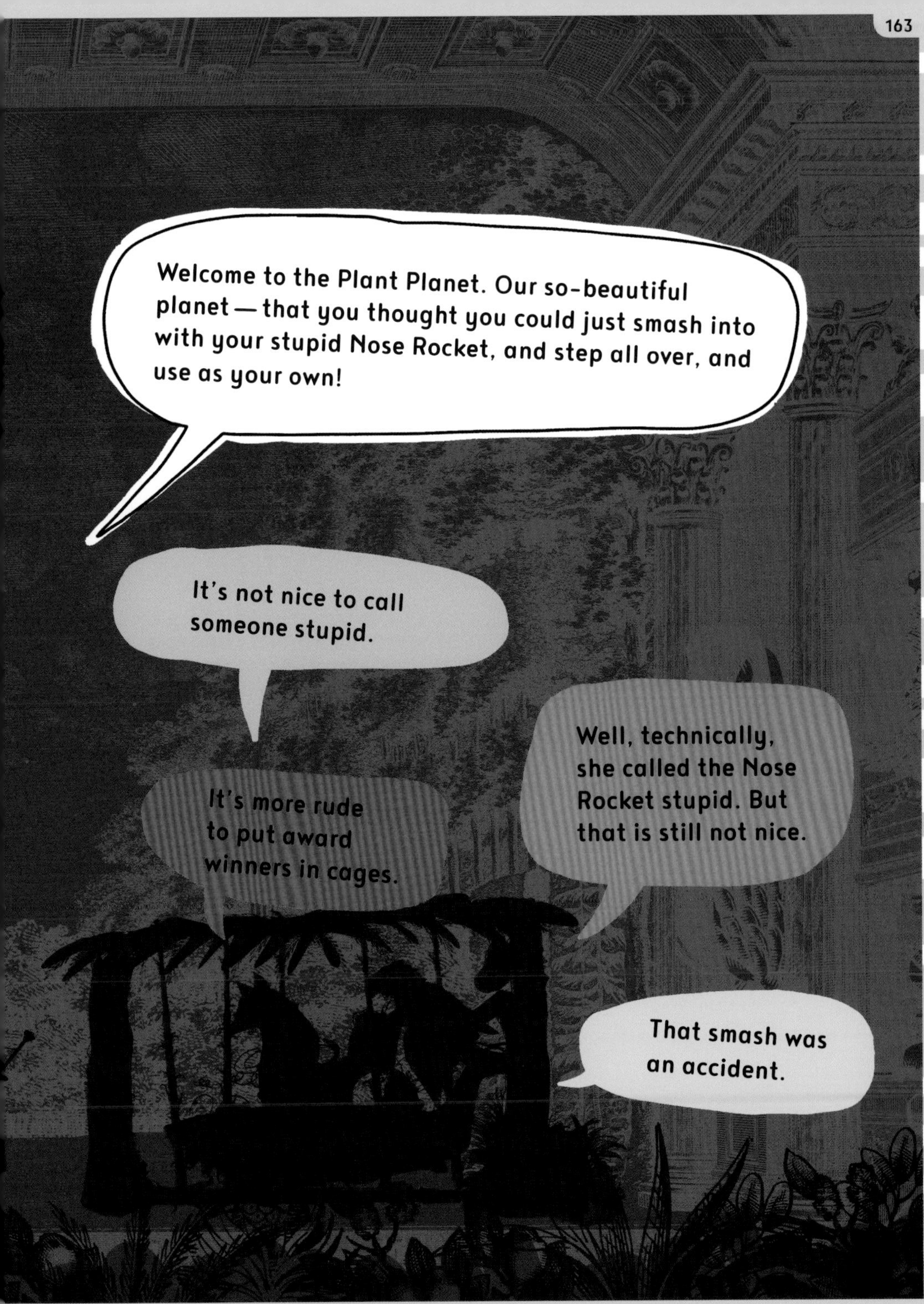
Welcome to the Plant Planet. Our so-beautiful planet — that you thought you could just smash into with your stupid Nose Rocket, and step all over, and use as your own!
It's not nice to call someone stupid.
It's more rude to put award winners in cages.
Well, technically, she called the Nose Rocket stupid. But that is still not nice.
That smash was an accident.

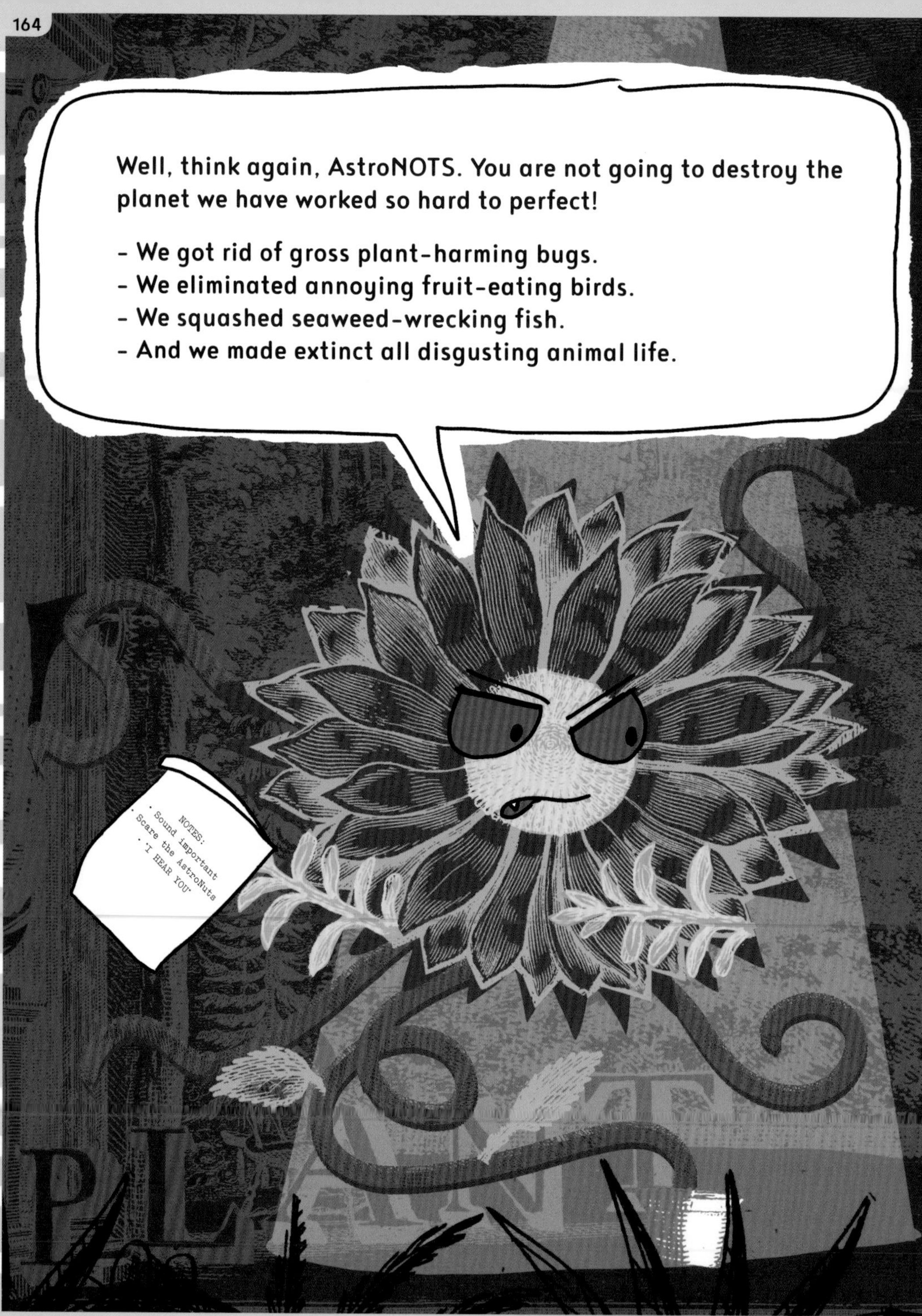
Well, think again, AstroNOTS. You are not going to destroy the planet we have worked so hard to perfect!
- We got rid of gross plant-harming bugs.
- We eliminated annoying fruit-eating birds.
- We squashed seaweed-wrecking fish.
- And we made extinct all disgusting animal life.
NOTES:
• Sound important
• Scare the AstroNuts
• 'I HEAR YOU'

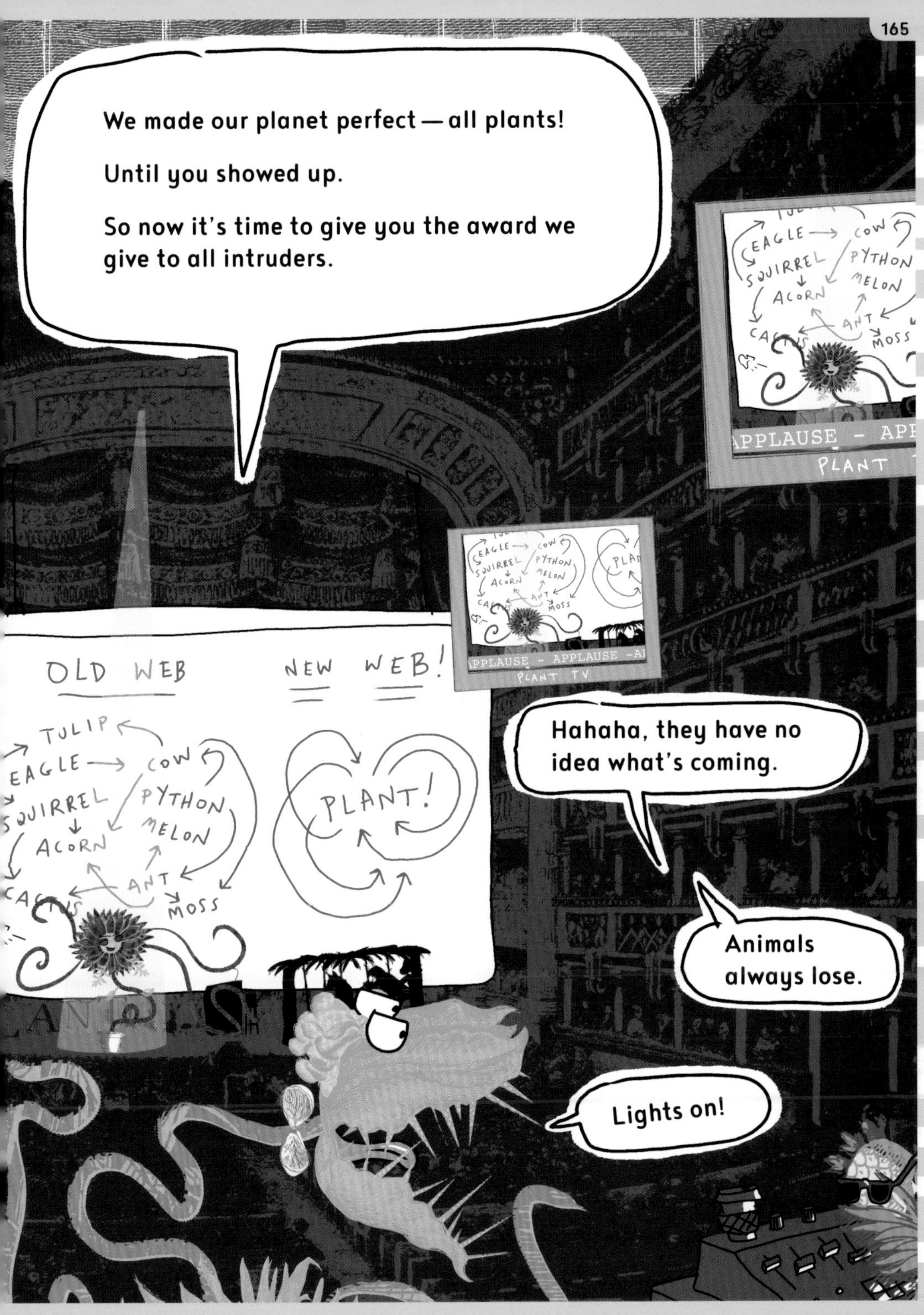
We made our planet perfect — all plants!
Until you showed up.
So now it's time to give you the award we give to all intruders.
OLD WEB
NEW WEB!
TULIP
EAGLE
COW
SQUIRREL
PYTHON
MELON
ACORN
ANT
CACTUS
MOSS
PLANT!
APPLAUSE - APPLAUSE
PLANT TV
Hahaha, they have no idea what's coming.
Animals always lose.
Lights on!

Here's your award.

That's right, my friends. You are looking at 22 feet of sharpened steel.

Called the Headge Clipper. It trims giant hedges—and it clips off heads. Normal-sized clippers are used for flower heads. But we are going to use these to clip off your heads and replace them with much smarter, much better PLANT HEADS.

Then you New and Improved AstroPLANT-HEADS can get back to your Exciting Activities: weeding, trimming, and rebalancing our lovely planet. Making it perfect for us with your superpowers. Using them the way they were meant to be used.

Forever.

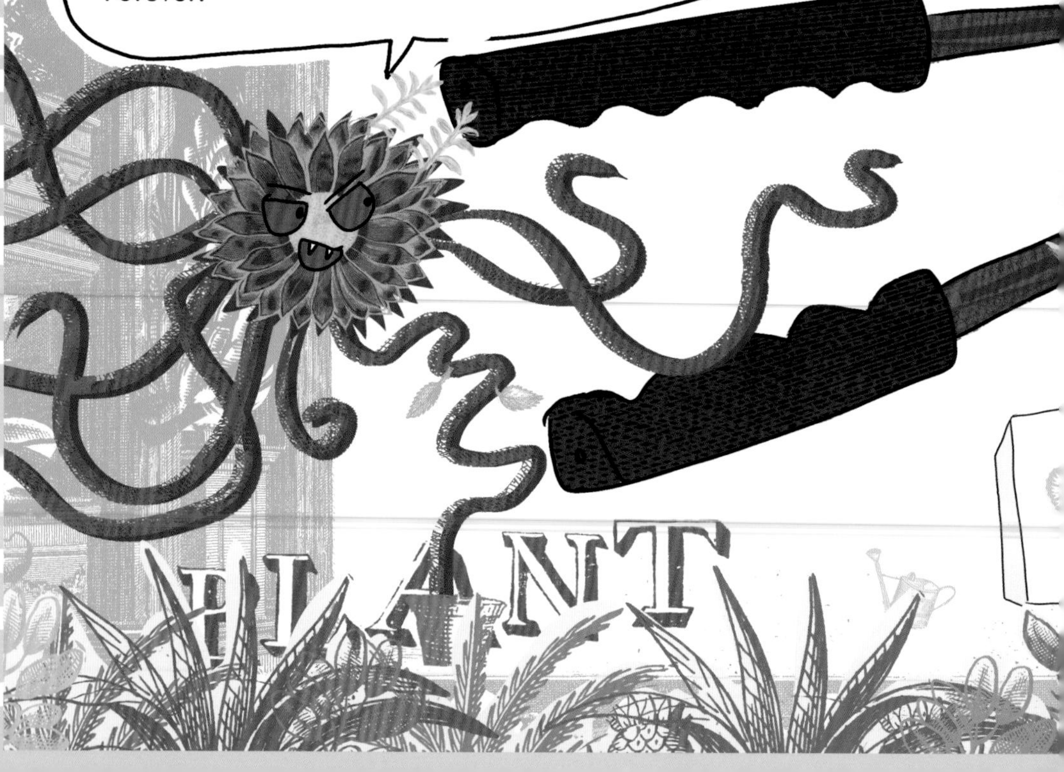
PLANT

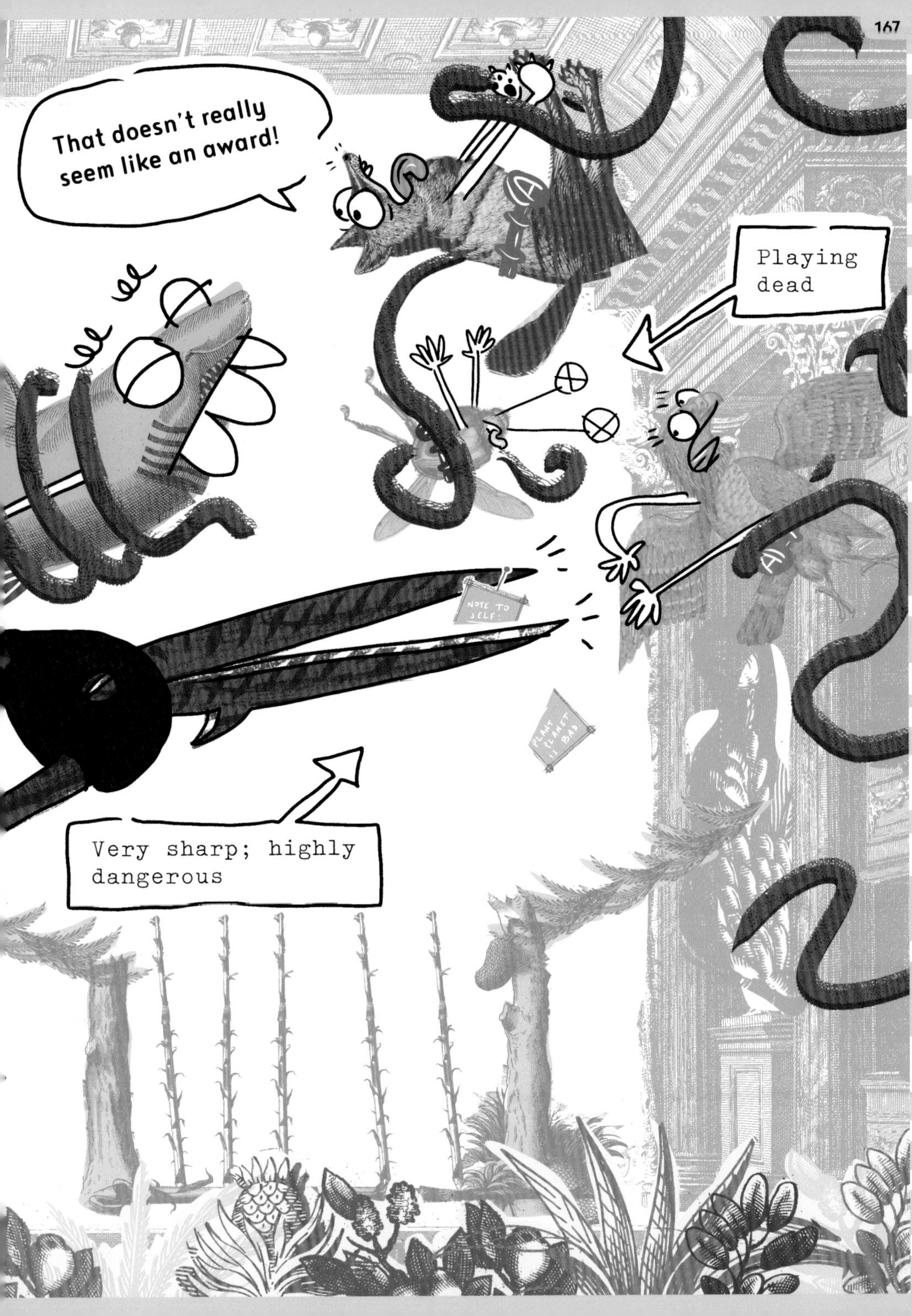
That doesn't really seem like an award!
Playing dead
Very sharp; highly dangerous

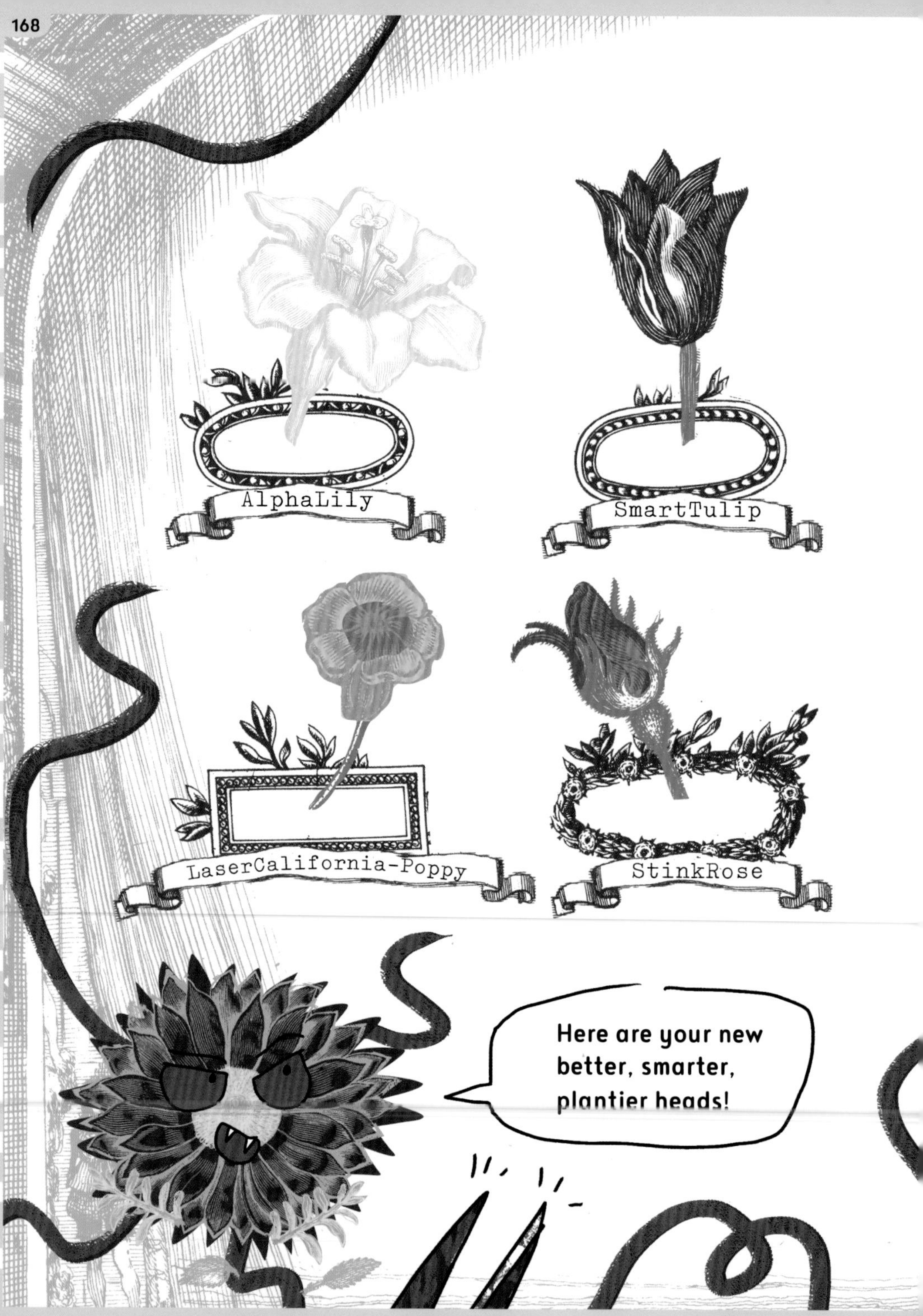
AlphaLily
SmartTulip
LaserCalifornia-Poppy
StinkRose
Here are your new better, smarter, plantier heads!

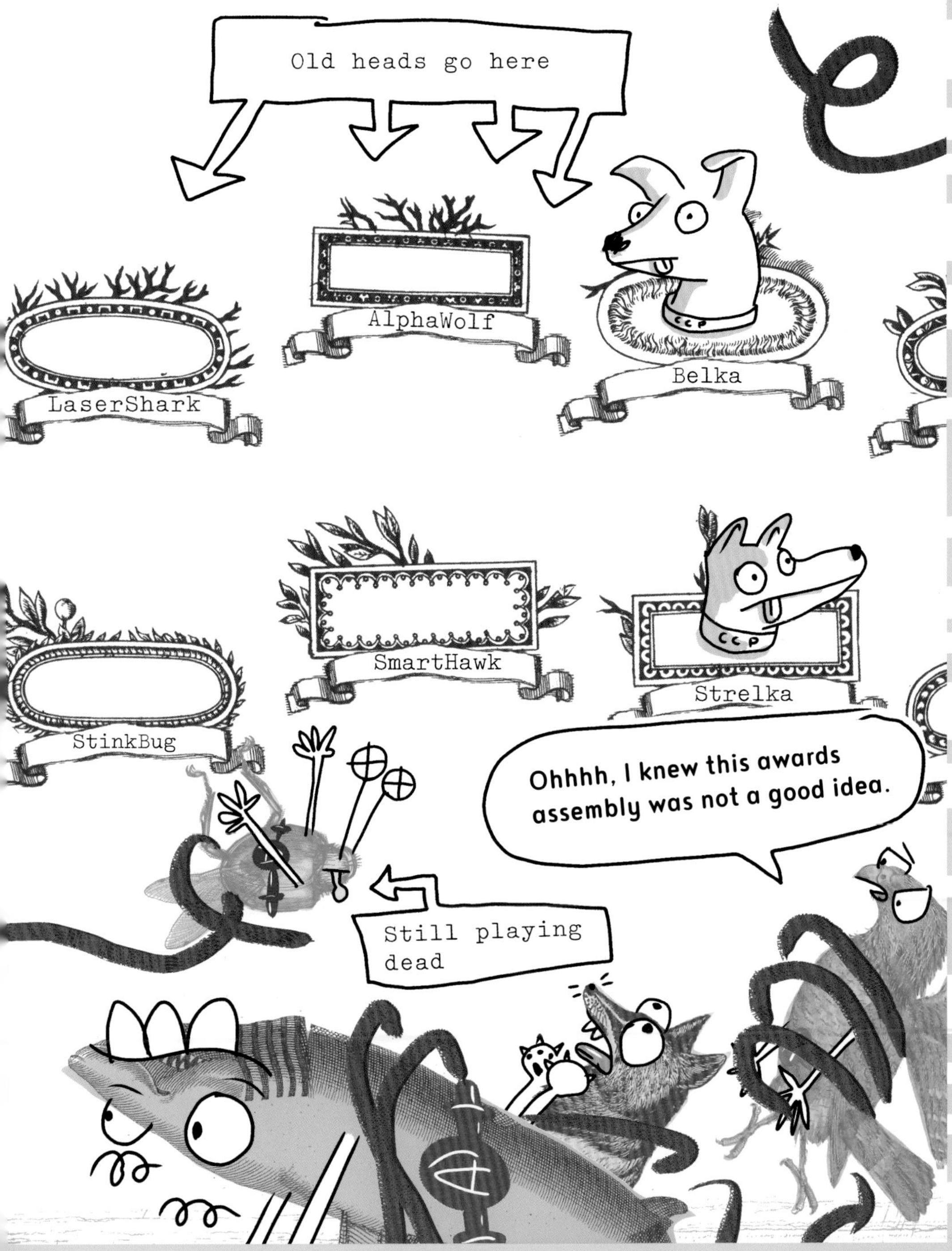
Old heads go here
AlphaWolf
Belka
LaserShark
SmartHawk
Strelka
StinkBug
Ohhhh, I knew this awards assembly was not a good idea.
Still playing dead

CHAPTER 23:
Clipped

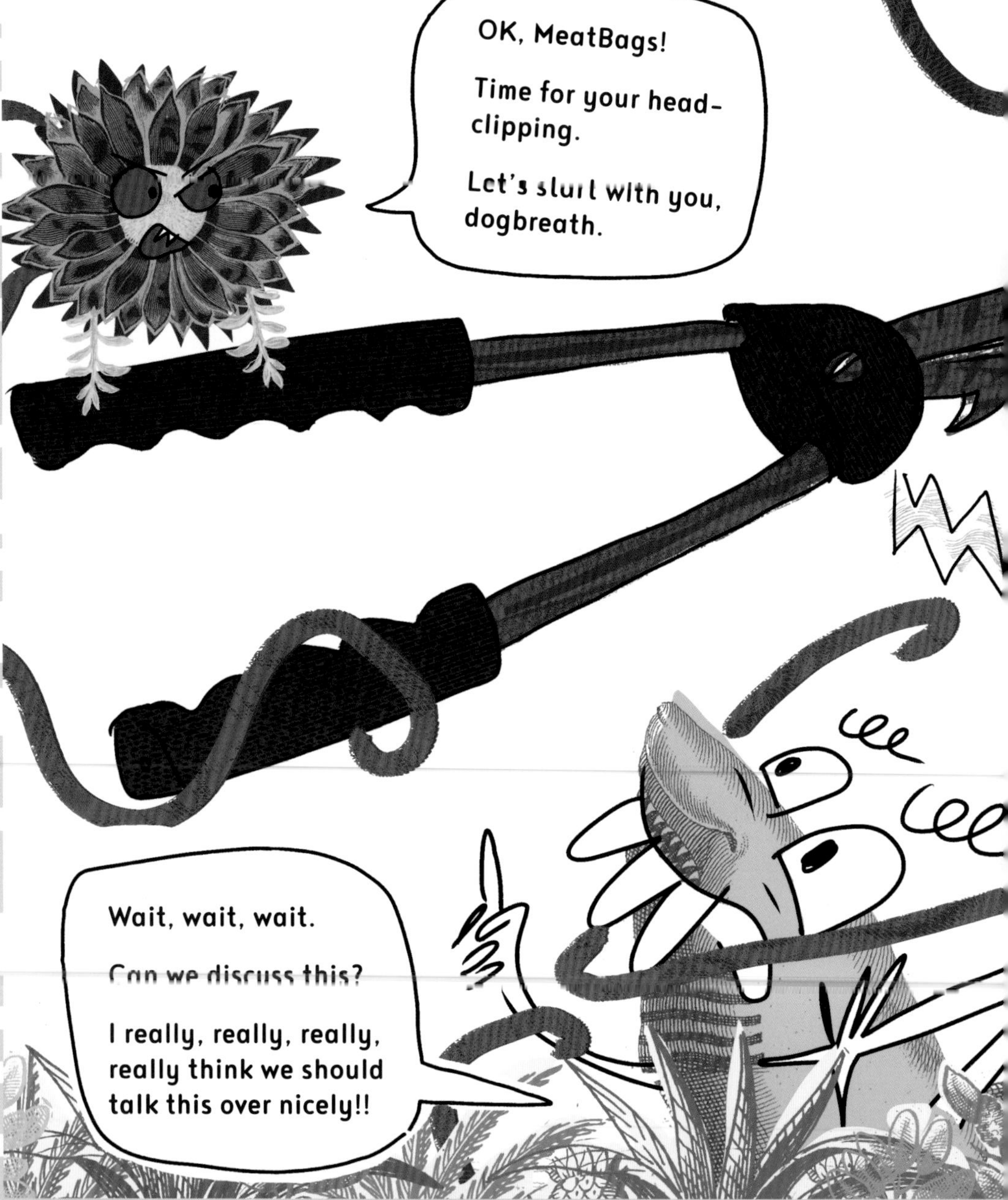
OK, MeatBags!
Time for your head-clipping.
Let's start with you, dogbreath.
Wait, wait, wait.
Can we discuss this?
I really, really, really, really think we should talk this over nicely!!

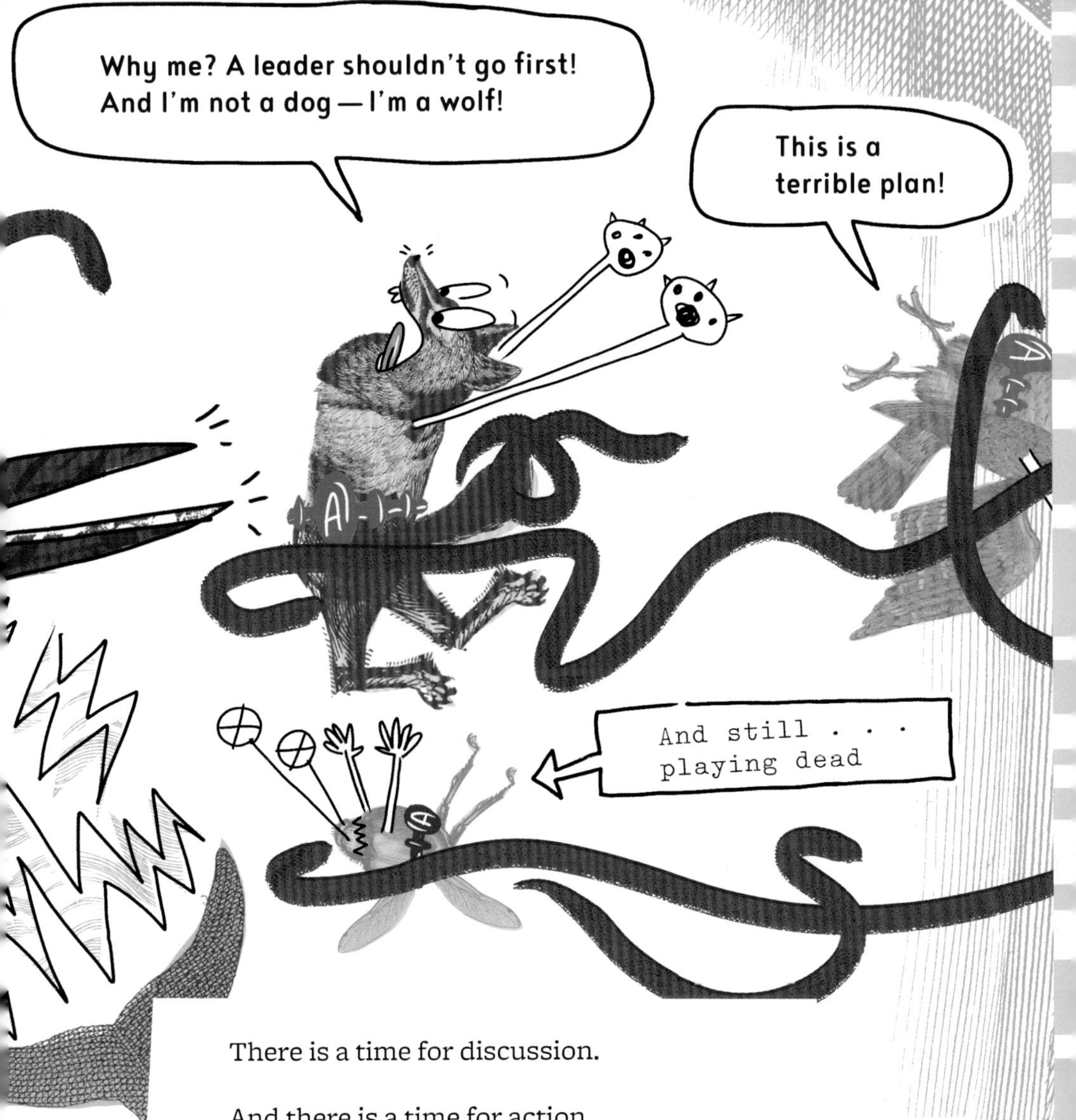
Why me? A leader shouldn't go first! And I'm not a dog — I'm a wolf!
This is a terrible plan!
And still . . . playing dead

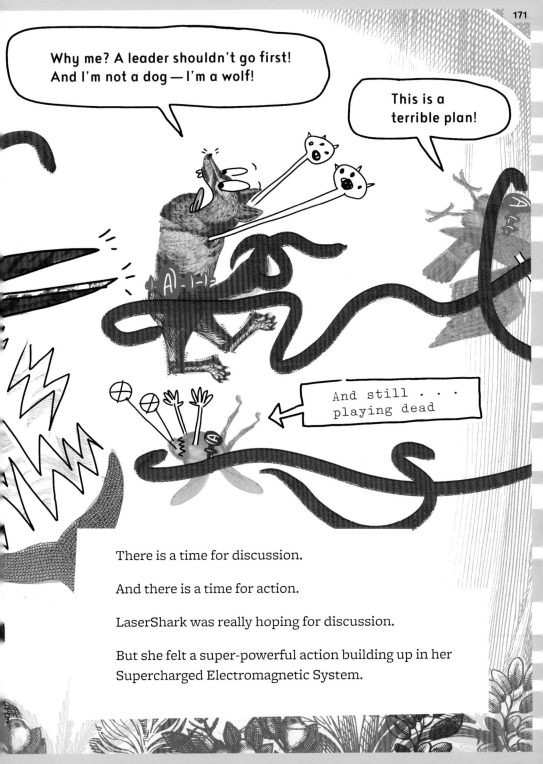

There is a time for discussion.

And there is a time for action.

LaserShark was really hoping for discussion.

But she felt a super-powerful action building up in her Supercharged Electromagnetic System.

LaserShark looked out into the audience for help.

She was faced with a super-powerful bunch of super-angry plants. It was enough to scare even me. And I have some pretty angry plant life of my own. Like Nettles. And Nightshade. And Jumping Cholla.

LaserShark took a deep breath.

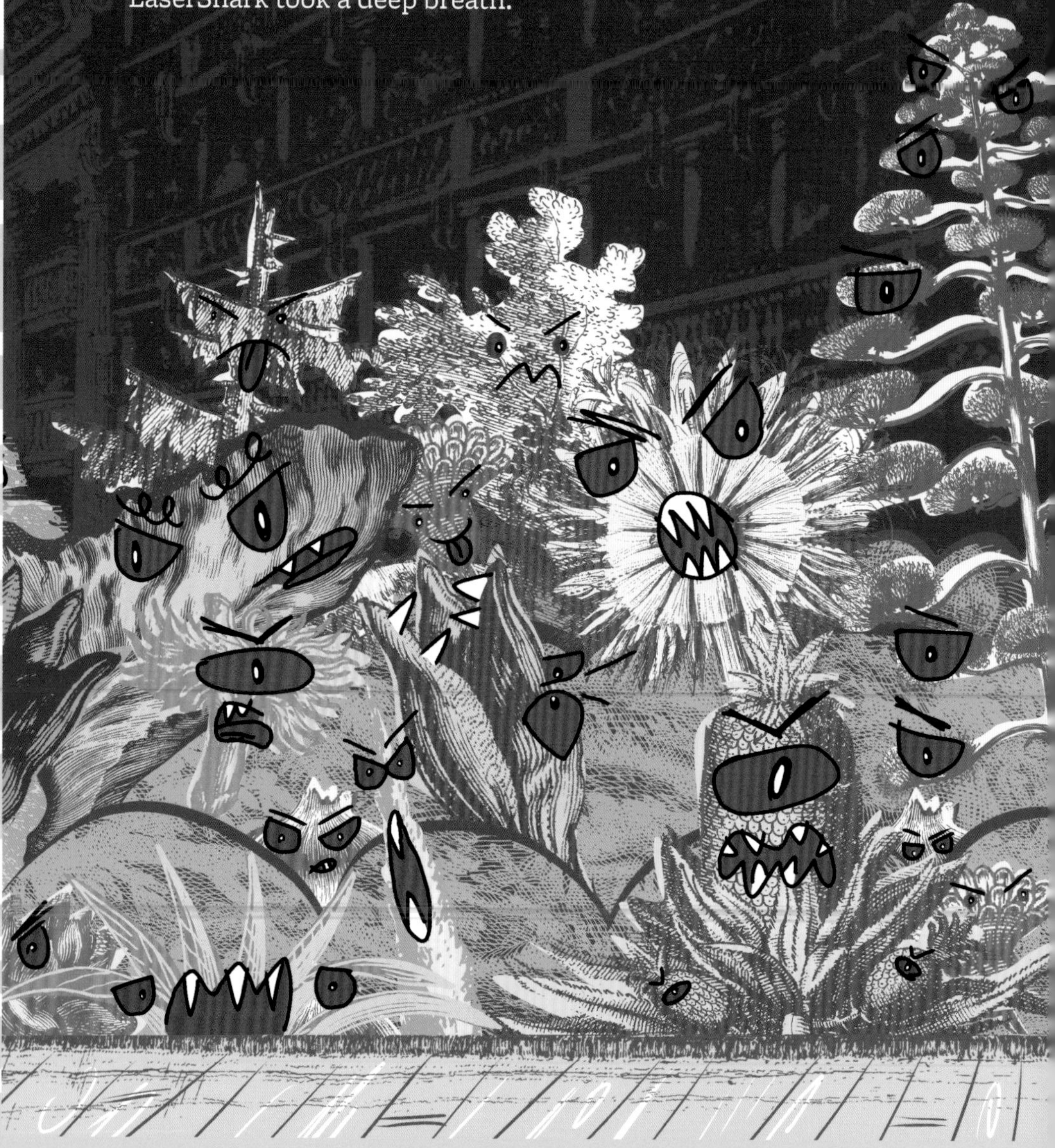

She tried her best to calm down and keep her laser bolts to herself.

She really did.

But when Supreme Leader Daisy started to count down, LaserShark thought about her dear friend AlphaWolf about to lose his overinflated head.

And LaserShark completely, electromagnetically lost it.

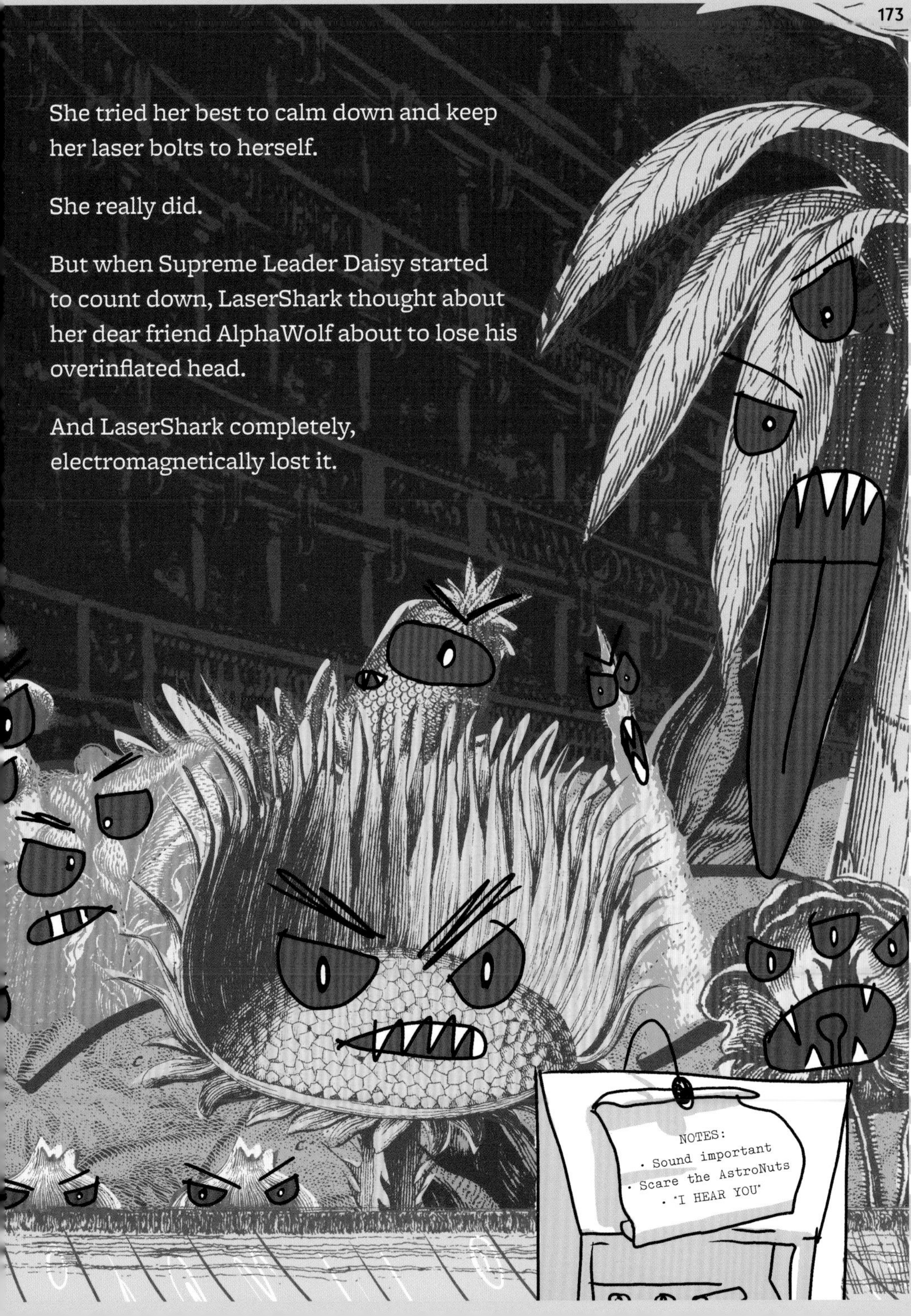
NOTES:
· Sound important
· Scare the AstroNuts
· "I HEAR YOU"

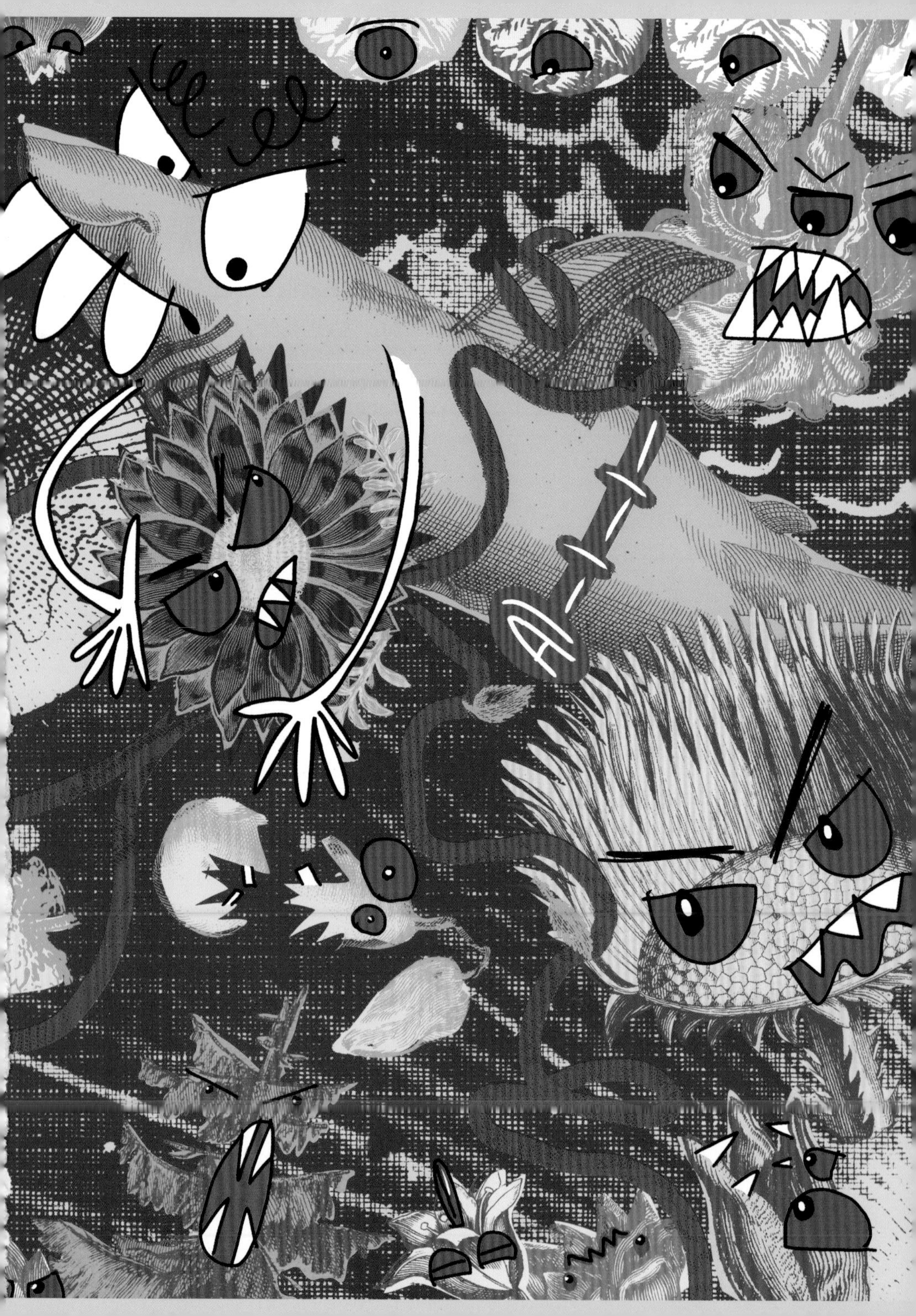

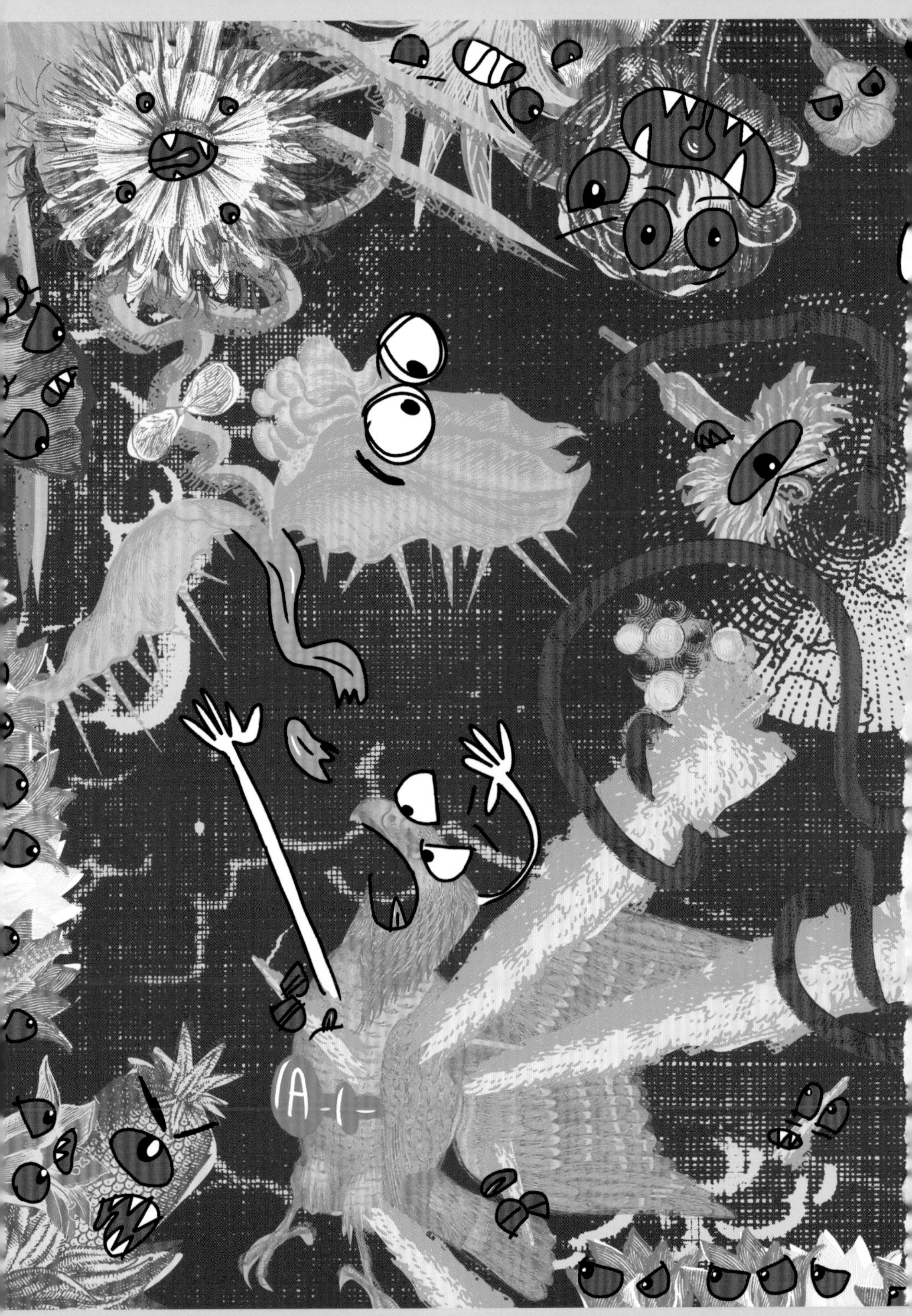

LaserShark zapped. The Headge Clipper dropped. A swarm of angry plants charged the stage to save their leader.

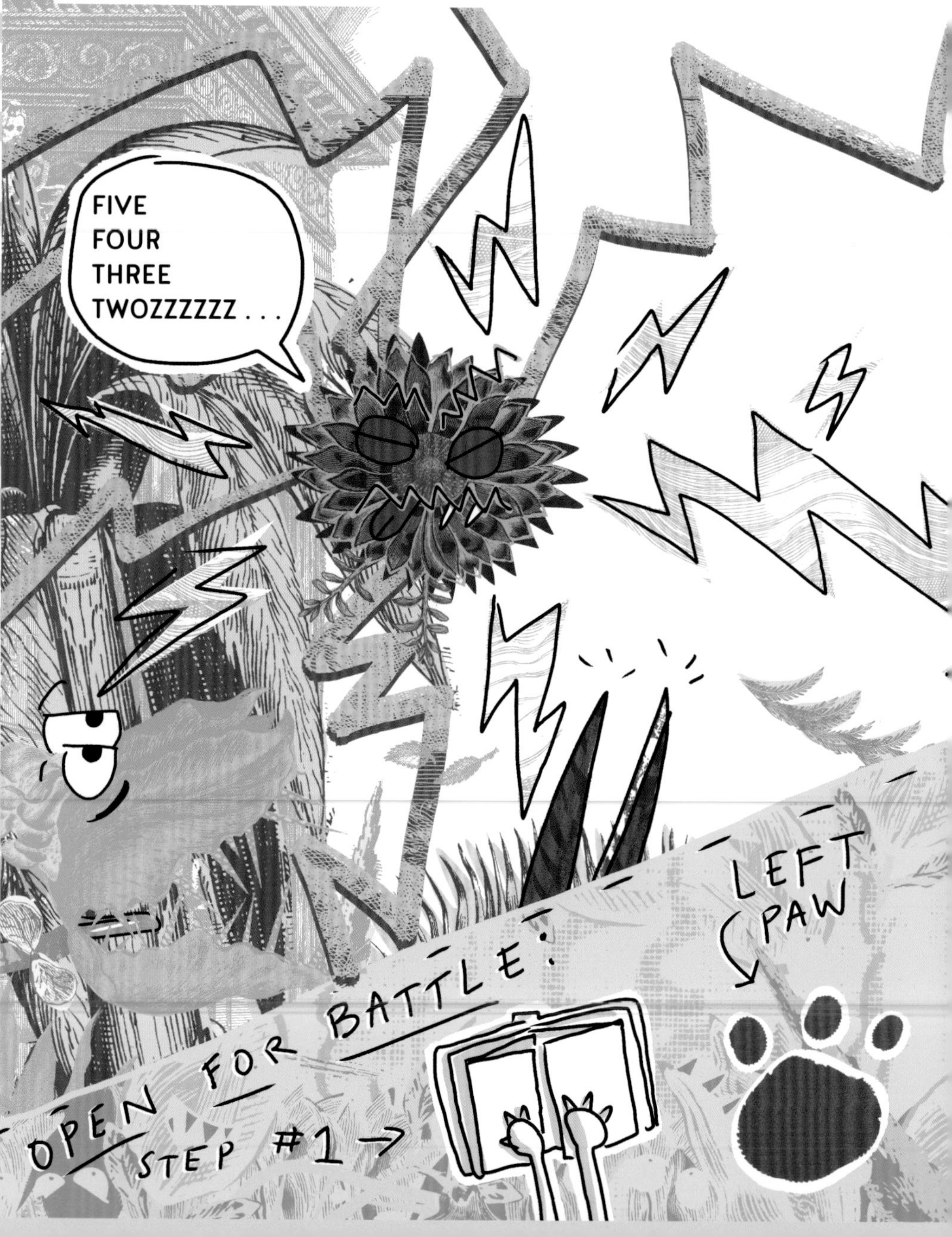
FIVE
FOUR
THREE
TWOZZZZZZ . . .
OPEN FOR BATTLE:
STEP #1 →
LEFT PAW

And the whole awards assembly turned into the BIGGEST BATTLE I HAVE EVER SEEN. (And I have seen them all.)

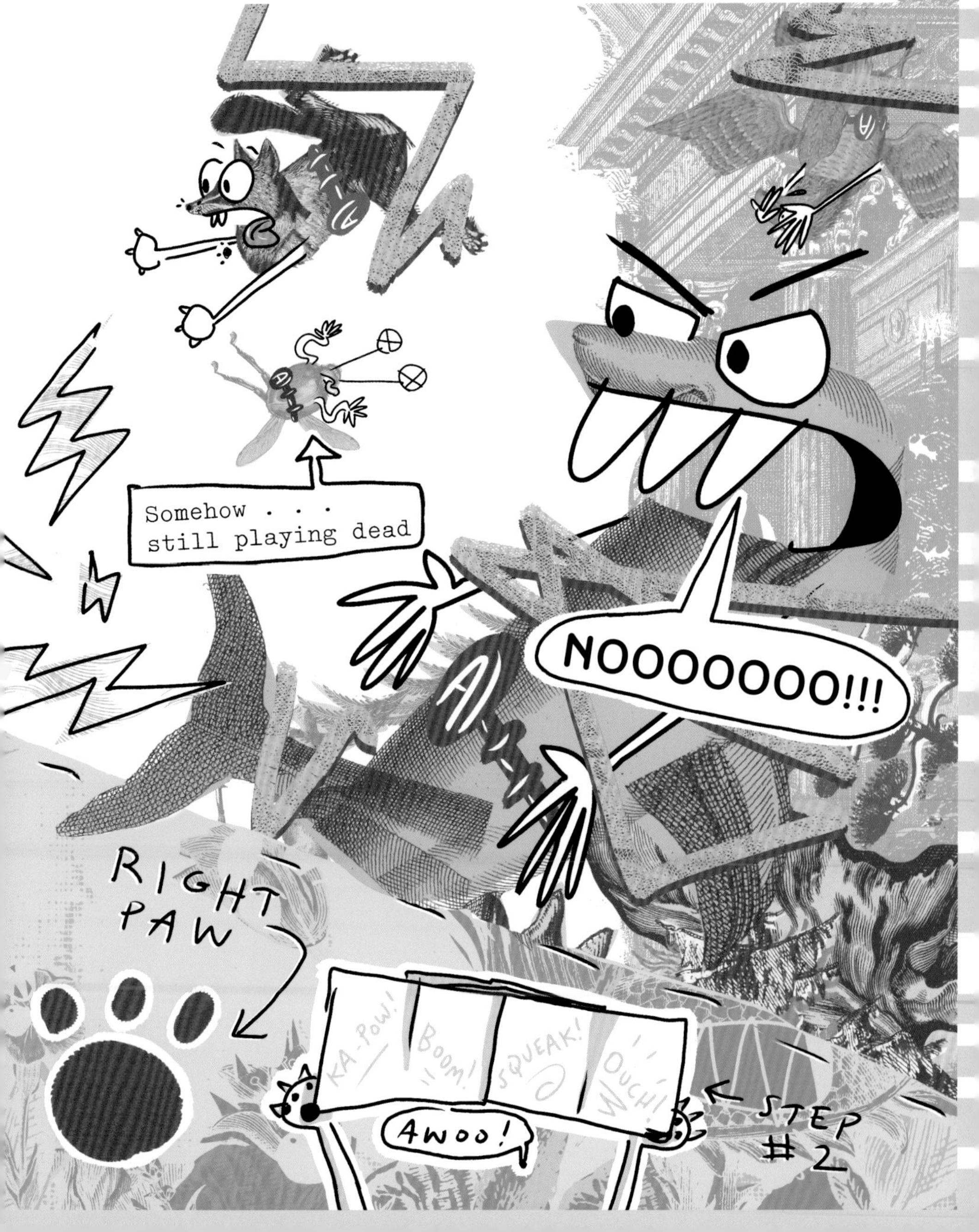

Somehow . . .
still playing dead
NOOOOOOOO!!!
RIGHT PAW
KA-POW!
BOOM!
SQUEAK!
OUCH!
AWOO!
STEP #2

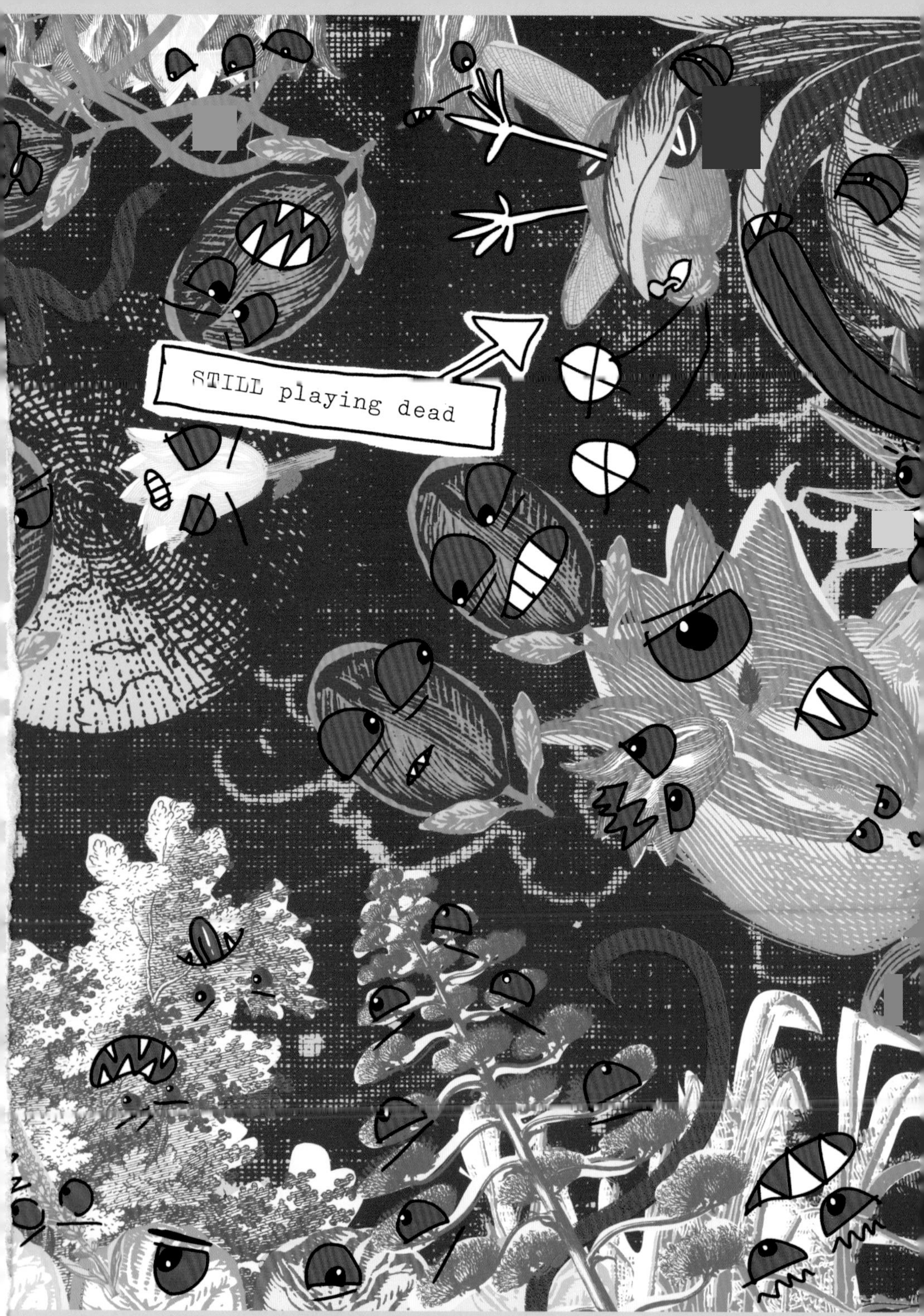
STILL playing dead

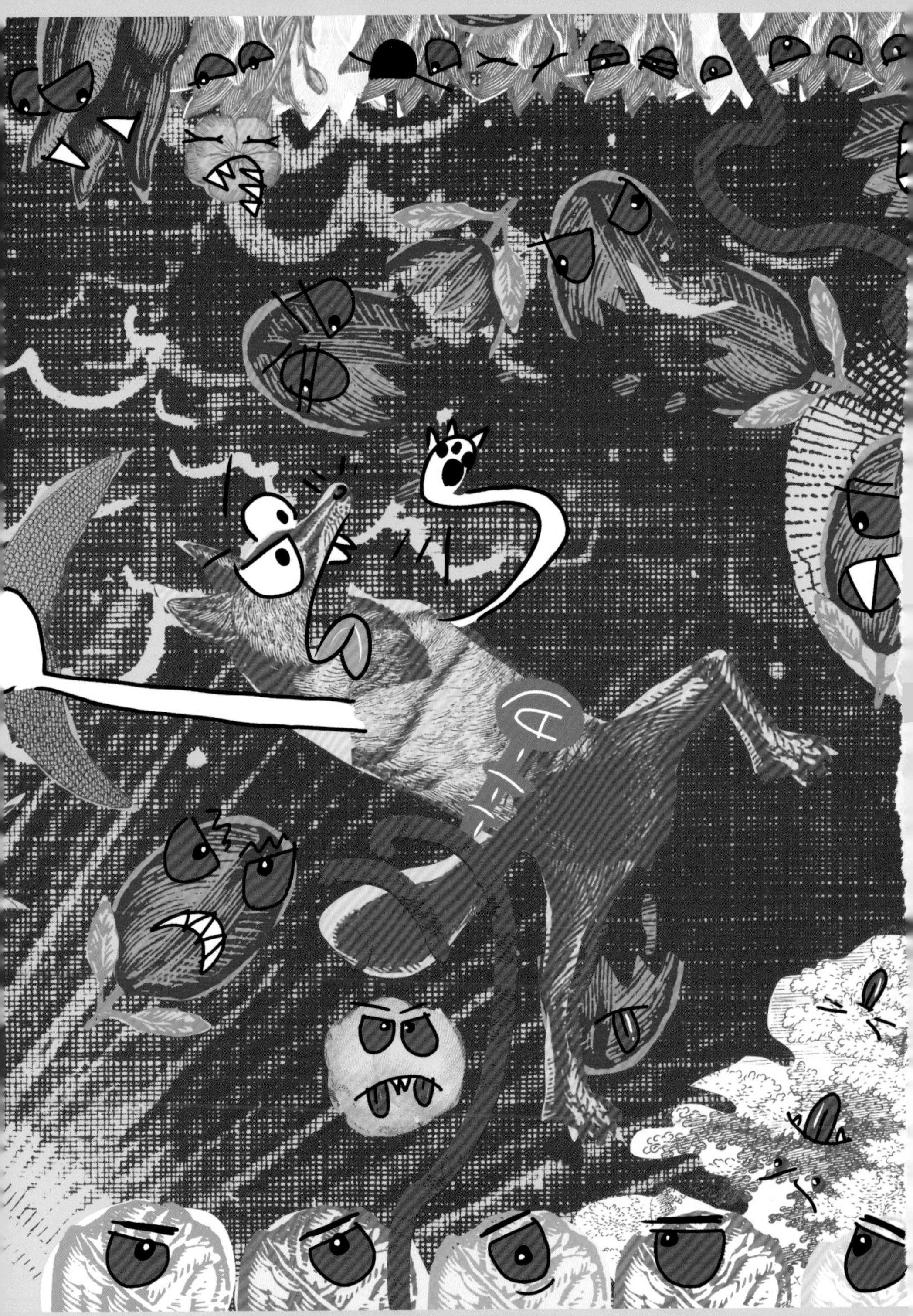

The fight went long. The fight went hard. The fight went back and forth.

Our brave AstroNuts, fighting against the entire Plant Planet, almost escaped five separate times.

Almost.

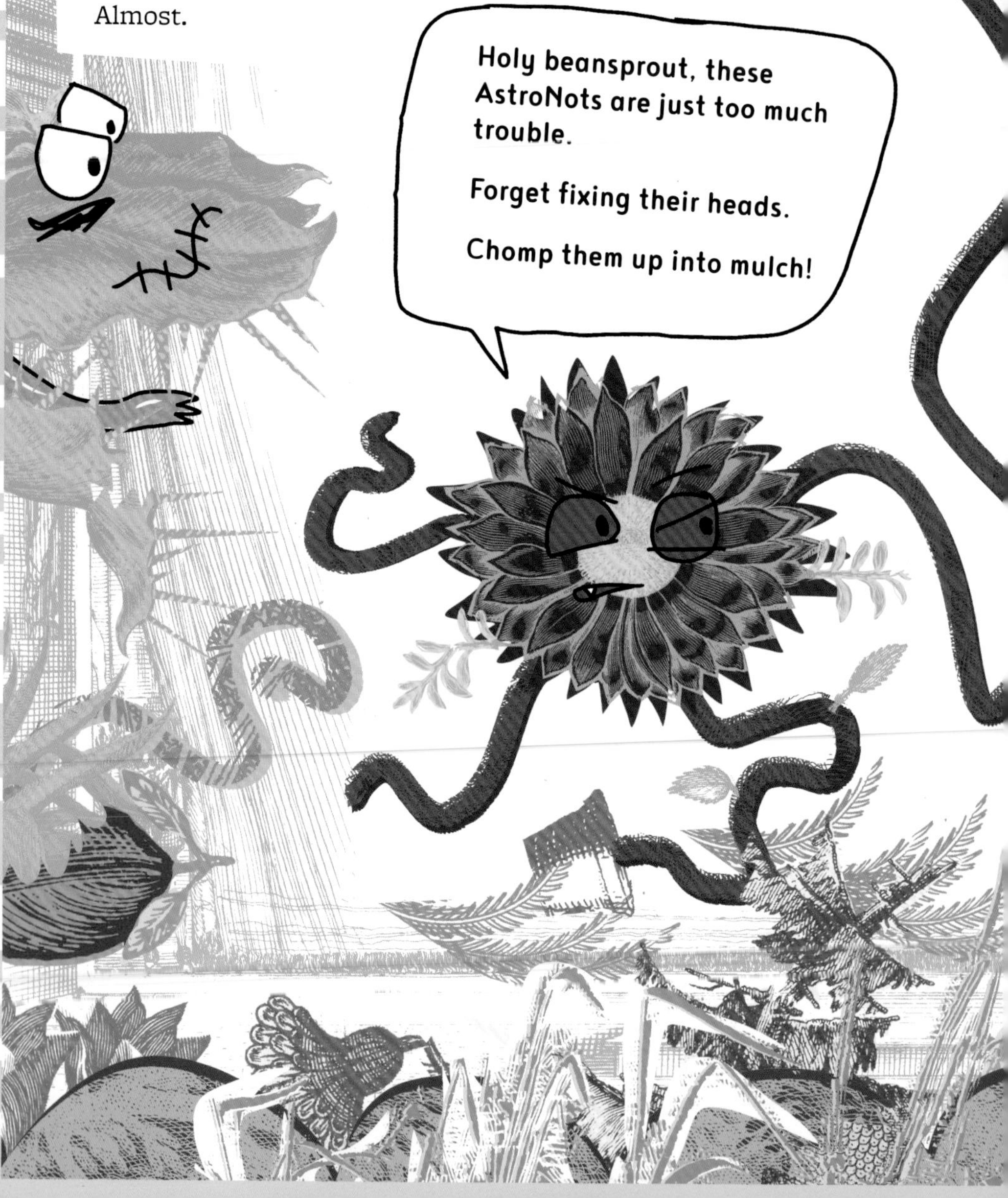
Holy beansprout, these AstroNots are just too much trouble.
Forget fixing their heads.
Chomp them up into mulch!

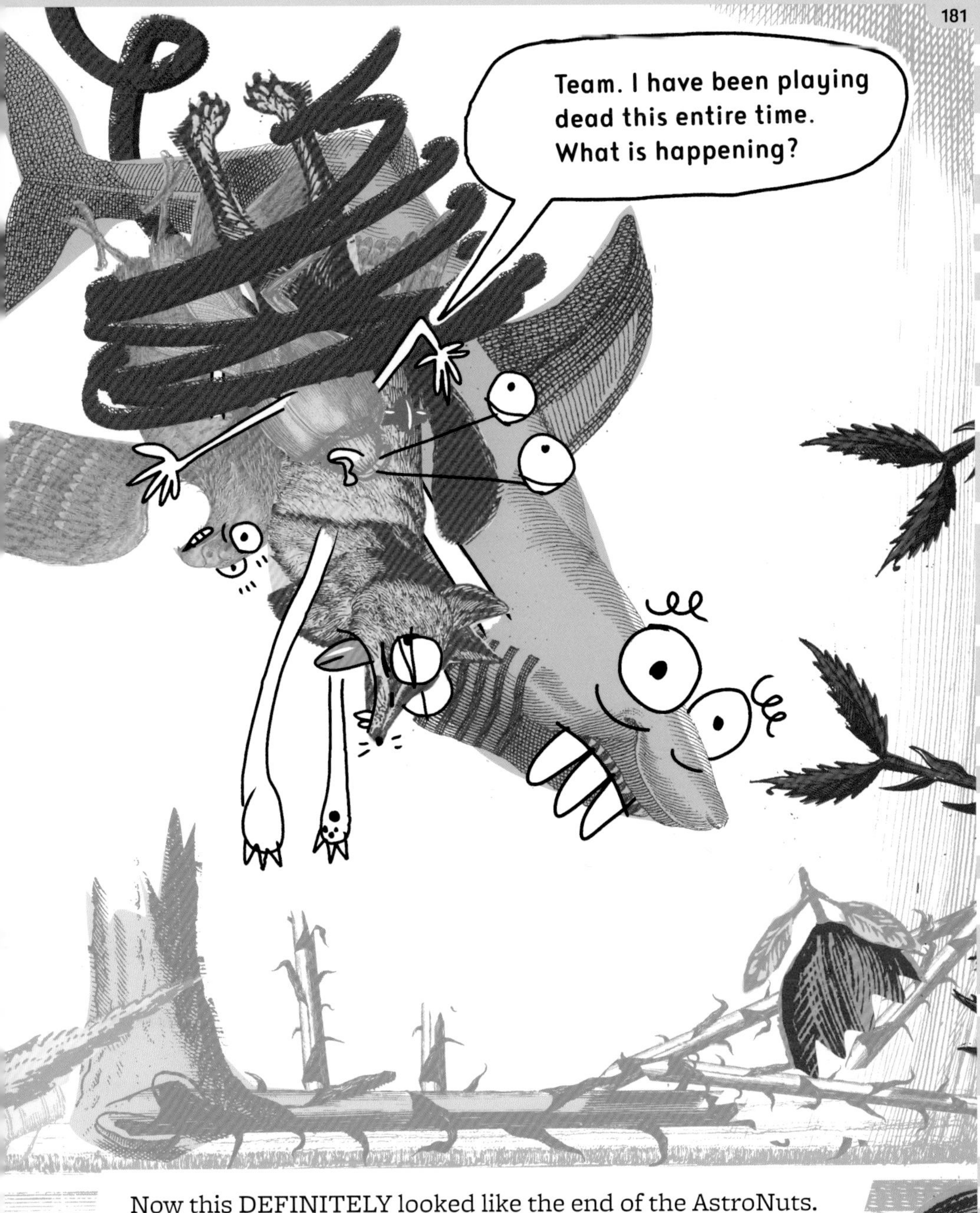
Team. I have been playing dead this entire time. What is happening?

Now this DEFINITELY looked like the end of the AstroNuts.

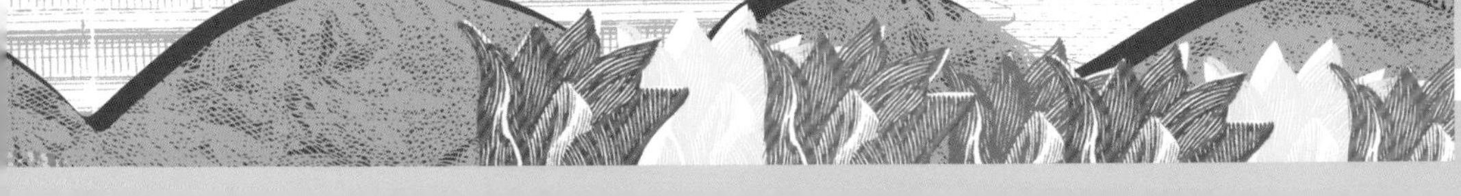

CHAPTER 24:
Never Give Up

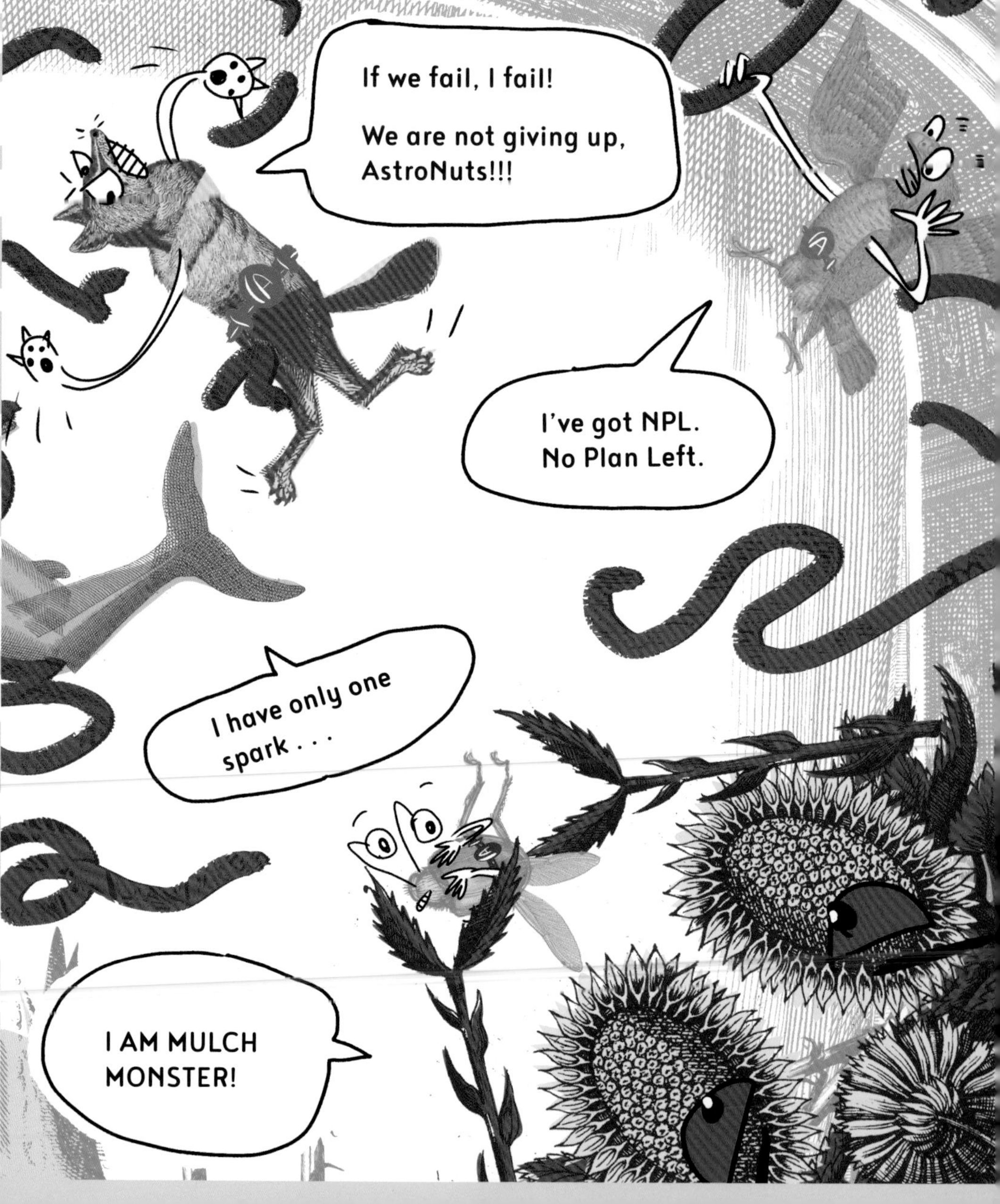

If we fail, I fail!
We are not giving up, AstroNuts!!!
I've got NPL. No Plan Left.
I have only one spark . . .
I AM MULCH MONSTER!

AlphaWolf's REAL-STRONG-IUM claws were dull. SmartHawk's Dark Energy Tornadoes were spent. LaserShark was down to her last spark.

And StinkBug, unfortunately for everyone, was getting seriously shaken.

And you know what happens when StinkBug gets shaken. Wait. What? You don't know what happens?

Good heavens! Listen up.

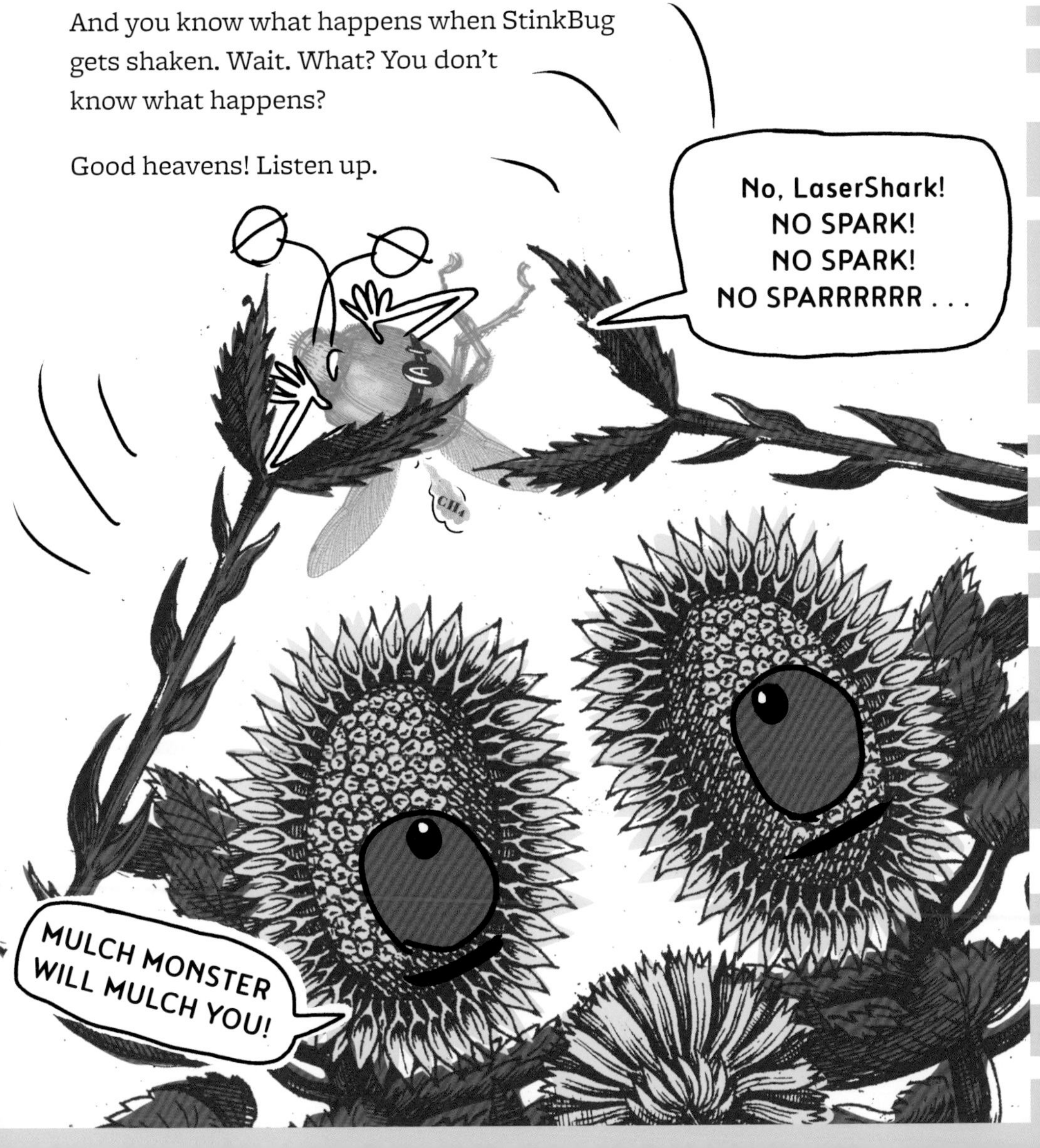
No, LaserShark!
NO SPARK!
NO SPARK!
NO SPARRRRRR . . .
MULCH MONSTER WILL MULCH YOU!

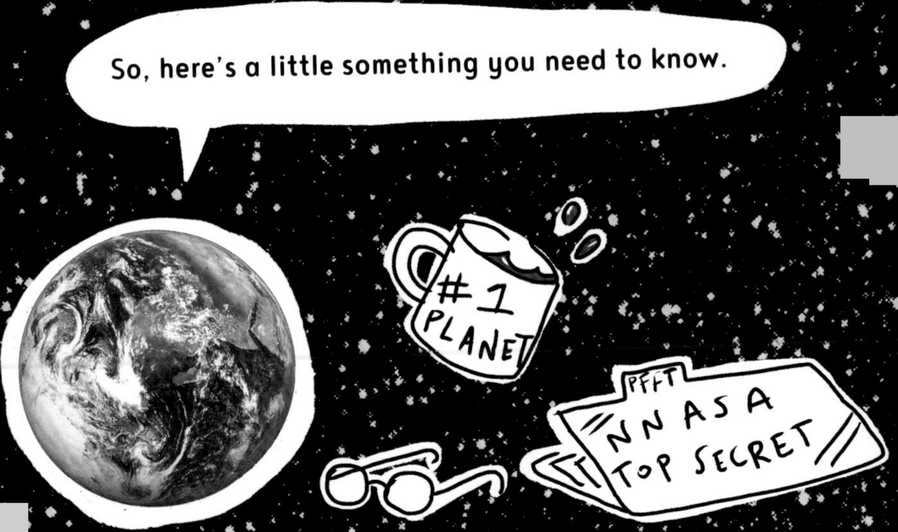
So, here's a little something you need to know.
#1 PLANET
PFFT
NNASA TOP SECRET

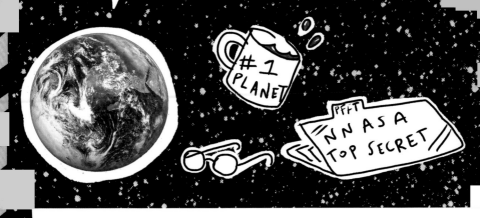

Back in 1988, when StinkBug was originally built by NNASA scientists, no one could figure out how to correct one of his design flaws:

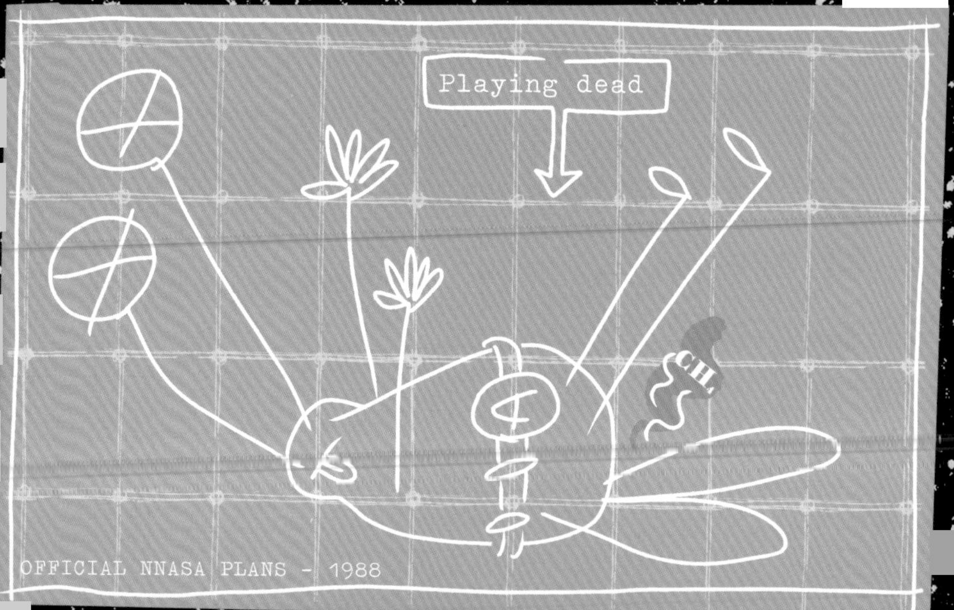
Playing dead
CH.
OFFICIAL NNASA PLANS - 1988

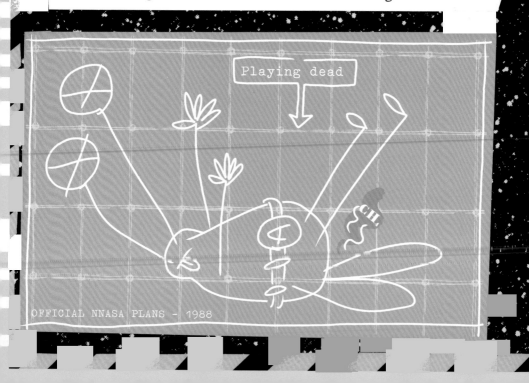

Whenever StinkBug played dead, his PFFT Gas Defense System created extra methane.

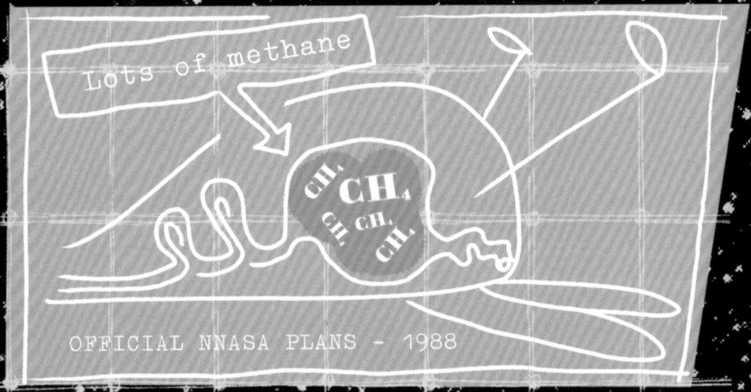
Lots of methane
CH_4
CH_4
CH_4
CH_4
CH_4
OFFICIAL NNASA PLANS - 1988

The longer he played dead, the more methane he built up. This didn't seem like such a big deal at the time, because all he had to do was shake his butt . . . to activate his Release Valve.

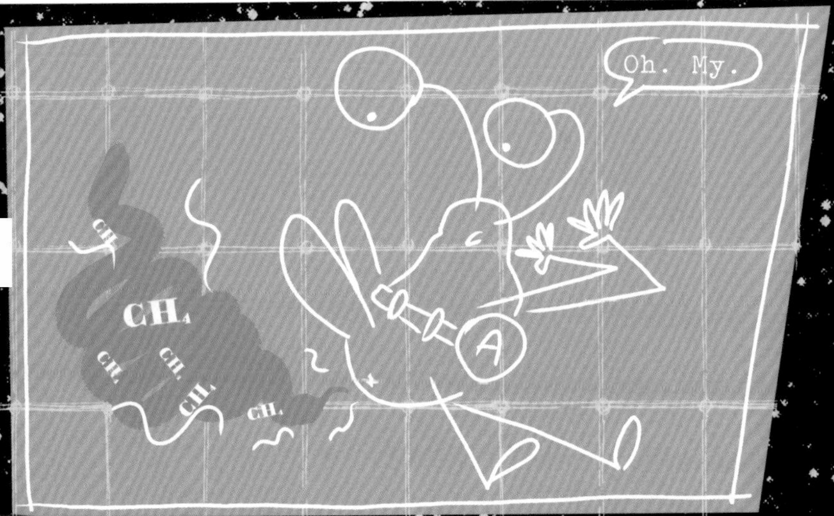
Oh. My.
CH_4
CH_4
CH_4
CH_4
CH_4
CH_4
A

The Release Valve simply blows out the extra methane to mix into my nicely balanced atmosphere.

Harmlessly.

Who could have ever imagined what might happen if that methane was released into an atmosphere already overloaded with oxygen and methane?

And then exposed to a Super-Electromagnetic Laser Bolt spark?

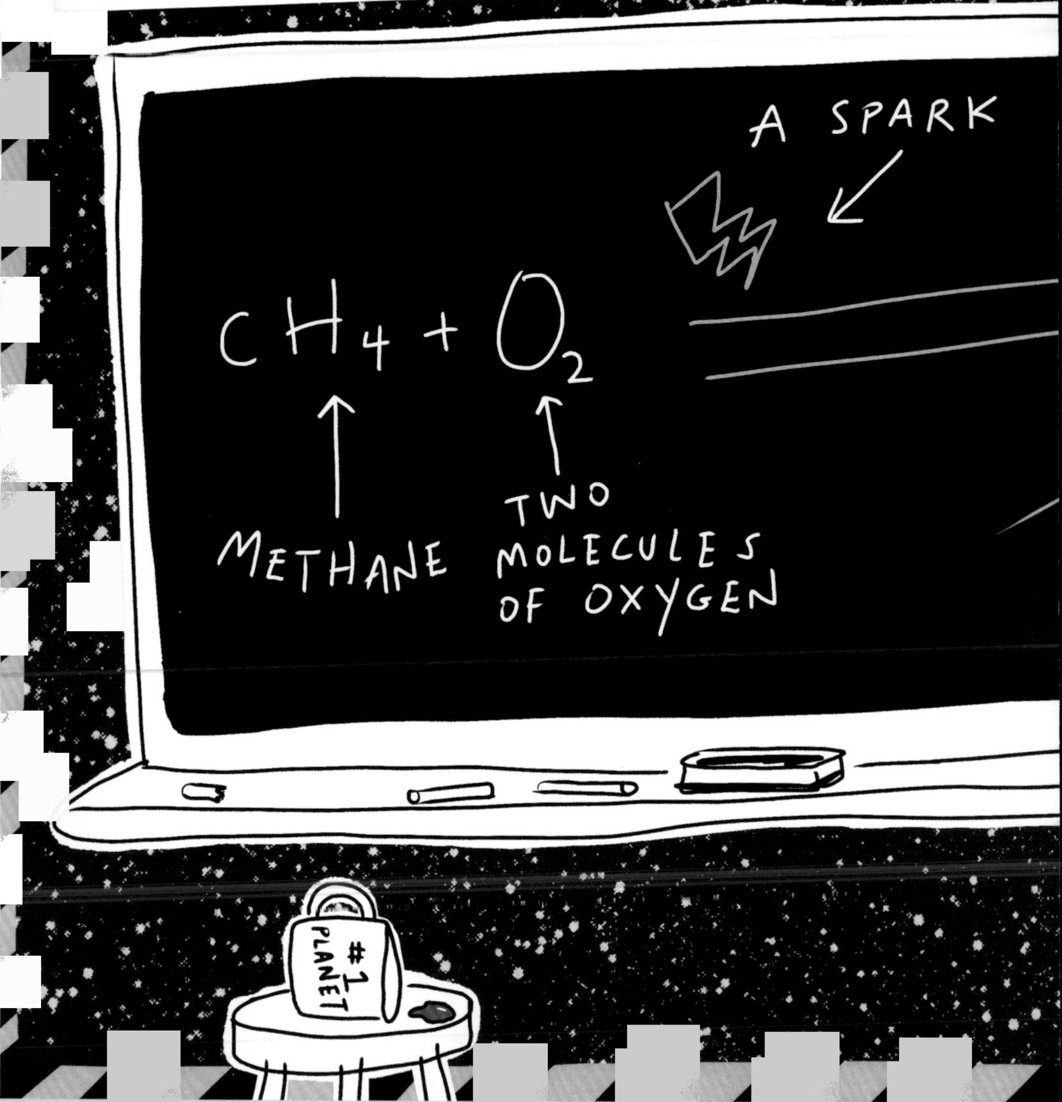
A SPARK
$CH_4 + O_2$
METHANE
TWO MOLECULES OF OXYGEN
#1 PLANET

Well, actually, that's some pretty basic chemistry.

We know exactly what happens.

The chemical equation looks like this:

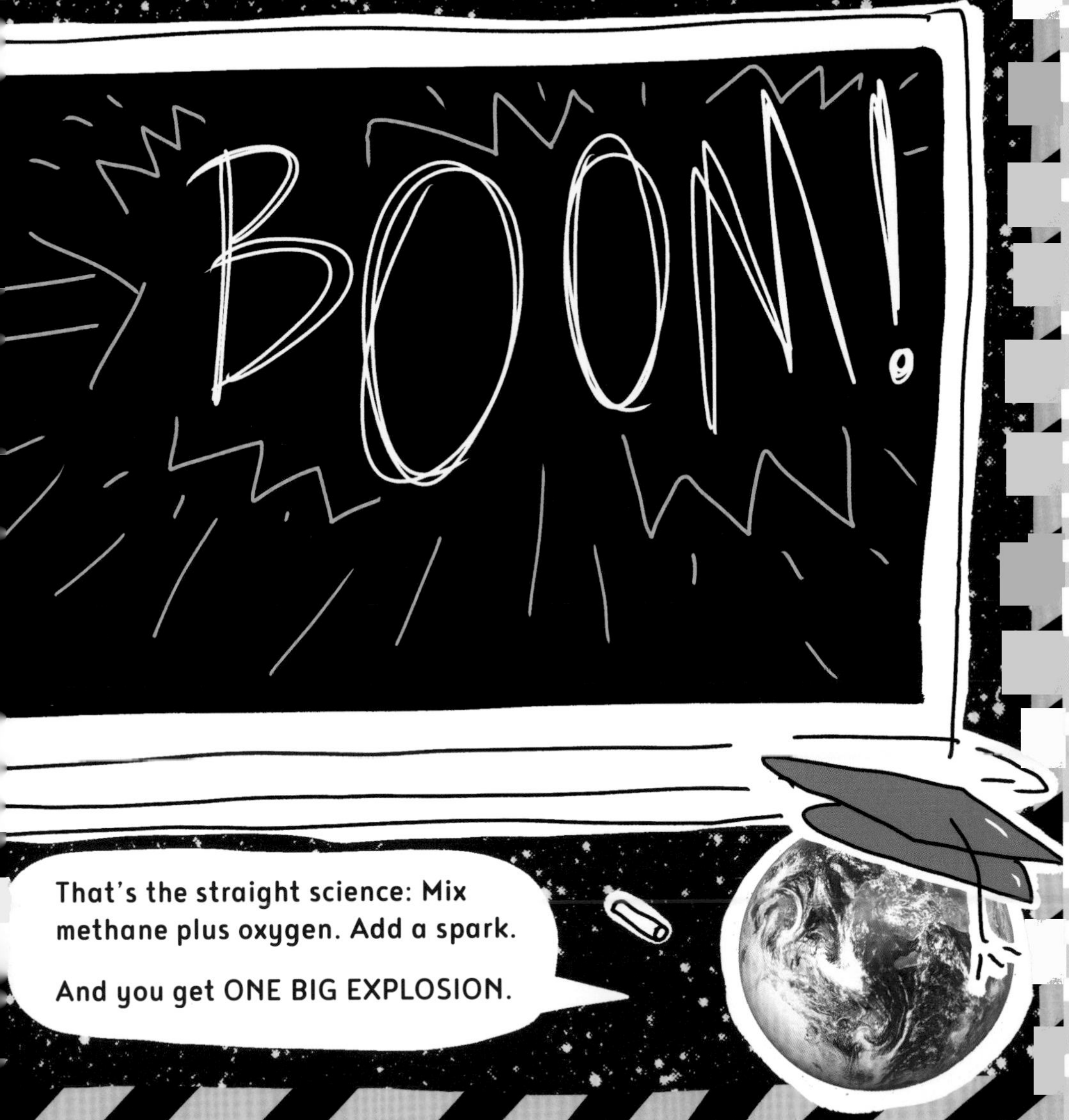
BOOM!
That's the straight science: Mix methane plus oxygen. Add a spark.
And you get ONE BIG EXPLOSION.

And that, dear humans,
is precisely what happened on the Plant Planet.

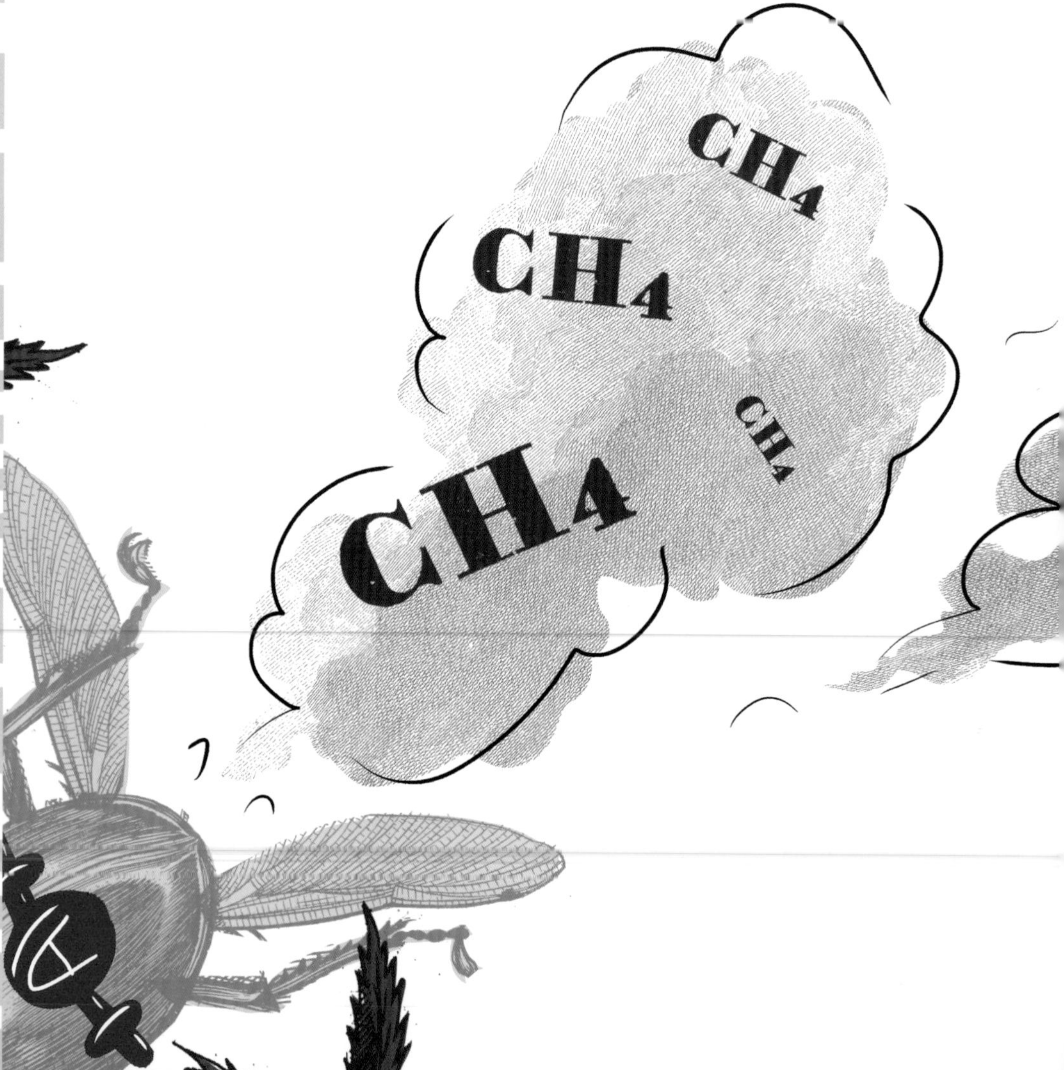
CH4
CH4
CH4
CH4

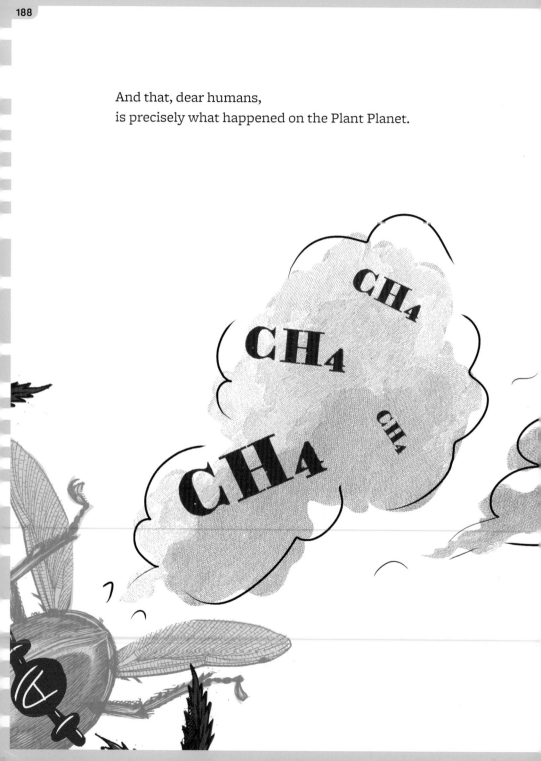

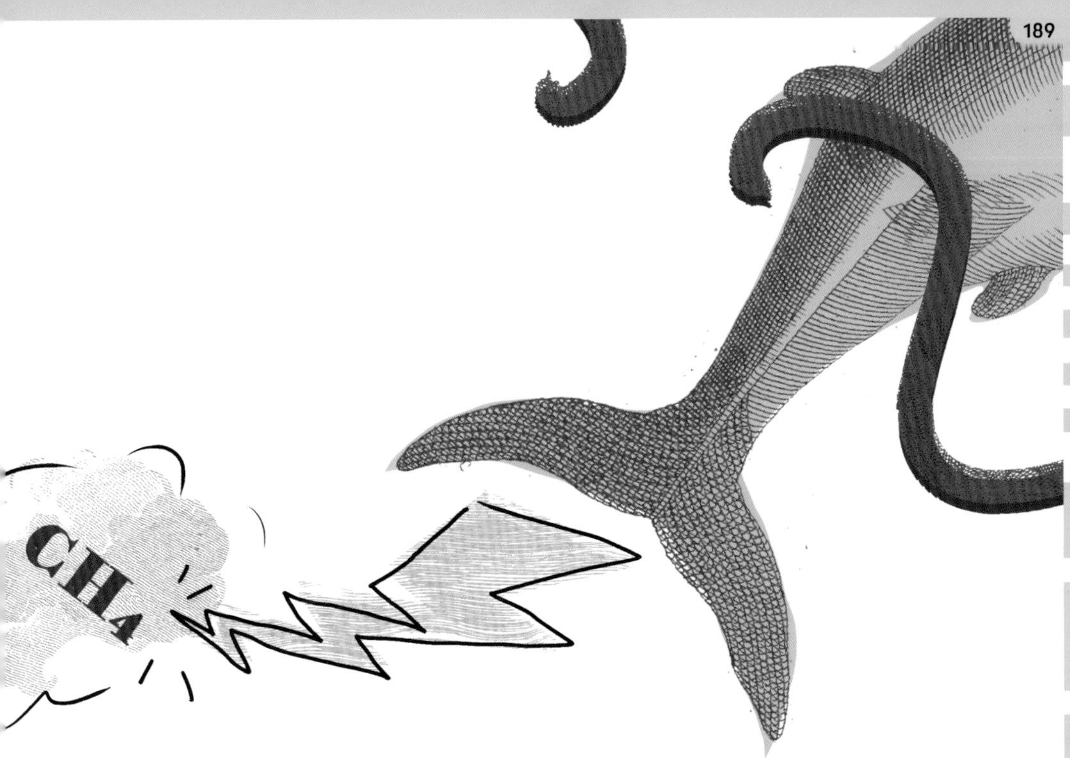
CH_4

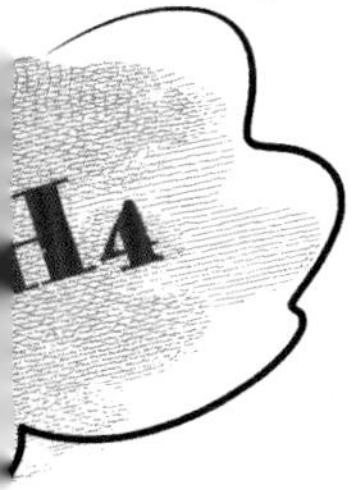
H_4

After playing dead for half of Daisy's speech and the whole crazy AstroNut vs. Plant Battle, StinkBug and his faulty PFFT Gas Defense System got shaken up and released a whole lot of methane.

LaserShark sparked her one last spark.

And everything went . . .

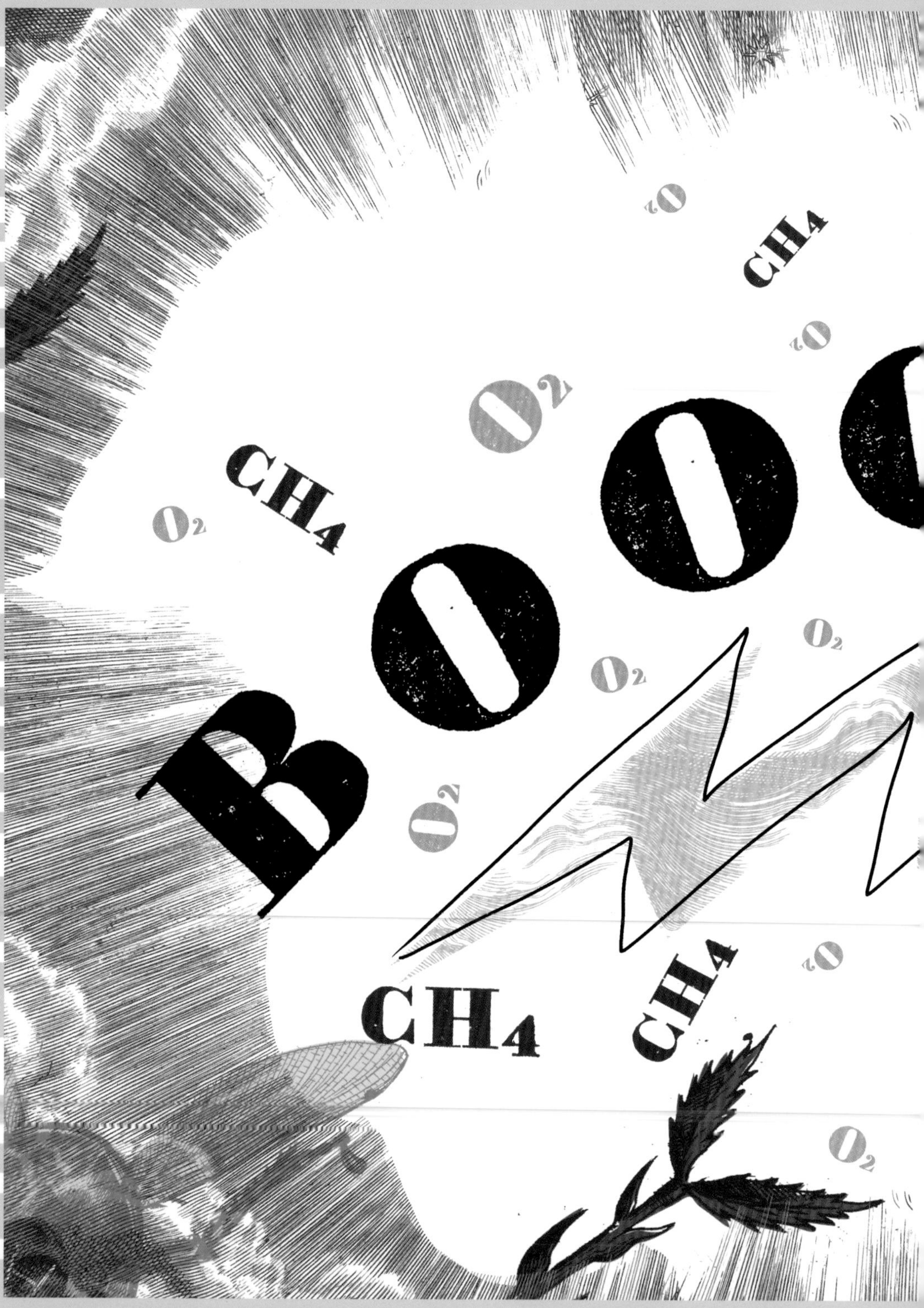

BOO
CH_4
O_2

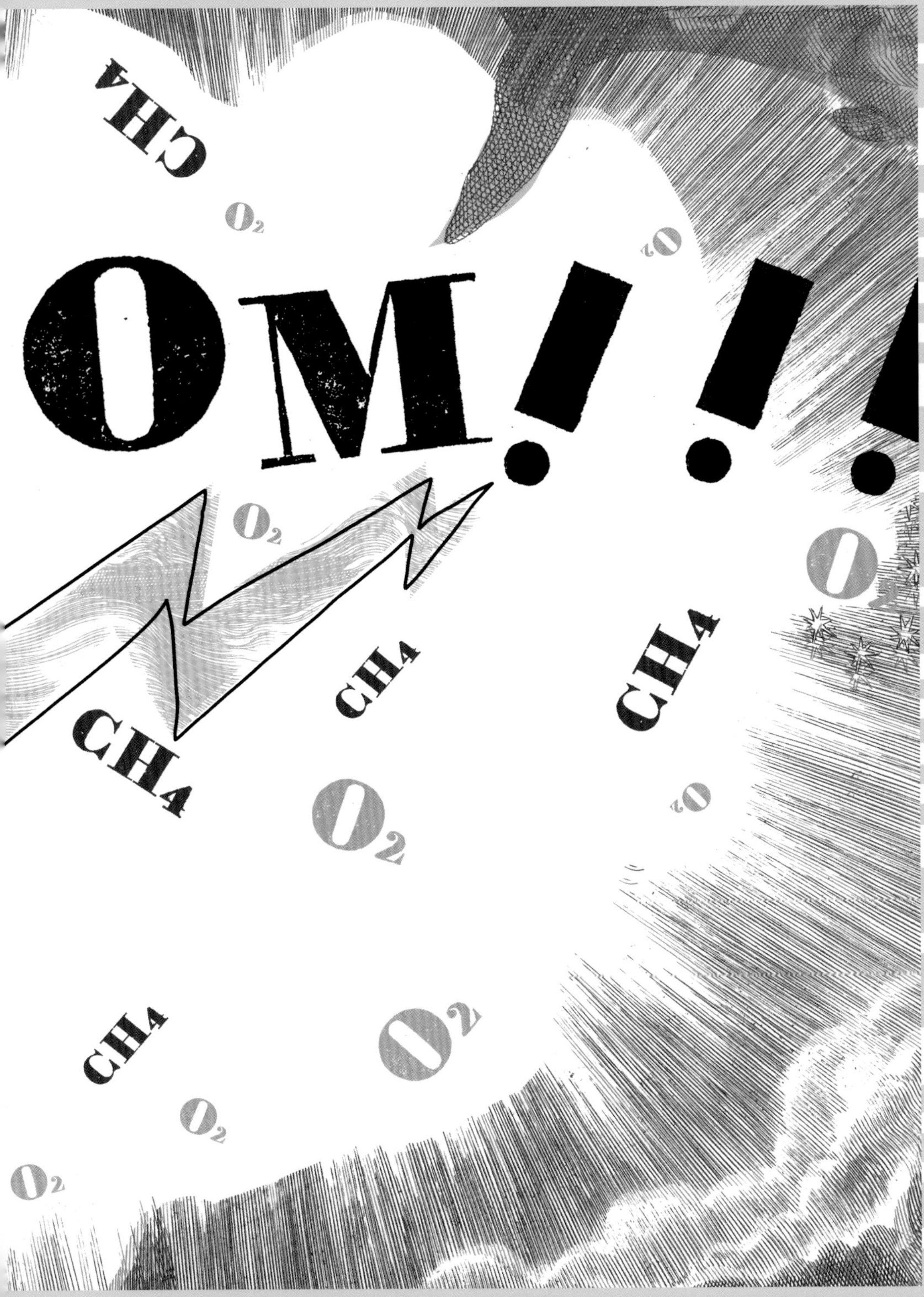

OM!!!
CH4
O2
O2
O2
O2
CH4
CH4
CH4
O2
O2
CH4
O2
O2
O2

CHAPTER 25:
THIS IS NOT A DRILL

Remember that bit I told you about balance? How it's key to a planet's survival?

Because the Plant Planet atmosphere was already so overfull of methane and oxygen, the explosion at the awards assembly also set off a chain reaction of explosions—around the entire planet.

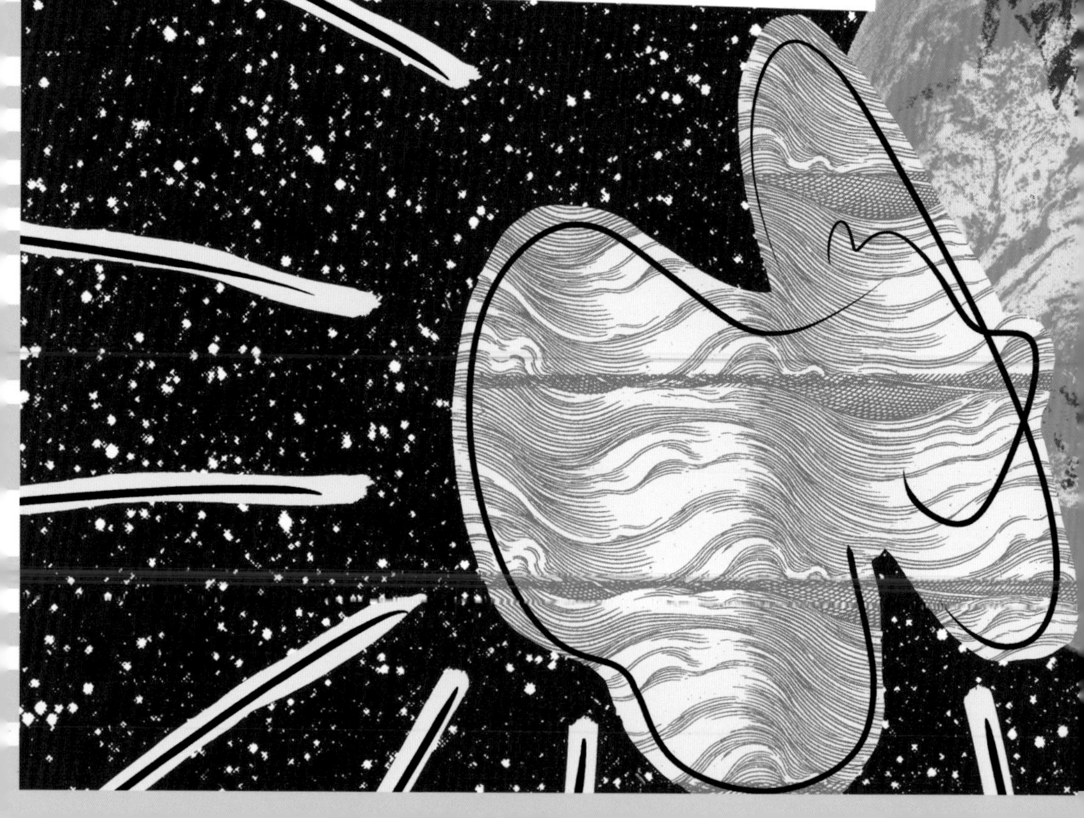

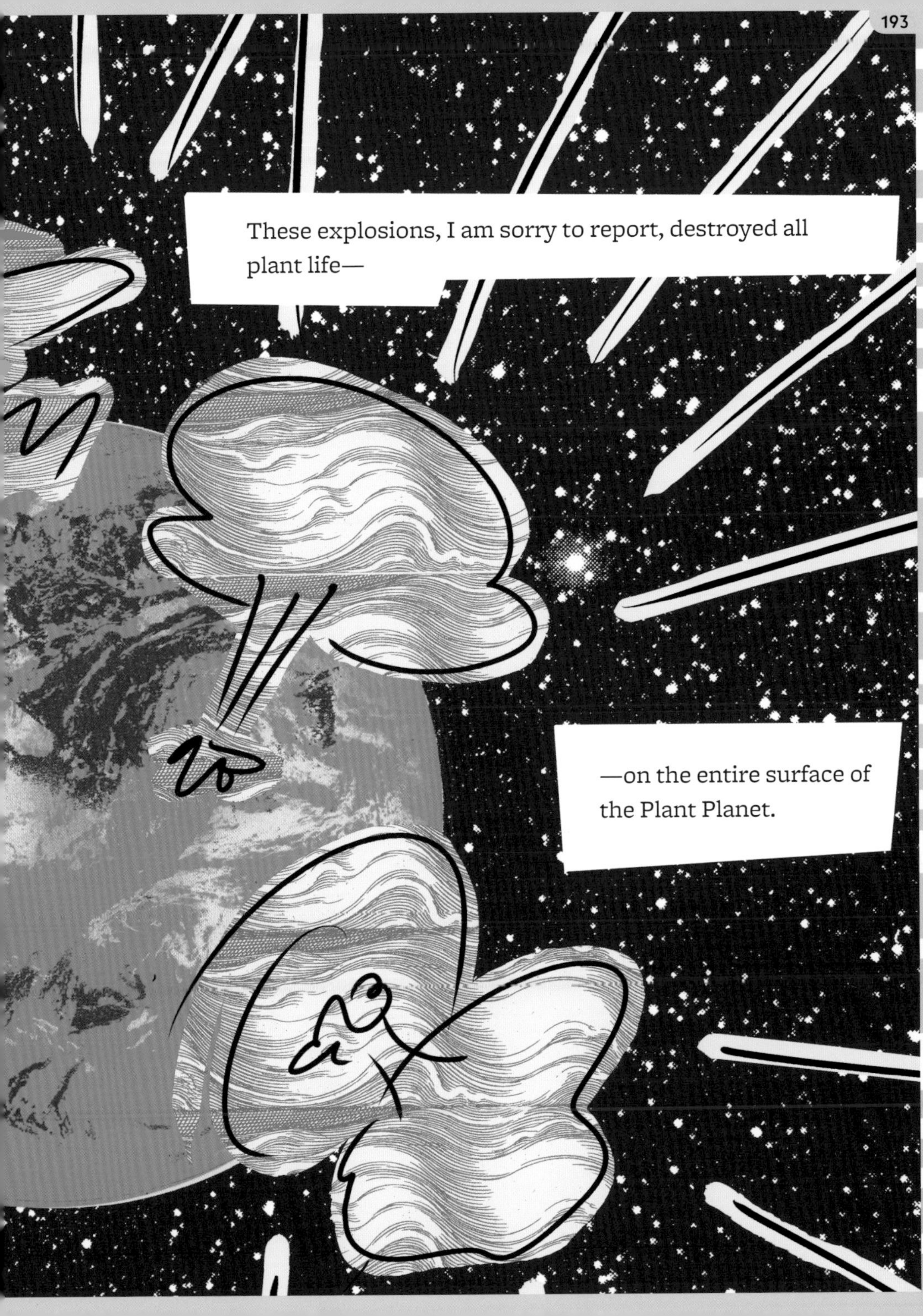
These explosions, I am sorry to report, destroyed all plant life—
—on the entire surface of the Plant Planet.

It did not, however, destroy four NNASA-designed AstroNuts.

So this Mission did not turn out the way anyone was thinking it might. From any planet's point of view, it was downright terrible.

But from *this* planet's perspective, it was also perfectly educational, because it showed the AstroNuts exactly what can happen when one species takes over a planet. Like what humans are doing on me.

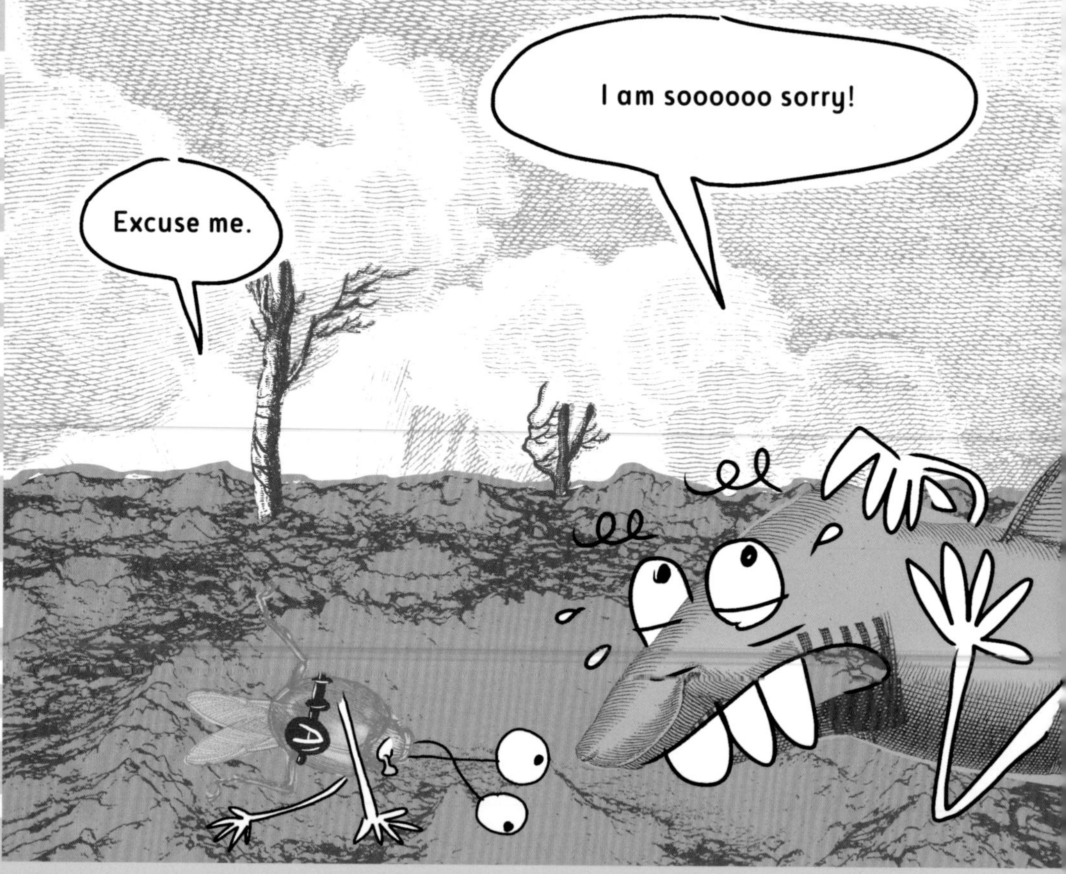
Excuse me.
I am soooooo sorry!

The AstroNuts gathered themselves together, made their way to the Thomas Jefferson Nose Rocket, and blew off for home thinking about planets—and pretty sure that they were in big trouble.

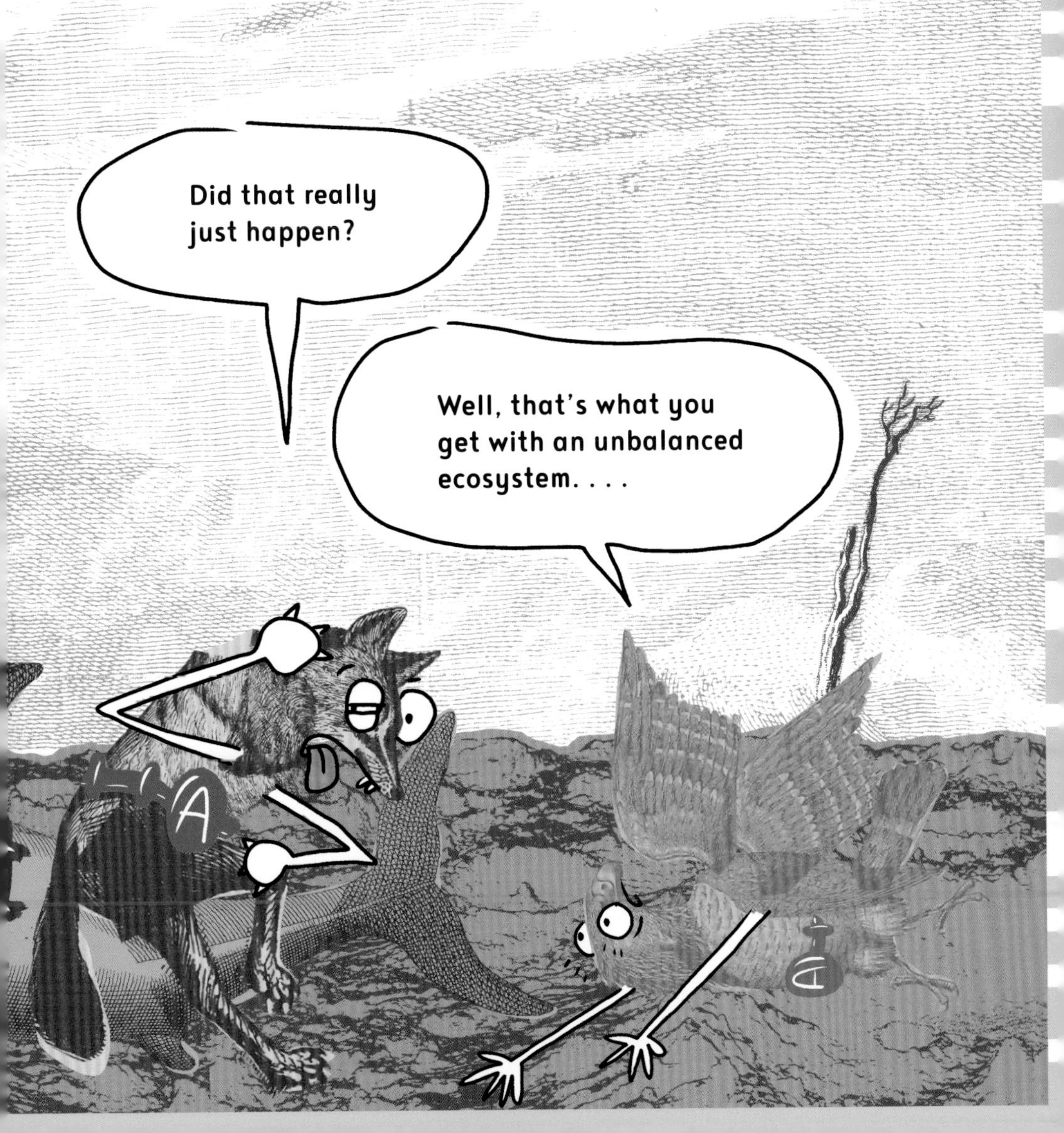
Did that really just happen?
Well, that's what you get with an unbalanced ecosystem. . . .

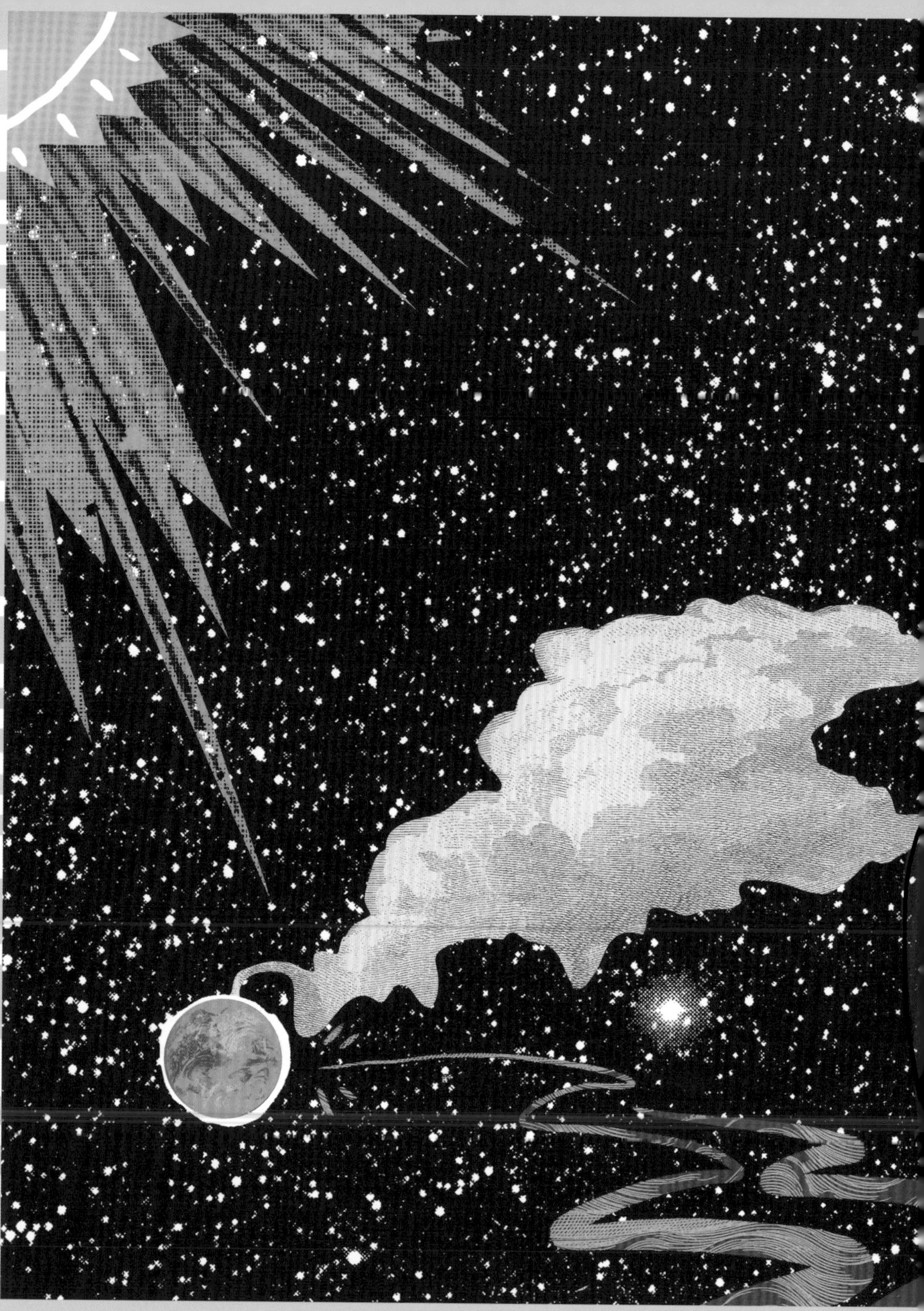

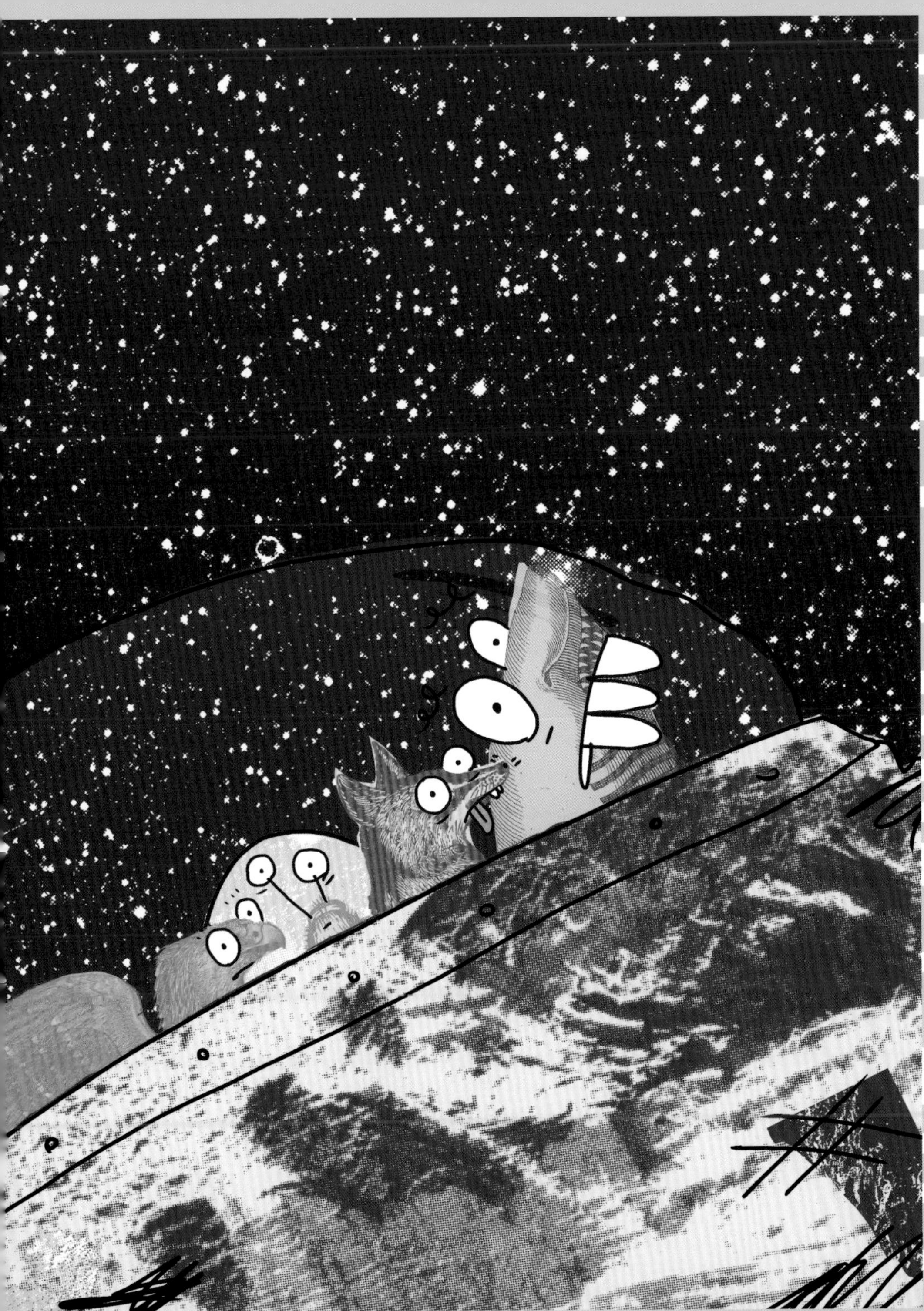

CHAPTER 26:
Go Home

In the 3 hours and 26 minutes it took to travel the 39 light-years back home, the AstroNuts had some time to think over their first mission to find a Goldilocks Planet.

And it was a lot like that time your mom told you not to swing your baseball bat inside the house because you might break something and you said no you wouldn't break anything and you had the bat in your hand so you took just a couple easy swings to show yourself how right you were that it was completely safe but then the glass lamp somehow got completely smashed and you had to decide how you were going to explain what happened.

That's how the AstroNuts were feeling when Command Escape called.

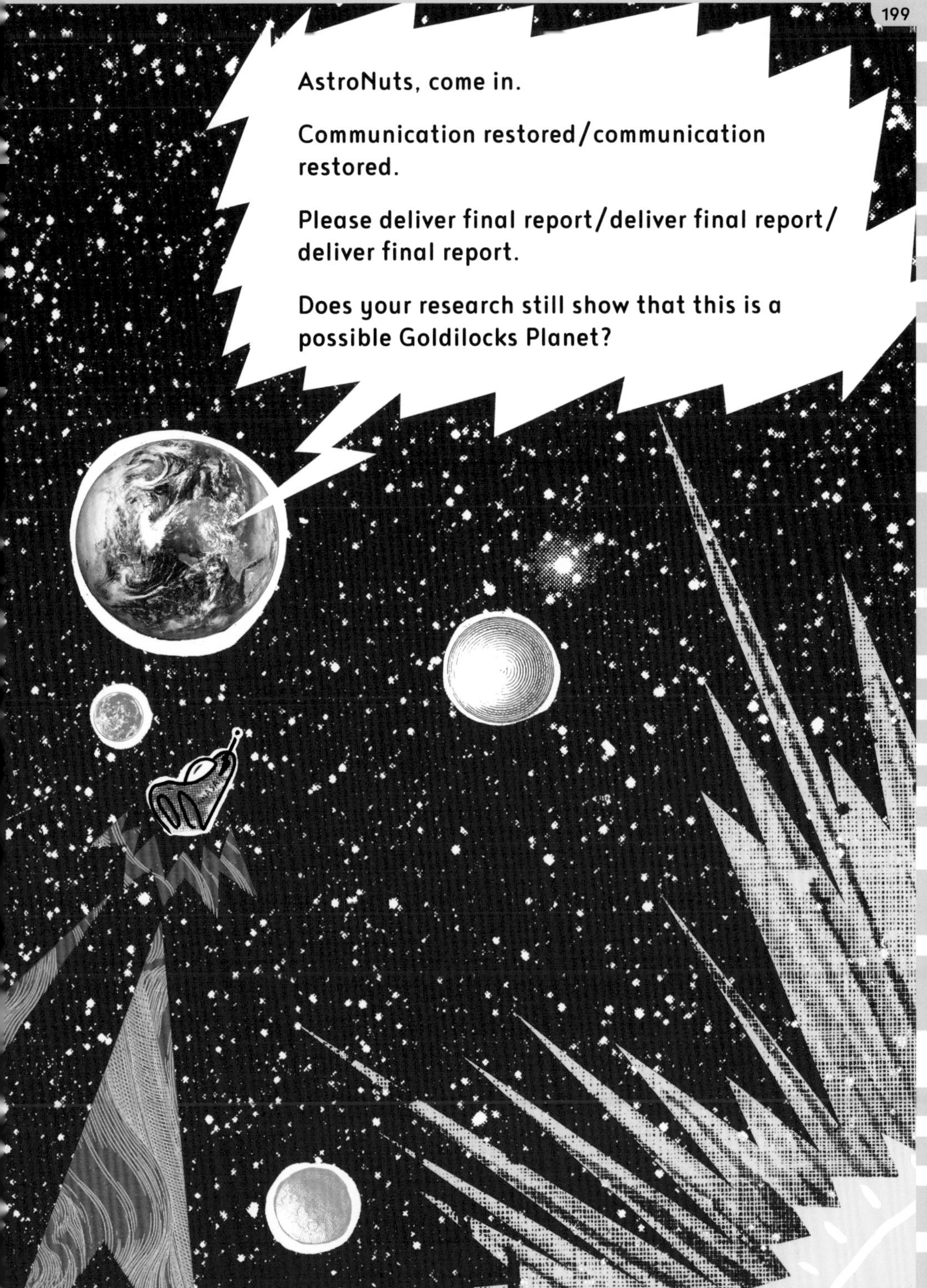
AstroNuts, come in.
Communication restored/communication restored.
Please deliver final report/deliver final report/deliver final report.
Does your research still show that this is a possible Goldilocks Planet?

The AstroNuts hustled to the AstroTorium.

Mission Leader AlphaWolf quickly filled out Form 35-FGPR Final Goldilocks Planet Report in a way that seemed a bit like he was trying to sweep a broken lamp under a rug.

FORM 35-FGPR

FINAL GOLDILOCKS

Name of planet: Nevrmind

Temperature Range: Not Good

Atmosphere: nope

Describe inhabitants: Gone...

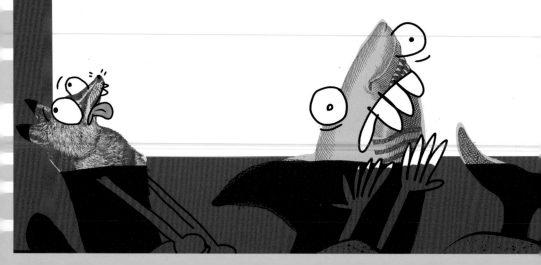

PLANET REPORT

~smelly~

Planet has liquid water: TRUE/~~FALSE~~

Humans could find Food and Shelter here: ~~TRUE~~/FALSE

Planet ecosystem well-balanced: TRUE/FALSE

No intelligent life harmed: TRUE/FALSE

OVERALL RATING:
a) Great
b) OK
c) Not good
d) Terrible
e) Your head explodes

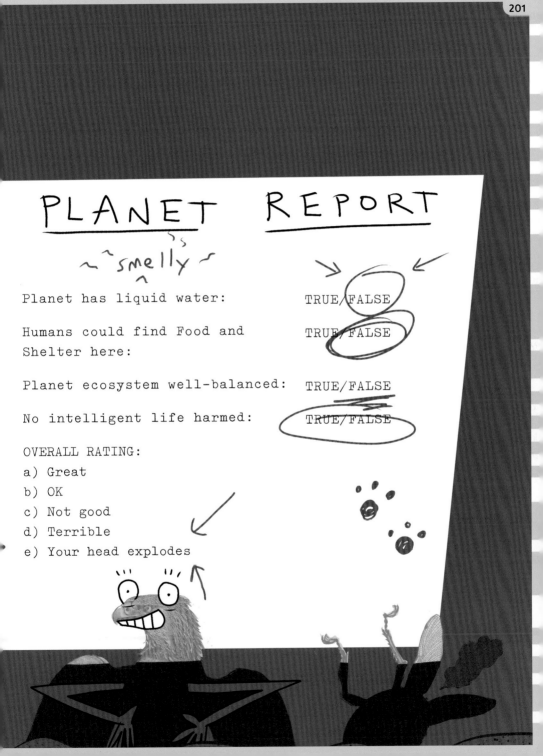

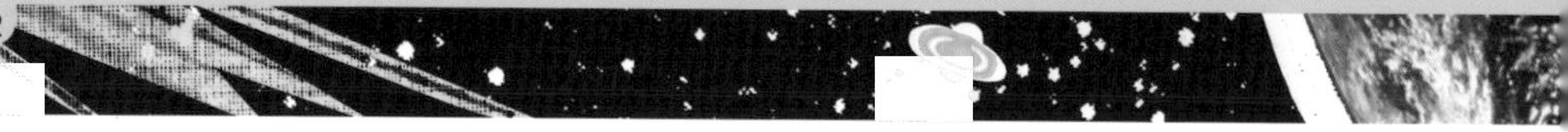

///// Official NNASA transcript /////
//// of ASTRONUT MISSION 1 ////

Command Escape: The Plant Planet does not sound habitable after all. What happened? Initial report sounded perfect/sounded perfect/sounded . . .
SmartHawk: Well, we ran all tests according to plan.
LaserShark: Yeah, we totally covered that planet. And we really wanted it to work.
StinkBug: Too many . . . system problems. Terrible roots. Awful tubers.

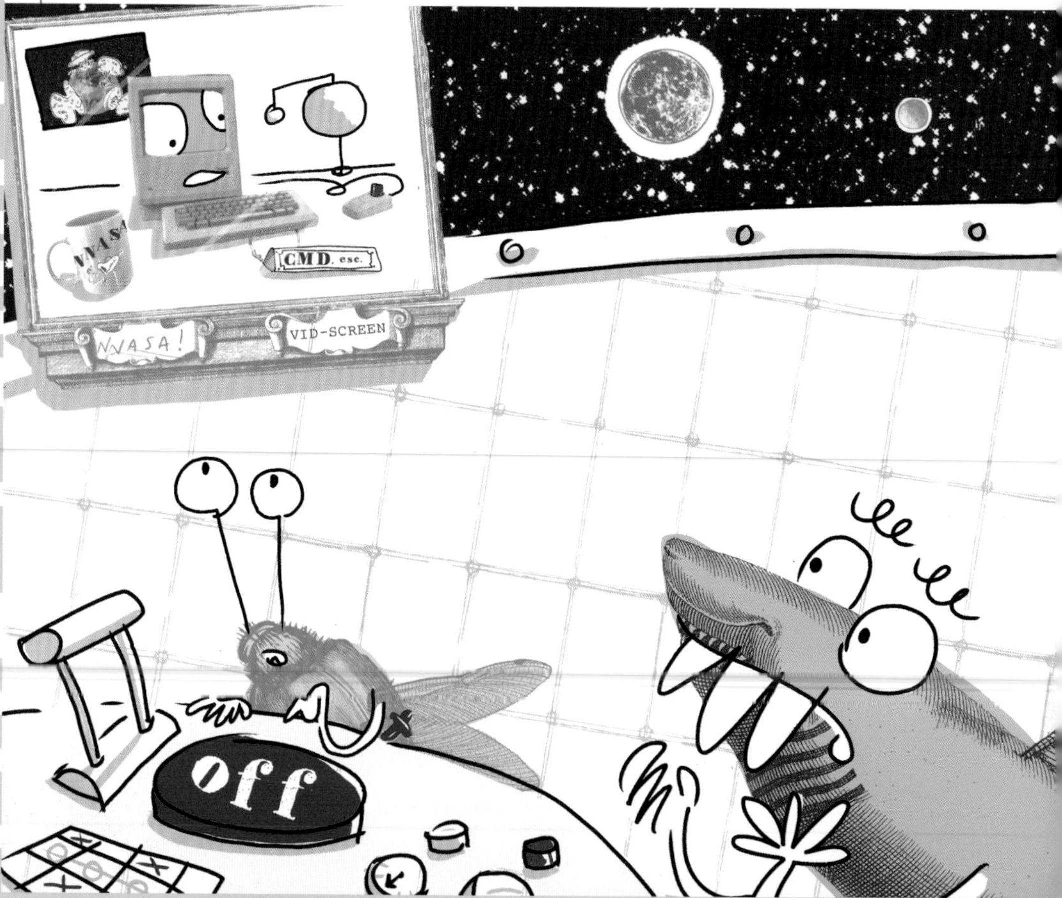
NNASA
CMD. esc.
NNASA!
VID-SCREEN
off

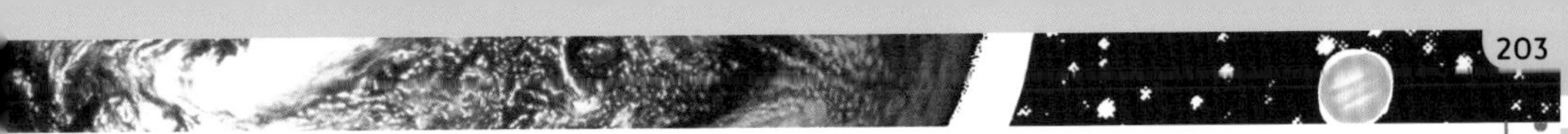

AlphaWolf: I don't know what happened. I think we messed—

SmartHawk: Very messed-up METHANE LEVELS. Just much too high for human life.

LaserShark: And what a super-unsafe place. So mean. And fighty. And not at all friendly.

Command Escape: OK. Input received. Are you sure you did not alter any of the life/the life/the life of the Plant Planet/Plant Planet/Plant Planet—

//// Further Transmission Cut Off ///

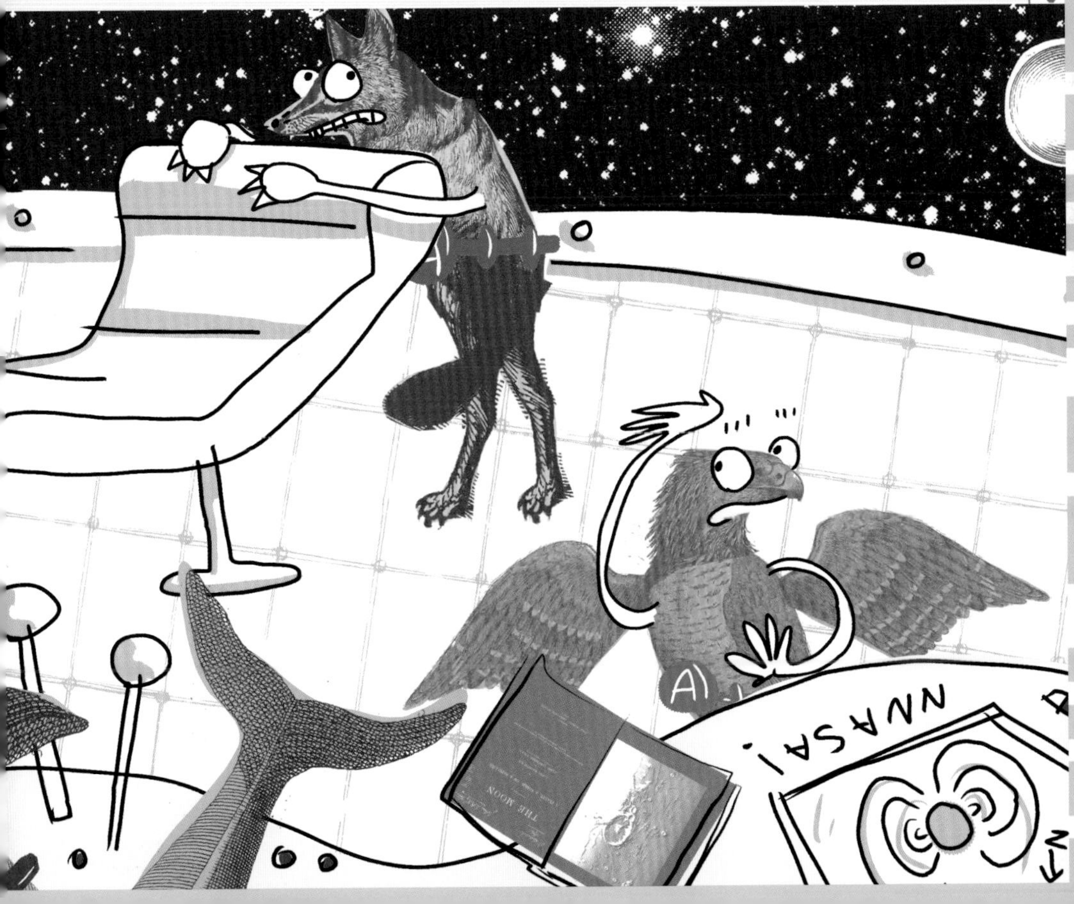

The AstroNuts held their breath. I'm not exactly sure why they did this. But if I had to guess, I would say they were worried about answers to questions like: Would their future missions be scrubbed? Would they be put back in cold storage?

The Thomas Jefferson Nose Rocket reentered the atmosphere.

Command Escape squawked back ON.

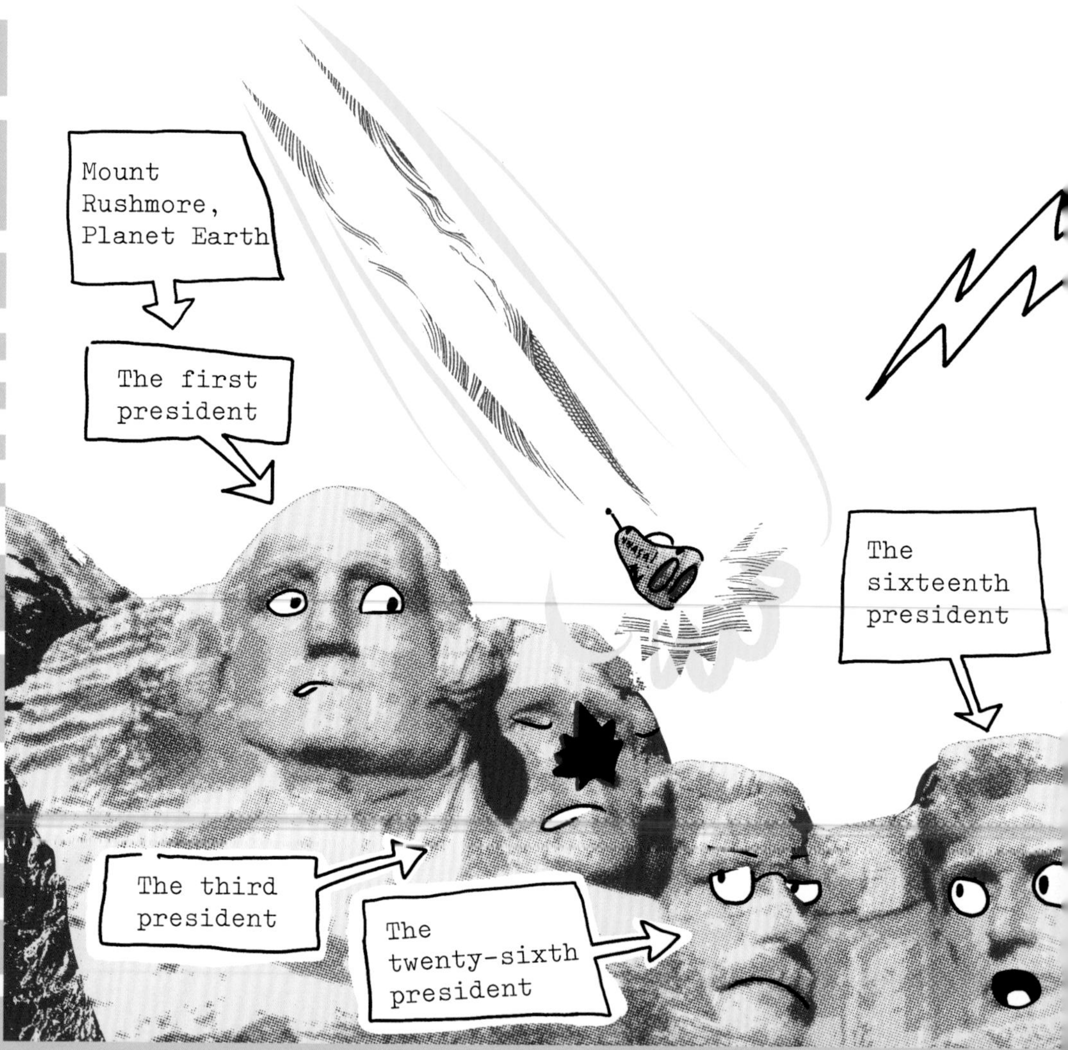
Mount Rushmore, Planet Earth
The first president
The sixteenth president
The third president
The twenty-sixth president

This is not good/not good/not good, the way my OFF button keeps shorting out. I will get that fixed/fixed. Now what was I saying?

Hmmm. I will check my Memory Banks later.

AstroNuts: Return to Thomas Jefferson Face Base. Reset. Refuel. And prepare for Goldilocks Planet Search, Mission #2.

The Water Planet/Water Planet/Water Planet/Water Planet/Water Planet/Water Planet!

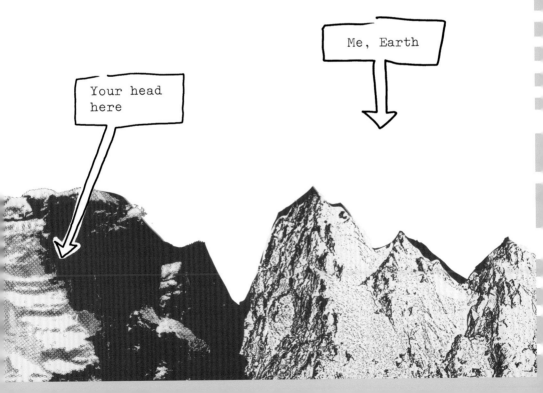

Me, Earth

Your head here

Mission Accomplished.
Well, we did go to the Plant Planet, complete our tests, and make it back in two weeks. But I don't know that I would use the word "accomplished."

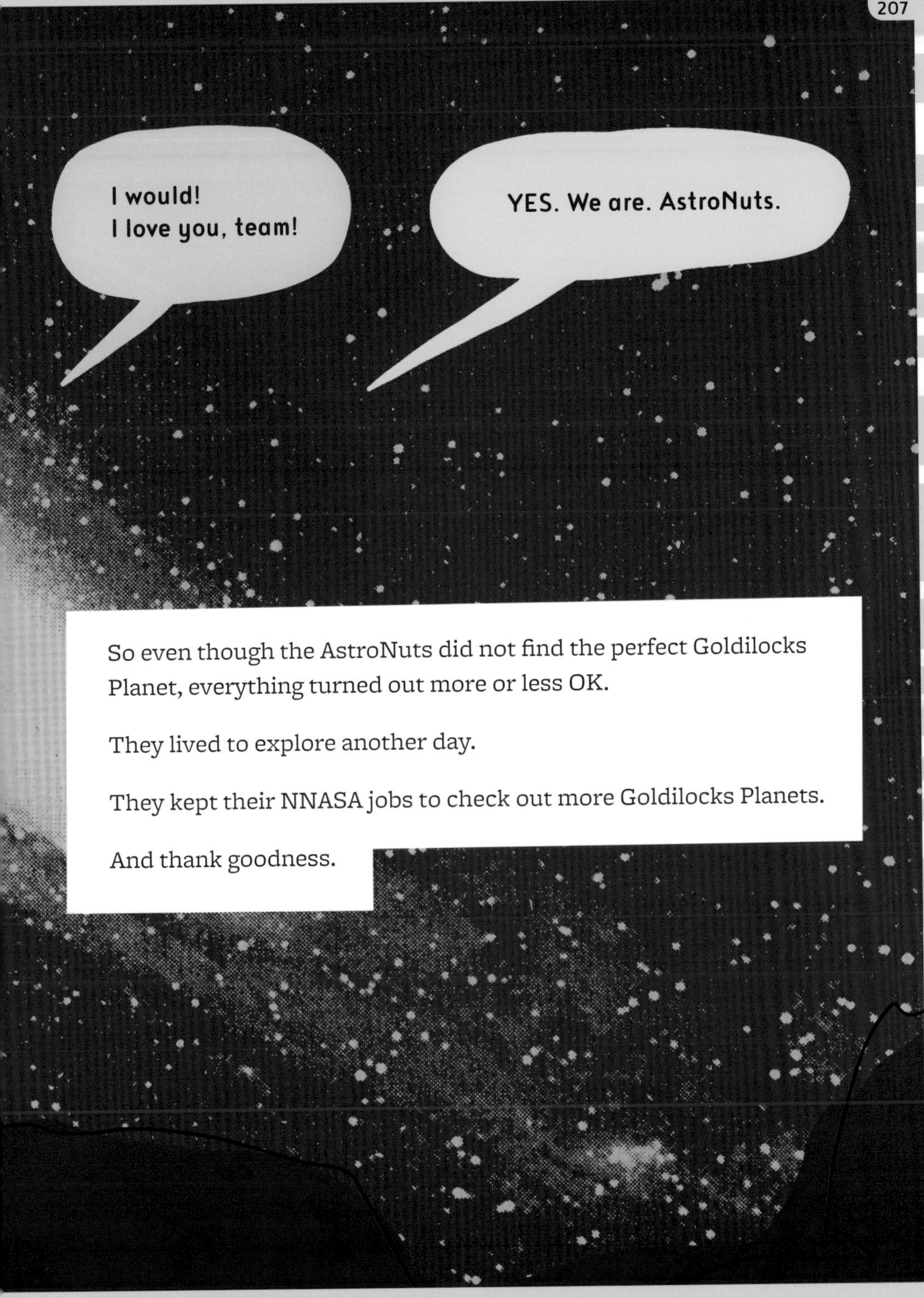
I would!
I love you, team!
YES. We are. AstroNuts.
So even though the AstroNuts did not find the perfect Goldilocks Planet, everything turned out more or less OK.
They lived to explore another day.
They kept their NNASA jobs to check out more Goldilocks Planets.
And thank goodness.

Because are you feeling a little carbon-sick? And greenhouse overheated?

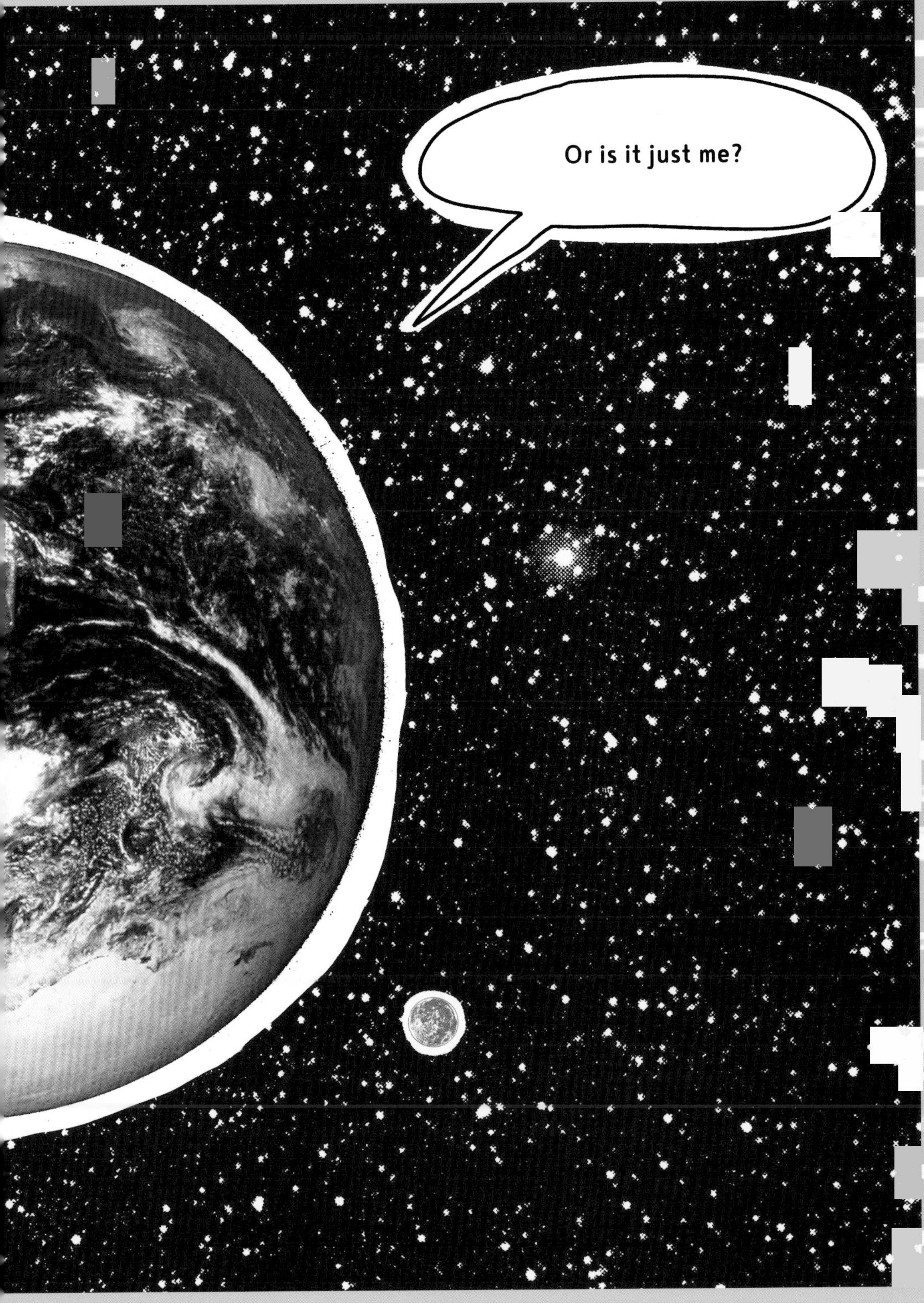
Or is it just me?

EPILOGUE:
Some Good News

Oh, and a little bit of good news and some more straight science—you might not know this, but sometimes the best way to help new growth is to get rid of old growth.

Ask any thoughtful gardener.

That's how you produce life that is new and healthy.

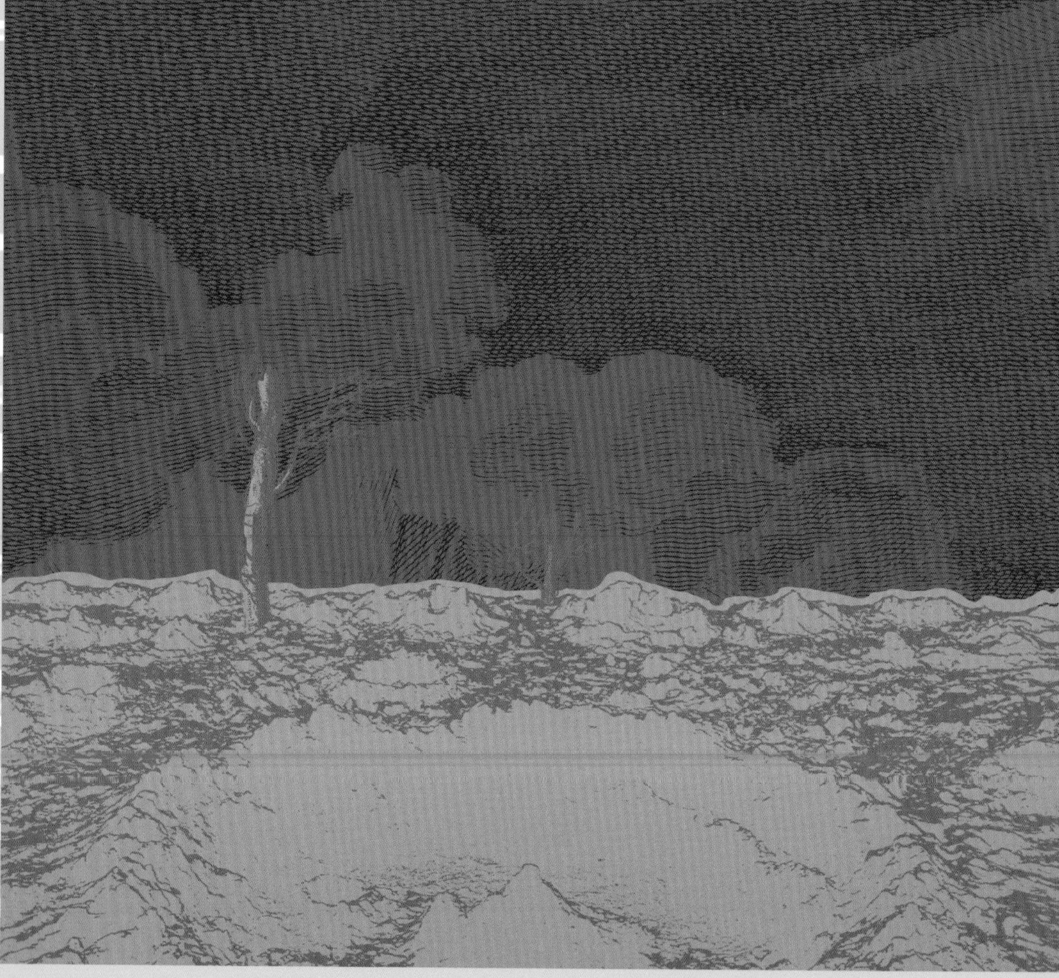

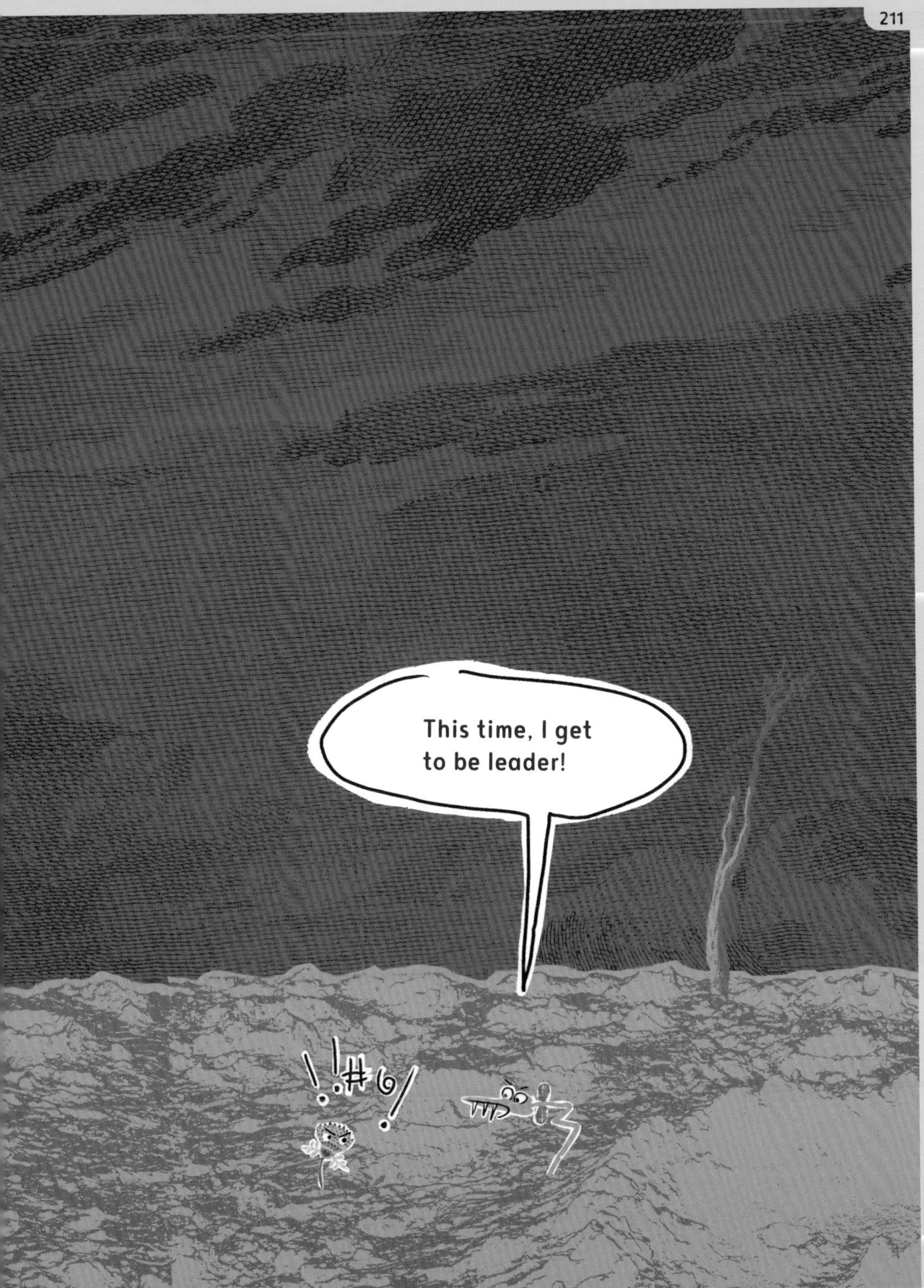
This time, I get to be leader!
!!#@/!

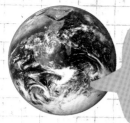

So you might have noticed that the illustrations in this book look like they were cut out of other artworks and reused. Well, that's because they were. Illustrator Steven W. took art from the Dutch national museum (the Rijksmuseum) and cut and pasted and colored it. That's called "collage."

So LaserShark is collaged from an engraving by Johannes van der Spyck from around 1736-1761.

CHAPTER 4:
LaserShark
I am LaserShark! I am super! I protect and feed everyone.

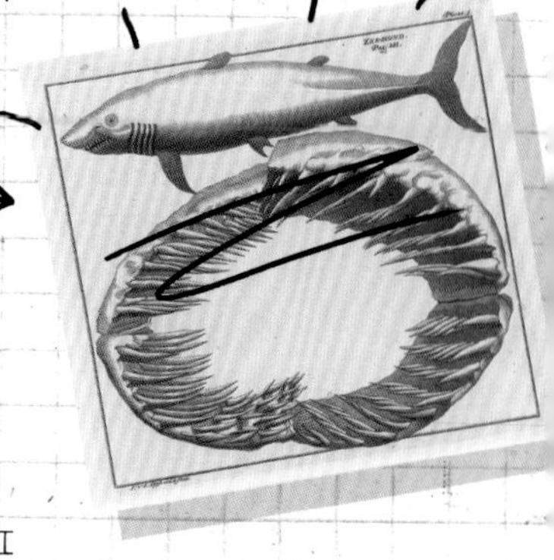

This crazy flower monster is collaged from an engraving by Noach van der Meer II from around 1741-1822.

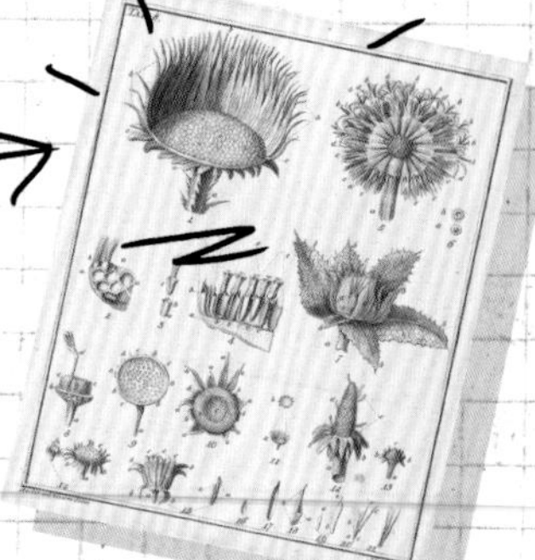

And even outer space is collaged!
Does this 1888 photograph of the Andromeda Galaxy look familiar?

YOU CAN COLLAGE TOO!

MAKE YOUR OWN!
GO TO: ASTRONUTS.SPACE

Just to get you started, we have 8.5" x 11" printouts ready for FREE download at our website AstroNuts.Space where you can make your own AstroNuts!

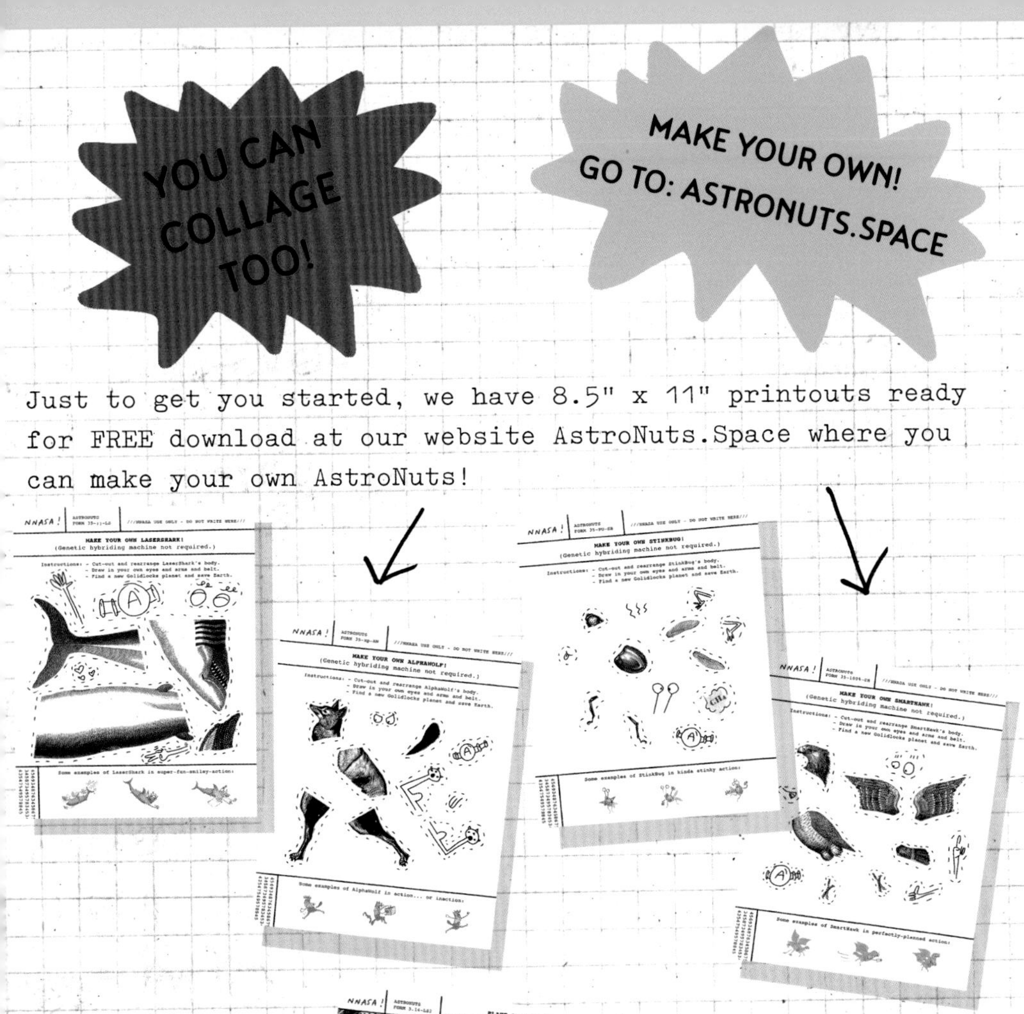
NNASA!
MAKE YOUR OWN LASERSHARK!
(Genetic hybriding machine not required.)
MAKE YOUR OWN ALPHAWOLF!
(Genetic hybriding machine not required.)
MAKE YOUR OWN STINKBUG!
(Genetic hybriding machine not required.)
MAKE YOUR OWN SMARTHAWK!
(Genetic hybriding machine not required.)

You can use some backgrounds from the book too!

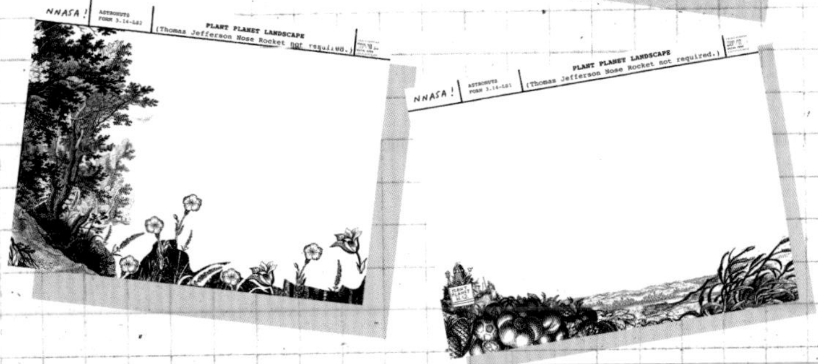
NNASA!
PLANT PLANET LANDSCAPE
(Thomas Jefferson Nose Rocket not required.)

Don't worry. Steven is not breaking any laws. The Rijksmuseum wants people to see and use their amazing collection of artwork. So they have put almost all of it online.

For more information, go to: RIJKSMUSEUM.NL

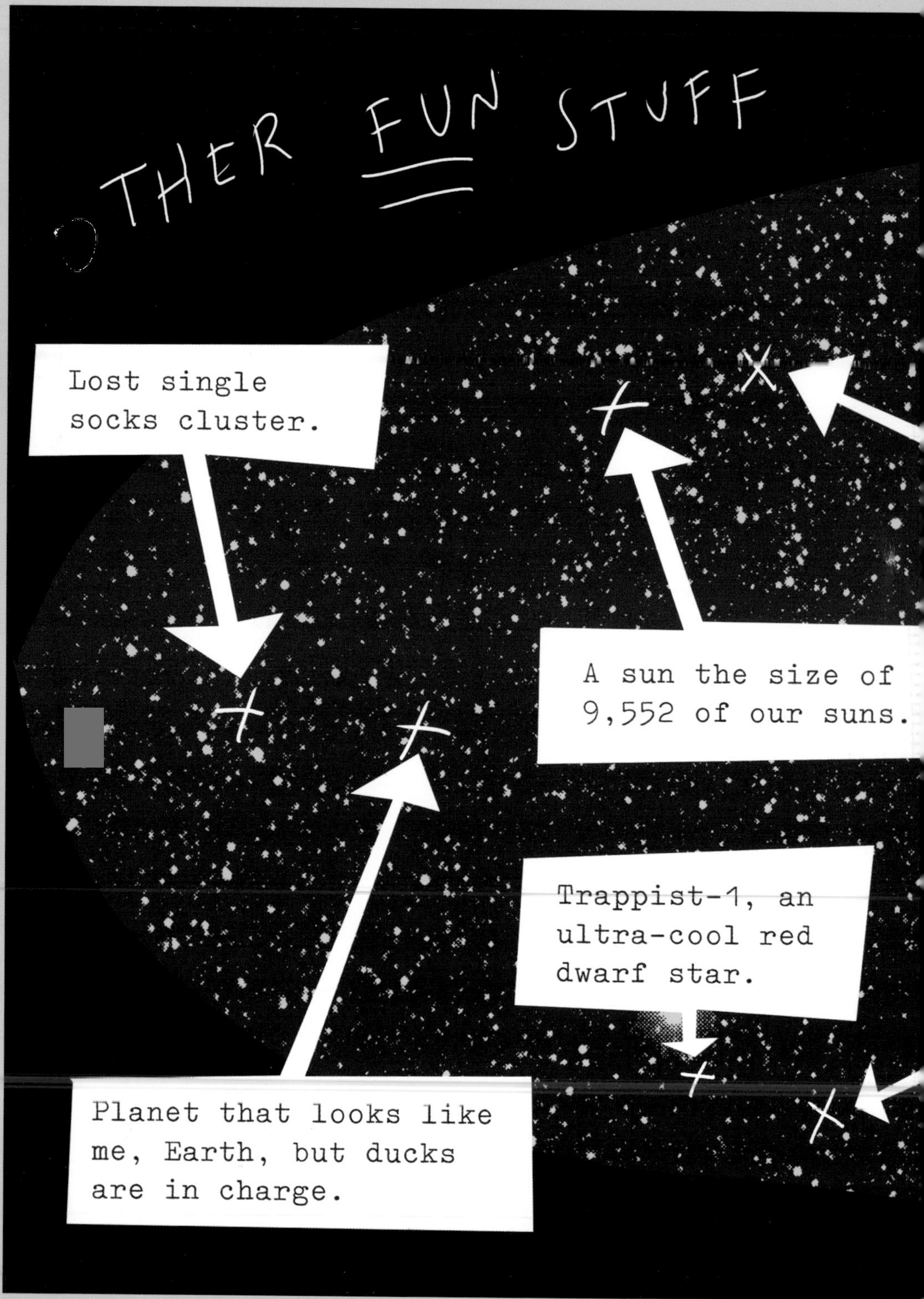
OTHER FUN STUFF
Lost single socks cluster.
A sun the size of 9,552 of our suns.
Trappist-1, an ultra-cool red dwarf star.
Planet that looks like me, Earth, but ducks are in charge.